Isaac Henderson

Agatha Page

A parable

Isaac Henderson

Agatha Page
A parable

ISBN/EAN: 9783744750622

Printed in Europe, USA, Canada, Australia, Japan

Cover: Foto ©Andreas Hilbeck / pixelio.de

More available books at **www.hansebooks.com**

AGATHA PAGE

A PARABLE

BY

ISAAC HENDERSON

AUTHOR OF "THE PRELATE"

FOURTH EDITION.

BOSTON
TICKNOR AND COMPANY
211 Tremont Street

CONTENTS.

PART FIRST.

PART SECOND.

PART FIRST.

AGATHA PAGE.

A PARABLE.

———•———

PART FIRST.

———

CHAPTER I.

IN THE BRIANZA.

IN charming verse, one hundred years ago, the poet Monti wrote of a villa in the Brianza,—the rich plain which has its beginning between the two arms of the Lake of Como. The villa lay upon the table-land above the town of Erba, and was now (in the year of grace eighteen hundred and seventy-eight) the property of the Duke Faviola of Rome, who occupied it with his wife and young daughter during the summer months. Like most Italian villas, the house was of stucco painted white, and its lines were symmetrical and stiff; but the grounds were beautiful, and as worthy as ever of a poet's transport, the mellow sunshine melting flower, cropped lawn, and distant landscape into an exquisite mosaic.

The Duchess Costanza Faviola was seated in an easy-chair upon the lawn, talking with a man a few years her junior. Her merry eyes twinkled at the slightest cause, and the finely-cut lips parted constantly, as though eager to smile. Yet she could be as haughty as Juno when she chose. Her companion was her brother, the Marquis Loreno. He had been in Berlin for five years as Charge d'affaires of the Italian legation, and this was his first visit to the villa, which the Duke had inherited two years before.

Filippo Loreno was a manly, handsome fellow of eight and twenty. His face, clean shaven, resolute, and earnest, was of the old Roman type rather than of the new. His eyes, large and gray, shone now with unusual brightness, for he was indignant. Some neighbors of the Duchess had lunched with her that day, and while drinking their coffee upon the lawn had indulged in intemperate gossip. The Duchess had early noticed signs of growing indignation upon her brother's face, and knowing the impulsiveness and directness of his nature, was rather relieved than annoyed when she saw him rise, bow ceremoniously to the group, and retire toward the house; nor did he come out again until she was alone, and now she had playfully taken him to task for his rudeness. He freely acknowledged his scant courtesy, but his wrath against the visitors was in no wise assuaged.

"Why can't women enjoy themselves without their incessant gossip?" he demanded.

"Why can't men enjoy themselves without their incessant politics?" she replied.

"But you can't compare the two."

"Why not? The only difference is, that a woman slanders her friends and a man his opponents."

"But," he persisted, keeping his mind upon the true inspiration of his protest, " if these friends of yours really think so badly of the people they spoke of, why do they keep them up? But they do, and they will!"

" Of course; and that proves that you solemn men take us too seriously."

" And what talk for those young girls to hear! It's monstrous! "

" Ah, that's another matter: now you speak like a prophet."

The Marquis was a man of the world, — above all, of the Roman world; yet his very soul would sometimes revolt against the hypocrisy which society finds convenient, perhaps necessary. He did not suppose it practicable for a woman of position to shut her door against all men and women whose presence was an affront to her home, but he had not yet acquired that complacency which accepts without protest what it cannot cure. He had lofty ideas about consistency, and by these he occasionally measured his associates, with the result which had now kindled his righteous wrath. He knew that certain honorable women, whom he had that day heard confess their knowledge of the dissolute characters of certain men, would to-morrow recognize these same men publicly, or greet with a kiss some woman they had to-day affected to despise; he knew, moreover, that others among these same virtuous critics were themselves just targets for the tongues of their sisters. Yet many of these women were mothers with daughters to train, " from among which wise virgins," he thought, " I am expected to choose a wife."

He said nothing more, however, and the Duchess was glad to let the subject drop.

" What time is it?" she asked presently.

He looked at his watch. " Nearly four o'clock."

" Then I must leave you," she said, rising. " We will dine a little later to-night. Good-by."

As she passed him she paused, and tapping him on the shoulder with her fan said, " You don't know much about women. I'm curious to see the sort of wife you 'll choose."

" I suppose I must eventually have a flower for my button-hole," he replied; " but I don't think I 'll choose from your bouquet."

She tapped him smartly across the ear for his impertinence, and with a bright nod left him.

He was in no humor for reading, and lighting a cigar decided to stroll over the hills as far as Alzate and return by the high-road. Walking through the long avenue of cypress-trees to the entrance-gate, he crossed the highway and began the ascent of a range of low hills dotted with villas and hamlets stretching toward Milan. He was a strong climber, and soon reaching the top turned to enjoy the view. Before him the shadows were lengthening on the highlands beyond Erba, but the sunlight still bathed the rich plain at his feet, bringing out every shade of green, from the deep tint of the fir-trees to the lighter shades of the mulberry and olive, while the sterile rock-ribbed mountains that blocked the way to the north made the wealth of the southern sweep more striking.

" It 's the modern Eden — for Eve's daughters !"

he exclaimed half aloud, as he turned to pursue his way.

The country was generally open and the walking easy, so he made rapid progress. At length·he came to a chestnut-grove, and after noting his course entered it. Presently he paused and listened to a distant sound, but in a moment went on again. The brisk exercise, the soft breeze, and the liquid notes of the nightingales along his way, calmed his nervous mood, and he acknowledged that he had often before heard, without even a mental protest, criticism quite as bitter as that which had offended him to-day.

"Yet with every allowance," he declared, " time given to such society is wasted, and I'll keep away from Costanza's neighbors as much as I can. The fact is, I don't interest them and they don't interest me. The men are absorbed in the women, and the women — are like so many sparrows, who feed, plume themselves, and chatter."

He stopped again and scanned the woods to his right. He thought he heard a soft strain of music; but the breeze rustled the leaves and the sound was lost, so he went on. Soon, however, it reached him distinctly, rising— falling —and again almost inaudible. He was passionately fond of music, and stood listening until the gentle strain died away; then he pushed on again, until suddenly, quite near him, a violin lifted its voice in the opening phrase of a nocturne. He could hear every note distinctly, and critical as he was, the player's skill charmed him.

"How exquisite!" he exclaimed, his interest excited, and the possibility of unearthing a second

Paginini occurring to his mind. "The musician is evidently just above me. I'll have a look at him."

He changed his course, and after a few steps found himself at the upper edge of the wood, along which ran a strip of meadow about twenty yards in width, skirted by a high gray wall overgrown with moss and vines. To his left it formed an abrupt angle on the edge of a steep incline, and to the right, as far as his eye could follow, there seemed to be no opening. He stood gazing at this barrier undecided what to do, when the touch of the bow upon the violin and the low sound of a man's voice reached him.

"He's just over the wall," thought the Marquis; and he again scrutinized it closely, feeling a strange confidence in his power to look upon the player in spite of it.

He was seldom daunted when pursuing a purpose, either serious or trivial, and in the end he usually succeeded. Some persons called him lucky, others believed him uncommonly clever. He never thought about the fact, but like an Alpine climber was only stimulated by difficulty, and seldom looked back. With such natures high purpose usually brings rare results; but Loreno as yet had no high purpose, and was in consequence merely wilful. Anything he wished to possess he grasped at. If it were out of his reach he moved nearer: sometimes this was difficult, but he moved nearer all the same.

Therefore, as his clear gray eye scanned the wall, he became more interested than ever in his search, and more determined than ever to succeed. Had no

other method presented itself, he would in all proba-
bility have scaled the wall (for he had already measured it with his glance); but his "luck" served him
and made the way clear.

A dozen yards below, near a thick growth of ivy
upon the wall, some cattle were grazing, and Loreno's
quick eye saw an ox catch the vine upon one of his
horns.

"The ivy in that spot does n't grow against the
wall," he said to himself; and going quickly forward
he discovered that the vine was a mere screen for a
gate formed of iron bars.

Through great oaks that cast long shadows upon a
velvet lawn he caught a glimpse of a spacious park,
and upon a distant plateau he could see the upper
part of a large villa. Sloping down from the house
were terraces of flowers and stretches of woodland
leading gently to the gate at which he stood. Within
the shade of a tree near him a silver-haired priest
was seated upon a rustic bench, his fine pale face
upturned in rapt attention to that of a young girl
who stood before him in the full splendor of the
golden sunlight, playing upon a violin.

Her form was tall and slender, and her dress was
white. Her golden hair fairly romped over the well-
poised head, escaping from two demure bands of
velvet which tried their best to hold it; some daring
tresses even dancing down the forehead to catch a
glimpse of the deep-blue eyes beneath, then turning
aside to scamper down the neck and join the flowing
mass that swept around the farther shoulder and
hid itself under her violin. The face, while im-

mature, was eloquent of latent strength. The reflective eyes, the delicate nostrils, the arched lips, the round firm chin, told an observant eye that had this girl lived in ancient Rome, she would have stood in the arena undaunted in her faith.

She played with much feeling, sometimes swaying with the rhythm, or again inclining her head toward the instrument until her cheek seemed to caress it; but now her bow scarcely touched the strings as the tone grew fainter and fainter, and when it died away the player looked down upon the silent violin as a mother gazes at her sleeping child.

With a quick motion she dropped her bow to her side and turned toward the priest.

"Can't you praise me even a little?" she asked.

The old man, his face glowing with satisfaction, put out his hand to her. She ran forward impulsively and dropped on her knees beside him.

"That's the dear old hand that began it," she said, stroking the white fingers. "Now tell me if I've improved."

"Wonderfully!"

"Are you proud of me?" and the upturned eyes looked very bright and happy.

"Even Tagliani, great master that he is, has n't many such pupils, I'll venture to say!"

She was about to protest, sincerely enough, but caught herself in time. "Very few of his pupils come from such a master as I had."

"Nonsense!"

But she saw how pleased he was. Rising, she seated herself beside him, still holding his hand.

"Tagliani said I already had a good tone when I first played to him; but did n't I write you that from Rome?"

"Yes, child, yes. But I did n't teach you your tone; it was God's gift."

"You can't deny that you improved it," she said decidedly.

He held up his hand deprecatingly, his kind eyes grave.

"Caro Padre! I 'm always shocking you. I 'm very sorry," and she looked into his face penitently. "But," she added quickly, "you have n't told me how you like my new violin."

"It 's a fine instrument; indeed, I 've seldom heard one so good."

"It has n't so lovely a tone as yours, but perhaps it is more brilliant."

"It 's altogether a different thing," and he shook his finger at her hypocrisy. "Mine was cheap and served its purpose well, but this is fit for the bow of an artist;" and he examined it with admiration, lightly touching the strings.

"Play something," she pleaded.

"I? My playing would sound very tame after the artists you have been hearing in Rome."

"Your playing sound tame to me? Never! You play much more to my heart than Tagliani, or any one else. Do try something."

In spite of his absurd nervousness at the presence of his former pupil, Padre Sacconi played uncommonly well. As the young girl watched him her thoughts flew back to the first lesson she had taken

from him four years before on that same spot. It
was also on a day in May, and he had stood before
her, as now, his tall form erect, his long hair shaking about his neck, his brown eyes glowing with the
fervor of his work.

"Bravo!" she cried, as the priest lowered his bow.
"I never enjoyed your playing more."

Unusually excited by his performance, the old man
examined the violin with a tenderness that did not
escape the notice of his watchful companion.

"It's marvellous!" he said, as if to himself. "I
never knew an instrument so responsive, so really
sympathetic." He stepped toward the young girl
and held out her treasure. "Many thanks, my
child; it has given me true joy."

"I hope it may often do so—but not enough to
make me jealous of it."

"Thank you," he replied. "Then I may use it
sometimes?"

"Always—for my sake;" and stooping she picked
up the case and held it out to him, pointing to a
silver plate bearing an inscription.

He looked at it soberly, and read the words—

"TO PADRE GIOVANNI SACCONI,
FROM HIS GRATEFUL PUPIL
AGATHA PAGE."

His eyes were raised to hers, then sought the instrument; drawing her head nearer, he kissed the
fair forehead gently, then looked again at his violin.
Patting it, he said huskily, "I'll love it chiefly for
thy sake—Agatha."

A few moments later the old priest locked the iron
gate behind him and walked down a path which the
Marquis had discovered as he turned away. It was a
short cut to a little hamlet at the foot of the hill,
and Padre Sacconi, who had been the priest of the
village for twenty years, often used it when he went
to see Agatha or her uncle, the Count Ricci, who
owned the villa.

The Count's sister had married an American named
Page, who was at the time of his marriage in the
diplomatic service at Rome. When Agatha, their
only child, was four years old, her father died, and
seven years later she lost her mother; whereupon
the Count, for love of his sister and from a sense of
duty as the child's guardian, took Agatha to his own
home. His daughter Mercede, two years Agatha's
senior, was at a convent, but in obedience to his
sister's instructions the Count had Agatha educated
at home. Thus the cousins saw but little of each
other until Mercede's seventeenth year, when she
returned to Rome. While the kind Italian made no
difference in his demonstration of love toward them,
his heart inclined much more tenderly toward his
own child, not only because of the closer tie, but
because he understood her character better. His
raven-haired, black-eyed daughter, impulsive and
often wilful, belonged to a type with which he was
familiar. He could comprehend her moods (and they
varied from ecstasy to sullenness), because her mother
had possessed the same temperament; and he gloried in her warm Southern nature. Even when
she sometimes became jealous of Agatha he appre-

ciated her suffering and comforted her wisely, or if she disregarded his commands he understood her and was lenient. Agatha was calmer, stranger, farther away; more lovely of disposition certainly, and in her way quite as interesting, " but," he would say with swelling pride, " not so Italian ! "

When one evening his beautiful daughter, leaning upon his arm, made her entrance into society, he felt that no father had ever juster reason for satisfaction and high expectation. Nor was he disappointed in the reception accorded Mercede. Her dark beauty and exuberance of spirit. won her many admirers, and within two months the Duke Bramante broached the subject of a union between the two families. No alliance possible to his adored child could have been more agreeable to the Count; but he was not yet prepared to lose her, and smilingly bade his good friend be patient, for his daughter was very young.

In the mean time, however, a young officer, dashing but poor, made love to Mercede under the very eyes of her father and aunts, whose minds failed to grasp the possibility of her making an independent choice. But she did so, and at last a dim suspicion of the fact was forced upon the Count, who questioned her about it, although without serious misgiving. She boldly avowed her love for the lieutenant and her determination to marry him. Pleading was of no avail ; indeed, nothing served to shake her decision, and the old aunts could conceive of no better plan than the ancient one. Therefore by their advice, and in despair at Mercede's obstinacy, the Count decided to send his child away from Rome for a long visit.

In three weeks he received a despatch telling him that Mercede had run away; and a week later a letter from her announced that she was the lieutenant's happy wife. The tone of this letter showed plainly her immaturity and her confidence of speedy forgiveness.

But she had not measured her father well. His love was indeed great, but so were his pride, his ambition, and his sense of authority; no one of which was so powerful as his love, but the union of which guided his action in this crisis. He did not answer her letter.

Beside all else, his heart was sorely bruised by his daughter's disloyalty. He had always supposed she must needs be persuaded to marry; that his love and protection constituted her chief happiness: the sudden disillusion shocked him severely, awakening a feeling of resentment toward her and of jealousy toward her husband; and with the intensity of his Southern nature he became as bitter as he had before been doting. When, therefore, Agatha attempted to plead in Mercede's behalf, he told her sternly to be silent, and never again to mention the name of her cousin in his presence.

Thus it was that the impecunious lieutenant waited in vain for the dowry which he daily expected would be given his bride with the parental blessing; and although the religious ceremony was performed, the civil marriage — which by Italian law cannot be contracted by an officer unless the bride possess a certain capital — was indefinitely postponed.

Mercede, however, did not mourn seriously; she

believed that her father's anger would burn itself
out, and her Ernesto told her that if worse came
to worst, he would some day inherit enough money
to give her the requisite dowry, and then the second
ceremony could be performed.

" But, after all," said he, "what is the civil marriage ?   A mere form in compliance with an arbitrary
law of recent date.   The essential service — that
which truly unites a man and a woman — is already
accomplished, and you hold a certificate duly signed
by the priest who performed it."

Thus he reassured her, while she waited patiently
for time to bring back both her beloved father and
her accustomed luxury.

Month succeeded month, and still the Count remained obdurate.   Finally came the news that
Mercede had a son, and Agatha ventured to tell
the grandfather.   If he felt any emotion, he hid it.
Facing Agatha, he said coldly: " You had no right to
speak of this subject ; have my wishes no weight with
you either ? "   Then he left the room, and for the rest
of that day remained in his own apartment.

It had been the lieutenant's custom to keep
Mercede near him in his changes of station, and
his marriage was only officially a secret.   He provided her with a modest home, and she took her
position as in all respects his true and lawful
wife.   There were only two drawbacks to their
otherwise smooth life : one was Mercede's unbal-
anced temperament, and the other a lack of money.
Mercede at first had lived in an ecstasy of bliss,
and her new joy, combined with a certain awe in

which she held her idol, enabled her to control the
variable moods which later, swinging backward and
forward, often led her from beatitude to misery.
She had never known until now what it was to
need money, and inevitable anxiety regarding the
common necessaries of life had a marked effect upon
her.

Instead of their financial state growing more comfortable, as the lieutenant often predicted that it
would, each year it became more straitened; and certain loans which Mercede was induced to make from
Agatha, under the illusion that at quarter-day the
lieutenant would be able to repay them, now repre-
sented an amount equal to her husband's pay for a
year.

Mercede never understood where all this money
went to; but she handed it to the lieutenant, who
kept the accounts, and whose technical explanations
only served to confound her. She economized as
closely as she could both upon herself and the child,
and anxiously awaited the day when this dreadful
load of debt might begin to be reduced.

Suddenly the truth was made known to her.
Her husband was a gambler; and his pay, together
with Agatha's remittances, had been lost at baccarat,
while creditors besieged their home from every side.
The effect upon so intemperate a nature as Mercede's was sure to be serious. Outraged and full of
scorn, she followed the first surging impulse that
flowed over her. Taking her child, she left the home
which she felt no longer belonged to her, and wrote
bidding the lieutenant sell its contents and pay what

debts he could, and not to hope for her return until all were cancelled. She took a room near by and began publicly to support herself by sewing and teaching. This open disgrace was more than her husband could stand, and he went to see her. Mercede was unbending, and a stormy interview ensued. At last she ordered him to go, and when he refused she left the room.

Desperate, and with the purpose of bringing her to terms, he took her marriage certificate and departed, and when a few days later he was ordered to Como he took the paper with him, leaving her to come to her senses; but she continued obstinate, and by means of the work given her by sympathetic friends, managed to keep out of debt. She had not, however, the heart to write to Agatha, with whom she had until now kept up a weekly correspondence; and it was of this strange silence that the latter was thinking as she sat under the oak-tree after Padre Sacconi had departed with his precious gift under his arm.

CHAPTER II.

ALTHOUGH the Marquis Loreno was commonly accounted impulsive, he succeeded, not only during dinner, but afterward while smoking with the Duke, in restraining an impulse which had taken strong hold upon him. He did not approach the subject which engrossed his mind, but talked with the Duke about his three hobbies; namely, hunting, New Guinea, and his daughter Gaeta, who was now twelve years of age.

The Duke was a tall, broad-shouldered man of five and forty. He wore a long black beard which, together with heavy eyebrows above a pair of keen black eyes, gave him a somewhat ferocious appearance, and strangers passing him often looked a second time at the striking figure, with everything black about it except a bit of collar and warm olive skin beneath the crushed felt hat.

Early in life he had gone to New Guinea on an exploring expedition, which had won him distinction. Since his marriage he had curbed his love of adventure; but occasionally he would don his hunting-suit and with his dog and his gun wander about the great Campagna for several days. He was a very silent man, yet his silence was not oppressive, for it seemed to fit his personality, and when he chose to speak he spoke well; but he did not refer to his adventures except upon rare occasions and at his own fireside. Other hunters, however, told wonderful tales of his indifference to danger and exposure, and gave ample testimony to his force of will and remarkable prowess with his rifle.

When they muffled themselves in great-coats to keep out the biting cold, and protected their faces from the brambles by thick visors, they would sometimes be startled by the sudden appearance of the stalwart Duke — his soft hat pushed back from his torn face, his hunting-coat unbuttoned, and his breast bared to the air, as he stalked rapidly along, bearing lightly his trusty weapon, and followed by his tired dog.

An accidental witness testified that once when he was challenged by three brigands in one of the wildest parts of the Campagna, he haughtily fired his rifle into the air and then dared them to molest him. The bravado of the act was disconcerting, and as he dashed at them with his gun clubbed, two of them fled incontinently, and only the third fired upon him. But the fellow's aim was hasty, and ere he could escape he was in the clutch of the thoroughly aroused giant, who dashed him to the ground, spurned him with his foot, broke his gun like a reed, and only pausing to recover his own weapon, walked unconcernedly away.

Yet this same nature could be swayed by that of little Gaeta with a certainty and force that were almost pathetic. He would listen to her words with the deepest interest as she poured out her sorrows and joys. He was proud of his wife, but he adored the child, and the two seemed to form his world. He had a hearty liking for Loreno, and showed it by occasionally relaxing his habit of silence and permitting himself to be drawn into conversation by him, as in the present instance.

Soon, however, the father and daughter went off together, and then Loreno lost no time in approaching the subject which engrossed him.

" Whose villa is that, Costanza," he asked, turning to his sister nonchalantly, "higher up the ridge, about three kilometres beyond here? It is directly above the church with a tower."

" I suppose you mean the Count Ricci's."

" Yes, that's the name;" and in reply to her quick glance of surprise, he added, " I remember asking some one this afternoon. Don't you know the Count?"

" Yes, quite well."

" But I've not seen him here."

" Very likely; his wife died some years ago, and he seldom goes anywhere. I have almost given up asking him."

" He has a daughter, has n't he?"

" Yes, — surely you must have heard about her; she ran away with a lieutenant."

"Indeed! is *that* the Ricci?" and his face fell. " I presume, then, that the daughter has repented and come home again."

" Not that I have heard; is there such a report?"

" I don't know anything about it — except," and

he avoided her gaze, " that I happened to see a young girl there to-day."

" You did ? I did n't know that you knew them."

" I don't; only while walking over the hill near the Count's villa I heard the sound of a violin coming from the grounds, and my curiosity prompted me to look through a gate in the wall, and I saw a young girl playing to an old priest."

She folded her hands in her lap and regarded him quizzically.

" Oh, did you. And now that same curiosity impels you to come to me to find out all about her." She laughed softly, adding, " You are not very skilful in such matters; directness is much more in your line."

" Do you think it 's the daughter? " he asked.

" How should I know ? "

" Has the Count any other daughter? "

" I won't tell you."

" Answer that question, at least."

" No, he has not."

He waited, hoping she would continue, but she remained silent. This was an occasion when he would not have run away from a little gossip.

" You don't think she has left her husband ? " he asked presently.

She laughed quietly. " I doubt it."

His face fell, and he seemed to be musing. " Perhaps her father is reconciled to him," he suggested.

" I doubt that also ! "

And so she parried his questions until, tired of chaffing him, she told him who it was he had seen, and related Agatha's history.

"The poor child," she added, "goes nowhere. Her uncle has no heart for society, so she devotes herself to her violin. She is charming, and I have her at luncheon occasionally; although were she not charming I should invite her as a charity."

"Invite her to-morrow, and include me as a charity," he exclaimed.

She laughed lightly, and sat toying with her cup of coffee.

Her hesitation gave him the clew to her thought. "You don't relish the responsibility," he said.

"Well, I don't deny that she interests me."

"Shall I tell you frankly how I feel about it?"

"By all means."

"Miss Page is very sincere, as well as lovely, while you are lovely but not so sincere. I ought to know; I've watched you often enough."

He looked amused. "And what do you make out of me?" he inquired.

"If a thing interests you it's your nature to go close and have a good look at it, just as a child would. This principle was well enough while you were a child, but when as a man you apply your habit to susceptible young women, it's misleading; and when, having satisfied your curiosity, you calmly turn away, you seem to forget that their young hearts are not made of wood or china, and that what is to you a mere episode may be their —"

"Last straw, poor things!" he interrupted. "But this is different, really it is, and after such a warning you may trust me."

"That's the strangest part of it all," she said

helplessly. "I do you the justice to believe that you don't realize what a flirt you are, and that you are innocent of most of the hearts you 've broken ; but I can't tell Miss Page that, and I don't wish to put her at a disadvantage."

He laughed quietly. "I 'm awfully sorry about myself," he said ; "but can't you keep an eye upon me, and whenever I begin to flirt strike your table-bell ? It might also put her on her guard."

At first the Duchess was obdurate ; but he urged her so earnestly that at last she began to yield, and before they parted he won her to his wish, and she agreed to invite her young neighbor to luncheon during the week.

The next morning, as Agatha was arranging some flowers upon the breakfast-table, the mail was brought in, and she hurriedly tore open an envelope addressed in Mercede's handwriting. As she read the letter her color grew faint. The Count's footstep sounded upon the stairs, and bidding the servant tell her uncle not to wait breakfast for her, she hastened from the room. Going into the air, she crossed the lawn, and entering a deeply-shaded path went to an arbor where she felt comparatively safe from interruption. Drawing the letter from her pocket, she eagerly read the remainder of it, and then sat pondering, her hands in her lap, her eyes fixed upon the distant landscape. The breeze caught the paper and it fluttered to the ground. Aroused by the act of recovering it, she sighed and slowly re-read it.

It ran as follows : —

My dearest Agatha,—In my alarm I turn to you. My husband disgraced himself and me, and I left his house. He came to my rooms and begged me to return, but I refused and left him alone. Afterward I discovered that my writing-desk, which was in the room with him, had been forced open. I don't know why, but I instantly thought of my marriage certificate. It was gone! Yet it was there, for I remember — such a sickly fool was I yesterday! — I remember kissing it.

I am certain he took the paper, but for what purpose? Agatha, I beg of you to think for me. If you can reassure me, do so; if not, then help me.

The civil marriage was never performed — never mind why; we are dealing with the present. I telegraphed to him instantly, and just now a trifling reply has come *addressed to my maiden name*. Agatha, I fear serious trouble is near. In the disgrace my father put upon me my husband sustained me; but if he is gone, to whom can I look? My husband is at Como, and Erba is so near that perhaps Padre Sacconi would go and talk with him. He must give me back my certificate. Think it all over, Agatha, and telegraph me something, for I am almost wild.

MERCEDE.

Agatha raised her head, and looking through the long vista of over-arching trees that edged the path to the brow of the hill, gazed upon a distant mountain tipped with snow.

"As well ask Padre Sacconi to melt that snow with words," she said. "What that scoundrel needs is a visit from Mercede's father. He might bring him to his senses."

She sat and revolved many plans having this

purpose, and at last arose with the decision that she would seek her uncle.

Walking rapidly in the direction of the house, she reached the edge of the lawn, and pausing looked toward a palm-tree where the Count often had his easy-chair placed in the morning, while he smoked his cigar and talked with the head gardener. She saw him, and fortunately he was alone.

The Count was sixty years of age, and a stranger glancing at his gray mustache and decided face would probably have taken him to be a soldier. Indeed, there was much of the military in the Count, — that is, much that is popularly associated with a soldier's character; but having determined this, one would have decided further that he was accustomed to a general's plume.

"Good-morning," he said as she approached; "I fear you are not well."

"Perfectly, only I —" and she paused.

His eyes twinkled as he added, "Only you! So long as you can come back and say 'Only I,' Padre Sacconi may remain your sole confidant. Now give me my morning kiss."

She laid her hand in the one he held out to her, and bending down kissed him lovingly. She dreaded to speak, yet felt that the moment was opportune, and that there was danger to Mercede in delay.

The General patted the hand he still held, and looking into her face smiled kindly. As he noted the seriousness of its lines and the gravity of her eyes, his own expression changed, and he regarded her with more attention.

" Uncle — " she began.

There was a pause.

" Yes, dear."

She tried again, but her throat was parched and her voice failed her.

She was frightened at her position. The General, unsuspecting, was looking at her sympathetically, and she was on the point of dealing him a blow the result of which she could not foretell. Was it necessary? In any event, would it not be better to get Padre Sacconi's opinion before taking such responsibility?

She looked into the kind eyes raised to hers, and tried to smile and gain time for thought. But suddenly Mercede's position came sternly to her, sweeping away indecision as death devours hope.

" Uncle," she said clearly, — " Uncle," and she clasped his hand tightly, " I fear I must make you terribly unhappy ! "

He half turned and searched her face with sudden dread. The old love for his Mercede welled up and overwhelmed all bitterness for the moment, and he could not control his trembling.

" Is she dead ? "

Agatha looked upon his quivering lips and could not answer.

" Is she? Is she?"

How dare she tell him worse than this ! She shook her head without speaking. But it was enough ; Mercede lived, and his terror passed. Dropping back into his chair, his gaze remained fixed but less strained. His child was not dead. He could bear anything else.

Agatha felt that this moment of reaction was the moment of his greatest strength, and she hastened to speak.

"He has left her!"

The soldier's expression did not change for fully a minute as he eyed Agatha and smoked rapidly. But gradually and painfully he comprehended; then he swung his chair away a little and laughed scornfully.

"Deserted his wife, has he?" he said in a quiet voice, — "deserted the Count Ricci's daughter; it's perfect!"

"There is something worse."

"Ah! something worse, is there? What else has my son-in-law done to annoy his wife besides deserting her?"

Agatha moved a little that she might see his face and if possible soften the blow.

"He has deceived her," she began; "he never —"

"Deceived her!" he exclaimed, turning suddenly. "How? Wasn't that letter hers?"

"Yes."

"Then she was married, for my daughter was never a liar. Had he another wife?"

"No; but the civil marriage was never —"

"Agatha!" and his eyes blazed.

"Here is her letter; will you read it?"

As she held it out he looked at it but did not take it. While he hesitated she anxiously watched his eyes, as their expression changed slowly from eagerness to indecision and then to haughtiness.

"No," he said.

She dropped the letter upon the table helplessly, while tears filled her eyes.

" Then what can she do ? "

The words were spontaneous, but they could not have been better chosen. They appealed to the obstinate man as no pleading or upbraiding could have done. They were simple and graphic, and they went straight to their mark, touching both his manliness and his pride.

He arose and paced back and forth, while the bitterness that had controlled him during the past few years battled with the emotions Mercede's position had awakened.

At last, reaching out his hand, he took the letter and walked firmly to the house.

An hour later Agatha sat in the broad corridor at the foot of the stairs, listening to the footsteps of her uncle as he paced his room. How closely connected with the human drama is a measured tread!

As the clock struck the half hour after ten, the Count rang for his valet and ordered the dog-cart to be brought at once. In a few minutes he came slowly down the stairs, and as the strong light from a window fell upon his face Agatha's heart throbbed with pity. He had evidently suffered much since she had last seen him. His manner was unnaturally deliberate and formal, and the expression of his eyes was cold.

" I am going to Como," he said quietly.

" I am sure it is best," was her reply.

" Then I am going to Mercede, and so is he."

Agatha was thinking rapidly but said nothing, and presently he added, —

"After the civil marriage I will send Mercede to Rome."

The carriage was announced, and while waiting for his overcoat to be brought he lit a cigarette and smoked calmly.

Agatha walked with him to the carriage, and as he bent and kissed her she found courage to speak.

" Suppose he objects?" she said.

The Count raised his eyebrows slightly and continued to pull on his gloves as he replied quietly, —

"He and I will settle our relations before we go to Mercede. Those once settled he won't object to anything!"

She was silent again, while he mounted to his place and gathered up the reins.

" I hope he won't give you much trouble," she sighed anxiously.

The General showed animation for the first time. He turned quickly and his eyes grew bright.

" Don't imagine," he exclaimed, " because a girl once trifled with me, that now a man may!" He struck his horse savagely and it sprang forward.

CHAPTER III.

WHEN Filippo made his bow to Agatha before luncheon a few days later, he was glad that her face fulfilled the measure of his expectation.

"Miss Page is a neighbor of mine," said the Duchess, diplomatically.

"I know that she is," was his astonishing reply.

"Yes?" and although her tone was neutral her face betrayed some vexation.

"Yes," he continued in answer to Agatha's look of inquiry; "I saw you, Signorina, the other day playing the violin to an old priest. I have felt ever since that I behaved rather shabbily, and I am glad of this chance to apologize."

"Where were you?" she asked, and as he hesitated the expressive eyes opened wider. In truth, he was not thinking of her question, but of the liquid quality of her voice.

"I beg your pardon," he said presently; "I was walking up the — that is — it was through a little iron gate in the wall." He actually showed embarrassment, to the delight of the Duchess.

"It was the day on which I arrived from Rome," she said simply, "and I was trying a new violin with

Padre Sacconi, who was my first master; did you
listen long?"

"That's just it," he replied; "I am ashamed to
say I lingered much longer than was necessary."

Her face grew bright. "Then you saw his pleasure perhaps?"

"Yes, I did;" and there was marked deference in
his manner as he added, "the whole thing touched
me very much."

"*Was n't* he sweet about it?" she said.

"His happiness and gratitude were certainly as
sincere as could be."

"Yes, it also made me very happy;" and she gave
a little sigh of contentment.

"I don't wonder!" and as the Duchess noticed
his tone and eyes she maliciously struck her bell.

The footman came, so she asked him if the Duke
had returned.

"Has he gone out, Signora?"

"That's what I wish to know," she replied; "however, let us have luncheon as soon as possible."

Filippo had sometimes believed that he was becoming blasé. The novels of Matilda Serao, Daudet,
and others, which his friends discussed with enthusiasm, awakened in him only a languid interest,
and he was conscious of preferring the society of
his sister, to whom he was devotedly attached, to
that of any younger woman. He still enjoyed the
companionship of children, and he and his little niece
Gaeta were great friends; but this fact he regarded
as additional evidence that he had drifted unscathed
through the rapids in which most of his companions

had lost their identity. He believed the reason of this to be that he was exceptionally impervious to the influence of feminine charms.

But the young stoic had not been in Agatha's presence fifteen minutes when he found his eyes constantly seeking her face ; and at luncheon, as a ray of sunshine fell across her hair, revealing its gold, he was betrayed into an undisguised stare, that caused the young visitor to flush slightly, and presently her hand stole over her locks to discover if one of them had escaped.

After luncheon the Duke excused himself and, as usual, disappeared with Gaeta. The Duchess watched them affectionately until they were out of sight, and then proposed a stroll to the coffee-house, a suggestion which Loreno warmly seconded. Although Agatha's slender figure and erect carriage made her appear tall, Filippo stood well above her as he walked at her side past the flower-beds and across the lawn.

"They make a striking couple," thought the Duchess.

When they reached the coffee-house, a picturesque little building overhanging the valley, the Duchess seated herself on a bench upon the veranda, while Agatha and Loreno went on a few yards farther to a wall upon the brow of the hill, leaning upon which they gazed at the peaceful scene far below. Presently the sound of children's voices floated up to them, and Filippo saw his companion's face brighten.

"You are fond of children," he said.

" Yes, of course; and the children about here are such pretty little things."

" Everything connected with this place seems especially lovely to you, I suppose."

" I am very fond of it all, for I live here fully half the year."

" I begin to think I also might become very fond of it."

She turned and looked at him with frank pleasure. " I 'm glad to hear you say that, for I take a personal pride in the place. Just look at the plain as it sweeps far off toward the south like a great green sea! Does n't it appear to be broken into waves by the breeze from those rugged old mountains at the head of the valley? Then see those two little lakes that seem to be looking right up at us, — the blue eyes of the Brianza, I call them, — and those towers and steeples on the horizon! I suppose they are mere silhouettes to you, but I know each one intimately. And see that picturesque old monastery up there to our right, — that building with the square campanile on the hill toward Como; and beyond the hill see that distant bank of white, like clouds: it is the Alps. Is n't it beautiful? Do you wonder that I delight in it?"

" Indeed I do not!" he responded heartily.

He had watched her with growing interest and pleasure, and as her enthusiasm had tempted her out of her quiet of manner and speech, his admiration had been squarely challenged. The Duchess smiled quietly at his absorbed interest, and began to think she had no need to waste sympathy on her little neighbor.

Filippo glanced toward his sister but did not notice her amusement, for he was looking beyond her at the lawn, and contrasting the women he last met there with this lovely girl.

"I was unjust to Costanza," he thought; "for she *has* some neighbors who interest me."

The following day a dog-cart drove up to the Villa Ricci, and Loreno left cards for the Count and his niece. While driving back through a grove of chestnuts that lay between the house and the lodge he came face to face with Agatha and Padre Sacconi. The young girl had been visiting a sick woman in the village, and the priest meeting her had walked home with her by the high-road.·

Loreno pulled up, and throwing the reins to the groom sprang out.

"Good-morning," he said; "have you been for a walk?"

Agatha held out her hand. "Only a short one," she replied. "Padre Sacconi, let me present the Marquis Loreno. This is the gentleman who attended our matinée."

"Indeed!" said the priest, heartily; "then, Marchese, you are fortunate, for we are exclusive. But you must have been very quiet."

"A young peasant in my part of the country," he replied, "chanced one day upon a maid who was painting the reflection of the clouds upon the glassy surface of a stream. Fascinated by her charms, the youth drew nearer and nearer until he stood almost at her side. Turning quickly, the fair artist saw him and instantly disappeared. Nor did he ever look upon her again, although he hovered near the same spot day after day until at last he became mad through lamenting the folly which had cost him the vision of an angel."

The priest smiled. " Well answered," he said, pronouncing his words deliberately. " And you, profiting by your neighbor's experience, win the chance of turning a pretty compliment. From your accent I judge you to be Roman."

" So I am, though I have a villa near Varese and am very fond of Lombardy."

Padre Sacconi believed Lombardy to be the loveliest spot in the world, and this sentiment of Loreno's confirmed the favorable impression which his frank face and easy bearing had already made upon the old man.

" Yes," he said in reply, " God has indeed blessed Lombardy without stint. And so you prefer our northern lakes to the stretches of sea around Naples? So do I. Sorrento, Castellammare, and the rest are charming for a time, but I always rejoice to get back to these quiet scenes."

" Won't you return to the house ? " asked Agatha, turning to Loreno. " I regret that my uncle is away from home, but Padre Sacconi will represent him. I have promised to give the Padre a granita, and perhaps you will join us."

Filippo expressed his pleasure, and Agatha led the way. She turned into various paths winding through the venerable grove, until suddenly they reached a circular opening, no larger than a room of moderate

size, containing a table and arm-chairs carved out of
granite. From this little resting-place the path ran on
with gradual ascent through a dense arbor of holly.
Peering up the long vista framed by this arbor, Loreno
discovered a flight of steps rising lazily until only a
distant spot of light marked the level of the terrace
to which they led.

Entering the arbor, they walked slowly to the
steps, having mounted which they emerged upon the
green terrace dotted with spreading palms and mag-
nolia-trees.

Loreno looked about him with interest. The terrace was large and nearly square. In front of him
was the house, on one side were green-houses, on
the other a row of old oak-trees, while in the centre
a fountain of clear water cooled the air. Under a
palm stood a table and two or three wicker chairs,
to which Agatha led them.

As she walked toward the house Filippo followed
her with his eyes, and when she disappeared he cast
an observant glance at her home.

"It's a comfortable-looking house," he said to
himself, "and that ivy is rather an English touch.
I wonder which room is hers? Probably the one
with the flowers in the window and the blue curtain-
ribbons."

The fact that he had a companion flashed into his
mind, and thereupon by way of conversation he asked
his opinion concerning the attitude of the Vatican
towards Germany.

Agatha presently came across the lawn followed
by a servant bearing ices, and stood behind the chair

of the priest listening to his final words. She loved
at such times to watch his face brighten under the
influence of his thought. As she heard him speaking
of European politics, quite unconscious of Loreno's
intimate knowledge of the subject, she glanced furtively at the young Marquis. She saw only serious
attention, and was glad; for she was inclined to like
him, and it would have offended her had he appeared
indifferent to the opinions of one for whom she felt
such respect.

CHAPTER IV.

MERCEDE.

As the days passed by and Count Ricci neither came home nor wrote, Agatha grew more and more anxious. She longed to write to Mercede for news, but the silence of her uncle, as well as his continued absence, convinced her that serious and absorbing measures were in progress, into which mere eagerness for information had no right to intrude.

On one point her mind dwelt constantly, with varying hope and misgiving, and that was upon the question of Mercede's return to Erba.

She was confident that the love between the Count and his child had not been seriously weakened by their estrangement. She could not believe that the Count's bitterness could withstand the presence of his daughter and her child, nor could she doubt that Mercede's pride would be subdued by this evidence of her father's affection. Even if the Count should succeed in having the civil marriage performed, Agatha did not believe that her high-spirited cousin would consent to remain with a husband she must despise, nor did she believe that the Count or the lieutenant himself would favor such an adjustment of the matter. Therefore Mercede would be thrown upon her father's protection, and where would he so naturally bring her, and where would Mercede's heart so naturally turn, as back to her old home?

In this hope Agatha caused her cousin's former room to be set in order, and prepared an adjoining room for the child. Each morning she had them opened to the sunshine, and with her own hands placed flowers about them. It was with keen expectation, therefore, that one night she received a telegram sent by the Count from Rome announcing his return on the following day. The telegram said nothing about Mercede; but this fact did not discourage her, and she caused the same preparations as before to be made for her cousin's return.

At the appointed time the Count arrived, but he was alone.

Agatha welcomed him at the door and tried to hide her disappointment. He stepped out of the carriage heavily, seeming tired and worn; yet his face was calm, and she concluded that he had been successful. He went immediately to his study, where she followed him. Laying a paper upon the table, he looked into her eager face and said quietly, —

"That is Mercede's marriage certificate. She is in Rome with her child."

"I hoped you would change your mind and bring them home with you."

"No," he replied, "not here, — at least, not yet."

His tone as well as his words led her to hope that his feeling toward Mercede was less bitter, and she was more than ever at a loss to understand their continued estrangement.

But it was not so difficult to understand, even theoretically; indeed, a less charitable mind would quickly have fathomed the reason.

The Count's determination to obtain justice for Mercede had not been prompted entirely by quickened love, since a few moments' reflection had shown him that unless she were made a legal wife her disgrace would fall upon his name. Yet his heart was wrung by her misery; and had she shown ample penitence and made it easy to reconcile proper regard for his outraged authority with full forgiveness, he would have welcomed the chance of restoring her to the old place both in his heart and home. But Mercede was morally unable to appreciate the extent of her wrong-doing. She had never been taught that she actually owed consideration to either duty or authority. She failed, except in a feeble and sentimental way, to recognize that she had any obligation to others. She knew that she had disappointed her father in regard to her marriage, and at first regretted the depth of the wound she had inflicted; but she soon began to think that he was nursing his hurt, and as weeks went by she decided that he was sulking, and at her expense. His quick response to the news of her disgrace did not touch her heart, for she reasoned, correctly enough, that no father would be inactive when the honor of his child was at stake. She loved him deeply, however; and had he given ample evidence of the regret she believed he must feel when he learned what she had suffered, and when he looked upon the grandchild he had ignored, she would have been disposed to meet him part way, and make such acknowledgment as was consistent with her notions of her own self-respect.

Is it strange, therefore, that they did not renew the old relation? In the beginning each waited for the other, and as the days passed, each stubborn heart justified itself at the expense of the other, while love, rebuked, shrouded its face.

Agatha, divining little of all this, longed to hear something of his visit and of Mercede; but she waited for her uncle to speak.

He stood by the table with his hand upon the paper and seemed lost in thought. Presently he placed the certificate within his safe, which he closed and locked.

"Have you any news for me?" he asked, with assumed spirit, seating himself upon the lounge.

"Nothing of importance; every one is well; I have some letters for you; Padre Sacconi has been here almost every day, and — Oh yes, I have a piece of news, after all!"

He tried to appear interested.

"Yes, and what is it?" he asked.

"I have a card for you, left by the Marquis Loreno."

His interest became more genuine.

"I met him at the Villa Faviola and he called the next day."

"The Marquis Loreno, indeed! I have heard of him," he paused, and she waited with fixed gaze, "favorably. How were you impressed?"

"Padre Sacconi and I liked him."

"Oh! Come sit here and tell me about it. Was Padre Sacconi at the Duke Faviola's?"

"No — he — that is, we met the Marquis after he had left cards here."

"And the Marquis came back with you?"

"Yes."

"And the Padre and you talked him over afterward?"

"Yes, we spoke of him the next day."

He smiled slightly. "Then the gentlemen left together the day before?"

"Yes, they did; but how could you know this?"

"Did the Padre think the young Marquis handsome?"

"Yes — that is, he said he was fine-looking and intelligent."

"And have you usually found the Padre's taste good?"

She hesitated and flushed slightly.

"I don't remember ever having asked him before."

"Was your own opinion so uncertain that you needed the priest's?"

She glanced up quickly and caught a merry twinkle in the Count's eye.

"Oh, Uncle," she exclaimed, "what a shame to make fun of me!"

He passed his arm around her and kissed her forehead. "When do you expect to see this young man again?" he asked.

"Never! now don't try to tease me any more. I really did n't talk to him much; he and Padre Sacconi seemed to take a great fancy to each other."

4

" If he likes old men, possibly I may interest him ; may induce him to come here occasionally, and even — "

" Please, stop ! " — her tone was quite serious, — " he isn't just the sort of man to joke about. But you don't think I was silly in speaking about him to Padre Sacconi, do you ? "

" Not at all, my child ; not at all," he said. " Always speak your thoughts honestly and be your simple transparent self."

He stroked her fine hair, and each remained quiet for some moments. Presently the old man sighed. She believed he was thinking of the child he had so often caressed in the same way, and she yearned to profit by the moment and speak of her.

" Uncle," she began gently, " why did you bring me to your home when I was alone ? "

" Because I pitied you, and you were my sister's child," he answered unsuspiciously.

" You pitied me because I was alone ? "

" Precisely."

" And protected me because I was your niece ? "

" Naturally."

" Would you do it now ? "

" Now I would do it for your own sweet sake."

" Uncle ! "— she leaned forward and gazed wistfully into his face, — " some one else is alone and has sad need of you. Some one else — No, dear Uncle, don't leave me ; don't be angry ; you just told me to speak my thoughts honestly. Mercede is the same old Mercede. She has the same intense love for you, the same pride in your name. She has been misled, but

what of it? Can't you forgive a mere girl a sentimental folly? You know what *you* have suffered;
she can't have suffered less. I feel sure that she
longs to come home and that you long to have her
back. It should be so; nothing is right as it is.
Every one is unhappy, and there seems to be no
reason for it."

As he listened he was swayed alternately by pride
and self-condemnation. His was an arbitrary nature,
and false shame taught him that to relent was weak.
Therefore, while his heart yearned for Mercede, he
nevertheless sought to justify the position he had
taken. She had given no token of repentance, so he
told himself, and how could any one reasonably ask
him to restore her to her old place? But why should
he be called upon to discuss the matter, much less to
justify himself? His reasons were his own, and he
had given Agatha plainly to understand that he desired to have the subject dismissed. That she should
now attempt to stir it up again and unsettle his mind,
produced a feeling of sudden irritation which overshadowed all other considerations. He turned indignantly and looked her full in the eye.

Had she faltered he would have reproved her
sharply for her temerity, but her gaze was as steady
as his. The issue was simple and sharp. He intended to bury the subject here and now; she would
not permit it. It was a conflict of will, and hers was
the stronger. Although his eyes remained fixed upon
hers, his lips were dumb.

The decisive moment passed, leaving her the victor.

Yet he could not yield without making terms; few

men can. The young girl whose calm eyes were
searching his did not fathom his mental process;
she merely felt keenly and trusted her intuitions.
Something told her that she had won, but she believed
it due to his innate goodness. He also knew that the
victory was hers, but he sought solace for his pride
in capitulation.

"I should have been better pleased," he said, "had
you let this subject rest for the present. It has absorbed me for some days and I am tired of it."

"Then don't let us speak of it any more to-day,"
she replied. "But may I write to Mercede and give
her your love?"

He hesitated.

"And would there be any harm in my saying that
I'm dying to see her, and that she mustn't stay in
Rome too long?"

"I don't know that there would."

"And that you also want her?"

At another time her persistency might have irri-
tated him; but having yielded what he had, to yield
the rest was easy, for his heart leaped at the thought
of again having his child. As Agatha folded her
hands around his arm and looked into his face like an
angel of mercy, his pent-up love and his manliness
responded to her silent plea and swept away the
remnant of his pride.

"Tell Mercede I want her," he exclaimed, in a
broken voice. "Tell her to come home!"

Mercede sat in her old home, after an absence of
five years, reading her cousin's letter.

The palace was one which had been in her father's family for generations, and did not differ essentially from the majority of solid old structures which contain the homes of the Roman aristocracy. It was built of brick and stone around a large paved court. The stairs were high and imposing, and at every landing an ancient and mutilated bust seemed either to appeal for a merciful judgment upon its deformity, or to bear its suffering in the jaunty spirit of its compatriot Mucius.

The rooms of the Ricci apartment were large, and furnished in rather sombre colors. There was an air of dignity, or better, of seriousness, pervading the place, which, judging from the portraits distributed along the panelled walls, was characteristic of the Count's family. The room in which Mercede sat was what had formerly been her sitting-room, and its warm color made a rich setting to her dark beauty.

She was a typical Roman in the first years of womanhood, with full figure, thick coils of black hair, fine eyes and teeth, rich color, and possessing by nature the rapidity and range of expression of a finished actress.

The letter affected her in quite a different way from that which Agatha had anticipated.

" The erring child may return, may she ? " was her bitter exclamation. " Turned off for years because she preferred to choose her own husband, and only invited to resume her rights when she must return without him ! No, sir ! your daughter has some of her honored father's pride, and will send you a message that will open your eyes."

Her unhappiness, especially during the past two weeks, had worn sadly upon her nerves, and the letter excited her unduly. She felt this, and struggled to be calmer. She tried to read ; to amuse her boy ; to sew ; but it was useless. She could not banish thought, and soon abandoned herself to the bitterness which possessed her.

" Think of it !" she exclaimed passionately. " I — a Ricci — am one of your women to be pitied. *Per Dio !*" and springing to her feet, she paced the room, uttering her scorn audibly from time to time. " Even my father receives me as a Magdalen, so what need I expect from the rest of the world ? Yet I don't blame them. They judge according to their standard, and," she added, laughing bitterly, " my marriage can't be called dazzling."

She threw open the window to get air, and stood for a moment looking into the street.

" Come, Francesco," she said, " let us go out. Mamma needs to walk."

The child had been quietly watching some fish in a globe upon the table, quite unmindful of her excitement, to which he had grown accustomed during the past year.

They walked aimlessly but rapidly until, at last, her passion was cooled, and being near the Ponte Sisto she yielded to the child's wish to go upon the bridge and see the boats.

They stood for some time on the footway, watching the dredging of the river.

" What are they doing, mamma?" asked the child.

" Digging up the clay."

" What for ? "

" To make the river deeper."

" What is clay ? "

" Clay ? It 's damp earth."

" What do they do with it ? "

" Oh, they make marbles for little boys to play with, and pipes ; and some men make pretty figures with it."

" Figures, — what are they like ? "

" Why, they are shapes ; some are little boys just like you."

"I should like so much to have one to play with!" exclaimed the child. " Won't you get me one, mamma ? "

" You don't understand yet, caro mio ; you are too young." ¯

" But I 'll try to understand if you 'll get me one. Can't you make them ? "

Mercede smiled slightly, but suddenly grew serious.

A train of thought had been awakened which, although interesting, made no strong impression at first. In her childhood she had shown cleverness at modelling in clay and wax ; and without other instruction than that gained by repeated visits to the galleries of sculpture, she continued to improve, until, during the year before her marriage, she had made several busts which gave evidence of decided talent. During the bitter experience following her marriage she had had no inclination for such work, and later she was engrossed in earning food each day for her child and herself. She recalled and reviewed these ·facts, and the more she dwelt upon them the more intent she became, until her thoughts, gliding swiftly and uncontrolled, left the past and swept forward, and presently a sigh of regret was stifled by an exclamation of wonder.

The child looked up. " What is it, mamma ? "

" Hush, dear; mamma wishes to think ! "

If she could do something with her talent, what then? was the question she kept asking herself. And now her mental vision eagerly scanned the path her thought had taken, until her head grew hot and dizzy. It seemed to her that a way had suddenly been illumined, which afforded her a chance of escape from the hopeless misery of her present life. Her position was indeed insupportable. Her disgrace was already an open secret, and in the autumn would be public property. Everywhere she showed her face she would be pointed at with disrespect, and her story would be whispered from one to another, while her old associates would regard her either with pity or a sneer—she cared not which, for the thought of one was as galling as the other. She could not go to her father, for even he offered her a home as though it were a refuge. She had her dowry now, on which both Francesco and she could live comfortably, but where could she live happily? Where could she live with any hope except that after many years, when both she and her story had become musty, her presence might be tolerated by a few good-hearted friends?

But, on the other hand, suppose she should leave Rome and cultivate her talent? Even if she failed, she would lose nothing, for her time had no value.

Indeed, she would even then have gained a respite from her unceasing despair, and though the result were disappointment she could not be sadder than now.

But suppose she should succeed? Suppose she should even be able to return to Rome some day, no matter how far away, when her talent might turn pity and sneering into acclamation? Was this not an object worth striving for? Was this chance, even though desperate, to be thrown away? Having once nurtured the thought, could she sink back into the old, aimless, hopeless existence? She clenched her hands until the fingers ached, and muttered fiercely, "No; never! never!"

Then she gave herself up to enchantment, and as was natural to her wilful nature refused even to consider further any reasons which might modify her transport. Presently, however, some details bearing on her plan forced themselves upon her mind, but she banished them when they began to be troublesome. It was time enough to ford a torrent when it was reached. Upon one thing, however, she was determined, — to drop her name and assume another in its place; and then, as often happens at such moments, her mind was occupied with this unimportant question.

The name André suggested itself to her, and she repeated it several times, — "Madame André! Mercede André!" It sounded well, and would do unless she thought of a better, although it sounded French. Yet why not? Would Paris not be the best of all places for her object? It would take her away.

from Italy altogether, while the advantages for her work would be good, and the city was large enough to hide in.

Then London suggested itself, since she spoke English quite as fluently as French; but her heart inclined more toward the brighter city, and she was in no humor to weigh reasons. Yes, to Paris she would go! Then her thoughts were turned again toward the distant future, and her enthusiasm mounted once more until it swept away all restraint of imagination, and she was confident that a splendid career was open to her.

She felt, not for the first time, that she was no ordinary woman. Circumstances, bad luck, inexperience, — something, had hitherto kept her down; but it mattered little now, for her time had come. The thought overwhelmed her, and for the first time in many days she thanked God.

"Come, Francesco!" she said excitedly, her beauty radiant as of old, "come! let us hurry home, for mamma must stop on the way."

Her step had its old firmness, her blood seemed to rush through her veins, as she walked swiftly toward the Corso. An hour ago how dark her future seemed! Then there had been nothing—worse than nothing — to look forward to. Now, how different! Remembering how the new idea was suggested to her, she bent down and gratefully kissed her child. Stopping at a shop, she bought some iron supports and some clay, and then hurried home. She awaited their arrival as patiently as she could, in the mean time arranging a provisional studio and posing Fran-

cesco in various attitudes, her heart at one moment
throbbing with wild hope, at the next faint with
despair. At last the clay arrived. She kneaded it
lovingly, and then began her momentous task. She
was very serious, and firmly holding herself in check,
worked slowly and carefully. The afternoon was
fast passing, and little Francesco needed frequent
rest. Mercede urged and commanded, then begged
him to be quiet, and he did his best; but the light
began to grow dim before she had finished blocking
out the head.

She worked all the next day and into the afternoon
of the day following; then stood back and critically
surveyed the bust. To her eye it seemed like the
child. In any case she had no patience to work
over it longer. She must have relief for the strain
upon her mind; the matter must be settled without
further delay; the work must stand as it was, — a
silent witness before the judge to whom she would
intrust her fate.

She drove to the studio of a sculptor whom she
had known before her marriage, and whose skill and
judgment in art were not excelled in Rome. She
knocked with a trembling hand, and it was a new
sensation to her. Formerly when she had visited
this studio she had felt that to some degree she was
patronizing the place, but this was before she had
attempted any serious work of her own; now she
wondered at her former arrogance, and felt a becoming sense of humility as she stood upon the
threshold of Genius.

The artist was still at work, and came immediately

from his modelling-room to receive her. He recognized her and greeted her kindly. She briefly stated
her wish; would he come and look at a bust of her
boy she had at home? He told her that he never
judged the work of other artists. But this work, she
declared, was not by an artist. He frowned slightly
and begged to be excused; he really had no time to
criticise amateur efforts.

Her disappointment was so great that she had difficulty in restraining her tears. He noticed this, and
although surprised, was touched by it; his manner
softened, and he asked her to follow him to his modelling-room, where they could speak more privately.
This respite restored her courage and enabled her to
form her decision, and when they were seated she
told him briefly as much of her story as was necessary to explain her position, and then acknowledged
that the work was her own.

Without further delay the kind-hearted man took
off his blouse and prepared to go with her. Ten
minutes later they stood before her work.

As she watched him calmly studying the figure, all
that the moment portended rushed over her and she
grew faint; but she would not, she must not distract
his attention at this supreme moment, and by force
of will she conquered.

At last he spoke: "You say you have never
studied; is that literally true?"

"Yes."

"It's almost incredible!" she heard him say —
and then her will gave way.

CHAPTER V.

MIGNONETTE AND ORCHIDS.

THE promise of a genial season, written upon the hillsides by the spring primrose, seemed at last fulfilled. This flower and its sweet sister, the violet, had long since disappeared with the hepaticas and anemones, but the air was still fragrant with wild lilies-of-the-valley, locust-trees, and golden laburnum blossoms.

Agatha raised her eyes from the plant she was watering not far from the house, and scanned the branches of a tree near by from which the song of a nightingale came.

" How perfectly you have placed your nest, you vain little thing ! " she said half aloud. She knew the spot well, with its famous echo.

The half smile still lingered on her lips, when she was startled by a voice just behind her.

" Good-morning, Signorina."

She turned and looked into the face of the Marquis Loreno. She was glad to see him, and returned his greeting cordially.

" What an odd plant to cultivate ! " he said, glancing at the vervain she had been watering. " Do you

drive away ill spirits with it as our respected ancestors did, or do you use it to unveil the future?"

"Neither," she answered gayly; "I'm too practical by half — my Anglo-Saxon half. My sensible
English ancestors tied it around their necks to ward
off disease. Why, in their day it cured nearly thirty
different complaints, and quite thirty when tied with
a white ribbon."

"Then by all means give me a spray," he pleaded;
"in common humanity you can't refuse."

"Unfortunately this is an Italian vervain."

"But don't you think it worth trying, — say with
a double quantity of white ribbon?"

"I'm afraid not; but I'll give you a spray of
mignonette instead; it heals bruises."

He laughed quietly. "I must say your language
of flowers is a practical one," he remarked, walking
with her toward the bank of mignonette a few steps
farther down the path.

"I am half American, and that must be my
excuse."

"But you have sentiment enough when you are
with your violin."

"That depends," she said slyly.

"Oh, upon your audience — yes, I see!" and he
was amused at his own discomfiture.

Agatha's heart misgave her lest she had hurt his
feelings, so she tried to soften the impression he
seemed to have received.

"Perhaps what I mean is rather this," she said
seriously: "different natures find different responses
in flowers as well as in music. As I can't interpret

all music equally well, perhaps the appeal of certain
flowers escapes me."

Her kind effort had a more cheering effect than
she intended, for her companion broke into a hearty
laugh.

"Upon my word, Miss Page," he exclaimed, "I
ought to be ashamed to find your soft-heartedness
amusing; but don't let mercy spoil so pretty a prick
as you gave me. If I induce you to fence, I must
abide by the consequences."

Plucking a spray of mignonette she divided it, and
putting one part in her dress handed him the other.
"I hope this spray will heal the prick," she said.

As he took it he watched her eyes; but when they
were upturned to his frankly, he caught no subtle
expression to give her words additional weight.

He held the flower a moment before speaking.

"Your spray seems a little bigger than mine," he
said. "Would you mind changing, — simply upon
medicinal grounds?"

She flushed slightly, but without hesitation loosened
her spray.

"There!" she said; "country doctors, I believe,
not only give their own drugs, but in big doses, and I
suppose I ought to be consistent."

He placed the flower carefully in his button-hole.

She held in her hand the spray he had given her,
and he wondered if she would throw it away.

"Let us go to the house," she said presently; "I
wish to present you to my uncle."

"I have already presented myself," he replied. "I
called this morning to pay my respects to the Count,

and he received me most kindly. While we were talking, the gardener came to consult him, so he sent me out here, saying that I should find you and that he would join us presently."

He was conscious of pleasure as he spoke the word "us," and wondered if he had spoken it quite naturally. Self-consciousness is like yawning: it seizes its victim suddenly, and there is no use trying to browbeat it. Strict silence helps to disguise it, but to speak is to be lost. Unfortunately Loreno spoke.

"It's curious," he said impulsively, "to find myself here talking to you."

Agatha showed surprise. "Why?" she asked.

"Because —" He paused and began to cast about for an answer. What could he say? He dare not risk telling her that he had thought of her constantly since the hour he discovered her, nor in fact was he prepared to go so far. He was ashamed to turn his remark into a bald compliment, and yet he must make some reply.

Agatha was distressed as she watched his embarrassment, but suddenly believed she had fathomed it.

"I think," she ventured, "that you are a little too sensitive about having chanced upon me the other day while I was playing. I really don't see anything so dreadful in it; was there?"

He accepted with alacrity this chance of extricating himself.

"Any way, it's very good of you to treat it so leniently," he replied.

"Do you play any instrument, or sing?" she asked.

"I sing a little, and I paint in an amateur fashion."

" What do you paint, — landscapes, or portraits ? "

" Portraits, usually."

Agatha's eye brightened with pleasure; she had felt sure that he had a talent for something.

" What are you working on at present ? "

His eyes twinkled. " A combination of both," he replied.

She was thoroughly interested and was about to ask more concerning his work, when the Count joined them.

" Have you shown the Marquis the orchids? " he asked, turning to Agatha.

" Not yet; but we might go and see them now if the Marquis wishes."

Loreno declared that he should be delighted ; and they all went to the conservatory, where the Count had many specimens of this weird flower.

" After all," said Agatha when they had looked through the collection, " while I admire orchids, I have n't the peculiar sympathy with them that I have with other flowers."

" I feel the same," said Loreno. " An orchid seems to me more like an animal than a plant."

The General nodded his head. " That 's just it," he said; " their splendid colors and their seeming wilfulness have a great fascination for me." He chuckled quietly and then added, " They remind me a little of my daughter."

Agatha was delighted to hear him mention Mercede so familiarly, and turning to Loreno, who was searching the distant horizon as though a thunderbolt had fallen, she said, —

5

"The next time you call, my cousin, Signora Finelli, will be here."

"There has evidently been a reconciliation," thought Loreno with a tinge of regret; for he did not consider a woman under a cloud a fit companion for the young girl into whose clear eyes he was looking.

"Indeed!" he said aloud.

"Yes; she has been away a long time," said the Count, "and at last she's coming home again." Then he added in a lower tone as though to himself, "It will be very pleasant to have her here in the old way,— very."

"When do you expect your daughter?" Filippo inquired, conscious that he had not said enough.

"We don't know definitely, but I almost hope for her to-morrow; still, something may keep her a day or two longer in Rome."

"I shall be curious to see how closely she resembles the orchid; but," he continued, deliberately leading the subject to less perplexing ground, "do you really find that the colors of the orchid are more admirable than those of the usual garden flowers?"

Then they debated again this much debated question, Loreno finding a secret pleasure in joining forces with Agatha. He watched her closely, and began to think that he had never seen a face combining so many of the qualities which he admired in a woman. Then, too, while holding to her point firmly, she argued with so much modesty and such becoming deference to her uncle's opinions, that Filippo, in thinking over the conversation on his homeward ride, pronounced her conduct to have been perfect, indifferent to the fact that ninety-nine young women in a hundred would have acquitted themselves quite as creditably. But Filippo was developing a tendency to idealize everything that Agatha did or said, throwing over her all the charm of his glowing imagination and intemperate nature.

The next day, although Agatha was up very early, she found that the Count was before her. He was walking in the garden picking flowers, — a most unusual thing for him, — and as Agatha drew near she heard him humming an old song of Mercedo's. When he caught the sound of her footstep he looked up brightly.

"So here you are!" he exclaimed. "I began to fear I was doomed to solitude this glorious morning. Come, a fresh rose for a kiss!"

Agatha went to him and kissed him affectionately. "You deserve two," she said, "for the improvement in your hours."

"To-morrow, perhaps I shall receive two," he replied. "But we must not be too sure, for it's not so easy for a woman to run off to the country at a day's notice, especially a woman with a child; and, by the bye, Agatha, that's a fine little boy of hers, — a very pretty child indeed."

"I have his photograph; did he not remind you of dear Aunt Teresa?"

"Very much. Is the photograph here, or in Rome?"

"I brought it with me; let me get it."

"Never mind now, dear," he said. "I'm going

to Erba for the morning mail, and we ought to have
our coffee immediately; won't you hurry it, and
bring the picture to the table?"

She went to the house, and a few minutes later
the Count followed. As Agatha busied herself with
the coffee, her companion bent affectionately over the
face of his grandson.

" I suppose that Francesco will sit here beside
me?" he said.

" Yes, and I'll sit opposite, in my old place."

" No, you must stay where you are."

" I don't wish to," she said. " I shall feel it much
more of an honor to be near you."

He laughed nervously. " Well," he said, " arrange
it all as you think best;" and after a pause he added
fervently, " it will be even pleasanter than it used
to be, for now we shall have the child."

After breakfast Agatha watched him drive away,
and then went to Mercede's rooms to see that
they were in order. Upon the sitting-room table
were the flowers which the Count had so carefully
selected.

" Dear uncle!" she said half aloud; " I hope he
won't have to wait another day."

She went down to the lawn where she could watch
for his return, but as soon as she saw him knew that
he had been disappointed.

" No letter from Rome," he said as bravely as he
could. " I suppose it was unreasonable to expect
her so soon, but I hoped that at least she would send
a line."

In spite of her own disappointment Agatha tried

to comfort him. Putting her arm through his she said, —

"She probably missed the post.. I'm sure you will hear from her this afternoon."

"But if she had written immediately we should have received the letter last night."

"Yes, but she probably waited to decide when she could come."

He seemed to be considering this explanation.

"That's true," he said presently; "I think you are right. I hope we shall know to-night."

But neither that day nor the next brought any news from Mercede, and the Count's growing disappointment was sad to see. Agatha was at a loss to understand her cousin's silence, and determined, if no letter should come the following day, that she would telegraph to her.

When she met the Count the next morning, he was pale and haggard, and it was evident that he had not slept. His nerves were at a high tension, and she dreaded the effect of another disappointment. After watching him furtively for a few moments she made up her mind that he ought not to go to the post-office alone, for he could scarcely guide the cup to his lips, because of the trembling of his hand.

"Would you mind taking me with you this morning, Uncle?" she asked. "It's very hard to bear the suspense here all alone."

The reason appealed to him, but at the same time he was conscious of less power to bear stoically another fruitless errand.

"In case we don't hear anything this morning, I might telegraph," she suggested desperately, seeing his indecision.

This seemed to impress him favorably.

"Yes,—it might be well," he replied.

"Then I may go?"

"Well, I don't know,—perhaps."

She chose to accept this as final, and when the carriage was announced, sent for her hat.

They arrived at the post-office before the postmaster, and waited for him half an hour. There were a dozen or fifteen contadini present in the dingy little room; the men smoking and speaking occasionally in guttural tones, while they stared with curiosity at the Count and Agatha, whose faces they knew well. The Count talked rapidly and incessantly during the sorting of the letters, and as his excitement continued to increase, Agatha grew more and more anxious.

As the window was swung open, she saw her uncle turn pale. He suddenly stopped talking, but stood stolidly, with his back toward the letters.

The contadini waited for him to advance.

"Buon giorno Eccelenza," called the official, "only two papers for you this morning — and a letter."

The Count turned quickly and his face flushed.

"Let me get them," pleaded Agatha, laying her hand upon his arm.

"I will get them," he replied firmly, as he moved forward.

Taking the letter with eager eyes and compressed lips, he scanned it, and with an exclamation of delight handed it to Agatha, to whom it was addressed in Mercede's handwriting.

She tore open the envelope, and standing close together, each read as follows: —

MY DEAR AGATHA, — Thank my father for his eleventh-hour consideration. Were I not his daughter it would be ungracious to decline his invitation; but with his blood in my veins and his pride in my heart, I should disgrace him did I so humble myself.

My father turned his back upon me for years; then he recognized his obligation merely to save his own honor. It would be undutiful to continue to offend that sensitive honor with the presence of the offender and her child born out of wedlock, and I propose to bury the past with more certainty than through death, — to disappear without need of a gravestone. In fact, Agatha, at the moment you read this I shall have begun a new life, with a new name; I here and now renounce the old, *absolutely*.

If at some future day I should return under new conditions and my father and you, like the rest of the world, will receive me for my new self alone, I shall then be truly grateful and happy.

With abiding honor for my father and love for you,

MERCEDE.

The old Count staggered and uttered a cry of pain, then with a ghastly struggle he conjured up a smile. "Come, Agatha," he said, offering her his arm gallantly, "come, my dear. We should be going; my early rising betrayed me into a yawn."

And as the villagers raised their hats to him, he courteously returned the salute, and passing through them went out into the air.

CHAPTER VI.

AT THE IRON GATE.

It was about eleven o'clock when Agatha, hearing from her uncle's valet that the Count was sleeping quietly, put on her hat and started out to find Padre Sacconi.

The sun shone as brightly as yesterday, yet somehow it seemed less joyous. The quiet about her, usually so welcome, oppressed her now. The memory of a distant day came back to her; on that day also everything and every one seemed horribly quiet, and her heart, as to-day, seemed numb. At that time her uncle had drawn her to him tenderly and tried to comfort her; now their positions were reversed, and to-day, when at last they had reached the house, and the Count's nerve gave way, she had been the comforter, stroking his hair and suggesting such hopeful thoughts as she could.

Yet this day was sadder than the other. The consolation of a tender parting had been hers, while the desolate old man yonder had no look of love to recall, no message to treasure. His cup was as full as hers, but filled with gall. In his surging grief he had moaned out each heartless phrase penned by Mercede, until with a shudder he cried, " They are

cold as steel, Agatha; they pierce like the stiletto."
And now, as the young girl recalled them, her in-
dignation grew hotter, until she exclaimed bitterly,
"Shame upon you, Mercede, shame!"

Reaching the iron gate through which Filippo had
first seen her, she flung it open vigorously, then
started back in surprise. She was confronted by the
easel of the young Marquis, and she saw its owner
stretched on the grass a few yards away, playing with
the Duke Faviola's dogs.

Her righteous indignation had given her unusual
color, and he thought she was annoyed at finding him
there. Rising hastily he turned his sketch, and then
held out his hand to her.

"Good-morning," he said.

She felt that her cheeks were hot, and her embarrassment was increased by his searching gaze.

"We seem fated to meet here," she said, seizing
upon the first words that entered her mind.

"This time I feel less guilty," he answered, "for
you must acknowledge that it's a pretty spot for a
sketch."

"It is very pretty, certainly," and her tone was as
gay as she could make it, "very pretty indeed."

"Have you started for a stroll, or are you going
somewhere — I mean, where I may not go with
you?"

"I am going to Padre Sacconi's, and think I had
better go alone, for I have something about which
to consult him; besides, I see that you are painting,
and I'll come back the other way to avoid disturbing
you."

"Then I'll not stay a moment longer," he said decisively. "I won't consent to drive you to the sunny high-road."

"If you really don't mind being disturbed, I'll come back this way; and now I must be going."

He watched her with surprise, for her manner was unnaturally gay.

"You are evidently in great spirits this morning," he said with a smile.

"And why not?" she answered; but in spite of herself she could not control the quick tears that sprang to her eyes, nor a premonitory little twitch at the corners of her mouth.

He was at her side in an instant, while something in his eyes and voice made her hold her breath.

"I wish I might know," he said, "that you hold me in enough esteem to call upon me if I can help you; for something has surely gone wrong, and very wrong."

Her nerves had been greatly strained by the events of the day, and she could scarcely choke back the tears. "I don't think you can help me," she replied in a low voice. "I fear no one can."

He looked at her earnestly. "Answer me but one question — may I ask it? Are you perfectly happy in your present home?"

"Yes," she cried quickly, "perfectly! I couldn't be happier."

He continued to look at her while he reflected.

"I don't wish to pry into your affairs," he said presently; "but because I don't press the subject I hope you won't think me indifferent."

She did not reply, for she was absorbed in thought. Intuitively she trusted this man, she was surprised to find how much. He seemed to her the most manly man she had ever met; as Padre Sacconi was the most saintly, and her uncle the kindest of men.

As she raised her glance to his earnest face and read the honesty and sympathy beaming in his eyes, how could she doubt him? She needed the advice of some one in this crisis, if only for the sake of her uncle, whose heart seemed broken and whose purpose seemed dead. Had it been a personal matter only, she might have remained silent; but she felt that she must share with some one her present responsibility. She did not believe that Mercede, could she but be found, would be inflexible; but where and how should they seek her? Padre Sacconi was the only person whom she had thought of consulting; but now Loreno's unexpected offer tempted her greatly. He was a man of the world, and his opinion upon such a subject would be worth more than that of the priest.

"Do you remember," she said at last, "that I told you my cousin was coming?"

"Perfectly; has she arrived?"

"No; and that is what troubles me."

"I'm very sorry; hasn't she written?"

"Yes, a terrible letter." She paused, and he watched her silently as her eyes filled with despair. "I don't know that any one can help me, and yet I can't be sure."

"Two heads are sometimes better than one. As I have said, I am entirely at your service."

"You are very kind. I was on my way to ask Padre Sacconi's opinion, but I am tempted to ask yours also. You have been more in the world, and might have better judgment about an affair of this sort." She looked into his attentive face. "Are you sincere? Do you really wish to help me, or are you merely courteous? Don't let me make a mistake!"

He stepped forward impulsively and looked straight into her eyes.

"Signorina," he said, "test my sincerity. I long to help you, and I promise to do everything in my power to justify — "

"Wait — " and she held up her hand; "first hear what it is."

"I don't care what it is," he replied, impelled not alone by his interest in Agatha, but by the natural impulse of manhood to aid a woman in trouble. "I invite your confidence, not to comfort you, but because I hope to serve you."

"I don't doubt it," she said firmly; "but I really have no right to draw you into my trouble."

He was silent a moment. "Can I say more than I have? Is it necessary to repeat what I have said already? Don't stand upon ceremony. Perhaps I can help you; I have said that I am more than anxious to do so; then why go backward? Why not take me at my word, and state frankly what your trouble is?" He paused, but she remained silent, and he added, "Indeed, I have already guessed it, — you fear your cousin has run away."

"We know that she has."

"With any one?"

" With her child."

"Simply run away from her husband, then?"

" They were not living together, and she was in Rome; as you know, we expected her here, but to-day a letter came from her saying she has run away. My uncle is heart-broken, and I must find her and induce her to come back."

She felt in her pocket and drew out Mercede's letter.

" Do you think any circumstances would justify my showing her letter to you?"

" Yes, but I can't judge whether the present circumstances would; you must decide."

" I must find her, and I have n't the faintest idea how to go about it. I feel utterly helpless, and don't dare to speak her name to my uncle. I wish I knew what to do!"

Without further hesitation he began to question her, thus, to her great relief, drawing the main facts from her; and the ice once broken, she readily handed him the letter and without reservation told him whatever she thought would throw light upon the affair.

He was indeed puzzled. What could have induced this flight? Mercede, as he learned, had no need to work, and dishonor was unlikely, since her letter spoke of a new life from which she might some day emerge with the respect of the world. Could she then have run away only to escape humiliation? Perhaps; but mere absence would not win respect: there must be something more active in her intention.

" You say she is beautiful and romantic," he said, after further reflection ; " she may intend to go upon the stage."

Agatha shook her head. " Possibly, but I doubt it ; my cousin never would consent to play a minor part."

" Would she, perhaps, try to do something with her taste for sculpture ? "

Agatha considered well before replying. " Possibly, but I doubt it. She had done so little at it."

They both remained silent, conning the main facts.

" I think I would simply be patient," Loreno said presently, " for you don't wish to make the matter public, and to search for her without attracting attention is impossible. Her experience in facing the world alone, may force her back to you ; but you can't touch her feelings even if you find her, — her letter convinces me of that. Her head is full of a new idea, besides which, she thinks she has a grievance. She will not come back until she has tested her experiment and is ready to bury her grievance. Leave her alone for the present ; but should further reflection suggest anything to be done, I shall be ready to do it."

" In the mean time," said Agatha, " what about her father? He 's terribly broken down."

" He will pull up again ; although, of course, such a wound must leave its mark. His breaking down was the best thing in the world for him ; it relieved the tension, and now his old pride will come to his aid."

" I fear that he will never be the same man after such a blow."

"How does my opinion about your cousin strike you?" he inquired.

Agatha silently reviewed what he had said; then with a deep sigh that went to her companion's heart she replied, "I'm afraid you are right."

"You don't know how it cuts me," he exclaimed, "to feel that anything I have said should make you sigh like that; I would ask no happier life than to—" the sudden fright that came into her eyes checked him, and he stammered in a changed voice, — "to always say pleasant things to people."

"Yes, I am sure of it," she found voice to reply, and then moving quickly to the gate seemed about to dart within its friendly protection, but on second thought came forward and gave him her hand frankly.

"Good-by," she said. "I feel scarcely at liberty to invite you to the house to-day, but I hope we shall see you soon, and I thank you again and again for your kindness."

He clasped her hand in both of his and she let it lie passively for a moment. Then she withdrew it slowly.

He went back to his canvas, and turning it sat with fixed gaze regarding the figure of a young girl playing upon a violin.

Not far away Agatha paused, and opening a locket which hung from her watch-chain looked upon a spray of mignonette that lay within.

CHAPTER VII.

UNDERTONES.

THE growth of love is inexplicable. We may recognize certain conditions which favor it, but who can tell how its complex tissues are spun? The love which sprang up and blossomed in Agatha's pure heart became a blessed fact which she accepted not without emotion intense and absorbing, but without marvelling. The growth of a flower or a tree " in the teeth of gravity " had often filled her mind with wonder; but this new growth in her very soul seemed not only natural but inevitable. It did not occur to her to analyze either the reason or the method. She simply accepted her joy as a nun accepts the " peace of God which passeth all understanding." It was the result of a condition for which she should be, and was, devoutly grateful.

Loreno was sensible of her charm, even conscious that she had awakened in him a deep regard. While he had never been truly in love, he had several times before been strongly attracted toward some young girl, until a trivial offence to his fastidiousness, or a premature token of conquest, had chilled his interest.

At the time his sister had spoken, half in sport, regarding his treatment of young women, he was conscious of the general truth of her words, and now he wished and intended to profit by them. He respected Agatha to the depth of his nature, and would on no account compromise her by aimless attention; nor would he even approach nearer and run any possible risk of awakening her interest, unless prepared to offer her everything. Therefore he decided that he ought to go away without delay and test the strength of his feeling.

"There is no telling what I might have said had her frightened face not stopped me," he murmured, as he sat at his window the night after Agatha's confidence, pondering until the stars grew dim, and the rattle of market-wagons blending with the sharp crack of whips, floated up from the pallid plain.

Where he should go was now to be determined. The first place he thought of was his own villa near Varese; but this did not meet with unqualified approval, for he feared the quiet of the place would not favor his experiment. One plan after another was canvassed, but he arrived at no decision. The reason for this was clear,—he was working from the wrong end; but as soon as he permitted his mind to consider freely his yearning to aid Agatha, he began to draw nearer a conclusion. He had promised to help her, and was in honor bound to make his promise good. The first thing to do was to go to Rome and search for a clew to the refugee's movements. Thus he would redeem his promise and yet be away from Agatha's spell.

Hollow as was this self-deception, it seemed to satisfy him, and he blithely dismissed his perplexity.

6

It is difficult for certain practical minds, with an habitual and almost puritanical sincerity of self-examination, to realize the power of optimism, both material and moral, which a certain type of mind possesses. It exists, nevertheless, even under the shadow of many a New England church-steeple, and thrives luxuriantly in the sunny atmosphere of contentment-loving Italy. Loreno was sincere, and opening a door to a balcony went out to see the first shafts of the rising sun touch the distant Alps, and after enjoying the pageant threw himself upon a lounge and slept peacefully.

The Duchess was surprised when her brother announced at luncheon his intention to leave for Rome the following day, and she protested, as did the Duke and Gaeta.

"Have you finished all your sketches?" asked Gaeta, innocently.

"Yes; although I've some last touches to put on one of them after luncheon."

"Which one? The head of that peasant woman at Erba?"

"No; a — landscape with a figure in it."

"And a gate," added the Duchess.

"I have n't seen that one," said the child.

"No; the gate is in the foreground," replied her mother, "and it's usually closed."

"What does mamma mean?" Gaeta asked, turning to Loreno.

"Have n't you heard, little girl, of certain Bible truths that you will understand better when you are older?"

" Yes ; but what of that ? "

" This is one of the same kind."

The Duke smiled, and Gaeta was encouraged to persist.

" Try me," she said ; " I think I 'm old enough to understand."

" Not quite yet," and he patted her dark curls.

" But mamma was talking of a gate in a picture, and about it 's being closed; I understood that."

" The modus operandi ? "

" What is that ? "

" There, I said you would n't understand."

The crestfallen child remained silent, and the Duke remarked upon the evidence furnished by the Paris Exposition, of the wonderful recuperative power possessed by the Parisians, considering the recent date of the Franco-Prussian War.

Within an hour Loreno started for the hills toward the Villa Ricci, with his faithful companions, the Duke's four dogs, circling about him.

As he approached the villa he saw Agatha and her uncle together on the veranda overlooking the lawn. The Count was reclining in a long wicker chair, while Agatha sat at his side reading aloud. As she glanced up and saw the visitor she spoke to her uncle, who turned his head listlessly, but instantly lowered the foot-rest and pulled himself together. Agatha arose, and walking to the end of the veranda greeted Loreno cordially and invited him to join her uncle. The old man was upon his feet, and stood erect, waiting to receive his guest.

"I'm afraid I disturb you," said Loreno, taking the Count's hand. "I saw your niece reading to you."

"Not at all," was the hearty response. "Agatha occasionally reads aloud after luncheon while I listen, and sometimes," he added with a faint smile, "I fear I sleep a little."

"You don't mind my bringing the dogs up here?" Filippo asked, as he noticed the General's eye rest upon the big brutes, who stood wagging their tails at Agatha's flattery; for she was upon her knees patting each head in turn and praising all.

"Not in the least; and what fine fellows they are!"

"Are they not splendid?" exclaimed Agatha, looking up at her uncle. "What good faces they have!"

"So they have," he replied. "One may do worse than love a faithful dog."

. The General asked Loreno to be seated, and ignoring the easy chair offered him, chose one with a straight back. Then he asked after the Duke Faviola and his family.

"Isn't Gaeta a charming child?" said Agatha, still caressing the dogs.

"Charming," Filippo replied; "and her devotion to her father is touching."

The anxious glance which Agatha gave her uncle told the Marquis how careful he must be.

"She is very clever also," added Agatha hastily, rising and standing behind the Count with her hand upon his shoulder. "I think her musical talent is remarkable."

"She tells me that you sometimes play duets with her."

"But she told *me* something more important," and Agatha looked at him knowingly.

"And what, pray?"

"That she has been promised a new piano on her next birthday."

He laughed deprecatingly: "I'm glad she is pleased; but you also know the condition upon which I promised it?"

"Yes; that she learns the piano part of the Chopin nocturne in D flat, arranged for piano and violin; she came to ask me if I had the music," was the naïve response.

"Did you have it?" asked the hypocrite, soberly.

"Yes, indeed; it's one of my favorites. Why, I believe I was playing it that day when —" She paused, and then seemed to forget what she was about to say, which may have been the cause of her sudden color.

"So you, too, are fond of music?" said the Count to Loreno.

"Very; although I don't play at all."

"But you sing beautifully," said Agatha; "Gaeta told me so."

"That's in return for the piano."

"Would you mind singing something to us?" she asked. "My uncle is devoted to music, and I have some books of songs. Do you sing Schumann?"

"Sometimes, but I'd rather not reveal my German to you; let me try something in Italian."

"Something of Tosti's or Denza's?"

"Have you Rotoli's arrangement of Mendelssohn's 'Auf Flügeln des Gesanges'?"

"No, but I have Mendelssohn's songs, so perhaps we can manage it. Come, let us try;" and she led the way through a glass door into the music-room, and after a few moments' rehearsal the Count heard Loreno's rich voice singing the passionate strains.

"How lovely!" he heard Agatha exclaim at the close. "Strangely enough, I never heard that song before."

"It would sound charming on the violin," was the answer.

"Would it be troubling you too much to write the Italian translation?"

"I will do so with pleasure; and I'll do it now, for I am going away to-morrow."

He watched her closely, hoping to detect some sign of feeling at the thought of parting.

"Are you?" she said in a low voice.

He must have been blind; for although the cheeks lost color and the sensitive lips parted and even quivered slightly, he saw nothing. Perhaps he expected that she would start involuntarily and murmur, "'T is better so," as tears streamed from her eyes.

Had he detected her feeling, — such is the nature of some men, — he might not have appreciated so easy a conquest, possibly never have returned to her. The feminine instinct of coquetry has scarcely been given even to birds without reason.

"Yes," he added; "I'm going to Rome, and may then run on to the Exposition."

"How interesting! I envy you."

He glanced toward the open door and dropped

his voice: " But I shall not be unmindful of your cousin."

" You are very kind."

" How shall I communicate with you if I find trace of her?"

She touched the piano and appeared to be thinking.

" Send word to Padre Sacconi; I 'll prepare him for it," she said softly.

" Very well." Then he continued in his usual tone, " Can you let me have a sheet of paper?"

" Certainly; I 'll get it from the library."

The Count appeared at the door. "Sing something else, won't you?" he said. "You have a delightful voice."

"With pleasure," Loreno replied. " Miss Page will perhaps find something that I know, while I copy the words I 've just sung."

" You sing Schubert's songs?" asked the Count.

" Yes, some of them."

" Then sing this one to me;" and finding the book he turned its leaves. " Do you know it?"

" Yes."

"Come," he said to Agatha, who now returned, carrying a portfolio; "play this accompaniment for the Marquis."

She was pleased at her uncle's interest, but as she glanced at the song she grew grave.

" Oh, not that one," she said; "choose some other."

" But I wish that one," said the Count.

" It's so morbid."

" Come, begin!" he said.

So Loreno sang : —

> "' The storm hath rent asunder
>   The sky's thick robe of gray ;
> The clouds are cleft with thunder,
>   And roll in strife away.

> "' And blinding fires are flaming
>   The dusky clouds behind ;
> A morn like this resembleth
>   Mine own bewildered mind.

> "' My heart sees in yon heaven
>   It 's own dark image there ;
> 'T is naught else now but winter, —
>   Wild winter cold and bare.'"

The old man stood near the singer drinking in the wild measures with sincere delight.

"That 's a good song," he said as Agatha closed the book, "and admirably given."

Then he went out again upon the veranda.

"He is very bitter," Loreno said.

"Very!" and Agatha's face was troubled.

"Don't be down-hearted; he 's not half as bad as I expected to find him. Try to get him away for a few weeks; a change would do him a world of good."

"Yes, it might; I 'll think it over. Shall we go outside ?"

"Won't you play something first ?"

She hesitated. "Willingly, if you wish it; but before I begin I 'll go and see if my uncle needs anything."

He watched the graceful outline of her figure as she walked toward the light, and felt a sense of pleasure at the thought that presently she would be coming back to him. He stood by the piano turning over some music mechanically, his thoughts upon the new interest that had come into his life.

"What a restful personality she has," he said to himself, "and how gently and naturally she does everything!" Then he wondered how it would seem to have her always about him as the Count had. "Probably I should get used to it and cease to appreciate it, — that's the way of the world;" and he smiled at his wisdom. "And then?" His face gradually grew serious as he thought rapidly and earnestly. The rustle of Agatha's dress at the door aroused him. "Yes, much better go away," was his mental conclusion.

"I'm sorry to have kept you waiting," she said, going to her violin-case and taking out the instrument.

"Don't mention it: how are the dogs behaving themselves?"

"They are all lying about my uncle's chair, trying their best to keep awake. What shall I play?" she asked.

"Almost anything," he said indifferently.

A shade of disappointment touched her face.

"Then I'll play a little thing of Wieniawski's," and instantly her bow struck the strings and she dashed into a brilliant waltz full of technical surprises, but without a pretence of sentiment.

"What fire you have!" he exclaimed as she laid the violin away.

"But surely you prefer another kind of music?" and her voice was almost pleading.

"Certainly I do; but I am glad to have heard you in that kind."

She was penitent for having misjudged him even for a moment, and turning took up her bow again. Poising it for an instant she began the nocturne he had before heard her play.

Thrilled by the force of its new associations, she gave to it a depth of pure sentiment that finds a fitting means of expression in the music of Chopin. He was too musical to be insensible to such a rendering, and with eyes riveted upon the player, sat motionless, oblivious to all save the swelling notes that flowed from a full heart.

Suddenly, in the midst of a phrase, the music ceased. The spell was broken, and he searched the face of the musician eagerly.

She stood with her head bent low, her bow at her side; her breathing was distinct and tremulous; she struggled bravely for a moment, then raising her eyes to his, smiled deprecatingly, and turning laid away her violin.

Neither spoke while she busied herself over the case, but when she turned her face Loreno rose impulsively and went toward her.

"Why did you stop, Agatha dear?" called out the Count, who appeared at the window.

"I couldn't go on," she answered.

He came forward solicitously.

"You're tired out, my child," he said, "and need rest. Come out into the air and let me show you how to be comfortable."

"I feel very well, thank you," and she took his

arm ; " but the Marquis, I am sure, will enjoy a cigarette with you. I 'll get the tobacco ; " and disengaging her arm she hurried into the corridor.

" The fact is," the Count explained, " my niece is
in need of rest; she has had some affairs to worry
her of late, and such a nature as hers can't stand
much wear and tear."

" Why don't you take her away for a little
change ? " suggested the other.

" Not a bad idea," was the answer. " I 'll consider
it ; but Agatha does n't often care to run away from
Erba."

" But if she needs change of air, and you urge
it, she will probably yield."

" No doubt. I 'll think about it."

Agatha soon rejoined them, bearing the tobacco
and paper, and having deftly rolled two cigarettes,
handed one to each gentleman.

A little later Loreno rose and offered his hand to
the Count.

" I must bid you good-by," he said; " I leave to-
morrow."

The Count glanced quickly at Agatha and was
glad to see that she showed no feeling, for he dreaded
the thought of losing her, now that Mercede was
irreclaimably gone from him.

" I hope we shall have the pleasure of welcoming
you again," were his words ; for he liked Loreno.

The Marquis thanked him and turned to Agatha.

" Good-by," he said, holding out his hand.

" Good-by," and she looked him bravely in the
eye.

He strode homeward with his brow contracted, his eyes upon the ground.

"She doesn't seem to have a heart except when she plays the violin," he muttered as he turned into the gate of the Villa Faviola.

CHAPTER VIII.

MADAME ANDRÉ.

MERCEDE knew that a sculptor, like a pianist, must acquire technique; that a stranger in haste takes the highway, leaving short cuts to pleasure-seekers; that genius, like electricity, must be guided. Therefore she attended an art school, and entered the studio of M. de Valro, a distinguished sculptor to whom her patron in Rome had given her a letter. She put her boy at school near Paris, and took a room for herself near the studio. Although the Count had given her the dowry required for an officer's wife, strict economy was necessary. At last she was fairly started in her new career, and felt the exultation which a true sailor knows when the land is growing dim and he feels the blue water under him. Before him are anxious watches, tempests, calms, and possible disaster; he is not unmindful of them, but braves them gladly because they are part of the life he loves.

Her progress in her work was astonishing, and she had already attracted the attention of her master at the school, while M. de Valro began to take a genuine interest in her. Her industry was exceptional; she studied constantly, getting her only exercise in going to and from her work. In her waking hours she thought only of art. Her enthusiasm for her new profession was so great, that for the pleasure of doing something for those who had chosen such a life, she actually mended the torn blouses of the men employed in the studio, while they were at luncheon.

They could not understand her motive, and at first were wary of her; but she gradually won their confidence by her quiet, workmanlike manner, and now she was on the best of terms with them all, although as a rule they did not take kindly to students. They gave her many a useful hint, and often came for her when there was some simple work she could do under their direction. She had a delicate sense of touch, combined with a boldness of method which these rough fellows were not slow to appreciate, and they did not fail to remark her progress, nor were they insensible to her beauty and her gracious manner. They began to take a pride in her, and over their bread and wine at a neighboring café told their fellow-workmen from the other studios of the beautiful lady with the great talent.

" Now we help her," said the assistant foreman; " some day she will have work for all of us ! " And his prophecy was hailed by a chorus of, " Truly, Jacques, truly ! "

Loreno's common sense told him that the most likely place to learn Mercede's whereabouts would be at her recent home, and consequently he went directly to Rome. The next morning he went to the Count's palazzo and presented his card to the concierge. This august personage uncovered his head as he read the name of the visitor, and his stately manner seemed to slip from his portly body like a shirt, leaving only his natural servility. The Marquis asked if there were any servants in the Count Ricci's apartment. Yes, there were two. Very well; the Marquis desired the concierge to accompany him and secure him an interview with them.

This was easily done; but, to his disappointment, the servants seemed to know nothing more than that Signora Finelli had caused her luggage to be sent to the railway station and had gone with her child, and without leaving any address. In reply to his minute cross-questioning as to anything un-usual in Signora Finelli's conduct or movements be-fore her departure, neither of the servants could recall any fact worth mentioning, until suddenly the housemaid remembered that the Signora was locked in her room with little Francesco for a day or two just before she left the apartment, but she was only amusing herself making a bust of the child in clay. Oh, yes, the maid had seen it twice, — when doing the room, and once again when Signora Finelli fainted. Oh, the faintness was nothing. An old man had come in with the Signora, and the Signora faint-ing suddenly, the man rang the bell and waited until the Signora recovered, when he finished his business and went away; she thought now that he had come to arrange about the luggage of the Signora.

Loreno made many inquiries in other directions, among them at the railway station, but without success; still he had learned much. To what city, he asked himself, would Signora Finelli, wishing to study sculpture, naturally betake herself, Rome being out of the question? He decided against Florence, because of the acquaintance she must have made while there with her husband. Indeed, he could see no object in her remaining in Italy, and there were several strong reasons why she should go to some other country. Paris naturally suggested itself as possessing excellent art schools, while it was big enough to hide in. Then he canvassed the rival claims of Vienna, Munich, Berlin, and London, but decided that if Mercede were allured by art, the chances were in favor of her having gone to Paris.

In any case, to Paris he would go; the Exposition was now open, and there, if anywhere, he could amuse himself and really try to be less absorbed by Agatha.

He did not, however, ask himself whether, had the Exposition been in Berlin, he would not have gone to Paris all the same. He avoided that line of thought, for he was not unconscious of a certain inconsistency in a man's running away from a girl, and then choosing a refuge where he should constantly be upon her service. But many another man has turned his back upon desire — and looked over his shoulder.

Among his Parisian friends was the sculptor Rossier, at whose studio he had always been a welcome visitor. With the remote chance of learning something about Mercede, he availed himself of his old privilege immediately upon his arrival. M. le Chevalier Rossier, whom he made his confidant, knew

nothing of such a student in any of the studios; but
M. Rossier seldom paid visits, and the only chance of
help from him was through the casual inquiries he
might be amiable enough to make among such of his
confrères as he was thrown against. Filippo was
embarrassed in his search by the desire not to make
Mercede's flight a topic of public talk, and he soon
found that this need of secrecy practically tied his
hands. He had presented cards from M. Rossier in-
troducing him to many of the principal studios, and
while passing through them used his eyes diligently.
He caught no glimpse of any one who resembled
Mercede closely enough to give him even a moment
of hope. He went to several schools of art and examined the names of the students, but gained no
light. He frequented the brasseries of the Latin
Quarter, but without result. He never chanced to
hear the men of M. de Valro praise the talent of
their prodigy, nor had he visited that sculptor's
studio, owing to the fact that a few days after his
arrival, when M. Rossier, meeting M. de Valro, asked
concerning the latter's pupils with an interest that
excited his suspicion, M. de Valro mentioned only
two blockheads, upon whose dulness he discoursed
at serious length.

M. de Valro, who knew Mercede's story, immediately told her of this incident with much glee, and
they agreed that the circumstance was suspicious.

Had M. de Valro been content to leave well enough
alone, Loreno might have gone out of Paris without
hearing news of Mercede; but desiring to serve his
charming protégée by discovering, if possible, what

had incited the Chevalier to show this uncommon
interest in his neighbor's students, M. de Valro decided to pay the Chevalier Rossier a visit. He timed
this visit so that M. Rossier should have finished his
work, and as an excuse for his call pleaded the affairs
of a committee, of which they were both members,
connected with the Exposition.

While the gentlemen were together in M. Rossier's
room, Loreno dropped in at the studio to confer again
with his friend and counsellor.

"M. le Chevalier is engaged for the moment," said
one of the men.

"Then I'll wait here," Loreno replied, seating himself in a large room, where some of the men were still
at work.

"I'd send in word that you are here, Monsieur,"
said the foreman, "but it's M. de Valro, and they
have shut the door."

" M. de Valro the sculptor?"

" Yes, Monsieur; but he's not likely to stay long;"
and the man busied himself at his work.

" That," remarked another workman, dryly, "depends upon whether M. de Valro is as wild as his
men about his new student. They have talked of
her for a fortnight, and don't seem to have finished
yet."

This sally was greeted with a general laugh : nor
was it lost upon Loreno.

" Of 'her'?" he said. "Is the new student a
woman?"

" Yes, Monsieur," responded the same speaker, the
acknowledged wit of the building ; and as he paused,

each workman stayed his hand and listened expectantly. " For beauty, worthy to be the model of M.
de Valro's Juno; and for talent, worthy, — oh, mon
Dieu! what can I say? — worthy to be blessed daily
by her master's smile!"

This sally was received with positive enthusiasm.

" Have any of you seen her?" Loreno asked.

" 'Seen her?' No, Monsieur: in the street she
wears a heavy veil; in the studio they put her under
a cage."

Loreno waited for the merriment to die away.

" She is French, eh?" he asked as indifferently as
he could.

" I don't know, Monsieur. Does any one?" and
he looked at his comrades.

" I can't be sure," an old man answered, " but I
think some one said she is Spanish."

" What is her name?" asked Loreno.

" André, they call her, — Madame André."

" That's curious Spanish," was the wit's comment.

" Is she only a student, did you say?" inquired
Loreno.

" That's all, Monsieur," the wit spoke again; " began only a month ago, and probably M. de Valro has
come to hire this studio for her."

" In that case," said Loreno, " I don't think I'll
wait for M. Rossier;" and he strolled leisurely toward
the door.

When he reached the street his leisurely manner
disappeared, and he strode rapidly toward the studio
of M. de Valro.

" Now is my time," he reasoned. " If she be Mer-

ccde, he is hiding her; otherwise why did he deceive
M. Rossier, and why does she wear a veil? Should
he know I am anxious to see her he might prevent
it. Yes, now is my time, while he is away; it is still
light, and she may not have stopped work."

Arriving at the studio he knocked loudly.

A workman came in answer.

"M. de Valro has returned?"

" Not yet, Monsieur."

Loreno glanced at his watch. "Humph! I will
go to his room," he said, " and as soon as he comes,
mind you tell him that the Marquis Loreno is
waiting."

The peremptory tone and the title smothered the
simple fellow's doubts, and doffing his square cap of
paper he led the distinguished visitor across a large
room full of statues and casts, and thence through
several smaller rooms, into one which was evidently
the modelling-room of the master.

" Shall I send for M. de Valro?" asked the man,
placing a chair for Filippo.

" That is scarcely necessary; he is with M. Rossier,
and will probably come soon. In the mean time I
will have a chat with Madame André. She has not
gone yet?"

" No, Monsieur, not yet."

" Where is Madame?"

" In her own room, Monsieur,—the second beyond
this. Shall I announce M. le Marquis?"

" No, I'll announce myself," he said carelessly;
" but don't forget to inform M. de Valro of my
arrival."

"Monsieur may rely upon me;" and opening the door of the adjoining room the man waited for the nobleman to pass.

Filippo walked without hesitation to the second room beyond and knocked.

"Entrez," was called in a woman's voice.

The intruder obeyed, and closing the door behind him, stood in the presence of a young woman of striking height and beauty, whose large black eyes regarded him with surprise. She had a silk handkerchief of bright colors bound about her head, and wore a blue blouse to protect her dress.

"She looks like a gypsy queen," thought Loreno, as he went toward her.

Regarding him calmly she waited to hear his business.

"I think I have the pleasure of addressing the Signora Finelli," said Loreno, in Italian.

Her dark eyes opened and her figure reached its full height.

"Who are you, sir?" she demanded.

"The Marquis Loreno. I come in the name of your cousin, the Signorina Page."

The artist's eyes closed slightly, and she watched the stranger without replying. He bore her scrutiny stoically, noting the quick impulses recorded by the expressive face, and gave her time to think. She was evidently disconcerted, and uncertain what to do.

"Why do you intrude upon me?" she demanded finally.

"Out of consideration for those to whom you sent your letter."

" You have made a mistake, sir; my name is André."

" Is your father not the Count Ricci ? " was the firm inquiry.

The dark eyes flashed with sudden fury, and the full lips trembled.

" That, sir, is my affair, not yours. I decline to submit to this impertinence." And pointing haughtily toward the door, she added, " Leave the room ! "

Loreno bowed slightly. " Signora," he said, " you have a perfect right to dismiss me, and I will go; you will permit me, however, to add that I have no further reason to remain, since my only object was to assure myself that you are well, and not in need of friends."

She had supposed he came to upbraid her, and if possible to compel her to return to Rome, therefore the spirit of his answer perplexed her.

" But I do not know you, sir," and her tone was less imperious.

" That is scarcely my fault, Signora ; " his face was lit by a faint smile, " and I have little encouragement to try again."

" What ! are you an amateur detective ? " she asked scornfully.

" I should rather say a house-breaker," he replied amiably.

She was in no humor for banter, and her softer mood vanished. She tapped her foot impatiently.

" This is no time, sir, for nonsense," she exclaimed, " and I will speak plainly and finally. I *am* the daughter of Count Ricci; I have for reasons of my own come to Paris; I do not intend to leave, and I will not be hunted down like an escaped convict."

Loreno's face was now grave enough.

"No one questions your right to be in Paris," he responded; "no one intends to trouble you. One who loves you is anxious concerning your safety and happiness, and this is the reason for my visit."

His pacific words calmed her again.

"You mean my father, of course."

"No, Signora; I do not represent the Count, only your cousin."

The effect of this declaration was twofold. While relieved that her father had no intention of embarrassing her new ambition, she resented his apparent indifference to her flight.

"I might have known that my father would not trouble himself about me," was her bitter comment.

"How about your cousin?" he ventured.

She remained silent for some time, and when she spoke her voice and manner were changed.

"I am not indifferent to my cousin's good intention," she said calmly, "and you may tell her that I am well, where you found me, and what I am doing. But tell her, also, not to come here, nor to send to me again;" she hesitated, and then added resolutely, "for I have done with the past!"

"And with the past you mean that you renounce your father and your cousin."

"It is necessary!" and her voice was hard.

His thoughts flew to Agatha. "It is inhuman!" he exclaimed indignantly, "and if you really mean it, you will live to regret it."

She was aroused again, and laughed scornfully.

"I 'll risk that."

"Risk it,—risk what?" The words which followed were spoken slowly and impressively. "You propose to stake everything upon your health, your chance of success, and the rapture success will bring; heedless of conscience, indifferent to proved love, risking even the future of your own child. Believe me, Madam, few gamblers would be so reckless!"

"Mere words!" she sneered. Then her eyes half closed and she spoke vehemently: "Why should I fear conscience? Am I not more sinned against than sinning,— dishonored by my father and deceived by my husband? You call me indifferent to proved love! Who loves me? Who merits my consideration?"

"Agatha Page!"

She stood silent, with her hands clenched; presently the fingers opened, and she folded her hands before her.

"Agatha has been true to me," she said, as though thinking aloud.

"And is true still; what motive under Heaven except the knowledge of her great love for you would have impelled me to come here? However, it is best now that I should go."

"Wait a moment," she said quickly, as he moved toward the door. "I wish to think."

He turned and waited for her to speak. She was evidently considering something which troubled her, for her face grew anxious.

"What do you mean," she asked, "by what you said about my child,— about risking his future?"

"Even should his material interests not suffer, he will, by your act, be cut off from the position your family would give him, and his future thus be greatly handicapped."

" He should be willing to sacrifice something for the sake of his mother's pride."

" For your sake I hope he will be, but — "

" Well, I 'll risk even that," she declared.

" Very well, Madam ; I have nothing more to say."

" One moment ! "

" I cannot wait any longer," he replied. " M. de Valro is likely to come in upon us at any moment. I am a stranger to him, and must be prepared to meet him."

" He is coming now," she whispered hastily ; and Loreno heard footsteps approaching the door. " I 'll present you as a friend of mine ; stay until he goes. I can't decide anything at this moment."

The door opened and a small man with bushy gray hair and pointed beard entered. He looked at Loreno curiously, and then came forward.

Mercede presented the Marquis as though he were an old friend.

It was so amiable of M. le Marquis to come, the sculptor declared with much effusion, and he should never forgive himself for not having been in his studio to receive Monsieur; but he consoled himself because Monsieur had been able to find their common friend Madame André.

Filippo was not to be outdone, and apologized for his intrusion in the master's absence ; and then the two gentlemen bowed again and eyed each other suspiciously. After a little general conversation which dragged wofully, the sculptor excused himself, saying that such old friends must have much to say to each other.

Mercede did not speak until the sound of his foot-steps had died away.

" How did my cousin come to consult you about this affair ? " she asked.

Then Filippo gave her a brief account of the circumstances, and while Mercede listened she found herself modifying the unfavorable judgment she had formed of him. A few more questions enabled her to place him socially, for she knew his sister by name, and was familiar with his family history, although she had never happened to meet Filippo during her short Roman season.

She felt decidedly less aggrieved at the intrusion of the young Marquis, now that she understood his motive, and with a woman's intuition having jumped at a just estimate of the relations which existed between him and her lovely cousin, she began to feel even kindly toward him. She tried by suavity of manner to make amends for her previous behavior, and her success was rapid; because Loreno not only failed to resent her indignation, but thought it not extraordinary, considering the cause he had given her.

" You haven't done me the honor of even glancing at my work," she said, smiling; "if you are indifferent, my cousin may not be so."

" On the contrary," he protested, " I am most eager to see it."

He stepped before her work and examined it critically. She was copying a head of Goethe.

"The original is in Weimar, is it not?" he inquired.

"I really don't know; I found the cast here and was fascinated by it."

"It is my favorite bust of Goethe, and you are making an admirable copy."

"Is it not a beautiful, a fascinating face?" she exclaimed rapturously. "Do you suppose it is like him?"

"Somewhat idealized probably, but still a likeness."

She gazed upon the bust for fully a minute before speaking, her large eyes full of light, her face bearing the intensity which often distinguished it. Presently she turned to her companion. "Think," she said, "what a delight it must have been actually to look upon such a man and hear him speak. Is there any Italian or French translation of his works?"

"Oh, certainly;" and he mentioned the best in each language.

"Let me write down the names."

This she did with a girlish enthusiasm quite in contrast with her usual maturity of manner.

"What a superb creature!" she exclaimed, as she stood again in rapt admiration before the poet. "I can't imagine such a man ever doubting the strength of his genius, can you?"

"No, I don't suppose Goethe ever truly doubted the strength of his genius. Yet such natures, you know, live among the clouds; and it is but natural that they should sometimes lose sight of their broad horizon, and even wonder if they are ever to see it again."

She listened eagerly to his words, applying them to herself; but her only answer was a trembling sigh.

Her ambition was intense and her self-confidence unlimited; it was easy to stimulate her by praise, but it would have been impossible to shake her conviction that she had a great career before her. True, she had occasional trepidation, intense while it lasted but sure to pass, for the feeling was but superficial, — the result of temperament, not of consciousness. " The book is written to be read now or by posterity, I care not which," calmly wrote John Kepler. " I can well wait a century for a reader, since God has waited six thousand years for a discoverer." And yet who that is familiar with his life can doubt that John Kepler suffered days and even weeks of apprehension while he was gathering immortality from the stars? There are natures as far above the plane of common comprehension as the planets are above the earth. Their light shines down upon us and we gaze up to them, while our wise men gravely weigh and measure and compare them, even mark their spots and count their satellites. But after all, the strongest telescope has failed as yet to pierce a planet.

Mercede sighed; but whatever the cause, it was not from consciousness of being ordained to dwell unto death in the land of Moab.

CHAPTER IX.

AT THE VILLA D'ESTE.

Both Agatha and her uncle considered carefully the suggestion which Loreno had made to each in behalf of the other regarding the benefit of a change of scene.

Agatha confessed to herself that personally she would welcome a change, for she was thoroughly unhappy and restless. Yet she acknowledged that the Brianza had never been more beautiful than now, and that the opportunities for pleasure and usefulness which had before occupied her time still existed. She did the same old things, visited the familiar spots, called on the sick and aided the poor. But the old-time joy was gone out from these things, and her nature yearned for something which her eyes seemed to seek in the shadows of the distant Alps or among the stars. But she shrank from suggesting a journey to her uncle lest he might divine her wish to get away. She could not propose to take him where he must mix with the world whether he would or no. The General, on his part, only hesitated to make the suggestion, thinking that perfect quiet and the old associations would do more for Agatha than change of scene with its attendant bustle and discomfort. She appeared to go about her customary occupations as usual, but he saw that she did not regain her color. Therefore he decided to sink his own preference for home in his duty to her, provided Padre Sacconi should agree with Loreno that she needed a change. He sent for the priest, with the result that he took occasion, that same day at dinner, to suggest a trip.

Agatha received the idea with unfeigned delight, supposing that he made it on his own behalf; and they occupied the remainder of the day studying guide-books and examining maps, with a view to a little trip into Switzerland by way of the Italian lakes.

" But," said the Count, " we don't want to go alone; we need a party."

In making this proposal the old gentleman was truly unselfish, for the last thing in the world that he desired was to have strangers about him. Agatha felt that her own preference ought not to count against that of her uncle, and therefore she heartily seconded his suggestion, and against both their wills they blindly determined to invite the Duke Faviola and his family to accompany them.

The next morning the General drove over to see the Duchess and unfold the plan. She received it with surprise, but was not averse to the idea, and agreed to consult the Duke about it, and late in the afternoon sent a note to the Villa Ricci acceding to the proposition. Thereupon, to Agatha's increasing astonishment, her uncle bade her invite the Duke and Duchess to luncheon the following day, that the trip might be talked over and its details arranged.

On the morrow, therefore, the plans were completed. The party was to leave in the General's coach two days later; drive as far as the Villa d' Este, on Lake Como; remain there until the early part of the following week; then drive to Varese, and after a few days go on to Lake Maggiore. Whether the Count should send his horses back from Stresa, or drive the party over the Simplon Pass into Switzerland, was left to be determined by circumstances.

On the day appointed, having made an early start, they reached Como before the heat of the sun was oppressive, and skirting the lower end of the lake went gayly toward Cernobbio.

The Count Ricci drove the four-in-hand, with Gaeta beside him. Agatha sat with the Duchess, and the Duke was facing them. The bells upon the harness and the merry notes of the horn cleared the way of small vehicles, and the spirited horses whirled the coach steadily over the smooth road.

" By the bye," remarked the Duchess, " I received a letter from my brother yesterday, and he asked to be remembered to you; he is in Paris, and seems to be enjoying himself immensely."

"The Exposition must be very interesting," Agatha ventured.

" He does n't say much about that. He has apparently been devoting himself to the studios."

Agatha's heart beat fast and she did not trust herself to speak.

" Perhaps I have the letter in here," the Duchess said, opening her hand-bag. " Ah, no, I put it in my pocket. Ecco! it may amuse you."

Agatha opened it with peculiar sensations. She knew the characters well, for she had studied every slant and twist in the translation Filippo had written for her. She read the letter deliberately, and with keen admiration for its tripping naturalness ; but one passage she read with special interest; it ran as follows : —

" When I came to Paris, I had only a dim hope of meeting a certain artist who had left Rome, but for what part of the world I had no way of learning. This is but the fourteenth day since I left you, and yet already the artist referred to and I have twice gone together to the Exposition. When I mentioned the strange chance which had favored me, my friend asked if on the day which brought us together I had brushed against a hunchback; and I recalled the fact that I had been so fortunate about that time, and I believed it was upon that very morning."

Agatha had no smile for this popular Italian superstition, but re-read the passage with great earnestness.

"He does n't really say whether this artist is a man or a woman," she said musingly, and with a wild hope that it might be Mercede.

"Does n't he? Let me see." The Duchess suspected that Agatha was a little jealous, and having examined the passage critically, thought to comfort her.

"You are right, he does n't," she confessed ; "but it 's accidental, for if it were a woman, why should n't he say so, especially to me, with whom he is always so frank ? " But all the same she thought Loreno had gone out of his way to avoid mentioning the sex of his friend.

"I merely observed the fact," Agatha responded, trying to hide her excitement behind a smile and a careless manner.

The horses left the highway, and the coach rolled past the lodge at the entrance of the Villa d' Este grounds, winding through a charming grove, to the imposing building which had once been the home of a Buonaparte, and in which the great Emperor had been entertained.

They found that the salon of the apartment reserved for them opened upon a balcony from which they could look into the clear water of the lake. There were easy-chairs upon it, and an awning protected it from the sun. Here they soon gathered and were refreshed with granitas.

"Where shall we have our meals?" asked the General. "The ladies must decide."

"I vote for the table d'hôte," said the Duchess. "It's amusing, — at least for a few days; don't you think so, Agatha?"

"Yes, by all means the table d'hôte; we have come for diversion, and that's the place for it."

So when luncheon was announced they went to the public dining-room. Agatha sat between the Duchess and her uncle, and upon glancing around the table saw that the guests were principally forestieri, the majority of whom were English or American.

Opposite her sat a gentleman, tall and lean, whose age was from thirty-five to forty, but whose fringe of

closely-cropped hair, encircling his small burnished
head, was prematurely white, — suggesting chalk-
cliffs around a peaceful bay. His short beard also
was quite gray, and his voice, when he addressed
his neighbor, seemed to Agatha almost as neutral.
His skin was fresh and soft, his manner studiously
prim, but his eyes were small and black and bright.
His name was Dow — Mr. Peter Dow, formerly of
Boston, U. S. A., where he had made a snug fortune in trade, which enabled him to come abroad and
establish his headquarters in Rome, — " nice old
Rome," as he was wont to apostrophize her, " where
one sees everybody, and yet is able to pick and
choose."

Mr. Dow had no prejudice against America; indeed,
he recognized, and upon occasion acknowledged, the
solidity of her commercial claims ; but in America,
or rather in the only spot of that excellent country
where a *gentleman* would care to be born, he found
that the picking and choosing were not left to one
who had no grandfather or father whom any one
really knew. This fact he fully accepted, nor did
he resent it ; on the contrary, he thoroughly approved
of the spirit upon which it rested, and in the relations
which he was carefully establishing in the Old World,
he studiously applied the pick-and-choose principle
which had driven him from the New World. There
was no more rigid social disciplinarian in Rome than
Mr. Peter Dow ; he was a veritable martinet in the
matter of birth, and had been decidedly wary of his
neighbor (a practical middle-aged Englishwoman of
quick, nervous manner, whose words shot from her

tongue like peas blown from a tube) until he over-
heard her say that Lady Croftly, of Croftly Manor,
was coming down from Menaggio to pass the next
day with her.

Mr. Dow had been scanning the hotel register,
and was deeply sensible of the possibility which now
presented itself, of making the very desirable acquaintance of some real aristocrats of Rome. But there
was a serious drawback; for among the names of
the new arrivals he had read that of plain "Miss
Agatha Page," and the golden-haired, reserved-look-
ing girl opposite, was undoubtedly she. Her presence
made him suspicious of the whole party. He believed himself inclined toward impulse, and as he had
an almost morbid fear of becoming the slave of any
habit, he rigidly disciplined himself against acquiring
the habit of acting without proper prudence. His
experience in life had taught him that haste was
disadvantageous nine times in ten. Indeed, he had
formulated a maxim which he held in great respect,
"Often the quickest way of getting there, is to sit
down." Moreover, his experience in Italy had taught
him that titles were too abundant to be taken without
ringing.

Mr. Dow's intuition that he was impulsive was not
without foundation; but his impulse took a form
upon which, curiously enough, he prided himself.
In other words, Mr. Dow had a settled habit of
jumping to conclusions, which habit he cherished
as sagacity.

His first glance told him that this young girl was
probably English, — more than likely of the middle

class ; her father in trade, as a matter of course. Or,
if she were American, her home was in New York, or
possibly Philadelphia, but certainly not in Boston ;
for he knew all the Pages of Boston, — at least he
knew all about them, — and there was n't an unmarried Page girl of her age, unless of the Springfield
branch, and he was inclined to think that the Springfield Pages had sent their eldest girls to Vassar, while
this girl must have been in Italy a long time to be
able to talk Italian so fluently as she was now doing
with the Duchess. She could n't be the sister of the
Duchess, that his sharp little eyes told him ; and his
ears discovered presently that she was called " Miss
Agatha " by the child, and plain " Agatha " by the
old man, who was registered as a general, — probably
the father of the Duchess. He believed this girl to
be either the companion of the Duchess, or the governess of the child. Her dress was unquestionably
simple, which indicated companion ; but her face,
while certainly lovely, was intelligent, and probably
meant governess. The marked courtesy with which
the Duke treated her was not lost upon Mr. Dow, and
he forthwith decided that the Duke was a thorough
Italian, — which meant that in certain respects he
was no better than he should be. Take it all in all,
the party was one to be watched carefully for future
developments, as their acquaintance might prove to
be a fair business risk.

While these judgments were forming, a young man
entered the dining-room, and passing behind Mr. Dow
took his place near the head of the table. Agatha's
eyes followed him with interest. He was evidently

an Italian, — a Neapolitan, she thought, when she heard him address a gentleman opposite him. His age was about twenty, yet his face, when in repose, seemed older. Its expression was frank, and the features told plainly that he was keenly sensitive and proud. His manner was courteous, even elegant; his eyes were large and brown, and showed a high degree of sensibility; his hair would not admit of parting, and like his delicate beard and mustache curled tightly. His teeth were noticeably good, and altogether, he was a decidedly handsome and refined-looking young fellow. Agatha's admiration was not like that which she felt for Loreno's stronger, more virile beauty; it possessed, rather, the abstract quality which one bestows upon a portrait.

On their balcony after luncheon the party chatted about their neighbors, and Agatha drew upon herself the mild chaffing of the others by her partiality for the young Italian.

In the quiet of the afternoon Agatha and the Duchess went for a walk, and while following a path which stretched up the wooded hill behind the hotel, came upon a fountain, surmounted by a colossal statue of Hercules, from which a broad band of velvet grass swept like an unwound scroll to the terrace overhanging the lake. A long flight of stone steps bordered this scroll on either side, each balustrade forming an aqueduct to guide the overflow of the generous fountain to a large basin of gold-fish far below; and drops of rushing water sometimes leaped over these shallow channels and sprinkled the unwary climber.

They stood for some moments looking upon the

lake and the mountains bordering its opposite shore, until the Duchess turned at the sound of a footstep behind her. The young Italian stood near, gazing with delight upon the same scene.

"Come, Agatha," said the Duchess in Italian, "let us look for the Grotto."

Agatha turned. "Do you know the way?"

"No; but it is above us somewhere."

"That seems a trifle indefinite."

The Duchess glanced at the young stranger, and after hesitating an instant, asked if he could direct them.

He lifted his hat and seemed to be thinking. "In truth, Signora," he said, "there are so many intersecting paths that it is a little difficult to direct you; but if you will permit I will accompany you."

"I do not like to trouble you."

"It will be a pleasure; pray permit me," and he led the way.

"You must have been here for some time," remarked the Duchess to their guide, "to know your way so well."

As he turned his face Agatha was confirmed in her favorable impression.

"I have been here a week," he said, "and the Park, like any other puzzle, is not difficult to make out when once you know it."

The Duchess gave him one of her bright smiles. "Pardon me," she said, "but you speak like a Neapolitan."

"I was born in Calabria," he said simply, "but I have been much in Naples."

"I am very fond of Naples," was her answer. "My husband and I often go there for the opera season." Something in his face led her to add, "You are fond of music."

He became grave. "Sometimes," he replied.

"'Sometimes'? That is a strange answer."

"Still, it is a true one." And as he spoke his face was almost sad. Then as they turned a sharp bend he added, "Ecco, Signora! the Grotto."

The entrance was formed by two columns, one of granite, the other of large stones roughly put together surmounted by a rich capital, the whole well covered with ivy. It looked black and uninviting, and the ladies held back.

"You will find it interesting and quite safe," said their escort, "and you may explore it without fear."

"What do you think, Agatha?" and the elder lady turned doubtfully.

"It looks ghoulish," Agatha replied.

"Let us explore it to-morrow with one of the gentlemen," suggested the Duchess.

"As you choose. Still, it's absurd to be afraid, — let us see it now."

The youth stood waiting to bid them adieu, but seeing their hesitation, proffered his further services as their guide.

"But we are imposing upon you," protested the Duchess.

"Pray don't think so, Signora," was the courteous reply. "Permit me to enter; I have a box of tapers and will strike one."

In a moment the cave was illuminated, and they

entered boldly, and by means of the tapers went easily through the various passages and chambers, connected by stone steps. The general effect was of cloisters; and among its other chambers was a little chapel lighted by a dome, while in the stalactite passages were round windows of red glass through which the light from without struggled uncertainly. There were also Gothic windows, overtopped with ivy, opening into courts containing stone busts upon pedestals, and in the centre of one of these courts stood a grim obelisk. Presently they came out again into the daylight, some yards higher than the entrance.

The young guide had duly pointed out the various objects of interest, and both ladies thanked him warmly as he left them.

An hour later, as they entered the broad corridor of the hotel, the sound of a piano reached them, and walking to the music-room, they glanced in to see who the performer was. To their surprise they saw the young Italian. He played superbly; a rich strong personality coloring each phrase.

When he had finished, Agatha went forward impulsively.

"Oh, thank you!" she said, with a gratitude so sincere that the musician flushed with pleasure. "How wonderfully you play Schumann!"

"I have only recently taken up Schumann," he said, "but I feel a peculiar sympathy with his music; you know the Novelette?"

"Yes, but I never before understood it; I never before heard its majesty and its aching coldness so brought out. You are indeed an artist!"

" I am a piano-teacher," he replied, an expression of sadness crossing his face, " and that kills the artist." Then looking up brightly he added, " But you also are musical, Signorina ? "

" I am fond of music," was the answer.

" The Signorina plays the violin beautifully," said the Duchess, who had followed Agatha to the piano.

His expressive face grew wistful, yet he said nothing. Agatha interpreted his silence correctly.

" I will play to you willingly," she said, " if you will give me the pleasure of hearing you again."

In her judgment social barriers were levelled by art.

The rich color of the musician's face deepened, and the eyes lost their habitual hauteur. He was surprised and touched, for aristocratic Romans, like their cousins over the broad earth, are, with rare exceptions, prone to exalt blood above brains.

" I shall hold myself at your command, Signorina," were his words.

Agatha thanked him, and at the suggestion of the Duchess it was agreed that in the evening they should meet again in the music-room.

Thus it happened that while Mr. Peter Dow was drinking his after-dinner coffee upon the terrace he heard the piano, and peering in at the open window discovered the perplexing English girl sitting near the Italian music-teacher, while the other members of her party were gathered around the instrument. Presently he saw her take a violin and begin to play.

" It 's as plain as the writing on the wall," he muttered. "' Governess, either resident or daily, competent to teach Latin, Greek, Hindu, or Zulu, French,
German, mathematics, and needlework. Special attention given to deportment and music. A good
home more desired than a large salary; willing to
go abroad.' Lord bless my soul! you read of a
dozen just like her in every copy of the London
'Times.' And now she has found a congenial spirit.
It 's ten to three she 's not friend but governess,
and I think I 'll risk their acquaintance."

Thereupon he went into the room and seated himself near the General, with whom presently he started
a conversation. Mr. Dow, while eccentric, was rather
nimble of wit, and possessing also an amiable personality succeeded in making a good impression
upon his companion. Conscious of this, he reflected
with satisfaction that he held in reserve an effective
characteristic; namely, the knack of embellishing his
social intercourse with apt poetic quotation. Gifted
with an excellent memory, and ambitious to take
the taste of trade out of his mouth; desirous, moreover, of affecting a habit of mind which was the
farthest possible remove from that which the European world ascribes to the practical American;
touched, perhaps, by the knowledge that culture is
commonly associated with the city of his birth, he
permitted himself much license in the reading of
poetry, and was sometimes fearful that his propensity
to quote apt titbits was really becoming a habit.

When the music was over, the two gentlemen
strolled into the air together. Presently the Duke

joined them, and ere the group parted, Mr. Dow felt that he had laid a firm foundation for a friendship which should prove serviceable to him.   The conversation had not been personal, and therefore he had discovered nothing concerning Miss Page's position, but he hoped for more light on the morrow.

CHAPTER X.

LUITELLO.

THE moonbeams lay lightly on Lake Como ; the air was sweet, the sky unclouded, and the distant glimmer of lights upon the mountains opposite Cernobbio seemed a reflection of the glowing planets. The calm silence was broken only by the swash of the gentle waves, the occasional sound of an oar, or the mellow exclamation of a nightingale.

Upon the terrace overhanging the lake, a short distance from the hotel, sat the Faviolas, the Count Ricci and Agatha, Signor Veltri the young musician, and Mr. Peter Dow. They had sauntered here to enjoy the night, and for many minutes no one had spoken.

Agatha was seated upon a low vine-covered wall, watching the waves as they touched its base, and wondering why she should feel depressed upon such a night. The scene should be restful and calming. Yet she felt the quick tears in her eyes, and turned her face farther away from the moonlight lest her mood should be betrayed to her uncle, who was standing near her. The others were resting upon two long benches set back a little from the wall, and while they missed the full path of the moonlight upon the water, they were recompensed by the greater comfort.

" What a night for music!" said Signor Veltri in a low voice.

" Perfect," answered the Duchess; and turning to her husband, she added, "Shall I send Gaeta for Agatha's violin? She might feel like playing if it were placed in her hands."

" It would be charming; I will go with Gaeta;" and he walked away with his child.

" A night like this makes a man of my age thoughtful," said the Count Ricci.

" It makes any one thoughtful," Agatha replied.

" But I mean something more; its quiet suggests the future."

" Its peace seems to me quite as marked as its quiet."

" Did you ever think, my dear, what different trains of thought such a scene suggests to one like you and to an old man like me? We both look into that streak of moonlight yonder, and wonder about the future; but your question is who? mine — whither?"

" The answer to both depends upon the Divine sympathy."

He pulled at his cigar in silence for several moments. " That is true," he said, — "that is true; but what lies beyond? We look into the sky, and powerless as we are to change the course of a star, still we can follow it. We look at the earth, and while unable to unravel its mysteries, we expect confidently the return of the grass and the flowers; yet my fellow-man disappears and the mystery is complete, neither his body nor his soul is ever known to me again. What is there beyond? Some persons guess and some assert, but no one proves anything."

"The very fact that puzzles you, I think, proves something. It proves that your fellow-man goes onward instead of following a circle; and as life comes from the sun, I love to think that in other worlds nearer the sun, where the conditions for growth are more powerful, germs of good within our souls will be unfolded that will make us more acceptable in the sight of God."

"Your theory has at least the merit of hope-giving," the Count remarked. "But you believe in future punishment?"

"Certainly, for Christ declared it; but I go no further: I simply have confidence that it will be with a wise purpose, and therefore not malignant or eternal. I believe it will be through repentance, as the development of the good in us increases our abhorrence of that which has been and is evil in us. Yet to whatever spot in God's universe He calls our freed souls, be sure, dear uncle, it is nearer the source of all that is most beautiful in Nature and in man. He calls us to Himself, and will punish us for past disobedience, as He has foretold; but He does not call us to feed an unholy desire for revenge, or to rejoice the heart of Satan. I cannot believe it of him who said, 'I, if I be lifted up from the earth, will draw all men unto me.'"

"Miss Agatha," said Gaeta, placing the violin-case in her hands, "won't you play to us?"

" Willingly," she replied; and taking the instrument she presently began the gentle strains of Mignon's song, " Knowest thou the Land ? "

As she finished playing and stood looking far off into the lake, the moonlight falling upon her face and white dress, no one spoke, and after a brief pause she raised her violin to its place and began the sweet strain of " Du bist die Ruh'." A boat glided into the track of the moon and she saw the oarsman held motionless by the spell of her bow. Endowing him for the moment with another's personality, she played to him, and to him alone. As she finished the last strain he dipped his oars softly and passed into the shadow. Her imagination was stirred; the conceit pleased her mood, and as if to follow him into the shadow and arrest his course, she turned slightly toward him and began the song by Mendelssohn that Loreno had translated for her. She played the first verse with growing fervor, repeating the words mentally, and after a moment's pause began the second verse, when, to her amazement, the rich tones of a man's voice rose like a bell from the deep shadow below her. He was singing the melody with the German words, and her heart gave a mighty bound. When the verse was finished and the singing ceased, Agatha repeated the short song from beginning to end, with a tenderness that electrified every listener.

In the moment of silence that followed, she heard the sound of retreating oars. The others had left their places at the sound of the stranger's voice, and gathered about her.

"He sang it beautifully, but you played it marvellously!" exclaimed Signor Veltri.

"I wonder who he is?" said Mr. Dow. "Did you notice that he sang in German?"

Agatha turned away, and the Duchess felt that she must rush to the rescue.

"Luitello, of course," she answered confidently.

"'Luitello'!" said the General, anxiously, "who is he?"

The Duchess laughed.

"Don't you remember who Luitello was?" and she thought rapidly as she asked, "who will enlighten the Count? Can you, Mr. Dow?"

"It sounds like a name I've heard somewhere," he rejoined.

She again laughed quietly, but remained silent for a moment.

"I'm afraid I must tell his story myself," she said; "but first come back to our bench."

They settled themselves comfortably, and the Duchess began:—

"Many years ago—or, to be exact, the year Apollo was born—the beautiful Queen of the Nymphs inhabiting the Brianza from the shores of Lecco to Como, was carried to Delos by command of Juno, to excite the jealousy of the vain Themis, who had incurred her displeasure.

"The nymphs were unable to agree who should be their new queen, and hearing that Neptune was at Olympus attending an assembly of the gods, they decided to ask him to come and choose the most beautiful among them, that she might be their sovereign. About that time a strange nymph came from the north to make her home with an old aunt who lived near the shore of Como. The rare beauty of the little stranger was undeniable, and it was equalled by the loveliness of her spirit. One day the news spread like wildfire that Neptune, who could not come personally in answer to their message, had sent a young Triton to represent him. His name was Luitello ; and when he arrived he proved to be not only well-born but handsome. He was not indifferent to the sensation he created, and slyly postponed naming his choice, on the plea that where so many were beautiful he found the task difficult. But he had not yet seen the new-comer, who performed her regular duties — such as changing the moss of her aunt's bed, preserving strawberries, gathering a stock of fig-leaves against the coming winter — without giving a thought to the dashing visitor.

Toward evening, when her work was done, she enjoyed going to the top of one of the neighboring hills to see the sunset, after which she would saunter home singing her Northern songs, until gradually the other nymphs learned to listen for the soft tones with which she accompanied her steps. At last there came an evening when she was later than usual, and the moonbeams were shimmering upon the lake before they heard her voice. As she reached the water near where they were gathered, she uttered an exclamation of delight and stood fascinated by the scene. Then her voice gently floated to them, and for the first time they detected something wistful in its quality. As they listened breathlessly, a form floated across the moonlight, and they saw Luitello, absorbed by the music. Every faculty seemed intent upon receiving the full measure of the golden notes, and each muscle seemed strained to carry him nearer the singer. Presently he dived, and rising just below the unconscious nymph, their eyes met. Then a spirit, exquisite and pure, appeared, and gliding over the water warned him not to go nearer the nymph lest she discover the unworthiness of which he was suddenly made conscious, and with a tremulous sigh he turned away and disappeared into the shadow.

" The poor nymph awoke from her short dream confounded. Her eyes, mercifully dazzled by the light of the spirit, had seen nothing of Luitello's defects. She only knew that he had come — that he was gone ; and her heart cried out with pain. Then her companions with sweet sympathy told her that the spirit she had seen was Love, and that it would again lead Luitello to her : so each night she waited faithfully by the lake until he should come. At last in the path of the moon-light she saw him approaching, led by the spirit Love. Now he was deemed worthy. Then the gods, who had given the nymph the spirit of a goddess, bestowed upon her commensurate power, and her companions by acclamation named her as their queen. In the first exercise of her new power, she ordained that whenever a worthy maid should stray to the lakeside and chance to stand where she herself had stood, Love, the guardian spirit of the lake, should bring to the maiden's feet another Luitello."

" Where is he, then?" asked Gaeta, seriously.
" Why did n't he stay?"

The Duchess laughed quietly, and caressing the child, said, "I only agreed to tell you what a Luitello is; not all the whys and wherefores that mere mortals are not privileged to understand."

"'In truth he was a strange and wayward wight,'" quoth Mr. Dow.

The Duchess saw that Agatha was still dreaming, and made a final effort to cover her preoccupation.

"I must go back to the hotel," she said, rising suddenly. "I have a letter to write, and besides, Agatha, I think it's a little damp here."

The young girl started slightly and turned. She had heard the words, but not consciously, and it took her a moment to apply them. She instantly thought of her uncle, and on his account was solicitous.

"I'll go with you," she said; "I should n't care to run any risk."

As Peter Dow walked home by the Duke he emulated his companion's silence. His mind was preoccupied. Could his theory, after all, be incorrect? He was almost certain that he had heard Miss Page speak of the General as her uncle.

The following morning Mr. Dow sat under the shade of a large tree within sight of the hotel, reading a newspaper. Hearing a step, he turned and saw Gaeta approaching. As the child reached him he looked up and greeted her pleasantly.

"Have you seen Mamma and Miss Page?" Gaeta asked.

" No; are they out of doors so early ? "

" They 've been out here somewhere for an hour. Perhaps they are in the grove; I 'll go and see," and she moved onward.

" How is your mamma this morning ? " he asked quickly.

" Oh, very well, thank you."

" And Miss Page — could she sleep after her adventure ? "

" Was n't it lovely ? " exclaimed the child.

" Yes, indeed ; " and then he added, at a venture, " he was probably some friend of hers."

This seemed a new idea to Gaeta, and presently a wise look came into her eyes: she smiled and nodded confidently. " I know now who it was, — I 'm sure I know ! " she exclaimed.

" Do you ? Oh, I think not."

" I 'm sure of it."

" Then some one has told you."

" No one. It just came to me this minute."

" Oh, then you 're probably all wrong."

" I 'll tell you," said the child, " and you see if he does n't come before night. It was Uncle Filippo; for now I recognize his voice."

" Oh, it was your uncle, was it ? What is his name ? "

" The Marquis Loreno."

" And he met Miss Page at your villa, of course ? " he said, feeling that now he should place her.

" He met her at our house first; but he called upon her afterward."

" Oh, that was the way ! He called upon her while she was at — " and he stopped.

"At home; at Erba."

" Then Miss Page has n't a home of her own ? " he continued.

" Why, of course not," and the child looked incredulously at her questioner. " She is n't married."

" So she lives with you ? "

"Oh no, she does n't; how did you get that idea?"

" I 'm sure I don't know ; " and Mr. Dow sank back, fairly discouraged. Then he added bluntly, " where *does* Miss Page live ? "

" In Rome."

" And at Erba she visits you ? "

" Certainly; we are awfully fond of her."

His curiosity was fast getting the better of his discretion. " Then she 's only your mother's friend ? " he said.

" Why, no, Papa likes her too."

" Of course he does ; I mean that she 's — that is, that Miss Page is not — " the nakedness of the words that sprang to his mind embarrassed him.

" There ! " and Gaeta clapped her hands as she looked toward the hotel. " I knew I was right; there 's Uncle Filippo looking everywhere for us." And she ran toward him.

He saw her coming, and raising his hand waved his fingers rapidly, — the universal token of greeting among Italians. " How do you do, little girl? " he called in his full rich voice.

" Oh, Uncle Filippo, how welcome you are ! " Mr. Dow heard her exclaim.

Then the interested observer saw him bend down and kiss the child, and without waiting to see more

walked toward the grove to search for the Duchess.
" There it is again," he thought; " I sat still and got
there ! "

A moment later Gaeta and the stranger followed,
hand in hand.

" How is everybody ? " he asked.

" Very well."

" Miss Page is with you, I hear."

" Yes ; is n't she lovely ! I just adore her."

" Do you ? " and he patted her head.

They turned into the grove and saw the Duchess
and Agatha seated upon a rustic bench, talking with
a gentleman who stood before them.

" Who is he ? " asked Loreno.

" A Mr. Dow ; we don't know him very well,"
she said judicially.

" I don't believe you adore him — at least not for
his beauty," he whispered.

After a quick girlish laugh she called aloud, —
" Mamma, Mamma ! see here ! "

The Duchess turned, looked at Loreno an instant,
and then hurried to meet him.

" This *is* a pleasant surprise," she exclaimed, kissing
him affectionately. " When did you arrive ? "

" Last evening at Como ; at Cernobbio, only a
moment ago."

Agatha, who had not gone forward, felt an unac-
countable impulse to run away, but compromised by
remaining where she was.

As he advanced toward her his eyes noted the .
effect of her soft white dress with a bunch of red
roses at the belt. She was very pale, but when she

touched Filippo's hand her cheeks took again the delicate color that belonged to them.

The Duchess presented her brother to Mr. Dow.

"I did n't go ashore last night," Loreno began; "there seemed to be such a large party."

The eyes of his sister twinkled at this characteristic directness, and she wondered how Agatha would meet it.

"I 've heard before," was Agatha's reply, "that the moonlight exaggerates. There were only two others besides ourselves."

"Indeed! I thought there were more."

"So you were the mysterious minstrel!" said the Duchess.

"Certainly! There was no mystery intended."

"Then I must say you were not very brotherly."

"My habitual modesty;" and he bowed suavely.

"It must be your latest Parisian acquirement. How did you know we were here?"

"Padre Sacconi told me; and I 've a pleasant surprise for you, — he will be here this evening. I 've persuaded him to go to Varese with me for a little visit. — Padre Sacconi is our confessor," he explained to Mr. Dow; "at least, he is mine."

"Oh, indeed!" replied that gentleman. "Well, I suppose confession is a matter of habit."

"More or less," Loreno replied.

"Where are you staying?" asked the Duchess.

"At Como. I had my luggage sent there from Paris before I knew you were here."

"We leave to-morrow morning for Varese; of course you 'll go with us."

"I hoped that you would stop at Varese!" he responded, evasively. "Naturally you are going to the villa?"

The Duchess laughed. "I took the liberty of playing hostess," she said, "and sent word to have the house ready for us. Am I not a thoughtful sister?"

He put his arm about her and looked fondly into her merry eyes.

"Where are the two commanders?" he asked; "I wish to pay my respects to them."

"The General was in the reading-room when I passed it," said Mr. Dow. "Shall I show you where it is?"

Presently the two gentlemen sauntered away together.

"You are an old friend of Miss Page's," suggested Mr. Dow.

"No; I only recently met her while I was visiting at my brother-in-law's villa."

"She lives with the Duke Faviola, then?"

"Oh, dear, no; she lives with her uncle, the Count Ricci."

"Her uncle — oh, indeed! I have only had the honor of knowing her since she came here."

"She is looking a little tired."

"Is she? Naturally, I'm not able to judge."

"Delightful old man — the General!" exclaimed Loreno, warmly.

"Delightful!"

"One of your prompt, frank sort, and devoted to his niece."

"Yes, indeed. He lives at Erba, I believe."

"He has a summer villa there, but in the winter they go to Rome."

"Oh, do they?" and Mr. Dow opened his eyes as well as his ears.

"You don't know many Romans, of course, — you are an American."

"I live in Rome now," Mr. Dow hastened to say, "but I was born in Boston."

"Boston; that's in America, is n't it?"

"Why, yes, *Boston!*"

"I've heard of it," Loreno continued. "They are talking of building a bridge from New York to Boston."

An expression of pain passed over Mr. Dow's face.

"No — that's a place called Brooklyn," he exclaimed.

"Ah! you see I'm not very clear in my American geography. But I intend to learn all about America; I'm very much interested in Americans."

Mr. Dow was placated. "It's a great country," he said, "although at present I prefer Italy for my residence."

"How strange! I cannot see how any one can prefer another country to his own. I was never more delighted than when I got back to Italy yesterday."

"That's just it. Your home is in Italy. If it were not, you would feel as I do."

"I'm glad to know that you like my country so much," said Loreno, courteously; "and now tell me, please, in which of these rooms was it that you saw the General?"

CHAPTER XI.

"Who else was with you last evening?" Filippo asked Agatha, by whose side he sat at luncheon.

"A young Calabrian named Veltri; he sits on the other side of the table near the top. He is charming. Here he comes."

Filippo looked up and regarded the youth steadily.

"He has an interesting face," he remarked. "He would be flattered if he knew the impression he has created."

"I don't believe so," she answered. "He does n't seem to be a vain young man."

The quaintness of her words amused and also charmed him. When a man listens to his "ladye love," his critical faculty is apt to be tempered "wyth alle good desyres."

"He seems rather solemn for one of his years," he remarked.

"He is down-hearted, poor fellow!" and she regarded Veltri with sympathy.

Glancing toward her his eyes met hers, and as he returned her bow he flushed and looked away quickly.

"Perhaps it's a case of the little tin soldier who saw and loved the queen," Loreno suggested.

" Perhaps it is," she replied unconsciously; " but I think his heart is filled with a passion for music." And then she told of his wonderful playing, and how sad his face had grown as he remarked that teaching killed the artist.

After luncheon Mr. Dow joined his new friends, who were gathered about a table on the terrace sipping their black coffee, and he actually accepted a cigarette, explaining that while he avoided the habit of smoking, he should make this occasion an exception in honor of the Marquis's arrival.

" By the bye, Marchese," exclaimed the General, "of course Padre Sacconi and you will go with us to-morrow on the coach."

" It would be charming," Loreno answered, "and I 'm sure Padre Sacconi will infinitely prefer the plan to a quiet drive with me ; but I expect my dog-cart to-night."

" Is it too late to telegraph and stop it ? " asked the General.

" Yes."

" Then it must simply go back without you," the Duchess announced calmly ; " you must come on the coach."

Filippo hesitated ; he had hoped to have an opportunity during the day of ending a suspense which he could scarcely endure. Yet the more he realized what he would ask of Agatha, the more he feared that a bitter disappointment was before him. If such were the outcome of their interview, he knew that the long drive proposed, would be most trying to her as well as to him. In short, should he accept the invitation of the Duke, he must sacrifice his ardent, almost irresistible longing, and postpone his declaration until they had reached Varese. But suddenly a new thought came to him with overwhelming force, and he was amazed that even the unexpected delight of having Agatha as a guest should have made him oblivious to the penalty of her visit. Yet now he saw clearly that he ought not to tell her of his love while she was his guest.

His sister watched his apparent irresolution with perplexity, and before he had time to reply, turned appealingly to Agatha.

"Can no one induce this spoiled young man to relent? Did ever one hear of anything so preposterous? Perhaps this is some more of his French modesty, or possibly he wishes us to go down on our knees to him."

"I accept, General, with many thanks," Loreno said.

The Duchess smiled happily and turned to Mr. Dow.

"It is a pity you are not also going to Varese," she said politely; "perhaps you would have joined our party."

"Oh, thank you," he replied, "but I may see you there. I intend to stop at Varese, and will do myself the honor to call."

"Pray don't forget, and I hope we shall still be there."

"We shall look for you," Loreno added courteously.

Signor Veltri now approached the group, and Agatha rose to meet him.

"Are you ready?" she asked.

"At your service, Signorina."

"Are you going to have some music?" asked the General.

"Yes; we had arranged to try over some duets for piano and violin."

"Do you object to an audience?"

"Not at all; any one will be welcome who cares to listen."

"Then I am one," said Loreno. "Will you please present me to Signor Veltri?"

The young Calabrian lifted his hat, but Loreno, going forward, offered his hand. "Do you also consent to our joining you?" he asked.

"With pleasure."

So the entire party adjourned to the salon and listened for an hour to the playing of the pianist and Agatha.

When they went out of doors again, leaving the young musician to his practising, Loreno surprised them by saying, —

"I've a little scheme about which I should like to consult Miss Page;" and turning to Agatha he added, "Would you mind going with me as far as the lodge?"

"Certainly not;" but her face showed surprise.

"Don't be gone long," called his sister, as they walked away together; "we are going for a row."

"I have something of importance to tell you," he began, after they had walked a few yards in silence; "but it's true that I have a little scheme in mind about which I wish to consult with you. I've taken a fancy to that young pianist, and I propose to ask him to come to the villa while you are there, if agreeable to you."

She flushed with pleasure. "You are doing this to please me," she said.

"And myself also."

"I should be very glad to have him there, so far as I am concerned, but I really know nothing about him except what I've told you."

"I had a little talk with him in the salon," Loreno answered, "and he told me that he came here to play to Rubinstein, who was expected at the villa of Baron von Feugel. But Rubinstein has postponed his visit for a week, and so young Veltri is waiting for him. He really interests me very much, and I should like to know him better. There is nothing to keep him here, and I hope that he will come with us. What I have to propose is that you should ask your uncle to offer him a seat on the coach."

"It's all rather extraordinary, isn't it?" she said, looking at him brightly. "Wouldn't it be better to consult the Duke and your sister?"

"Why? I'm master of my own house."

"But they may not approve."

"Have no fear of that. Costanza spoils me quite as much as your uncle spoils you; and as for the Duke — he isn't the least bit of a snob."

"Very well. And now what is it you have to tell me, — anything about my cousin?" and she searched his face eagerly.

"Yes; I have seen her."

"You have?"

"I found her in Paris. She is in the studio of a distinguished sculptor, M. de Valro."

Agatha's face was ardent. "She is studying sculpture, then. Did she seem happy?"

"Yes, because she is encouraged heartily by her master, and really shows great talent. I was surprised at her work."

Agatha laughed excitedly. "How splendid, and what a relief!" Then her face grew grave, "May I tell my uncle?" she asked.

"I will explain how matters stand, and then you must judge. When I first found her, she was inclined to resent my appearance; but before we parted she was more reasonable, and agreed that I might call again the following day. From that time I saw her constantly, and we had many a long talk. She can't bear the thought of living on in the old way, and is determined to make a new career solely on her merits as an artist. She has even adopted a new name, — she calls herself Madame André, — and her hope is to make this name known and respected through her work, and to enjoy the fruit of her labor. I must confess that after hearing all the circumstances, I understand her feeling and applaud her intention."

"What is her feeling toward her father and toward me?"

"Toward you most cordial; and before I left Paris her bitterness toward her father seemed to be greatly softened, — so much so, indeed, that she sent a message to you, in which she is willing to include her father if you think best."

" And that is — "

" That she feels that her present action, while wise, was not kindly taken. She hopes for your consideration (she could not bring herself to say forgiveness) regarding her method of taking up her work, and your sympathy in its result."

" That she will always have," exclaimed the fervent girl. " And I'm sure the Count will be very happy to hear of it all."

" Who shall tell him ? " he asked.

She thought for some minutes. " Would Padre Sacconi not be the best person ? "

" I think he would be : we will assign that duty to him, then."

She looked at her companion with undisguised gratitude.

" How can I ever thank you for what you have done ? " she said.

" The obligation is mine," he replied ; " I hope that by the little I have done, I have proved the sincerity which I bade you test."

She was silent as they walked side by side, each heart surging wildly.

" I cannot thank you, " she exclaimed presently ; " my uncle must do so."

They had turned and were approaching the rest of the party.

His step grew shorter, and lagged slightly.

" Do you realize " — his voice trembled with suppressed feeling, and the eyes into which she looked were intense — " do you understand, Miss Agatha, that your happiness is of real consequence to me ? "

"I really never thought of it," and she strove bravely to meet his glance again ; "but," — and now involuntarily her eyes sought his and her voice grew firm, — "I believe you, and am very grateful."

He stopped, and she turned inquiringly toward him ; but after a moment he moved forward and they walked for some time without speaking. Agatha was the first to break the silence.

"How did you like my cousin ? "

"Very much indeed. She is a splendid companion, so vivacious and clever. We tramped all over Paris, and examined every part of the Exhibition."

"You think her beautiful, do you not ? "

"Yes, indeed."

"Did you see little Francesco ? "

"Several times. He is a fine little fellow, but needs a less worshipful mother."

"Is he with her, or at school ? "

"At school ; but he passes every Saturday and Sunday with his mother."

"I must brush up my French, or he 'll laugh at me when we meet," she said gayly.

"Your cousin spoke of your French. She declares that you are one of the few foreigners who speak French like a native."

"My dear cousin is partial. But did she talk of me much, — naturally, I mean, and affectionately ? "

"Without the least restraint ; and as for her enthusiasm —" He made an expressive gesture.

"Oh, I 'm so glad ! "

Then she continued to question him rapidly about every detail concerning Mercede, and he succeeded in giving her quite a clear idea, not only of Mercede's present feeling, but also of her daily occupation and her home.

When they reached the hotel they found the party seated near the stone steps leading to the water. As they approached, the Duchess looked up.

"Well, what mischief have you young people been plotting?" she said.

"Out with it, Signorina," exclaimed Loreno.

"The Marquis says, Uncle, that he intends to invite Signor Veltri to go to his villa at Varese while we are there, and I think it would be pleasant to have him go on the coach."

The suggestion was met by a chorus of laughter.

"The same old Filippo!" exclaimed the Duchess. "He takes what he wants."

"And the same old Agatha!" added the Count; "nothing can curb her enthusiasm for musicians."

"Well, what do you think?" Agatha asked.

"I will leave it to the Duke and Duchess," the Count replied.

"Pardon *me*," said Mr. Dow, whose brow was stretched with amazement, "but do you know that this young fellow is nothing but a teacher in Rome?"

"No, I was n't aware of that," and Filippo looked at the speaker soberly. "It seems to me that he is much more, — that he is an artist; and as for his being a gentleman, I 'm again willing to trust my judgment."

"But he teaches."

"Because he is poor."

" Then you knew about it? "

" Of course ; but why do you ask? Is teaching disgraceful in America? "

" No, not disgraceful ; but music-teachers don't, as a rule, hold what I should call a good social position."

" I 'm not proposing to offer this young man a social position, but simply my individual hospitality. The first he might scorn ; the second I trust he will accept."

" Oh, you are quite right ; I merely thought you might be unacquainted with the fact."

The Duchess, who knew her brother's face so well, thought it time to interfere.

" Is n't all this rather off the point ? " she inquired. " The question has been left to the Duke and me, of inviting Signor Veltri to go with us to-morrow instead of following by train. If he can arrange to go, I should say by all means ask him to come with us ; should n't you, Luigi? "

" Certainly," said the Duke.

" Then my part is arranged," said Agatha, turning to Loreno.

" And mine shall be before night," he replied.

The sail upon the lake was most delightful to Loreno, for Agatha was by his side, her shoulder almost touching his, and when she turned and spoke to him he could look deep into the clear eyes he thought incomparable. With the knowledge that he would soon ask this girl to be his wife, to give him always the place by her side, came the realization that these hours might be the last during which he could treasure such a hope, or look into those eyes without despair.

As the boat returned to the quay, music floated over the water and roused Loreno from his dream. Could they have sailed for an hour already? He glanced toward the landing-place and his heart was heavy. His spirit yearned for rest; he chafed at delay, even though it deferred disappointment. His nature scorned the solace of ignorance and impelled him to grasp the truth. The boat rocked with the wave of a passing steamer, and Agatha's hand fell upon his; he caught a deep breath and his face paled.

" Why, Filippo, I believe you were actually frightened!" and the Duchess laughed.

" I'm frightened still!" he answered strangely.

The ladies went to their rooms to dress for dinner, leaving the gentlemen together. The Duke soon excused himself, and Loreno proposed to the General that they should light cigars and stroll in the park. After they had plunged into its seclusion, Loreno suddenly brought the conversation around to Agatha.

"Your niece, General, has great talent for music," he said.

" She really plays very well, does she not? "

" Beautifully! Nor is that all; her entire nature seems pervaded with music."

" My niece has a lovely nature."

In saying this the Count was not as naïve as might appear. He had recognized Loreno's voice the evening before, and now his suspicions were greatly strengthened.

" It would be a painful thought, therefore, to consider parting with her? " continued the Marquis.

" Very ! very ! "

" Yet, appreciating her as you do, you must realize that such a sacrifice is likely to be asked of you."

" You mean that she may marry ? "

" Precisely."

" She must love first."

" Certainly."

" Then I may have a long respite," and the Count smiled gravely.

Loreno abandoned circumlocution and dashed directly at his point.

" We probably understand each other, General," he began. " You mean to warn me that your niece does not care for me ? "

Knowing Agatha's tone so well, the Count had detected something in her playing the night before that he had never heard until then. He believed that she loved this young man, but it was not for him to tell him so, and he held his peace.

" I wish, with your permission, to find out for myself," Loreno continued, " and I respectfully request that privilege. You know who I am, and I need not assure you of my right to take a wife, nor need I assure you that in the event of success in my suit, I will take your niece with a full sense of my responsibility, and will cherish and love her as she deserves."

They had stopped walking and stood face to face. As the young man paused, the Count grasped his hand.

" Marquis," he said, " I need Agatha myself,—I really need her, — but I 'll not stand in the way of her happiness. If you should be fortunate enough to win her, I shall yield her up to you with less sorrow

than to any other young man of my acquaintance.
But I shall miss her beyond expression."

Filippo tightened his grip on the other's hand. His
warm heart went out to the brave old man, — half
laughing, half sobbing, as he realized that he was
now indeed to be left alone.

A few weeks before, he could have looked Loreno in
the eye and hidden his feeling like any other man ; but
now his nerve was broken and he was no longer himself. He was ashamed, and bowed his head slightly ;
and then as a big tear welled up from his heart and
dropped, without the chance of denying it, upon Loreno's hand, he confessed his weakness frankly.

" I realize now that I 'm an old man," he said, —
" really an old man, who must ask some indulgence
from a young fellow like you. Pray don't despise
the weakness that I have n't the power to control.
I 'm not my old self, — I 'm conscious of it ; but it
can't be helped, and I want your respect."

Loreno threw his strong arm around his companion's shoulder, not familiarly, but compassionately.

" Do me the justice to believe, sir," he said, " that
I honor you, not only for what you have been, but
for what you are. Every young man of Italy honors
General Ricci, and I honor doubly the tenderness of
the heart already distinguished for its courage."

" God bless you, Marquis ! " and the old soldier
raised his head proudly ; " you have come to me as a
strong friend ; I shall not often try your patience in
this way. Come, let us go back ; the others will be
waiting for us."

CHAPTER XII.

ALTHOUGH Padre Sacconi and Loreno were so different in their ages and pursuits, there existed between them a sympathy, the basis of which was their common love for Agatha; but irrespective of this feeling there was much to draw them together. The ardent nature of Filippo found rest in the calm presence of the white-haired priest, while Padre Sacconi admired the healthy vigor, both of body and spirit, possessed by the young nobleman; and the high-minded character of each found a ready response in the other.

On reaching Erba and hearing that his bird had flown, Loreno had gone to the old man for light. The conversation which ensued convinced the priest that an important hour in the life of Agatha was near, and a longing possessed him to be with her at such a time, perhaps to counsel her, or, if it might be, to bless her.

As if reading this longing, the young Marquis suddenly pressed upon the aged man a cordial invitation to go with him to Varese for a few days, stopping on the way at Como to see Agatha.

The simple old priest seldom took a holiday, and the responsibility of leaving the parish to take care of itself, or even of intrusting its manifold interests to another's keeping, filled him with dismay. But under the impetuous urging of Loreno, reinforced by the desire to be near Agatha, he at last agreed to apply to his bishop for the necessary permission, and, if possible, to join Loreno at Como on the following day.

He arrived, therefore, on the evening of Loreno's interview with the Count, and the following morning accompanied the Marquis to the Villa d' Este, where they found the coach already loaded for the drive to Varese. Having sent up their names, they seated themselves upon the hotel terrace. In a few moments Agatha appeared. She greeted her old friend affectionately, and then gave her hand to Loreno.

"I have to thank you for this pleasure," she said; "how shall I repay all my obligations?"

"A lady can pay any debt with a flower," and he glanced at the bunch of roses in her bodice.

She detached a bud and held it out to him. "'In hand to him paid,'—isn't that the technical phrase?" she asked gayly.

"Is this, then, payment in full?"

"No, indeed," and she looked happily into the face of the priest; "the whole bunch would not begin to pay this day's debt alone."

As she seated herself and began to chat with Padre Sacconi, Loreno watched her with admiration. Her dress seemed to him exceedingly pretty, with its whiteness, and its crispness, and its graceful folds, while the bow at the throat matching the bow in the coils of her hair quite fascinated his eye. Then the simplicity of it all caused him to wonder why other girls did not dress themselves so well; and as his glance, following the harmonious lines of the lithe figure, caught a glimpse of a foot which even among Italian women was noteworthy, he closed his eyes for an instant, as though to imprison forever the grateful picture which filled them.

The arrival of his sister broke the spell.

"Come," she said, after shaking hands cordially with Padre Sacconi, "everything is ready, and the General is impatient to be off."

The ride, which lasted throughout the day, was broken several times. At the last stage the General yielded up the reins to Loreno, who invited Agatha, from whom he had been separated since the first stage, to take the seat at his side. He was an excellent whip, and sent the horses along steadily and swiftly, and as they whirled around a bend which brought the long row of Alps in view, with Monte Rosa like an Amazon towering above her sisters, the sunlight was still playing over the snowy mountain-tops.

"How beautiful!" Agatha exclaimed.

"Yet," said her companion, "I think the sunlight upon Monte Generoso is the prettiest object of the landscape at this hour. You will be able to see it in a few moments. Now look out for it," he said presently, — "almost behind us."

The view across the plain to rugged Generoso

burst suddenly upon them. Loreno pointed out the town of Varese, while yet farther, removed somewhat from the cluster of houses, was a large hotel, and across the valley a villa upon the crown of a low hill. Around the latter were spacious grounds, and she could see that it was a beautiful estate.

"That is my villa," he said. "It stands at the head of the lake, and the grounds slope down to the water. What impression does this country make upon you?" he added earnestly.

"It is charming, — indeed, not unlike Erba."

"Then I hope that some of your affection for the Brianza may be transferred to it." And he looked into her face wistfully.

"Is Varese itself gay, or quiet?" Agatha inquired hastily.

"Neither; but in activity, of course not even a suggestion of what it once was. After Sforza introduced the mulberry-tree and the silk-worm into Lombardy, Varese took the lead in silk-making, and her silks and velvets were greatly prized even in France. To give you an idea of their prosperity I need only tell you that during the sixteenth century there was not a poor citizen in Varese. The next century, however, brought bad fortune, and a historian of that time says that any one of the Varese shopkeepers of the preceding century could have bought out all the shopkeepers of the town in his day."

"Poor fellows! how did they lose their money?"

"Through the great balances due them by France, especially Lyons, being paid in paper money instead of in coin, by which act Varese manufacturers lost ninety per cent of their investments. At first they despaired; but the generosity of the Duke of Modena during his residence in Varese gave them heart again. During the last one hundred years the town has had her ups and downs. Before the introduction of rail-roads, for example, it was on the high-road to France, Germany, and Flanders; but the railroads and the new passes changed all that. The citizens, however, still keep alive the traditions of Varese's former affluence, and always hope. Our wines enjoy a good reputation, and we have some excellent factories. I will show you my carriages, all made here; Varese furniture is well thought of, and our silk is even now sought after. We have four factories for making church organs, and you have surely heard of the bells cast by the Bizzozera. But the greatest pride of the modern Varesini I have kept for the last."

"And what is that?"

"That here was executed the first act of sovereignty for Lombardy in the name of Victor Emmanuel."

"Brava Varese!"

"At present my townsmen hope great things from the Milanese, some of whom are buying and building summer villas near the town."

"But how can you hope to bid for many of the Milanese against the incomparable attractions of Lake Como?"

"While no one exceeds your Milanese in his desire for a little country air in the summer-time, no one can be more bored than he at the end of three days, if he has not that which recalls his city life. He wishes to pay visits, go. to his café, read the newspapers, hear a little music if he may, — all of which require a sufficient population to make a demand for them. Our little city has this advantage over the silent hills of Como, — it can offer the charms of the country with a certain continuance of city habits."

" But do your rich visitors and residents do nothing except amuse themselves? "

" A few do more. My friend Dandolo, for example, belongs to a family renowned for its benevolence. His grandfather bought a convent which had been suppressed, and turned it into a villa. Here he delivered lectures upon agriculture to the inhabitants, and gave them the benefit of his personal experience; his son continued the work; and the grandsons in good time took it up. One brother, however, was killed in Rome while fighting the French, and Emilio returning from the war was left alone. Yet he has done much, both by example and by practical effort."

" And you ? " she asked, smiling archly.

" I ? Well, I confess that I do but little in proportion to my opportunity, and even that little becomes contemptible in the presence of one who does so much for the unfortunate ; " and he looked reverently into the face that had grown suddenly serious.

" My poor efforts," she said, with a touch of sadness, "don't even merit the recognition of an apology."

" Others think differently ; " and he paused before

adding, "if I had a good example always before me, I feel that I might really accomplish something. But there is no co-operation here, and my knowledge of what I might do is annulled by my lack of zeal."

In his preoccupation he had neglected his duties, and the Duchess found it necessary to call him to order.

"Hurry on, Filippo!" she called. "The horses can rest for the next week."

"Eu!" he called to the leaders, with the soft dove-like sound universal among Italian drivers. In the present instance, at least, the result was in the inverse ratio to the power of the sound, and just as the afterglow of the sun shot into the heavens the coach dashed into the villa grounds.

When the steps were brought, Filippo busied himself with his companion's wraps until his other guests had clambered down. The Duchess turned to wait for Agatha, but seeing that her brother lagged, discreetly led the way into the house. Then Filippo alighted, and taking Agatha's hand helped her to the ground; still retaining her hand he led her across the threshold of his home and bowed as she passed in front of him. She flushed slightly, and the hand which the Duchess now claimed, trembled.

"Welcome to my brother's home!" said the Duchess, kissing her affectionately. "In both our names, welcome indeed!"

It is an eventful moment when a sister first tacitly acknowledges her who has won the brother's heart, for they will be either sisters or opponents. When the bond is close between brother and sister, it is one not to be lightly loosened. Playfellows in baby-hood, companions in childhood, friends in youth and confidants in budding maturity; knit together by common interests and natural instinct, they have shared their joys and suffered the same sorrows until their hearts beat with peculiar correspondence. Through it all she has become more womanly, he more manly; and awakening to this fact each re-joices in the other and there continues between them the nearest approach to a relation of equality that is possible between the two sexes: when lo! some fine morning a little maid appears whose tastes, opinions, wishes, and even prejudices are counted more worthy of attention than those of the old comrade; whose fellowship is plainly preferred, whose adoption, in a word, is complete.

Yet she who is installed so confidently upon an-other's throne has need of a loving Mentor. Man-kind has not learned — and perhaps never will learn — to be reasonable regarding a young wife. The ancient Adam seems to have believed his Eve equipped with all the wisdom and self-denial that belong only to experience, and in consequence un-justly blamed his unhappy bride: the modern Adam, with corresponding thoughtlessness, seems to expect his Eve to understand his temper and his palate as perfectly as though she had rubbed against his rough edges and made his coffee since childhood. But the modern Eve has often a guardian angel in the guise of her husband's sister. Let her lay hold of that sister's heart and enjoy its sweet sympathy, profit by its wisdom, and woo from it sage hints born of experience.

The following morning was beautifully clear, and Loreno, rising early, sauntered to the garden. Upon his return, seeing no signs of his guests, he went to his room to write. He was restless, however, and soon threw down his pen and stepped out upon the balcony.

The villa had belonged to his family for several generations, and every summer of his youth had been passed here. The room in which he now slept was known as the Padrone's room, and his father and grandfather had occupied it before him; it was directly below his old one, and therefore the view from its balcony was familiar.

Sweeping down with a gentle curve, a lawn fell to the tranquil lake of Varese, a mile away, the waters of its farther shore seeming to bathe the feet of Monte Rosa, whose ponderous sides glistened in the sunlight. To the left the line of the snow-covered Alps led the eye far away to the needle-point of Monte Viso; while to the right, where the near Italian hills shut in the view, the famous chapels of the Sacro Monte stood out sharply against the summer sky. Ah, how he longed to go and ask the sweet girl his roof now sheltered to be mistress of these downs and groves, these flowers and splashing brooks upon which his eyes turned, but whose power to give him happiness was gone unless she should come and share their fellowship!

Presently his sister appeared upon the terrace and

stood breathing the pure air. His eye brightened with pleasure, and he watched her for a moment before speaking. She turned, and looking up waved her hand and answered his morning greeting. After chatting with her for a few moments he went below and joined her.

"I presume Miss Page is tired after her ride," he ventured.

"Very likely."

"It's a great pleasure for me to have you all here," and his gaze was fixed upon the tranquil view.

Her eyes twinkled as she replied solicitously, —

"You don't think, then, that I took too great a liberty with your hospitality?"

He turned quickly toward her. "Why, Costanza! you *cannot* impose upon me. You know how welcome any friend of yours would be at any time; but in this instance I am peculiarly happy to receive your friends."

She slipped her hand through his arm and looked into his face lovingly.

"You like Miss Page, Filippo?"

He answered her look firmly. "I have never known any one whom I admire so thoroughly."

Her hand closed tightly upon his arm, and with her eyes upon his she added, "A woman, dear, sees clearly through other women; and any one who succeeds in winning Agatha's faith will be very fortunate."

He paused for a moment and then said steadily, "I intend to try."

A door opened above them, and turning, they saw Agatha upon her balcony. She wore a bunch of fresh flowers in her dress, and a rose was fastened in her hair.

The Duchess smiled slightly and glanced at the bunch in her own belt. " By the bye," she said, " I suppose it is you I must thank for these exquisite flowers."

" Yes, I took a walk before my coffee was sent up, and picked a few flowers on the way."

The young girl above now caught sight of them, and bade them a cheery good-morning.

" Am I the last one ? " she asked.

" No ; you see all the early birds here," the Duchess answered.

" Then I 'll hurry down to shame the others."

" That won't be till the new year gets ahead of the old," called Padre Sacconi, as he and the General, arm in arm, came around the corner of the house.

The General had awakened early, and after lighting a cigar, had gone to the terrace, where in a few moments he was joined by Padre Sacconi, who proposed a stroll in the grove.

" Let us sit down on that bench yonder," said the priest, presently. " I have something to tell you."

They seated themselves, and the Count, turning to his companion, waited to hear what he had to say.

" I have news for you, General," Padre Sacconi began, "which its bearer, the Marquis Loreno, thinks you would prefer to hear from my lips rather than from his. However that may be, I trust it will be welcome."

The General's eyes twinkled; he believed Agatha

11

had consented to become Loreno's wife, and that they thought thus to break the news to him.

"What is it?" he asked; "out with it!"

"It is from Paris; from one of the studios—where students of sculpture are sometimes received."

The General's eyes grew bright and his face became serious, a spot of red mounting to each cheek.

"The Marquis," continued the priest, warily, "made the acquaintance of a young woman there, who gives unusual promise of success, and he bears a message from her to her father." Knowing the General's hot temper, and having been made acquainted with the circumstances of Mercede's letter, he paused, expecting at least an indignant protest.

"The message is from my daughter," was the quiet comment.

"Yes, from Mercede. She is showing wonderful talent, I hear."

The Count remained silent for some moments, looking up the path. "What is her message?" he asked presently.

"The spirit of it is this,"—and the kind-hearted old mediator permitted the message to receive the soft color of his own nature: "She realizes now that her life,—poor girl!—has again a ray of interest to her; that her leaving for Paris so suddenly, and writing so vaguely of her intentions was the result—quite natural, as it seems to me—of the strain (and it must have been a terrible one, poor child!) which had been put upon her by her girlish inexperience and love of romance,—for that, after all, is what it was. The dear girl hopes for her father's consideration,—that was the precise word, — hopes, under the almost insupportable circumstances, for a father's consideration ; and more, dear friend, this poor lonely girl, struggling bravely to win a name which her child may bear without shame, asks for her father's sympathy."

"Is that her word also?" asked the General, hoarsely.

"Her precise word."

The father's tone was full of feeling, and he was evidently touched ; therefore the priest thought it best to leave well enough alone.

After a long and profound silence the General rose and moved toward the house. His companion joined him, and they walked on without speaking for some minutes. When the Count spoke, his voice was steady and calm.

"Padre Sacconi," he said, " I'm a pretty old man to treasure either ambition or bitterness. Mercede has made me suffer, and a good deal ; but she too has suffered, and must suffer, I fear, in the many years before her. I shall write to her ; the Marquis has her address?"

"Yes."

"And Agatha knows of all this?"

"I think so ; indeed, I'm sure of it."

An expression of pain passed over his face.

"And Agatha didn't dare tell me herself?"

"She knew that the subject was painful, and that — "

"That," interrupted the Count with a sad smile, " her uncle's temper is untrustworthy ; but do you know, Padre, that seems a long time ago. While I

have certainly lost much in strength, I feel that I've
gained something. I think I'm a little less — well,
say impulsive — than I was. Not that it's all gone,
by any means, but that I seem to covet peace and
value good-will a little more than I did. I shall
write to my daughter, and — and I thank you very
much for your kindness, old friend, to-day and in
the past. But you don't wish to go in yet, do
you?" he demanded, with easy indifference to his
own leadership. "Why not take another turn up the
path and tell me all you know about Mercede; I was
always sure that girl had talent. She has a remarkable face. Did you ever notice an intense expression
of the eyes that seems to be the very essence of earnestness? It's really extraordinary; and when you
think of it, her temperament is a thoroughly artistic
one. I don't like, mind you, that a daughter of mine
should sell the work of her brain and hand to others,
but I suppose I've got to accept that with her new
life. It's a wonderful change from what I'd dreamed
would be my child's future;" and sadness again stole
into his face.

Then his companion recited the glory of talent,
and drew, as a result of Mercede's success, a picture
so wisely adapted to the Count's ambition, that he
became almost reconciled to her new life.

Then the General, whose heart was warmed, made
a confidence on *his* part, after which he stood and absorbed attentively an *ex-parte* and enthusiastic statement of the noble traits of a certain young Marquis,
meanwhile nodding his head emphatically, and uttering ejaculations of " E vero ! Certo ! Sicuro ! "

CHAPTER XIII.

" IL TRAMONTO."

THE next few days were divided between music, riding, driving, and roaming about the grounds. Loreno was sorely tempted to speak his heart to Agatha, but resisted firmly, although he put no restraint upon his devotion to her. The General seemed in uncommon spirits, while Padre Sacconi was rather inclined to censure himself when he found how contented he could be away from his flock.

Loreno soon discovered the old gentleman's weakness for books, and he established him in a big armchair near the open window of the library, with rows of rare volumes on all sides, and with a roving commission to delve among them to his heart's content. Now and again the scholarly old face would appear in the music-room, wooed by the magic fingers of Signor Veltri and the sound of Agatha's bow; or the sweet old priest would wander off for half an hour among the flowers or the big chestnut-trees, only to return soon to his easy chair and his books.

The young musician did not disguise his happiness. Treated as a friend, surrounded by congenial companions, neither persecuted by attention nor neglected, he walked and talked, practised his music, and rambled where inclination suggested, from hour to hour. Then, too, he often accompanied his host, Agatha, and Gaeta, upon a gallop over the surrounding country. The Duchess was everywhere, and seemed in her element as she watched over the pleasure of the guests; but she and the Duke sometimes jumped into her pony phaeton — at least, Loreno always called it hers — and went off alone for two or three hours. Although Loreno's guests had planned to push on to Stresa on Saturday, they had not yet visited the "Sacro Monte," a high hill upon which by the enterprise of a priest more than a dozen little chapels or "stations" are built at regular intervals, with a road leading past them to the hill-top.

"Why not go this evening?" suggested Loreno on the morning of Friday; "there is not a cloud in the sky."

The plan met with general approval, and thereupon he extended it.

"Let us," he said, "make an early start so that those who wish to push on to the Campo dei Fiore may see the sunset across the Alps."

They left the villa about four o'clock, and drove to the first chapel, beyond which a carriage could not go. The Duchess and Gaeta mounted ponies, but the others preferred to walk. Agatha was between her uncle and Loreno, while the Duke, Signor Veltri, and Padre Sacconi walked a few yards ahead.

"The Duchess told me, with much pleasure," said the priest to Signor Veltri, "that you have consented to accept her daughter as a pupil next winter."

" The obligation is mine," was the answer. " I am very glad to get pupils."

" But you can't take more than a certain number."

" My time has never been full."

" Is that possible ! " Padre Sacconi had never before heard any really good pianist, and this young artist's skill filled him with wonder. He had supposed that pupils would throng about such a master.

" Only artists have all their time taken, and I am merely a student."

" Dear me, dear me ! " answered the simple priest; " then what must they be ? "

" I understand," remarked the Duke, " that you taught the children of the Countess Casolini last winter."

" I have n't them any longer," and Veltri's brown eyes met the Duke's ; " I told the Countess that her eldest daughter had no talent, and that it was a waste of money to have her taught. She was offended, and dismissed me instantly.'

The nobleman smiled grimly. " Honesty is n't always wise."

" I 'm sorry, of course, for through the Countess I got several pupils, and two of them have already been withdrawn ; yet what else could I do? I thought I ought to tell her my opinion, but I said I was willing to teach the child."

" Have you heard Gaeta play ? "

" Yes, this morning."

" And you think it worth while for her to study music ? "

"Yes, I do, although I can't tell the extent of her talent; but she holds her hands well, and I hope has true feeling."

The Duke eyed him closely while he spoke, and then smiled slightly, but said nothing; presently their attention was attracted by an arch, and the conversation took another turn.

Loreno and his companions had fallen many yards in the rear, and fearing that the Count was growing weary, Loreno offered him his arm.

"What for?" demanded the General.

"It's rather a long pull, and I thought you might be a little tired."

The old gentleman drew himself up, his pride evidently touched.

"Not in the least, sir!" he said. "Am I walking too slowly for you?"

"No, indeed!" and then as the other quickened his pace, he added in a laughing tone, "Oh, come, General, don't hurry us; your niece and I have yet to climb to the top of the Campo dei Fiore."

The Count laughed contentedly. "I've been a good walker in my day," he said; "my niece can bear me out in that, for it's not so very long ago we walked from Erba to Bellagio — eh, Agatha?"

"And only a few weeks ago," Agatha added, readily comprehending the situation, "do you remember walking so fast from Inverigo across the hills that I cried for mercy?"

The old man chuckled at the recollection, and then grew grave.

"I doubt if it ever will occur again," he said presently; "an old war-horse must give way sooner or later — sooner or later."

The young girl regarded him with great tenderness. "Why, uncle dear," she said, "what are you thinking of? After this little change of air you will be stronger than ever."

"Yes, General," added Loreno, with the best of intentions, "compare yourself with Padre Sacconi, or even with a man so much your junior as Mr. Dow! You could give them a kilometer in five."

"Comfort myself by comparison with a priest and a slate-pencil!" exclaimed the nettled soldier.

"I mean," stammered Loreno, desperately, "that you could distance them both if their strength were combined."

"You didn't say that!" the other said suspiciously.

"Well, I say it now."

"And I believe my uncle could — easily," affirmed Agatha, coming to the rescue.

The Count remained silent for a moment or two. "I am getting old all the same," he said presently; "I know it because I'm so testy. I didn't mean any disrespect to my dear old friend Padre Sacconi, nor even to Mr. Dow!"

This evidence of his increased infirmity saddened Agatha greatly, and it was with difficulty that she could conceal the sudden depression of her spirits; but Loreno, in his turn, now came to the rescue bravely and effectively. He succeeded in starting the Count on reminiscences which wooed him into the most amiable of moods; and the old gentleman, either from a sense of requital or in obedience to that mysterious intuition which leads mankind when in a confidential mood to grasp the biceps of its fellow-man, slipped his arm through that of Loreno.

When they reached the top, Loreno found that only the Duke and Gaeta would push on with Agatha and himself, the others being contented with the view from the veranda of the inn. So the quartet started off, the Duke with Gaeta setting out at a rapid pace.

At first the ground was wet and slippery, but they soon entered a path which was dry and hard, leading toward the southern side of the mountain. Up this they climbed briskly for some time, until suddenly they came upon a cleft in the ground, from which a fresh breeze blew.

" How refreshing ! " exclaimed Gaeta.

"This breeze is said to be always here," Loreno remarked, "but in winter it feels warm and damp; there is a smaller cleft a little higher up."

" Let us push on," suggested the Duke ; " the sun is falling fast."

So off they started again, through fine grass and bushes, until presently they found themselves in the midst of a bewildering profusion of plants and flowers. They had, however, no time to linger, and with another effort were soon upon the summit. Gaeta found a seat, and availed herself of this opportunity to rest, her father standing near her absorbed in the splendid pageant.

Loreno led Agatha slowly away from them, beyond a high ledge of rock, passing around which they stood

silent, gazing over the vast plain of Lombardy framed
by the glowing Alps and the distant Apennines,
while below them the picturesque lakes reflected
different lights. Loreno watched the face he loved
as the sun slowly disappeared behind the mountain-
tops, its rays still penetrating the gloom, but losing
strength with every passing moment.

"How awful it would be," — his low voice was rich
with feeling, — "if we knew that it had sunk for the
last time! How willingly one would die!"

Agatha shuddered slightly. "What a dreary
thought!" she said.

"I don't wonder that you shudder," he continued,
"although at a mere fantasy. I too shudder, but I
have good reason." She turned and looked into his
face wonderingly. "Do you know," he went on,
"that from this moment I fear my life is to be
shrouded in a gloom as hopeless and even harder to
endure? I have known for some time that this moment must come, and dread has almost made a coward of me." His lips moved, but no sound came, and
he put his hand to his throat as though it were
parched. Then his eager eyes sought hers and held
them steadfast as he spoke again. "My heart, all my
being, has been illumed by a glorious hope; to-night
I fear it will sink and leave me in darkness." His
eyes grew wistful, while his tremulous breath gave
evidence of the deep passion that stirred him.

"I love you," he said, baring his head reverently;
"I love you deeply — eternally!"

He regarded her anxiously as her eyes grew frightened, and her hand sought a gold cross hanging upon

her bosom. Then he gently clasped both the symbol and the trembling hand.

"Is there hope of a morrow for me?" he asked, "or must it always be night?"

The whole intensity of her nature shone in the eyes that looked deep into his for a full moment. Then the light of a pure soul at rest came into her face, and he bent down and kissed her.

PART SECOND.

PART SECOND.

CHAPTER I.

AN INVITATION.

Do not judge your fellow-men too much by their masks. I have seen barbers with the faces of poets; I have sat near a red-faced fat priest whose thick lips trembled and whose bleared eyes filled with tears at the tender tones of an organ: nor because a face is stern does it follow that the heart it screens is hard.

There is an old man universally known, and at whom most of us look askance, of whom some hard things are said. He is often called " the Enemy," and treated accordingly. Yet behind his grim visage is a heart which lavishes gifts upon the young until their beauty rivals that of the angels. Abuse old Father Time, and he retaliates; treat him as a friend, and there is none better. This was the principle upon which Agatha and her husband ordered their married life, and now, although the fifth anniversary of their wedding day had passed, Time had evidently befriended them.

They were together in their home in Rome. The room in which they sat was large, and furnished with warm hangings and carved furniture showing Venetian skill. A bright fire blazed upon the hearth, in front of which a table was drawn, with a tall lamp upon it covered with a red silk shade.

Agatha was writing, while Filippo sat on the opposite side of the table reading. He looked up presently from his book and watched her affectionately.

" To whom are you writing ? " he asked.

" Mercede."

" Give her my love, and tell her how glad I was to hear of her Salon success."

" I included your congratulations with mine long ago. Is there anything else ? "

" I don't think of anything except kindest regards to the General. Are they still in Paris ? "

" Of course ; they don't go to Cannes until next week. What a memory you have ! "

He smiled amiably, and remained absorbed in thought for some time.

" What a change has come over things within the past five or six years ! " he said presently.

" Wonderful ! " and Agatha looked dreamily into the fire, her face bright with contentment.

Yet, after all, the changes were not so wonderful. Loreno had quickly become domesticated, while little by little Agatha had succeeded in interesting him in some of the plans which she had quietly and unobtrusively been carrying into effect. Her sympathy with the poor had been great, even as a young girl ; and after her marriage she availed herself of the broader sphere opened thereby to further the comfort of those who were less fortunate than herself.

Filippo, regarding this as suitable work for a woman, and interested in whatever was identified with his wife, gave a good-natured sanction to her efforts; but his main concern was with politics. He had early resigned his diplomatic post, and being chosen to represent the district of Varese in the National Parliament, had thrown himself with vigor into this new work, and was already one of the most prominent of the younger statesmen.

His views were broad, his words direct, and he won recognition from the leaders of both the Left and the Right.

Among all the politicians with whom he was thrown, no one appealed to him more as a thinker, or charmed him more as a friend, than the venerable Alfieri, "the democratic Marquis," as he was called. When, therefore, this statesman, during a brief visit at Varese, commended earnestly Agatha's philanthropic work, Filippo's interest in it was greatly quickened, and he discovered reason for the senator's approbation. He saw that the prizes which Agatha gave monthly to the contadini whose homes were clean and in good repair, and also to those who cultivated the prettiest plants in their houses, were agents not only of philanthropy but of good political economy, and that her sewing, music, and other classes were based upon a broad principle. Thereupon he adopted her plan and began with encouraging athletics by organizing competitions, and eventually presented to the town a fine gymnasium. In good time he subsidized the theatre, and prevailed upon the railroad to offer cheap excursions, — in short

12

did what he could to teach the poorer classes to amuse themselves rationally and healthfully. From this beginning grew more important endeavors, one of which was to teach the peasantry some essential sanitary laws. His most ambitious project, however, was the founding of a popular bank similar to those started by Luzzatti, Schulze-Delitzsch and others ; and he adopted the same plan which makes those institutions so successful in meeting the perplexing questions of agricultural credit.

He interested several of his influential neighbors in the scheme, and by agreeing to manage the cash department himself, induced them also to give their services without pay. The purpose of the bank was to receive and care for the savings of the poor, paying them good interest, advancing liberally upon produce and merchandise, receiving and issuing drafts upon other places, and putting an end to usury by discounting freely. Then it issued agrarian debenture bonds for sums of five hundred lire, to form a fund for the carrying on of agriculture. On these bonds it paid good interest, and the investment was felt to be safe by the purchasers, because the bank not only had a paid-up capital and reserve, but made an alliance with the other banks of the province to issue bonds under their collective guarantee.

Thus not only did the institution facilitate agriculture, but it circulated the unemployed savings of the people, facilitating work and production. Coin which before was hidden under hearthstones was now put at interest and kept in circulation. In this way political economy was illustrated practically to the community, and shopkeepers, farmers, workmen, and proprietors were associated together.

Thus Loreno found much in the new plan to engage his mind as well as his time, although after the machinery began to run smoothly he was relieved from his clerical work. In Rome he was naturally engrossed in his legislative duties, while Agatha was active in philanthropic works, to which she gave daily attention, in spite of the claims — never unhonored — of her son Sebastiano and her little daughter Teresa. Yet, as has been said, such changes as these in the life of the Marquis and his wife were not wonderful. On the contrary, they were quite natural to the ardent temperament of the one and the predisposition of the other.

In the mean time the General had carried out his intention of communicating with Mercede, and partly through the good offices of Agatha and Filippo, partly because the dawn of success cast a warmer glow over Mercede's horizon, she accepted, or rather she did not repel, her father's attempt at reconciliation, and sent a satisfactory reply to his letter. This led to a regular correspondence; and when she realized that he had no intention of opposing her artistic career, she showed her appreciation by the more unguarded tone of her letters. As the years went by, and the artist's hard work and talent began to bear fruit, she wrote frankly and with justifiable pride to her father, who in return did not stint his expressions of satisfaction; and thus they were gradually brought closer. Then came a stirring epoch

in the artist's career: her last work for the Salon
created a furore, and photographs of it appeared in
all the principal cities of Europe. The name of
Madame André was upon every tongue that spoke
of art, and naturally Rome was soon familiar with
it. Then came a report that the renowned sculpt-
ress was coming to pass the remainder of the winter
in the Eternal City, followed by a vague rumor that
Madame André had once been a student in Rome;
whereupon there were sanguine persons who declared
that they remembered having once met a little French
girl bearing the name of André whose attempts had
even then impressed them most favorably.

About this time Mercede wrote her father a
dutiful and cordial letter, begging him to pay her
a visit, and proposing that afterward they should go
together to Rome, stopping on the way for a little rest
at Cannes. As a matter of fact, while the old gentleman was perhaps "reformed," he had not become an
angel, and it is certain that he would have died without ever again laying eyes upon his daughter, had she
not thus asked him to come to her.

The General had now been absent about two
weeks, and in a letter to Agatha told of his surprise
at Mercede's genius and of his gratification at the
honor paid her. He was evidently very happy, and
wrote that the Parisian air agreed with him amaz-
ingly. Francesco he described as quite a young
giant; and as for Mercede — his impressions may
perhaps be best summed up in his own words: "She
seems older in judgment and manner, but I may still
say ' she is thoroughly Italian.'"

CHAPTER II.

A NINE DAYS' WONDER.

WHEN Mercede and her father arrived in Rome, they were received at the station by Agatha and Filippo. The General proposed that they should all dine together in the evening, and at seven o'clock the Marquis and his wife drove into the familiar court and climbed the long flights of stone steps, leading past the mutilated busts, to the heavy wooden door bearing the name of the Count Ricci. As they were ushered in, Mercede came forward eagerly to greet them, and Agatha had a better chance of observing the outward change that time had wrought in her.

She thought her cousin improved. Some of the freshness of her beauty had faded, but her face had undeniably gained in dignity and intellect. She was tall, graceful, and uncommonly striking in appearance; her carriage, moreover, had an ease and confidence that was beyond the promise of her maidenhood, — the result, no doubt, of her more developed character and of her success. In her presence not even the gracious Queen of Italy would have shone supreme; and indeed there was something in Mercede's manner and courtliness which suggested the

comparison to Agatha. She was stately, self-pos-
sessed, and vivacious; attentive to what was said
to her, intelligent and tactful in her responses. She
possessed also the gift of leading well, and during
the dinner and the long evening that followed chose
topics of conversation in which both Agatha and
Loreno were sure to find a responsive interest. She
was full of vigor, physical and mental, and under her
competent direction the conversation flowed genially
and incessantly.

Francesco did not dine with the others, but before dinner was the object of much attention. He
was a well-favored boy with pleasing manners. The
Lorenos were charmed with child and mother, while
the General seemed to be holding a mental jubilee.
What the last five years had added to his marks of
age, his trip to Paris and its sequel seemed to have
softened, — and where shall we find the true elixir of
life if not within our hearts? The hair may whiten,
the eye grow dim, and the joints stiffen; but all this
is not to be old, it is mere evidence of infirmity. No,
the Count was not old, — at least, not to-night.

Agatha and Filippo had already agreed upon a plan
by means of which Mercede should be introduced to
Roman society. Upon one thing only the latter
insisted, — that she should be presented and known
hereafter by the name of André; and this being
readily acceded to, she accepted gratefully the proposed plan. It was, that a large reception should be
given by the Marquis and his wife in her honor, until
which occasion Rome should be kept in ignorance of
her advent.

The invitations were sent out immediately, and for the ten days intervening, the city was full of the flutter which attends a new social sensation. And why not? Life, according to a well-known writer, " is composed of a series of small sensations ; " and surely this occasion combined the uncertainty of a début with the gratification of a most normal curiosity. All the elect studied anew the various productions of the distinguished visitor's work, on the chance of finding opportunity to rejoice her with their impressions. But beyond all other preliminary sensations was surprise at the auspices under which the artist was to make her appearance ; and social Rome craned its neck in every direction to discover some one who could explain the matter. But it remained a mystery even to Mr. Peter Dow. The Duke Faviola and his wife were undoubtedly the most likely persons to satisfy this curiosity, and to them Mr. Dow went. He found, however, that while sharing his interest they also shared his ignorance.

"When I spoke of Madame André," said the Duchess, " my brother merely laughed, and the Marchesa said that they entertain so seldom they feel justified in importing the latest Parisian novelty."

There was a pause, during which the Duchess thought of her forthcoming costume.

"It can't be your sister's long-lost cousin !" suggested Mr. Dow, verily inspired.

" No, her name was Finelli ; and besides, she has been living somewhere near Florence, I think."

" Well, we shall know next Thursday. But it is rather surprising that neither the Marquis nor his wife has ever mentioned Madame André to any one."

Tea was then served, and the visitor noticed that there were only two cups upon the tray.

"The Duke and Gaeta are off somewhere together," he said confidently.

"No; Gaeta is studying, and the Duke is cleaning his guns."

"Indeed!" and he thought what a bad habit it was to trust circumstantial evidence. "Gaeta has made wonderful progress in her music!" he added aloud.

"Do you think so? Signor Veltri is certainly a splendid master."

"It was a lucky day for him when he went to the Villa d' Este."

"I suppose the interest my brother and his wife have taken in him has helped him."

"Helped him! I should think so! Between you, you've made him. He told me himself that his time has all been taken since the winter Gaeta became his pupil."

"I am very glad; he merits success, and is so modest that there is no danger of his being spoiled."

Mr. Dow's eyebrows and lips indicated scepticism. "About his ability I agree with you, but as to his modesty — I must differ." Then in reply to the surprise on his companion's face he continued, "He is already a little spoiled,—indeed, very much spoiled; only last week at the Countess Fabiani's he left the piano because some people near him were talking."

"Do you blame him for that?"

"Certainly I do. What business has a young player

to insist upon people listening to his playing who prefer to talk?"

" Perhaps he feared he was disturbing them," she suggested gravely.

Mr. Dow laughed. " If that's the best defence you can make for your protégé, I think our opinions are not far apart."

" Was he paid to play?" asked the Duchess.

" I suppose not; I hear that he won't play for money in salons."

" Then he was a guest, and entitled to equal consideration with any other guest."

" In a certain sense, yes; but he was invited to play."

" And he was amiable enough to try. Suppose it had been my sister playing a violin, would those people have gone on talking?"

" Of course not; but that would have been quite different."

" You mean that she is an aristocrat and Signor Veltri is merely a music-teacher.

" Well, yes; that's about it."

" He holds a different opinion evidently, and took that method of expressing it. I think he was quite right."

" Do you really?"

" I do, indeed. Signor Veltri is a gentleman in every fibre, only he is poor and not high-born. His talent originally won him an introduction into some houses where he soon made himself welcome as a gentleman, as in my sister's house and in mine. When he comes as a teacher he is most punctual and faithful; when he comes as a guest he throws away the teacher. If he is invited to play he does so as a guest, not as a professional player, and if that fact is not clearly recognized he emphasizes it; and I say again he is right."

Her auditor regarded her with genuine surprise. "Et tu, Brute!" he exclaimed. "I begin to believe that the Marchese's democratic sentiments are infectious, and I won't deny that I look upon them as an unfortunate disease."

They did not continue the discussion, but on his way to his bachelor's apartment Mr. Dow carefully reviewed the Duchess's words.

"It's all very well for people in her position to talk so," he muttered,—"she can afford to; but all the same I'm not sure, if she's ever called upon to act up to her theory, that she'll stick to it. It makes a mighty difference whether one sits in the jury-box or in the dock."

The apartment of the Marquis Loreno was admirably adapted for a large gathering.

Upon entering it the night of the reception the guests were conducted through spacious ante-rooms with panelled ceilings, and floors of polished marble strewn with Eastern rugs, to a large hall having three doors, two of which led to dressing-rooms, the third — a wide double door — giving entrance to the drawing-room. Beyond the drawing-room was the ball-room, in the balcony of which the musicians were hidden behind a mass of plants. From one side of this immense room two doors led to a refreshment-

room, at the farther end of which was a conservatory.
The rooms were brilliant with lights and fragrant with
flowers. Servants in bright livery performed their
part of the pageant with appropriate unction; and the
gay uniforms of officers and the court dress of diplomats, mingled with the dazzling toilets of Rome's fair-
est women, combined to make a scene of uncommon
splendor. Loreno understood well how sensitive to
dramatic effect his countrymen are, and he used this
knowledge skilfully.

Agatha, in ivory satin, tall and lovely, Mercede
in garnet velvet, dark and majestic, stood together
before a superb marble figure of Destiny, — a repro-
duction of the work which had won Madame André
fame. It was the figure of a woman, the character of
whose face suggested that of the artist; but its lines
were broader, and the expression — wonderfully vivid
— was that of a sibyl inspired. The draped body,
though upright, was at rest, evidently borne onward
by myriads of angels to the place ordained of God. A
dark plush screen threw the figure into strong relief,
and covered jets of gas cast a mellow light upon it.

Its effect was electric upon the throng of guests who
pressed forward to be presented to the celebrity.

The striking beauty of the Contessina Ricci, which
Rome had remarked so well during the winter of her
début, was instantly recognized in the more mature
but added brilliancy of Madame André. The surprise was complete, the method dramatic.

Mercede, in spite of her apparent self-possession,
watched anxiously during the first hour for indications of the feeling which should follow that of sur-

prise. She noted closely the character of the glances directed toward her, especially those of the women.

In the mean time Loreno busied himself on all sides helping to form public opinion. He varied his words to suit his audience, but his general theme was regret that so great an artist should bestow upon the French capital the lustre of her name. This patriotic sentiment soon impregnated the atmosphere, sweeping before it all social misgiving; for Rome, like the rest of the world, finds it easy to condone the domestic eccentricities of its renowned children; and Madame André seemed to be, and was, practically, a different person from the tall dark girl who ran away with a lieutenant. If she had now run away from the lieutenant it mattered little; her success justified her. Such genius should not be confined to the limited span of a soldier's home. The Marchese was right: she belonged to the world, and the world had claimed her; now if Rome could content her, how fortunate for Rome.

Thus the first hour established her position. She felt it, she saw it; and as one after another pressed around her with pleas that she would remain among them, she recognized the guiding hand, and her gratitude went out to Loreno.

Now, too, she knew why he had urged her to finish the statue before she left Paris: it was for this occasion, this hour of triumph toward which her thoughts had turned yearningly for many years. She was excited, happy, exultant; and as Filippo joined the group surrounding her, her eyes sought his expressively.

"You have found quite as many old friends as new, I am sure," he said.

"Where all are so cordial, it is difficult to distinguish between them."

"I wish you could have heard all the comments that have reached me about the statue."

She laughed quietly as she said, "I think I have heard more than is good for me. I am reminded of what Goethe said,—that one never does a good thing but his friends do their best to prevent his doing another."

"Is your enthusiasm for Goethe as ardent as it used to be?"

"More ardent. I find him the most sympathetic of writers."

Several protests arose from her listeners, who advanced the claims of other authors, and Loreno took advantage of the discussion to slip away to Agatha, who stood near by.

"Marchese!" called Mercede, presently, "pray come to my assistance. These friends are quoting at me in all languages and dialects."

At this moment Loreno was confronted by Mr. Peter Dow, who apologized copiously for his late arrival.

Agatha presented him to Mercede, upon whom he beamed radiantly.

"I am not strong on poetry," Loreno remarked, "but my friend Mr. Dow is an authority. I commend him as a valuable ally;" and turning away, he again joined his wife.

In a few moments exclamations of pleasure from the group caused them to turn.

"Marchese — Agatha, dear!" Madame André called, "you must hear what a pretty translation one of the American poets has made to Grossi's words."

As Agatha and Filippo joined her, she turned to Mr. Dow.

"Come," she said, "we must repeat our recitations, but a little differently; I'll recite one verse at a time, and you must give its translation."

And thus they repeated alternately the poem of which the following is the English version.

"Swallow from beyond the sea,
    That with every dawning day,
Sitting on the balcony,
    Utterest thy plaintive lay, —
What is that thou tellest me,
    Swallow from beyond the sea?

"Haply thou for him who went
    From thee, and forgot his mate,
Dost lament to my lament,
    Widowed, lonely, desolate.
Ever, then, lament with me,
    Swallow from beyond the sea!

"Happier yet art thou than I;
    Thee thy trusty wings may bear
Over lake and cliff to fly,
    Filling with thy cries the air, —
Calling him continually,
    Swallow from beyond the sea!

"Could I too! but I must pine
    In this dungeon close and low,
Where the sun can never shine,
    Where the breeze can never blow,
Where thy voice scarce reaches me,
    Swallow from beyond the sea!

"Now September days are near,
    Thou to distant lands wilt fly;
In another hemisphere
    Other streams shall hear thy cry;
Other hills shall answer thee,
    Swallow from beyond the sea!

"Then shall I, when daylight glows,
    Waking to the sense of pain,
Midst the wintry frosts and snows,
    Think I hear thy notes again, —
Notes that seem to grieve for me,
    Swallow from beyond the sea!

"Planted here upon the ground,
    Thou shalt find a cross in spring;
There, as evening gathers round,
    Swallow, come and rest thy wing.
Chant a strain of peace to me,
    Swallow from beyond the sea!"

"What a charming translation!" exclaimed Loreno. "Whose is it?"

"It was made," Mr. Dow answered, "by our American poet Bryant."

"Indeed!" said Agatha. "How strange that I never have seen it! I thought my edition of his poems was complete."

"I think," was the answer, "that it is not included in any published edition of Mr. Bryant's works."

"Won't you write the translation for me?" urged Agatha.

"With pleasure."

Mr. Dow was elated. He felt that he had shone — a consciousness tending to induce good-will; especially toward that fellow-creature who tilted the

bushel. Therefore Mercede had bound Mr. Dow
hand and foot, so far as his social disapproval of
"mere artists" might have fallen upon her.

"I 'm sure you must be tired," said Agatha to her
cousin. "Filippo, won't you take Mercede to get a
glass of wine?"

Thereupon the artist slipped her hand through her
host's arm, the brilliant throng greeting her with compliments and smiles as she passed up the long aisle
made for her.

Her father, who was talking with the Duke Faviola,
caught her eye as she passed, and smiled fondly.
She paused and spoke to him, and he presented the
Duke.

"We have already been introduced," Madame
André said. "Even a less kind hostess than Agatha
would scarcely have withheld such a pleasure from
me."

The tall Duke merely bowed.

"The first time I met you, Marchese," she continued, turning to Loreno, "you had just come from
the Duke's villa. I remember the fact, because you
spoke so often of the Duke's charming home, and of
your little niece." She turned again to the Duke:
"Is your daughter here to-night?"

"Yes; she has just gone into the conservatory.
She has been dancing, and became heated." And as
he spoke of Gaeta his manner grew less frigid.

Mercede, perceiving this, followed the cue. "I
wish so much to see the child," were her words;
"after I have had my wine you must take me to
the conservatory, Marchese." And nodding brightly

to her father, and with a gracious bow to the Duke, she wended her way toward the supper-room.

Ten minutes later they found Gaeta seated upon a low settee in the midst of orange-trees, looking into the face of Signor Veltri, who was standing before her talking gayly. Loreno pointed her out.

" Who is her companion ? " asked Mercede.

" A musician named Veltri ; he is her piano-master."

" You are consistently democratic; " and she laughed quietly.

"If you please ; but this is a case of liking a man, and regarding myself as master of my own house."

"It must make some of your guests open their eyes."

"If they don't like it, they can easily open my doors."

Signor Veltri now caught sight of them. " Even the guest of the evening," he exclaimed, " deigns to follow our lead."

" It is a most fascinating retreat," Mercede rejoined, taking for granted that he had been presented ; " but I have really come to make the acquaintance of Donna Gaeta."

" Won't you sit down ? " said Gaeta, primly. Mercede took the proffered place, and devoted herself to the young girl.

Gaeta was a wide-eyed little maiden of the conventional Italian type, whose chief characteristic was her dignity. She was self-conscious on the present occasion, feeling the necessity of not betraying the fact that this was her first ball.

"Are you enjoying yourself?" asked Loreno patronizingly, when a pause in the conversation occurred.

"Immensely!"

"Is the music good — I mean for dancing?" Madame André asked.

"Perfectly splendid!"

"And the floor?" added Loreno.

"Divine!"

"What do you say to trying it?" he suggested to Mercede; and a few moments later they were gliding around the room together. As the excitement brought a rich color to Madame André's cheeks, many admiring glances were bent upon her brilliant beauty.

CHAPTER III.

A LITTLE LEAVEN.

WITHIN a few weeks Madame André was firmly installed as a resident and society pet of Rome. She hired a studio in a villa outside the Porta del Popolo, to which she transferred all her work from Paris. She threw this studio open one afternoon of each week, and her receptions became a marked social feature of the season. Commissions were pressed upon her, but success did not affect the care and thought which distinguished her work, and her artistic growth continued to be remarkable.

Although she seldom paid visits during the hours of daylight, she often passed the evening with the Lorenos.

It was during one of these informal visits that Agatha broached the subject of one of her charities. It was an organization following the general lines of the Girls' Friendly Society, of London, which she sketched briefly. In its behalf she proposed giving a performance of Schumann's " Pilgrimage of the Rose," and she asked Mercede to interest herself in its success.

"I like the musical idea," was Mercede's reply, "but choose another charity for its object, — for example, indigent artists or art students. I should not be willing to give my time or name to aid the charity you have sketched."

Then, as so often happens with ardent natures, her strength of conviction overpowered her judgment, moving her so greatly that she dashed on, not only impulsively but heedlessly. Exuberance of feeling always quickened her natural tendency to extravagance of expression, and, being intolerant of any opposition, when she was opposed in some pet theory her soul verily rose in arms. At such times, she would rush upon her opponent with an impetuosity that was effective solely because her thrusts were so vigorous that mere intellectual fencing (that delightful exercise of one's wits) became impossible, and there was left only a choice between earnest conflict and retreat. And thus it was now.

"What is it you propose to do?" she continued, — "encourage purity of life, dutifulness to parents, faithfulness to employers. You propose eventually — granting that your plan works out as perfectly as the dénouement in a fairy story — to establish a lodging-house, a bureau for servants, a hospital and a poor-house, disguised under prettier names, an emigration office, and a reading-room, — all good things, but plenty of them are already established and crying for patronage. But were this not true, — and I see that you already have twenty arguments each heavy enough to knock my poor opinion into atoms, — I should still oppose your plan upon its moral theory. I'm opposed to women banding together that they may lean upon one another. Women are feeble enough now, without creating a hot-house to force their flabbiness. What they need is to accustom themselves to stand firmly on their own feet, be it a question of judgment, will, or morals. This 'united we stand, divided we fall' principle for women, is in my opinion as pernicious as it can be."

"When you wished to perfect your talent for sculpture," Agatha replied, "you surrounded yourself with those whose aims were your own; you placed yourself in an atmosphere of art. But this did not weaken your individuality. This did not enervate your innate strength. And so with these girls: what applied to you artistically, applies to them morally, only with much greater force."

Mercede laughed impatiently. "The two things cannot be compared," she exclaimed, "and I am surprised that you should name them in the same breath. My art was a jewel, the unsuspected possession of which was revealed to me. I could not unlock its casket, and so sought some one who could. But virtue is a vastly different thing. All women are born with it, as with stomachs; they are as familiar with the penalty of trifling with the one as with the other. We all sneer at Adam for saying, ''T was the woman,' but I've no greater patience with women who snivel, ''T was the man.' Why don't you start an anti-indigestion society?"

"Surely, Mercede," and Agatha's voice betrayed both surprise and pain, — "surely you are not serious in regarding this grave question so flippantly. It isn't that the girls don't know, but that they are tempted. As the Milanese say, — 'You were not born with your eyes shut;' and you have now been in Paris for six years. Have you seen nothing there but what is faultless? Have you learned nothing of the world? If so, ask any candid man if such a society as mine would be useful."

Mercede shrugged her shoulders, but controlled any other evidence of irritation.

"I'm rather too busy a woman," she laughed, "to take my lantern and go in search of an honest man. No doubt some excellent results do occasionally come from such work, but it seems to me that a woman in your position has other duties quite as important in the social economy."

"I think most of us can make time for social duties as well as for graver responsibilities," Agatha replied. "Yet I know from experience that one needs to be watchful to keep an equitable balance."

"I'm glad to hear you say that," responded Mercede with emphasis, "for you are altogether too important a factor of this indolent Roman society to devote too much of your energy to interests outside of Filippo's career. I hear all sorts of prophecies for him, in which, naturally, I am deeply concerned. Nearly all the old giants are gone, and with a little patience and policy his place seems assured; but the social lever is unquestionably powerful, and should not, of course, be sacrificed to charitable work; above all, his own interests should not be too much divided."

"I think," said Agatha, gravely, "that no loving wife would be likely to lose sight of her husband's future, or of his usefulness to his country. But, after all, there are certain matters which each wife must determine for herself."

"Oh, of course!" and both relapsed into an awkward silence which Agatha broke in a moment by speaking of a new topic.

As Mercede walked home she had a feeling of dissatisfaction. She tried to throw it off by talking rapidly to Francesco; but her mind was like quicksand, — the more a fact struggled to free itself the deeper it sank. Upon reaching home she went directly to her room and threw herself into a chair.

In Paris she and Loreno had become fast friends, for in addition to her beauty and power of fascination, her kinship to Agatha had appealed strongly to the Marquis; and as it was his nature to reveal himself frankly, if at all, he had given Mercede every opportunity of knowing him quickly. She speedily discovered, of course, his love for her cousin, and this quickened her interest in him. Her own affection for Agatha was strong, and she threw herself heart and soul into the union of these two lives; the romantic quality of her nature finding courage to reassert itself in connection with experiences independent of her own bruised heart.

Whenever she thought of returning to Rome, she dwelt eagerly upon the almost ideal relation which would exist between the Lorenos and herself. Agatha would be even closer than before, while Filippo would be as a brother to her.

Agatha was glad that the cousin who loved her so well found her husband sympathetic, and from the day of Mercede's arrival she had done what she could to foster the cordial relations between them. Indeed, in her endeavor to demonstrate her idol's superior merits and peculiar virtues, she gradually overcame her reluctance to betray her innermost feelings to any other than her husband, and in moments of special confidence, responding to Mercede's eager interest with this sacred part of her life, she joyfully poured out her pure passion. But, alas! Mercede listened as did the rose in the sweet German legend, bemoaning the fate which denied her such joy. True, she had known marriage, but never unity like this. She listened with bated breath and drank in each syllable, coveting such sympathy as Agatha told of, and longing to yield the same worthy adoration.

> " For wintry bosoms too,
>   That seem of hope forsaken,
>   At thy sweet tones awaken,
>   And dream of joy anew."

The yearning was an abstract one. Without personifying it, she loved to yield to its fascination ; she bade fair to become its slave. Agatha, having no suspicion of this, continued to feed her cousin's eager interest, through gratitude for what she believed to be an unselfish sympathy.

There was, however, a potent factor of which neither cousin had taken account. Human nature sometimes has a way of backing and shying when we would guide it calmly ; and it was this unhappy fact that was partly responsible for the present state of Mercede's mind as she sat in her room and pondered. She had been conscious for some time of a feeling of dissatisfaction with the precise relations which existed between herself and the Lorenos.

CHAPTER IV.

A TÊTE-À-TÊTE.

SIGNOR VELTRI had just finished giving Gaeta her music-lesson. The Duchess was usually present during this hour, but to-day she had been summoned to receive visitors, and the two young enthusiasts were left alone. The master rose promptly as the hour expired; but Gaeta with one query and another detained him. At last a pause ensued, and he availed himself of it to bid her good-by.

"Why do you hurry?" she asked. "You often remain beyond this time."

"But to-day the lesson is finished."

"So it is; but I think I 've heard you say that you are sometimes glad to throw aside music."

"So I am, Signorina."

"Then why not sit down and throw it aside?"

He looked into the bright face unmarked by a line of care, and seemed tempted to yield.

"Come!" she urged, "treat me as a friend for once, and forget that I 'm your stupid pupil."

"I think I had better go," he replied, "for after all, I am only your music-teacher."

"You are our friend," she said.

He looked at her steadily as the color left his face. "I am not unappreciative, Signorina, of your kind disposition, but I must not permit myself to forget that I come at this hour in a professional capacity."

" The professional hour is past."

" And for that reason I should go."

" Nonsense ! " and she smiled and tossed her head ; " the truth is, you 're not interested in what I have to tell you."

" To tell me ? " and his brown eyes opened wide.

" Yes ; I 'm going to be presented at Court."

Instead of showing the interest she anticipated, his face fell.

" There ! " she said reproachfully, " you don't care a button."

" Indeed, I do," he replied ; " but — "

" But what ? "

His impulse was to say, " You will then be in a world still farther from mine ; " his spoken words were more wisely chosen.

" You will not lose a lesson for this reason," he said.

Her face fell.   " No," she replied, " and you wonder, therefore, why I bother you with this mere personal affair.   Pray don't let me bore you any longer."   And her manner was magnificent.

" Don't think I 'm not interested," he answered. " It is an important step in your life, and will introduce you into still another social world."

" I suppose it will ; " and she sighed slightly.

" Are your social burdens already so heavy that you dread this addition ? " he asked, smiling.

" I don't wish to be presented, if that 's what you mean."

" No ? " and his face bore genuine surprise.

" No; I only do it to please mamma."

He stood studying her face silently while she dropped her eyes and toyed with her rings; then looking up suddenly she said, " Signor Veltri, you don't understand me very well. I'm not half so fond of fashion and society as you think I am; but I don't care!" she added rather indefinitely.

" Surely, Signorina, it is no disgrace to be young and to enjoy one's self."

" But going out into society is n't pleasant unless one meets one's friends."

" One makes friends among those whom one meets in society. I'm sure you must already have met some charming companions of your own rank, and that you will meet many more before the winter is over."

" Perhaps I may," she said forlornly. " I'm sure I hope your wish may come true."

This way of putting it startled him. Did he wish that she might meet some charming young nobleman who would lay siege to her heart?

" Good afternoon, Signorina," he said suddenly, " I must indeed be going," and without further ceremony he bowed and walked toward the door.

At that moment it opened, and Mr. Dow's smiling face appeared. He held out his hand cordially to the musician, for since the " swells," as he called them, had taken to petting this talented youth, Mr. Dow had not only ceased to oppose him socially, but had even " cultivated " him a little. So easily is the tender heart of society affected by a good example!

Signor Veltri's face was set, however, and he hurried past the effusive visitor as quickly as he could.

"I heard you were taking your lesson," said Mr. Dow, greeting Gaeta; "your mamma has friends, and so I took the liberty of coming in here to wait for her."

"Won't you sit down?" said Gaeta, rather formally.

"Your master seemed in a hurry," continued Mr. Dow, who never quite knew how to talk to children or young girls; "and how solemn he was!"

"Was he?" was the cold answer.

Mr. Dow felt that he had not begun well.

"I don't suppose," he said, taking another tack, "that he would ever be cross with one of his charming pupils; yet it should n't surprise one if his head were a little turned."

"What should turn it, pray?"

"The way he's been taken up by people."

Gaeta folded her hands in her lap, and leaning forward gazed squarely into her companion's face. "Will you have the kindness to tell me what you mean?" she said calmly.

He saw that her calmness was only superficial, for her color grew brilliant. He cudgelled his brains to shape a course that might please her, but his usual nimbleness and certainty in arriving at a conclusion deserted him.

"I did n't mean to say a word which should reflect upon Signor Veltri," he began; "he is, so far as I know, a most deserving young man. I only thought that he was annoyed at something." Then shrewdly noting that he appeared to be rubbing her electric temperament the right way, he followed the clew.

"One can't help being interested in him," he continued; "he seems so frank and so — er —" He hesitated, disconcerted by this mere girl, and wished that he had gone directly into the drawing-room, visitors or no visitors.

"So what?" asked her ladyship.

"Well — so strange," he faltered; "in spite of his position, as Lord Byron would put it, —

> 'Still there was haughtiness in all he did.'"

"In other words," said Gaeta, "he respects himself, and so he should. If you happened to know as much about Signor Veltri as we do, you would understand him better."

"Is he so very deep?"

"I know nothing about that, but I do know that he has true manliness."

He could scarcely believe his ears. He thought that this young girl was repeating, parrot-like, some cant phrase she had heard. What did such a chit know about true manliness? For Mr. Dow little suspected the penetration and soberness of judgment that is often hidden behind the smooth brow of girlhood.

"What may be your standard of 'true manliness'?" and Mr. Dow looked at her quizzically.

"Self-respect and a kind heart," was the simple answer.

"Humph! and has our friend displayed these to you?"

"No; he hasn't *displayed* them, but his life shows them."

"Indeed!" and there was a color to his tone that made Gaeta clench her small hands tighter.

"You don't like Signor Veltri," she said calmly, "and I hope you won't think that what I'm going to tell you is told on his account, for I don't think he would mind what any one said who knows him so slightly as you do."　　　　　　　•

"Oh, I say!" ejaculated the discomfited listener.

"But I'd like to tell you something about him for *our* sakes; for *we* don't like to have *our* friends spoken ill of in *this* house."

"But you entirely misunderstand me!" Mr. Dow declared.

"Won't you hear me first, please?" and she inclined slightly her proud little head and raised her eyes steadily to his. He was quite awed by this revelation of unsuspected dignity, and leaning back in his chair waited attentively for her to continue.

"Signor Veltri is the youngest of five children, and when he was six years old his father died. His mother managed to get food for her family and to educate them, and when Signor Veltri was fourteen years of age he showed such musical talent that he was sent to Naples. After studying one year he managed (by teaching for one lira an hour, by copying music, and playing accompaniments at concerts) to support himself and even to help his mother a little. He did this for four years, working terribly; and at last became a little known, and played solos in two or three concerts. A French Countess who heard him and took

a great interest in him, persuaded him to go with her
to France, promising him no end of pupils and concert
engagements; even inviting him to be her guest. He
was made a great deal of by her and her friends, but
they did nothing to get him either pupils or engagements, and he found that he was simply the lady's
pet, like her dog or her saddle-horse; so he broke
away from it all, and taking a little room tried to support himself. But the French don't believe much in
the Italians as piano-masters, and he nearly starved.
Then, realizing that he must begin to work upward
if he was ever to be anybody, he came to Rome and
decided either to succeed or fail right here. But
the Roman school of music is all Liszt, while he had
been trained in the Thalberg school. He did n't care,
however, and went to work, and a very hard time he
had until the summer we met him at Lake Como.
You remember it, for you were there too."

Mr. Dow inclined his head.

"When mamma asked him his terms, he said five
lire an hour; and when she said she would pay him
ten lire (the same she had paid my other masters),
he would n't discuss the matter, but said simply
and decidedly that his price was five lire and no
more."

"But he charges ten now," interposed Mr. Dow.

"Yes; the following year he doubled his price:
First, because he wished to teach fewer hours that he
might practise and compose; and second, because he
had assumed the education and support of one of the
children of his eldest brother, who is very poor. And
through that little boy we learned to know Signor

Veltri's good heart. The little fellow is both deaf
and dumb, and Signor Veltri put him in a school for
deaf-and-dumb children, where, by paying well, his
nephew is made very comfortable. Every Saturday
he calls for the child and takes him off for the day,
never regretting a minute of the time it costs him.
Sometimes they go to the Villa Borghese, sometimes
to Frascati or Albano, or to the circus, or for a stroll
or drive in the city ; and Signor Veltri with his fingers
explains everything to the poor little fellow. My
dear lovely Aunt Agatha often invites them to her
home, and little Gigi passes the afternoon playing with
my cousins Sebastiano and Teresina. They are both
younger than he ; but the sensitive child is glad of
that, I think, for he feels less at a disadvantage.
Signor Veltri is always near him, but Aunt Agatha,
who learned the finger alphabet from Signor Veltri,
is trying to teach it to Sebastiano, so that he can talk
to Gigi. Gigi has a real talent for mathematics, and
now Signor Veltri (so he confessed to Aunt Agatha)
is saving his money to give the boy a thorough education in mathematics, and is trying to interest him
in astronomy. Uncle Filippo has promised that if
Gigi really takes to it, he will, in time, get him a
good position under a friend of his who is a profes-
sor. That's how the matter stands at present ; and
now you know what I call true manliness."

Peter Dow sat silent for several moments with his
eyes fixed upon the stern young girl.

"Will you believe me," he said presently, with evident sincerity, "when I tell you that I'm thoroughly
ashamed of myself? And I apologize humbly for

the injustice I did Signor Veltri — whom I'm proud
to know."

The haughty expression fled from Gaeta's face as
mist melts before sunshine.

"I do believe you!" she exclaimed heartily; "and
now I'm glad I told you."

"And what good people your aunt and uncle are!"
he added.

"Aunt Agatha is an angel!" Gaeta replied enthu-
siastically, "and she's just the woman for Uncle
Filippo. Mamma said the other day," she added
confidentially, "that Uncle Filippo was like a blooded
race-horse; if he had n't been well handled he would
probably have bolted the course and wasted all his
power."

"What does your father think of Signor Veltri?"
Mr. Dow asked, after a moment's pause.

"Papa admires him more than any other young
man he knows — who can't hunt."

Her companion laughed heartily, but controlled
himself as the door opened and the Duchess entered.

"I heard you were in the house," she said, giving
the visitor her hand, "and I pictured you here lonely
and sad; but Gaeta seems to have kept up your
spirits."

"Donna Gaeta has been most interesting. Indeed," he added significantly, "she has taught me
something."

The Duchess turned with a look of puzzled interest toward her daughter, who, blushing slightly, repeated the Italian proverb: *Sapia piu il Papa e un
contadino, che il Papa solo.*

14

"What is that?" asked Mr. Dow; "I did n't catch it."

She repeated a Venetian proverb which says that "the Pope and a peasant are wiser than the Pope alone."

He had the perception to see that Gaeta wished to avoid disclosing the character of their conversation, and he won her silent approval by aiding and abetting her.

CHAPTER V.

SMOULDERING FIRE.

" THAT's true ! " exclaimed Mercede, shutting her book vigorously.

" What's true ? " asked her father, looking up from his newspaper.

She found her place again. " This is Goethe's idea of a model wife : ' A wife who will everywhere co-operate with him [her husband]; who will everywhere prepare his way for him ; whose occupation spreads itself on every side, while his must travel forward on its single path.' That's precisely my idea. The woman should be content to co-operate, not to plunge ahead on her own career, leaving the man behind unless he chooses to grip her skirt and be dragged after her."

" That is almost an axiom."

" I know it; that's the reason I'm so astonished when women fail to let it govern them."

The General kept his thoughts to himself.

" True," she continued, " Goethe says a woman should prepare the way, — but *his* way, not hers ; and listen to this : ' And where is there any station higher than the ordering of the house, while the husband . . . perhaps takes a share in the administration of the

State? . . . What is the highest happiness of us mortals, if not . . . to be really masters of the means conducive to our aims ; and where should or can our first and nearest aims be, but within the house ? ' " and the reader laid special stress upon the last words. " ' It is when a woman has gained this domestic mastery that she truly makes the husband, whom she loves, a master. . . . Thus he can direct his mind to lofty objects, and if fortune favors, he may act in the State the same character which becomes his wife so well at home.'"

She closed the book again and flung it upon the table.

" Of course," she added, "general directions don't apply to special cases. My case, for example, is a fair exception. I have a career as natural as it is distinct. It is right, then, that I should follow it; but were I an ordinary woman, who had voluntarily assumed a position which carried with it certain domestic and social obligations, I should n't be doing right if I sacrificed everything, or at least made everything subordinate, to a cause consisting of a servant's agency and a cheap *pension*, some flowers in a pot — and Heaven knows what else ! " and she leaned back in her chair and drummed on its arms nervously.

"Heaven does know, I have no doubt," was the calm reply.

Mercede turned quickly, as though a sharp retort were on her tongue ; but as she looked into the dear face that smiled benignly into hers, her momentary excitement was allayed, and when she spoke it was gently.

" Of course, Papa, I don't really mean to belittle

Agatha's work, but I think she carries it too far, and my anxiety makes me a little bitter against the 'cause,' as she calls it, for which so much is sacrificed."

"And yet, Mercede mia, what is sacrificed, after all? Some social bustle and possibly Filippo's more rapid political advancement. Very well! In the first place, they entertain occasionally, and do it more than handsomely; and in the next place there are many men competent to carry on the public work, but few able men who are unselfish enough to devote themselves to the less brilliant but equally important tasks in which Filippo is engaged. What does your poet say about our first and nearest aims?"

"Where should they be, but within the house?" she replied.

"Precisely! and so Filippo is doing his part for Italy's good within Italy."

"But think of the career he may be sacrificing for this petty work!"

The General's face wore again the benign expression which it had gained rapidly with its increasing marks of age.

"My child," he said, "when a man of my age looks back upon the past, his chief solace for many sins of omission and commission is found in what he has done for others, not for himself. Believe me, the memory of such deeds makes the softest pillow on which an old man can lay his head each uncertain night."

His gentle words were not without effect; but as she pondered upon the undercurrent of indifference to

Filippo's career, which seemed to her to run in every mind except her own, she felt constrained to protest further.

"But my dear Father," she began, "a statesman's career redounds not only to his own glory but to the benefit of his whole country; and do you believe that such work as that of Cavour and our other great statesmen was less edifying to their souls than that of the best saint whose beneficence ever won him a place in the calendar?"

The blood mantled her cheeks and her eyes grew bright, while her voice took on a clear, bell-like quality which marked it when her blood was up; and, as usual, vigor rather than fairness distinguished her argument as she continued: "I surely believe, if you do not, that Cavour's brain and Victor Emmanuel's sword were means toward a righteous end quite equal to the best philanthropy the world ever saw. The latter has its place, of course; but I think it's a most perverted sentiment that would exalt the philanthropist above the others. Soldiers and statesmen created Italy, soldiers and statesmen must guard her! If they do not, God help you philanthropists; for you and your model peasantry will be shot, your incomparable banks will be plundered, and your prize flower-pots broken by a less sentimental and Utopian people."

As he listened the old soldier's face grew black.

"You go too far, Mercede!" he exclaimed sternly. "You know, without one word from me, that I am not the man to belittle the great king and the great statesman. You forget that you speak to a soldier, and to one who was made a general upon the field of battle! Let me tell you that we who fought for Italy were impelled by the same great principles that lead Filippo to continue the work our swords made possible. Civilization comes not by war, but is war's recompense. Yet while I would make swords into ploughshares, barracks into schoolhouses, and soldiers into husbandmen, do you think I am a man to be lectured upon patriotism?" He stopped, and extending his arm, pointed his trembling fingers at his sword which hung over the mantel. "I may be old," he said with flashing eye, " but I am still *General* Ricci, and with that sword hanging above your head, how dare you speak so to me!"

Mercede at first had seemed like one transfixed, but as he continued she involuntarily rose to her feet and moved toward him. Now throwing herself beside the chair into which he had sunk, she clasped him in her arms with surging reflux of passion.

"Forgive me!" she cried, tearing away the hand with which he had shaded his eyes. "Forgive me, Father!"

Self-willed, unyielding as she was, she had done that before which other attributes grow numb in women of her race. Kneeling beside the silent man, with broken voice and trembling lip she humbly poured forth her contrition, nor heeded the tears that streamed down her face as she realized that she, the daughter of an Italian patriot, had cast a slur upon her father's patriotism.

CHAPTER VI.

IN THE VILLA BORGHESE.

AGATHA was in her element. The fine green slopes of the Villa Borghese, dotted with venerable trees, lay on either side of her, and she was in the midst of a party of children. She was playing a game of catch with them, and a royal romp they were having. Presently two figures were seen approaching, and, in reply to a shout of welcome from the children, the new-comers waved their hats.

"Who will get to Gigi first?" called Agatha; whereupon the little ones scampered off to greet the boy, who leaving his uncle ran forward to meet them.

It needed no ears to understand their pleasure at his coming, and as they led him forward chattering like so many magpies, the red lips of the delighted mute parted and exposed his glistening teeth as he glanced happily from one to the other. As he approached Agatha he removed his hat gallantly, and, in reply to a few movements of her fingers, his big brown eyes grew eloquent with gratitude and he respectfully touched her hand with his lips.

Bending down she kissed him and turned to greet Signor Veltri.

" You got my message, then ?" she said.

"Yes, thank you; and Donna Gaeta is coming presently with Mr. Dow."

"Better and better! we 'll have a real frolic." Then she explained to Gigi what the children were playing.

He nodded with a quick, bright smile, and replied that he understood the game perfectly. So presently the fun began again, Agatha and Signor Veltri entering into its spirit quite as heartily as their juniors. They were both experienced enough to know that unless elders play with their whole hearts when they join a circle of children, they had much better hold aloof altogether — for how astute such little minds become in detecting a pious fraud! Veltri could remember distinctly the time when his efforts to imitate a distant locomotive whistle seemed to startle his father, who always awaited this signal before going to the adjacent station; and the result was a source of great glee to the child until one morning his father overacted his part, and the sensitive little mind felt the ignominy of being thus trifled with, and the whistle was never repeated. Therefore he now used all the tact he possessed to appear to be honestly enjoying the sport; but indeed, when it was his turn to catch some one and he started after Agatha, he had need of his best effort, for she raced across the lawn like a sprinter, darting here and there, doubling and turning, and foiling him so cleverly that the children were in ecstasy. But suddenly the pursuer turned and dashed at the youngsters, and then with redoubled shouts they scattered in every direction in a

wild panic. Gigi was caught, and now took up the
task his uncle had surrendered. Like a greyhound
he raced after the fleet-footed Marchesa, accompanied
by the renewed excitement of his companions, until
at last the victory was his and Agatha was caught.
Then came a scamper indeed, and the approach of
Peter Dow and Gaeta was unnoticed.

"What a race you and Veltri had!" Mr. Dow
exclaimed as Agatha came forward to greet them,
her cheeks glowing and her eyes sparkling. "But
don't you think it a little dangerous to make a habit
of exercising so violently?"

"You don't suppose that Signor Veltri and I play
this game whenever we meet, do you?" she responded
gayly.

"But I do really think that you ought to be careful
not to overdo it," he urged.

"Come; join in!" she commanded.

"I?"

"Certainly!"

"But I never run."

"Then it will do you good. Here, Sebastiano,
catch Signor Dow! Look out!" she called to that
discomfited gentleman, who, startled into his boy-
hood's instinct of self-preservation, found himself, ere
he knew it, rushing hither and thither, hatless and
breathless, his eye-glass bobbing against his back-
bone, and his long legs making wondrous play.

"Bravo! two to one on the Phenomenon!" cried
a clear voice before him, as he stopped, panting but
saved, — little Sebastiano being yards upon yards in
the rear.

" What a deer you are ! " exclaimed Madame André,
leaving her companion, the Duke Faviola, and reaching behind Mr. Dow's back to restore his eye-glass
to him.

He could not speak without breath, and therefore
smiled.wanly.

" Was it a level start, or a handicap ? " she inquired
earnestly.

" Whew ! " was the only sound he could utter.

" Is this the final heat, or do you run again ? " and
she looked up at him most seriously.

" Never ! " he gasped.

" I did n't know you were fond of athletics," said
the Duke, cordially, as he joined them.

" I 'm not ; this is n't a habit, it 's an accident."

" Then it 's the second lucky accident within ten
minutes," said Mercede ; " the first was meeting the
Duke."

Mr. Dow felt foolish. His admiration for Madame
André was great, and he flattered himself that she
always treated him with special consideration. Now,
to appear before her in this aspect annoyed, even
mortified him, for he was sure that a big man like
himself running away from a small boy like Sebastiano must have appeared ridiculous. He wished
to explain, and yet feared that the incident would
gather importance by being dwelt upon. There
seemed nothing left but to make a virtue of it.

" One likes to help the little ones amuse themselves," he suggested.

" It 's only a prig who never unbends ; " and Mercede's manner, as well as her words, greatly restored

his self-complacency. "Where is Filippo?" she added, looking around the group. "I thought that he usually came with the children."

"Filippo is with his sister," answered the Duke. "They will drive here later."

"Do you often come here?" inquired Mr. Dow of his bronzed companion.

"Occasionally; but the Campagna and the surrounding hills are more to my taste."

"Too much style here, and all that sort of thing," and Mr. Dow nodded knowingly; "I understand. These parks are not bad to stretch one's legs in; but, as you say, there's too much style."

"That's precisely what I come for," the bearded giant replied; "otherwise I'd always go to the hills. Sometimes I like to see my lady friends, and I find them here, well dressed, as women should be."

"Then don't look at me, please," said Mercede, "for I've just come from the studio; but feast your eyes upon Agatha. Isn't that a lovely costume of hers? Who would think that it disguises a reformer?"

They had been approaching Agatha, and she turned as she heard their voices.

"The Duke is admiring your costume, Agatha dear," Mercede exclaimed.

"I hope for his sake that he is: latest from Madame Tua." And Agatha turned completely around for his inspection.

"I've dressed more women that Mesdames Tua and Borla combined," the Duke replied, smiling in turn. "I found my clients universally arrayed in black, and apportioning to each a piece of every colored stuff I had with me, I soon brightened things up. I was also court jeweller, and bedecked my customers in every tint and variety of Venetian beads, and yards upon yards of Roman pearls."

"Oh, you mean the lady savages of New Guinea!" laughed Mercede.

"Precisely! For in such matters the Duchess and Gaeta despise my taste."

"Why, papa!" called Gaeta, turning from Signor Veltri, with whom she had been speaking rather apart, "you know that we agree perfectly in some respects, — for instance, about the sticks."

He laughed quietly. "Yes, that is true; you never admired those photographs much, did you? The ladies there," he explained, "distend their nostrils with sticks."

The children now began to protest against the interruption; so Agatha, reinforced by Mercede and by the Duke (whose reticence and shyness disappeared in the company of children), soon had them hard at play again, while Mr. Dow looked on benignly, and the young musician and his pupil again sat apart under the spreading branches of a fine old tree.

"You must be very proud of your father," said the youth.

"I am; I think he's heavenly."

Veltri sighed gently. "A woman must respect a man or she can't really care for him, I suppose."

"I don't know, I'm sure, how it is with other girls; *I* can't."

"I suppose not;" and he sank into an abyss of gloom.

"Yet I don't know that I ought to say that," and she became very judicial of manner, "for I *do* know a man whom I don't think I respect so very much, and yet I like him pretty well."

Veltri winced slightly. "I suppose I know to whom you refer."

"He made me awfully angry the other night after you left," she continued confidentially, "and I just hated him; but afterward he seemed so sorry that I liked him better than I ever had at all."

Her companion brightened as she spoke. "Oh, you mean Mr. Dow!"

"Yes."

"He is too old to think of getting married, and he is fortunate."

"Do you think so?"

"Yes; but let us speak of something more interesting. You are too young to think of such things."

The color came into her cheeks and she was evidently piqued.

"I wish you could get the idea out of your mind," she said, "that I'm an infant. I hate to have my youth and inexperience thrown at me as though I were no older than those children. Ever since I can remember, I've been told that I was too young to understand first this thing and then that thing; and just as mamma drops the words, the rest of the world takes them up. It's annoying, and I don't like it!"

"I'm very sorry. You must know that I would not willingly annoy you."

"I had supposed so until this moment," she replied haughtily.

"Perhaps I'd better go and look after Gigi," he suggested.

"As you choose ; but I don't see why you should n't try to amuse one child as well as another."

"Don't be angry with me," he pleaded ; "I did n't mean any offence. To tell the truth, I don't enjoy talking about marriage, because — well, because a poor music-teacher has no business to think of such things."

"Is that all you are ?" she demanded, looking him in the eye.

"Yes ; at least, so far as income is concerned."

"Is that all you intend to be ?" she continued, with the same full gaze upon his face.

He flushed and hesitated. "Frankly, no ! I'm going to be something more."

"Then don't begin by sneering at yourself. Your playing and teaching are very convenient rounds in your ladder, but I don't think those who know you mistake them for rounds in a treadmill."

He sat for several minutes silent.

"You may be young," and he smiled brightly as he spoke the offensive words, "but you are wiser than I am."

"Yes, I think I am — in some things," she replied.

So engaged were they with each other that neither saw the arrival of the Duchess and Filippo, and they turned with surprise as the voice of the Marquis greeted them.

" Were you quarrelling over Wagner, that you looked so serious ? " he asked.

" No, over his successor," answered Gaeta.

" And pray, who is he to be ? " inquired her mother.

" We wish that we knew."

" There seems to be absolutely no one to take his place," continued the Duchess, musingly.

" At present, Mamma, no," Gaeta said ; " but with time ' the mulberry-leaf becomes satin.' "

" Ah ! " and the clever mother, divining the drift of her child's thought, was amused at her girlish enthusiasm for her master.

But the Duchess seldom sneered, and besides, had too much respect for the young musician and too much consideration for her darling's feelings, to wound either by an unnecessary comment.

" What a good time the children are having ! " she said ; " and there is little Gigi too ! "

They followed her glance, and a few yards away saw the child and the Duke rolling round stones of the size of cannon-balls across the lawn, — a game Gigi evidently understood well, for he played it skilfully.

" Come," said the Duchess ; " Gigi deserves an audience."

As they skirted the lawn, Mercede, avowing fatigue, slipped away from the children's game and seated herself upon the grass. Looking up, she caught the eye of the Duchess, and bowed. Then

her eyes sought Filippo, to whom she nodded familiarly, whereupon he joined her, and was soon engaged
in a refreshing conversation. With Mercede he always found his thoughts led away from the subjects
which commonly occupied them; and although her
topics were not noteworthy in themselves, her treatment of them always interested him. Mercede's
usual mood was gay, her conversation pithy and
strongly colored, and he regarded less the under-
lying thought than the method and manner of her
communication. He delighted in her vivacity and
enjoyed even her extravagance of expression, while
the interest she appeared to feel in all that concerned
Agatha touched him deeply.

"No one, except myself, appreciates Agatha so
thoroughly," he often said to himself. "It's a pity
that Mercede thinks Agatha's feeling is less ardent
than her own. But I don't see what more she can
want, for Agatha treats her as a sister; yet even this
does n't seem to satisfy her. Upon my word, it
sometimes seems as though she aspired to share my
place in Agatha's heart."

He smiled complacently at the idea, and set it down
as evidence of his wife's charm and of Mercede's
loyal, warm nature. Nor was he mistaken in the intensity of her feeling. Its source may not have been
as pure as he thought, but its existence was none the
less a fact.

Mercede brooded constantly over her yearning to
become identified with the innermost life of Loreno
and his wife, and the more she dwelt upon this
desire, the less bearable became the thought of

disappointment. Her imperious will would not be reconciled to a sphere which, although intrinsically exalted, was inferior to that which she coveted. As the object subserved by her artistic ambition approached realization, this new object gained importance. She brooded upon it until she became morbid concerning it; it grew to be a necessity in her life. In art or society there was no door closed to her. Determination had accomplished this; and the same force, intensified by the closer relation which the new purpose bore to her inner life, was concentrated upon this yearning, the gratification of which she now deemed essential to her complete happiness.

Thus, in the graphic words of a proverb of her own country, as "eaten bread is soon forgotten," her success in breaking through the social and art barriers that blocked her impetuous course now lost their power of satisfying her, and she yearned for something more to fill her life, — something which should satisfy the longing of her humanity; something more restful, if not more masterful, than her art. She did not propose to rob, but to share. She believed that she could enrich the life of the Lorenos quite as much as they could enrich hers. She would not, she could not, realize that they were sufficient for each other when they were necessary to her. All that was in her, all that belonged to her, she consecrated to the fulfilment of her object. Did she recognize the truth? At this time, no. She desired to be the confidante of both Agatha and Filippo; to join forces with them both; to form, as it were, a triple alliance. Yet here was the rub; for she believed that to women as a

class friendship is a thing as colorless as the perfume
upon their handkerchiefs ; that they know as little of
the true glory of that affinity of which Goethe wrote
as they do of the possibilities of political science.

While she did not question the sincerity of
Agatha's affection for her, she began to fear that
her cousin might not be able to emancipate herself
from the limitations common to her sex, and, putting
aside petty jealousy and wifely selfishness, rise to
such a conception of friendship as that which Mercedo herself claimed to have, and which she believed
Filippo to possess. She did not base her opinion of
Filippo's friendship upon his responsiveness alone,
for, with blind inconsistency, while resenting deeply
Agatha's gentle opposition, Mercede gloried in the
frankness with which Loreno sometimes opposed her
when he believed her to be in error, either of opinion
or action. This was also Goethe's idea of a friend.
No one but Loreno dared beard the lioness in her
den ; but he seemed to have no thought of fear. He
opposed Mercede's views quite as frankly as he did
those of Agatha. With every one save Loreno, Mercede assumed the initiative ; him she seemed willing
to follow. Had she not been so inclined, the result
would have been interesting, for he would have gone
on in his own way just the same, there being but one
person on earth whom this young Marquis suffered to
lead him, that person being Agatha. Yet, so strange
is life, Mercede felt that in either judgment or power
of will Agatha was a mere child in her presence. For
this reason, although exasperated by her cousin's undefined but firm method of keeping the vantage-ground

of her husband and herself sacred to themselves, she had no doubt that in the end her desire would be accomplished. Nevertheless, it was rather a hurt to the pride of a woman so courted as she, to have even a small part of her friendship repelled. Had Mercede permitted herself to examine the facts coldly and judicially, she would probably have recognized the plain fact that her desire to occupy a relation toward Agatha closer than that of a sister would scarcely have been so keen had her cousin been unmarried. But her wilfulness was too great to permit her to stop and dissect her motives. If any suspicion of the truth ever perplexed her mind, she dashed it from her with an indignant disclaimer, prompted, she assured herself, by shame at having tainted the purity of friendship with an unworthy suspicion. Thus we ofttimes juggle with the truth as Hamlet juggled with the cloud, and our servile reason is as eager in agreement — and about as sincere — as was that other courtier, Polonius.

CHAPTER VII.

SOME PASSING FACTS.

ARISTOCRATIC Rome was gathered at a ball in the palace of the Spanish Embassy. Loreno and Mercede had been dancing together, and the latter, complaining of the excessive heat, asked if they could not get out of the crowd for a few moments. Filippo thereupon led her to an anteroom, in a recess of which they seated themselves.

"I'm glad to get away from it," said Filippo, glancing back at the room they had left.

"You don't seem quite yourself to-night;" and his companion looked at him anxiously.

"I'm a little tired."

Her eyes closed slightly, and she tapped her foot impatiently.

"That's not unnatural," she said. "Your parliamentary work is enough for one man, and you add to it half a dozen charities, not to mention your social duties."

"The charities count for very little, and," he added, laughing quietly, "the social duties for even less."

"But, Filippo,"—she leaned forward and gazed into his face earnestly,—"don't you know that you are burning the candle at both ends? You should take more exercise, and of a sort that will help you to forget your work."

" But I do exercise."

"You walk to Parliament and home again, — less than ten minutes each way. You should be in the fresh air at least two hours every day."

"'Two hours'! Where are they to come from?"

" From whatever you do outside of Parliament."

"Impossible! Before Parliament I arrange the accounts of Agatha's new society; and after I leave the House I join her, wherever she is, help her for an hour or so, and then bring her home."

"It's all very ideal and commendable, and I should n't like to interfere with it; but you must manage somehow to get more air and exercise, or you will break down."

" But how am I to do it? I can't neglect my parliamentary duties unless I resign altogether; and I have told you how the rest of the day is filled."

" Can't you take exercise in the morning and do your accounts in the evening?"

" On many evenings, yes; but I cannot rely upon them. The evening is my time for social duties and of preparation for my public work."

" You can if you will only make up your mind to it. Won't you try?"

" I won't promise."

"I think you are positively unkind! If you haven't any regard for yourself, you might have for your friends."

" There is no reason for anxiety about me. I feel

splendidly, as a rule, and when Parliament is not in session I have many hours in the air. Only to-day Agatha tried to make me promise to drive or walk with her three times a week, and I refused on the ground that I don't need it. Here she is now," he said, as he saw his wife approaching on the arm of Mr. Dow. "You and she can console each other."

"No, not now," she replied in an undertone.

"Come, Filippo," said Agatha, "I want a waltz with you."

Mercede's mouth grew serious, and she hastily addressed Mr. Dow, but she did not fail to notice the alacrity with which Filippo arose in spite of his fatigue.

"I'm invited to waltz," he said to Mercede, nodding familiarly as he moved away.

"Then I'll say good-night; I'm going in a few moments," she called quickly, scarcely knowing why.

"Going, so early!" and he turned with surprise.

"Yes, I'm tired; and the swing of the affair does n't catch me."

"Then jump into it," suggested Mr. Dow, practically. "Begin by giving me a waltz."

Her plan changed as quickly as it had been conceived.

"With pleasure," she said, rising.

Half an hour later Filippo found that her dancing-card was filled. He was surprised at this, for she usually declined to engage herself ahead, avowing frankly that she disliked to be compelled to dance whether she would or no. He complained good-naturedly at her not reserving another waltz for him ; to which she replied suavely that in future she would engage herself conditionally.

Mr. Dow, who was hovering near her, chuckled with amusement, and as usual drew his own conclusion. As her partner was a little tardy Mr. Dow joined her.

" That was a delicious answer you gave the Marquis," he said.

" Yes ? It was accidental then. But I 'm opposed to nepotism on principle."

" Well, the Marquis does n't seem to be. There he goes, dancing with his wife again. That 's the third time this evening."

" Why not leave the acts of the Marquis to the recording angel ? " she said haughtily. " You would entertain me better by telling me what you are smiling at."

He smiled more broadly than ever.

" A little verse occurred to me that I saw in a magazine the other day : it seems to fit the Marquis."

" Indeed ! What is it ? "

" It is called ' Moderation,' and runs as follows : —

> ' I ask not, oh my God, for worldly fame,
> For love, for fortune, for the thousand things
> My neighbors' restless prayers forever claim,
> Vexing thine ear with vain importunings.
> All these may pass, nor will they pass lamented ;
> Give me the moon, and I will rest contented.' "

Mercede laughed lightly. " It 's not inapplicable, is it ? " she said.

" No," he replied, with keen appreciation of his

humor. " For if he took a fancy to the moon he would n't hesitate to ask for it."

" There is certainly but little left on earth that the Marquis has need to ask for," she said proudly.

Mr. Dow was bewildered, and wondered if she quite knew which side she was on; but that was because Mr. Dow did not comprehend very well the feminine nature. It never entered his mind that Mercede's momentary and distinctly personal irritation would not give warrant to another's criticism. He was too blind to read the heart she had unguardedly laid bare to him, although even a moderately clever woman would have comprehended her feeling instantly. What we call " woman's intuition " is often logical although rapid deduction, and while her quickness may be surprising, our dulness is more so. No doubt she is prone to wonderful impressions, to which she commonly hangs with grim faith; but every mystery is not a miracle.

As they stood silent, looking at the dancers, Agatha again glided past, guided by the Duke Faviola.

" I did n't know the Duke ever danced," Mr. Dow remarked.

" I have seen him dance occasionally," was the reply. " He understands the arts of civilization, even if he does n't always practise them."

Her companion turned with genuine surprise.

" It *was* a rude remark," she said, meeting his eye, " but I 'm a little cross to-night; don't think of it again."

As a matter of fact, the Duke was one of the few men of Mercede's acquaintance who seemed imper-

vious to her charm. She had exerted all her power
of fascination upon him in vain. He remained always
sedate and unresponsive, although so perfectly courteous that she could find no just cause of complaint
against him. But with Agatha his manner was quite
different: he sought her society, he laughed with her
frankly, and seemed to find his tongue readily enough.
What occasioned this marked difference in his treatment of Agatha and herself Mercede could not fathom,
and she was tired of trying. Yet it was mortifying, and
it rankled. She had been too proud heretofore to resent
the fact, and was vexed at her present indiscretion.

A few evenings later, while Filippo was calling
upon the General and Mercede, a visitor's card was
presented, and Mercede, pleading a headache, re-
quested her father to excuse her. Then, turning at
the door, she suggested that Filippo should entertain
her until the visitor departed.

He promptly followed her to a sitting-room where
she had sometimes received him.

"Have you thought over my suggestion at the
ball?" she inquired.

"Well, I confess it has n't disturbed my dreams."

"I 've a new and brilliant idea," and she paused to
impress him duly. "I have not been practising what
I preach, and my sins of omission have begun to bear
fruit. So I consulted Dr. Maretti this morning, and
he says I must ride for at least an hour every day.
Now, I propose that we encourage each other by good
example, and at the same time avoid the monotony
of exercising alone. Come, ride with me; it 's the
very thing you need."

Loreno had been fond of the saddle before his marriage, but as other occupations claimed his time he gradually gave up riding. Mercede's proposition was tempting, and forgetful for the moment of his excuses to Agatha, he embraced it with characteristic enthusiasm.

" Do you propose to ride in the morning, or afternoon ? " he asked.

" In the morning, early, if you don't mind."

" Not in the least."

" About eight ? "

" Very well."

Mercede hesitated a little. " I don't suppose Agatha will object," she said.

" Why should she ? "

" She should n't ; but I did n't know."

" What a strange idea ! I sha' n't disturb her in the morning."

" Oh, very well ; then we will call it settled. And now, how about my horse ? Will you help me to find one ? "

" Why not use one of mine ? I've one that a lady can ride."

" You are very kind, but I want a horse of my own."

" Well, use mine until you find one that pleases you."

" Thank you very much ; I 'll think it over, and tell you to-morrow if you will meet me as I leave the studio at five. I 'm going to walk home every night— for exercise."

" I 'm afraid I must deny myself that pleasure : I

really can't spare the time; but use one of my horses, and let us begin to-morrow morning."

"I can't possibly; I haven't my habit yet."

"When will you have it?"

"I can't tell exactly; but drop in on Thursday evening. I think I shall know by that time."

Agatha did not receive the suggestion with the unreserved pleasure Filippo had hoped for. She was hurt that after refusing all her proposals looking to the same end, he should so quickly and complacently adopt Mercede's plan, and not even suggest that she should join in it.

He was not without consciousness of his inconsistency, but excused it on the ground that Agatha had never proposed a plan which, like this one, should not interfere with his regular occupations; and as for not including her in it, he would do so, of course, as soon as Mercede found a horse. He had but one that a lady could ride.

"I thought you would be glad," he said gloomily.

"I am glad; I'm really very glad that you will get the exercise."

"Then why are you so solemn about it?"

"I don't intend to be solemn. I'm sure I've urged you often enough to get more fresh air."

"Your approval seems rather reluctant."

Turning away, he went to his desk and busied himself with some letters until Agatha left the room. Then he brushed them aside and sat thinking.

CHAPTER VIII.

SHADOWS.

THE experiment of riding proved to be a success, and morning after morning Loreno and Mercede dashed over the Campagna for about two hours. Their intimacy could scarcely fail to grow rapidly under such favorable conditions, and at the end of a few weeks they both looked forward eagerly to the morning ride, and late hours at night never prevented them from meeting promptly in the morning.

The genuine light-heartedness which Mercede felt in Filippo's society made her a most charming companion; and as she rode well (the lieutenant having early taught her to be an excellent horsewoman), Loreno invariably found the keenest enjoyment in her companionship.

On her side, Mercede found in Filippo a companion far more sympathetic than any she had before known. His directness of method responded to her wilfulness, his breadth of judgment challenged her respect, while his genuineness commanded her confidence.

She believed him capable of taking a very high place in the State; and that he should expend his power and time upon extraneous work seemed to her little better than wanton waste. To convince

Agatha of this she felt to be impossible, and therefore gradually conceived the plan of herself being
Loreno's mentor, and of influencing him to sacrifice
non-essentials to essentials.

"I must be wise," she exclaimed to herself one
night as she sat pondering anxiously, — "I must be
wise and patient, for the work is worthy of me;"
and going to the mantel she stood looking intently at
a photograph of Filippo. Then with her eyes upon
his she repeated the lines: —

> "I am thy friend, and hold it for my duty
> To slow the speed that spurs thee to thy wrong."

Of course it is an open question how far the pretence of such a mission deceived Mercede; yet the
fact that she sought any justification of her course
indicates much. The keynote of her character was
self-exaltation, shown through a confidence, well-
nigh absolute, in her inability to think wrongly or
act unworthily. She was possessed and governed by
a belief that the spontaneous out-giving of her true
nature must be both lofty and right. If her opinions and conduct were sometimes at variance with
the accepted opinions and customs of the world,
this did not shake her faith in herself, but merely
proved her superiority. Even when she submitted
to Filippo's judgment, it was not because of uncertainty regarding her own, but simply because it gave
her joy to bend her will to his, and because it created a relation which it gratified her to bear toward
him. Hers was a character incompatible with a
quick conscience; therefore, though forced to admit

that her nature had two sides, she assured herself
that the bad side was distinctly subordinate, re-
quiring friction to make itself felt, — for which reason it could in no wise affect the infallibility of that
which was spontaneous in her. She believed herself
worthy to be a law unto herself. Consequently the
voice of self-condemnation had been quickly stifled
when it made itself heard, and her present studied
attempt at self-justification marked a new epoch in
her life. She had hitherto begun her campaigns by
burning her bridges behind her, and then carving
her way right through opposition to the object upon
which her mind was fixed; and quick success had
left no reason for retrospection. But now for the
first time she found herself baffled by a force mightier
than any she had yet attacked, — the force of Loreno's love for his wife. This necessitated a new sort
of warfare; she must substitute patient siege for sudden onslaught, — a form of attack so deliberate, combined with conditions so new (for she could always
retreat), that she could not prevent occasional out-
breaks of insubordination from the moral powers
which had heretofore been dominated by her will.
Like other commanders, after crushing the spirit
of revolt again and again, she was at last compelled to recognize, even to parley with it, and that
she might quiet it, often resorted to injudicious activity. Yes, Mercede was at last compelled to parley
with her moral forces, to listen to the voice of conscience protesting against her infidelity and ingrati-
tude to her cousin, — even against trifling with the
sanctity of marriage. Startled, she declared she could

not be so base as this; that her honest heart could not be unfaithful, her warm nature ungrateful, nor could her high principle be made to bend. She could have no motives save those which a noble nature like hers would naturally conceive. Besides, were not Loreno and Agatha equally dear to her?

To gain an accurate knowledge of one's bearings, one has only to note carefully the thoughts that press themselves upon the mind during a walk or any quiet hour of meditation. Had Mercede applied this test, she would have been surprised to find how constantly the image of her cousin's husband crowded out all thoughts of others and of her art. Her mind dwelt ever upon Filippo, directly or indirectly; for when she thought of herself or even of those near to her, it was in connection with him, or when she seemed to be absorbed by her art, still he was not shut out.

It was scarcely to be expected that Agatha, thrown so constantly as she was into Mercede's society, should fail eventually to catch some suspicion of all this. Yet her awakening was not so much the result of the growing intimacy between Mercede and Filippo, as of the change in Mercede's conduct toward herself; for conflicting emotions caused Mercede to blow both hot and cold toward her cousin, — the tokens of love given to-day being frequently offset to-morrow by undisguised annoyance at some thoughtless invasion of the privacy which Mercede coveted when with Loreno. Mercede did not believe these invasions to be intentional, but all the same they were annoying, and she resented them. This spirit, of course, aroused Agatha's wonder, and she was inclined to be watchful. Yet when stricken by misgiving, her apprehension would be allayed by some fresh token of love, to doubt which would be to believe her cousin a cool hypocrite. And indeed Mercede's affection for the woman who had stood by her so loyally was still strong, although as a directing force it had but little value.

From this point they no longer moved in unison, — Mercede striving with all the intensity of her throbbing soul to press closer to that ideal life the breath of which had fanned her; while Agatha, startled, drew away.

Filippo might have relieved the tension of affairs had he recognized the full import of the drama of which he was the central figure; but he failed to give the subject its due weight, and heedlessly led Mercede into fresh indications of her partiality, thus giving Agatha new cause for perplexity.

As the weeks passed, Mercede, forced on by her natural impatience of restraint, and influenced by the fact that Filippo seemed always to keep step with her advance, grew constantly more aggressive ; and there came a time, ere long, when there was a distinct lack of repose in the relation between herself and Agatha. Yet Mercede clung to her purpose, although the new conditions forced her once more to shift her ground. She compared herself to a magnet : Filippo was her armature ; and as the power of the magnet is felt through its armature, so should it be now : she would confine her power to Filippo and leave to him the task of drawing Agatha. Thus, at last, did she put away the theory of equality.

16

Following this new line of conduct, Mercede could scarcely fail to make her relations with Agatha more and more strained; and before another month had passed, the two cousins were exceedingly watchful of each other.

While the trustful wife by no means comprehended the actual condition of affairs, the little she did realize went a long way. The fact that any woman, and least of all her beloved cousin, should conceive it possible to separate Filippo from her in the warmth of friendship sought and given, was difficult to comprehend and almost impossible to accept. It must break upon her mind slowly. It must be a growth; and a growth it was, slow, very slow, — but yet a growth. With budding realization came great bitterness of feeling, — bitterness which at times almost made her forget the pain; for Agatha was not a saint, — and may Heaven keep all true wives from being saints under such circumstances, except in the exercise of saintly wisdom and patience, without which their chance of happiness is likely to be wrecked.

Probably no internal force so nearly destroys the mind's balance as that of jealousy, and yet it hangs over, most of us held by a mere thread. Once cut this thread, and the dread force falls, seeming to crush both heart and reason. Then must the sufferer have self-control and faith to a rare degree. Yet happily both are possible to all men and women, and even in a grave crisis a firm use of them makes the chance of happiness bright. It is, indeed, a combat of human nature, and hope lies in the fact that human nature is good as well as vicious. If the conditions be kept favorable through incessant vigilance and unfaltering self-control, and the result awaited with patience, while the result may be far from sure, the course of conduct chosen offers the best, almost the only, chance of happiness.

Many a stung heart is called upon to decide what to do when love, either from desire to roam or because enticed, seems about to fly out of the window; and, like a child in pursuit of a truant bird, it often crushes the life it is striving to retain.

This was the crisis approaching in Agatha's life, and she felt the chill of its shadow.

Mercede realized equally that an epoch of importance was at hand, and fortified herself by the assurance that her position was impregnable.

"It is surely not my fault," she reasoned, "that Agatha is less my friend than is her husband. I certainly had no wish to make a distinction between them, but Agatha would have it so. She repelled my advances, checked my impulses, and drew a magic circle around Filippo and herself, within which I was not to step. Nor did I; I simply stood back and waited, until at last Filippo has stepped without her circle and come to me. Is that my fault? Am I beyond my bounds? Not at all! Surely I have the same right as Agatha to think and speak, to live my life; and if any one comes voluntarily and wishes to share its pleasure, shall I deny him? What for, I should like to know? Because he is the husband of another? I am not seeking to estrange a husband, but to keep a friend. He knows it; I know it: no one is robbed, and there is no wrong. But suppose I banish him? Is there no wrong then? Should I permit Agatha's petty selfishness to stand in the way of duty to my friend, — a duty, too, the aim of which is to make him whom she adores more truly useful and happy? Moreover, is *my* happiness nothing? I can be as unselfish as any one when there is need, but am I to make the selfishness and niggardly desire of another woman my law and gospel? I cannot see why! Agatha has her rights as a wife, and I am the last one to dispute them ; but I have my rights as a woman, and she must respect them. I'll not encroach upon her territory, provided she keeps out of mine. But in my home, as in heaven, there is no marriage or giving in marriage. Friendship reigns there, and I'll not degrade it by putting it in a strait-jacket."

Agatha felt keenly Mercede's increasing absorption of Filippo's time and thought. His morning rides with her cousin was but one of a number of causes for this wifely suffering. The truth is that she had unconsciously absorbed almost all her husband's spare moments before Mercede's arrival, and had grown so accustomed to his constant companionship that she felt the present division of his free hours more than she otherwise would have done, and at times showed a soreness which, although not surprising, had an effect contrary to that which was desirable. Upon such occasions Mercede showed no resentment, and thereby, in Filippo's eyes, became a martyr to what he began to regard as Agatha's unworthy and unwarranted selfishness. He persuaded himself that Agatha, whose nature was not so social as his, had been somewhat spoiled by the entire devotion he had always given to her, and now that circumstances had brought their life into contact with another life, well fitted to give as well as to receive happiness by the union, she was unreasonable in her reception of the new conditions. He believed, however, that the goodness of her heart would lead her to overcome this ungenerous feeling, and teach her how natural it was that one whose life had been so clouded should creep into the sunshine of their life, and that then she would join in his full welcome.

While disapproving of Agatha's occasional signs of reluctance, he sincerely regretted the pain which prompted them, — a pain he felt to be none the less real because uncalled for. Therefore he often tried to palliate her moments of depression by including her in any plan which he and Mercede might have made; but while his attempt bore good fruit at first, he was puzzled to find that it was gradually becoming less effective. The reason for this, he was forced to acknowledge, rested in some part upon Mercede's shoulders, for of late when Agatha had appeared upon the scene, Mercede seemed to lose her spirits and to become unaccountably silent.

"What's the matter with you nowadays?" said Filippo to his wife one evening. "You don't seem quite yourself. I wonder if a ride in the morning air would n't do you good. Since Mercede has her own horse, why not join us, and keep the bay mare in practice?"

"Would you like to have me go?" she said eagerly.

"Certainly, it will double my pleasure; why not try it?"

"I have n't ridden for a long time."

"Yet you can try."

After a moment's reflection she looked up brightly, and said, —

"I will, — that is, if I can find my old riding-habit."

So the following morning, when Mercede came below to mount, she found a surprise awaiting her. She had, however, the good grace and good judgment to welcome Agatha cordially. They left the city by the Porta del Popolo, and dashed off at a rapid pace. As it was Agatha's first ride, she tired quickly, and after they had crossed the Ponte Molle she suggested that they should take the road to the left, which leads along the banks of the Tiber back to Rome. Mercede protested that it was too lovely a day to make their ride so short, and Agatha then declared that, while sorry to take them home, she did not feel equal to a longer ride.

"It is wise not to overdo it," Loreno said; "but in a few days you will be as eager as we are."

A shadow crossed Agatha's face instantly. "If you are so eager," she said, "I'm all the more sorry to disappoint you."

Why she said it she did not know, but in truth she was worn and consequently nervous. Filippo's first inclination was to correct her impression; but his pride was touched and it ruled him, so he said nothing.

Agatha thought he might have been more amiable, if only to keep Mercede from misinterpreting his silence. Her feeling was divided, therefore, between self-reproach and chagrin. They rode on without speaking, Loreno wondering what had provoked Agatha's caustic remark, and Mercede wondering if he would not contrast this ride with those he had taken with her alone.

" How lovely the shadows are toward Monte Mario ! " Agatha said after a time.

" Yes, are n't they ? " Loreno replied cordially.

But Mercede held her peace. She was not going to help her cousin redeem the effect of her presence.

" It will soon be time to think of going to Varese, won't it ? " Agatha continued, anxious to atone for her ill-humor.

It was Loreno who answered, —

" Yes; did I tell you that I had a letter from Varese ? "

" No; what is the news ? "

He hesitated before replying.

" I forgot," he said ; " I made a compact with Mercede, the first day, not to speak of my affairs during our rides. I suppose there is no exception to be made ? " and he looked toward Mercede.

" The only object," Mercede answered, " was to make this outing as complete a rest as possible for you ; but I don't suppose *our* rules should govern Agatha."

Agatha's cheeks felt hot. " I think the rule a very good one," she replied quickly.

Mercede made no answer, and again they all became silent.

" How are you getting on with that mysterious

new work of yours?" said Agatha presently, turning to her cousin. "We are wild to know the subject, are n't we, Filippo?"

He hesitated again, and Agatha looked at him with surprise.

"That's another of our forbidden topics," he said.

"Still, our rules are null and void now," Mercede remarked. "I hope to have it finished in a month or six weeks."

It was Agatha's turn to be silent. "Always *our!*" she thought bitterly. "'*Our* rules' and '*our* topics.'"

"If our rule is suspended," Loreno began, turning to Mercede, "I'd like to know something more about the statue; is it marble, or bronze?"

"When it's finished, I'll invite you and Agatha and a few others to come and find out."

"Won't you tell me so much now?"

"Don't you think, Filippo," Agatha broke in, "that you would make me feel much more comfortable if you would not suspend all your rules and regulations simply because I am with you? They are as wise this morning as they have been for the past month."

"We were taking a holiday," he said, with a propitiatory smile.

Again the objectionable plural pronoun. She wondered if Mercede were conscious of its effect upon her, and thereupon foolishly did what she could to emphasize this effect; for she made no further attempt to break the monotony of the homeward journey, and Filippo, out of patience with her ill-humor, left her to it and talked with Mercede.

CHAPTER IX.

QUESTIONS AND ANSWERS.

ANYTHING pertaining to Madame André interested Rome, and it was not to be expected that her growing intimacy with the Marquis Loreno could long fail to be commented upon. The criticism did not flower in a day, but, increasing steadily, had now become a full-blown bit of gossip.

It soon reached the ears of the Duchess, and she immediately laid the facts before the Duke.

" This thing will injure Filippo," was her sad comment.

" Not much."

" ' Not much ! '   How can it fail to do so ? "

" Because he 's a man."

" But he 's a husband ! "

" ' In men, mortal sin is venial ; only in women is venial sin mortal.' "

" But it 's disgraceful !   He 's no longer a boy, and should behave himself."

" Go tell him so ; it will console you."

" Can Filippo be flirting with this woman, indifferent to Agatha and the rest of us ? "

" No ; he 's probably as bothered as he can be with Agatha and the rest of us."

" Then why does n't he stop ? "

" Because he has n't got through." ‚

" Then he is contemptibly selfish."

"Not necessarily. It's the taste most men have for exploring."

" Did *you* ever do such things ? "

" I spent my proportion in New Guinea. In beaten tracks I use an atlas — or a guide," he added, smiling fondly.

" Do you mean to tell me that my brother is compromising himself with his eyes open ? "

"Men don't often compromise themselves with their eyes shut."

"Well, I believe it's more than half that horrid woman's fault."

" About half."

" And that Filippo is simply drifting."

"Probably. But he's in her boat."

" Oh, don't be so horrid ! "

" Now, I'm in her boat."

" Well, she *is* horrid; and you are as aggravating as you can be."

" So was Solomon ; at least in the opinion of one lady of his time."

She shrugged her shoulders impatiently and walking to the window stood looking into the street as she revolved the subject.

" I believe I'll send for Filippo," she said, turning toward the Duke, who had resumed his reading.

" Quite right."

She wrote a note asking her brother to call upon her during the day, and despatched it immediately.

It was late in the afternoon when Filippo appeared. She led him into her boudoir and closed the door.

" Filippo, my dear brother," she began, " do you know that you are making yourself talked about disagreeably ? "

" In what connection ? "

" Your intimacy with Madame André."

" Has she complained of it ? " and his voice was perfectly calm, his manner undisturbed.

" Of course not. Don't be frigid with me. You know how such a report would cut me."

He paused before speaking. " There is nothing in it," he said. " If there were reason to talk of us, I would tell you ; but while Agatha does n't object, who else should ? "

She sat and looked at him silently while she reflected. He puzzled her. " There are several reasons," she replied, " why Agatha may not object. The strongest is her confidence in you ; and another reason may be her wifely pride. But you certainly are imprudent in riding almost every morning alone with this lady, and in — "

" But Agatha often goes with us," he interrupted.

" Well, this is Saturday ; how many times has Agatha been with you this week ? "

He thought a moment. " Twice."

" And you have ridden every morning. In fact, you are always with her. Every one speaks of it, and I 've noticed it myself."

He made an exclamation, and seemed about to protest.

" Don't be annoyed, my dear boy," she pleaded ;

"remember our old relations, and what friends we have always been. Surely I may speak frankly without giving you offence!"

His mouth, which had become very firm, relaxed, and his eyes lost their sudden light.

"Well," he said, evidently struggling to suppress his anger, "I will listen to you, Costanza; but it is more than I would grant to any other woman living, even to Agatha."

"That's not right," was the firm answer. "Agatha, as your wife, has a peculiar right to speak to you of such a subject. Any way, I wish to speak, and that very frankly."

She went and seated herself beside him upon the sofa, and looking fondly into his face continued, —

"Filippo, dear, I'll tell you what I believe, and after you have listened patiently, then correct me if I'm wrong. I believe you, like most men, find Madame André very interesting. You are indulging your old propensity, and with no more restriction than before you were married. At that time your conduct occasioned gossip; now the same thing creates scandal. Then you were judged by the standard used to measure the conduct of young bachelors, while now you are judged by the standard used for men who are married. Your motives then and now seem to you identical; but their result is vastly different. Then it was called flirtation; now it is called immorality. I know it's plain speaking, Filippo dear, but we have always been frank with each other. Why not be more cautious in the future?"

" My dear Costanza," and his eyes looked into
hers with affection and truth, " I would not have
believed that I could sit quietly and hear any one
on earth speak as you have done ; but I understand
your motive and I appreciate it. That I am far from
indifferent to Agatha's feelings you know, and I am
scarcely less anxious to please you, for the simple
reason that my heart is instantly enlisted in whatever
affects either my dear wife or you. Therefore if my
intimacy with Madame André gave reasonable occasion for your disapproval I would modify accordingly
my relations toward her. But remember that she is
more than my wife's cousin ; they are practically
sisters. Mercede's history you know, and you must
sympathize with her misfortunes and admire her
courage. Probably the world thinks that her art
should absorb all her thoughts and aspirations, while
her success should satisfy every possible craving
of her soul. But how differently would the world
think if it knew the real woman! Her art is but
a means to a worthy end. She aims to create a
name that her son may bear without the shame that
belongs to her own, and to keep herself from being
a dependent. But while an artist, — and, you must
acknowledge, a great one, — she remains a woman,
longing, like Agatha or like you, for sympathy and
affection. To whom would her heart turn if not to
the sister who had stood by her in her darkest hours
with a loyalty that I never think of without my
pulse quickening ? It was glorious, and appeals
irresistibly to Mercede's warm heart. With Agatha
she naturally — almost inevitably — associates me.

She looks upon me almost in the sacred light of a brother, and I regard her as coming next to my own family and to you. Agatha fully understands and appreciates all this, and the only cloud that ever crosses the perfection of our relation arises from the disinclination of a peculiarly worshipful nature to lose a single hour or thought that might be hers. I only speak of this under the press of the unusual circumstances which have led to this interview; and I do assure you, Costanza, that according to my sincere belief this same feeling on Agatha's part, both in its quality and its extent, might apply as well to you as to Mercede. Shall I then obey the buzzing of careless tongues and disregard the silent pleading of a noble, suffering woman? Is that your advice, my other sister?"

The appellation shocked her, and a vigorous protest against dividing the cherished relation with this stranger rose to her lips. But her rare wisdom and good sense asserted themselves, and she held her peace, giving her mind to that which was really important, — the spirit which prompted the use of this sacred term concerning Madame André, and the outcome of the new-born scandal.

In view of her brother's evident sincerity she saw how hopeless a task it would be to urge him to regard the opinion of the world, clashing as it did with what she regarded as the sympathy and chivalry of his nature. While he never courted unpopularity, he was not afraid of it, nor would it disturb him. Her quick wit told her that there was but one hope, — his disillusion by Madame André herself. But this would be a question of time. Ebbene! One must be contented with what one can have, and this seemed the best that was possible; at least, it was the only reasonable hope that presented itself at the moment. She appreciated the need of making no mistake, and dared not follow up the matter. She desired, however, to leave the subject in a position to be reopened should she so wish.

"What you have said," she began, "requires, of course, my fullest consideration. It is evidently a conviction in your mind, but before accepting it I need time. Let us leave it so; and if in the future I wish to consult you again I may do so frankly, may I not?"

He hesitated, but after a moment's reflection told her that she might; so they spoke of other subjects, and when Gaeta entered the room a few moments later she found them chatting with their accustomed freedom.

"Well, little woman," said her uncle, cordially, "how is the music?"

"I think it would be more civil to ask after the musician," she replied pertly.

"I know *he* is well," he retorted; "I saw him in the flesh this morning."

Gaeta flushed slightly. "Our thoughts 'agree like the town clocks,'" she said with a little toss of her pretty head.

He enjoyed sparring with her, but never tried her scant patience too sorely.

"I stand corrected," and he held out his hand. "Now tell me how *my* musician is."

She kissed him, and then looking up brightly, replied, —

" Let me rather tell you again how much I enjoy the lovely piano. Every one admires it, and I 'm quite celebrated as the Signorina who owns the American piano. Signor Veltri says he is never tired of playing upon it."

" Your aunt Agatha will be jealous, for he never said that of her piano."

" That 's because he can praise her."

" Bravo ! I 'll remember to tell her your dutiful compliment."

" Don't forget, for I 've a favor to ask of her."

" Confide it, and win an ally."

" I want so much to hear 'Lohengrin.' It 's to be given a week from next Wednesday, and papa and mamma go to a dinner that night."

" By all means come with us. We have invited no one yet, and the box holds six."

" May I, Mamma ? "

" We will talk about it," was the maternal answer.

" I must be going," Loreno said, rising ; " I 'll leave the invitation open for a week, and you must tease mamma until she consents."

" Don't teach the child such nonsense," protested his sister.

" Knowledge is power, you know," he persisted. " Receive this testimony, Gaeta, from an experienced parent."

" I 'll try to be worthy of such an uncle," she said meekly. " I 'll try to give dear mamma no peace until she writes and thanks you as you deserve."

CHAPTER X.

IT was a bright warm afternoon at the end of April when Madame André's guests began to arrive. She had invited thirty or forty friends to see the unveiling of her last work, — the first important work she had done in Rome.

The building occupied by Madame André was in the grounds of a villa, several outhouses of which the needy proprietor had turned into studios.

As Loreno and Agatha left their carriage and walked up the short path leading to the building, they saw Mercede's guests seated at a number of small tables placed under the trees near the studio. A dozen pretty children, models in their gay costumes, flitted here and there serving tea from a table, at which stood the hostess looking very picturesque in a dull red costume of soft Indian stuff and a velvet turban of a darker shade. The company was chatting merrily, and Mercede while attending to her duties, addressed first one and then another near her, doing what she could to make the occasion informal.

Upon catching sight of her cousins, Mercede came forward eagerly, and immediately bespoke their assist-

17

ance, Agatha being put in charge of the tea, and Loreno instructed to make himself generally useful.

Agatha wore a spring costume, mauve in color, with a bunch of Parma violets fastened in her bodice, and Mercede was obliged to confess that she looked extremely well. The young wife, conscious of the curious glances that followed her, was quick to seize this opportunity to make a public display of cordiality toward Mercede. Filippo's neighbors found him formal in manner and unresponsive. He knew them well, and understood their furtive glances toward his wife. He was an uncomfortable companion, and they were glad when, presently, he urged the artist to lead the way to her atelier, and offered her his arm. The others rose, and falling into pairs followed Mercede and Filippo into the building.

" Why did you not come last evening? " she asked in a low tone as they passed through a suite of rooms filled with statuary.

"I did n't suppose you really expected me."

" I wanted you to be the first to look upon the finished work."

" I 'm very sorry to have disappointed you; but, after all, we could n't have seen it well at night."

" Oh, yes; I have a strong light thrown upon it; everything else is in shadow, the group standing out alone. It is strangely effective." She looked behind her. " One feels," she added in a still lower voice, " as though one became a part of it. I never before so entered into a work."

" Indeed! I 'm very impatient to see this mysterious 'it,'" he replied, as they halted before the atelier.

Disengaging her hand from his arm she pushed aside the portière.

The work was so placed that Loreno did not see it until fairly inside the room, where he was quickly surrounded by the eager guests. Mercede heard the hum of admiration that sounded around her, but she was indifferent to it. Laying her hand unconsciously upon Filippo's arm, she stood with fixed gaze eagerly searching his face.

"How beautiful!" "How exquisite!" were the words that resounded on all sides, but neither Mercede nor Agatha seemed to hear them.

"What is the subject?" asked Filippo presently, without turning from the statue.

"Tristan and Isolde;" and the artist's voice trembled.

He stood silent, intently studying the group for a long time, and then turning to her exclaimed cordially, "It is very fine!"

A look of disappointment and pain shot across her face, but she banished it instantly as others gathered about her to offer their congratulations.

Filippo's first glance at the group had startled him. The intensity of the subject so powerfully depicted was a departure from the severe classic that had hitherto characterized Mercede's work. She had evidently put into it all she knew of human passion, and the electric spark seemed to flash from the dead clay to the living flesh. A second glance convinced him that in Tristan his own features were clearly suggested. The incident chosen was the moment just after the drinking of the love potion, when recognition of their love first comes to the ill-fated pair.

While no one could look unmoved upon the group, since the breath of genius wedded to a woman's passion had created it, Loreno's sensations were not unmixed. It was more calculated to stir him than most others, because of his keen sensibility to art, the strong human element in him, and the fascination which the artist had for him: yet the first sensation which thrilled him was almost instantly suppressed by the chill of an undefined antipathy. He felt that he had been degraded. Even Mercede's genius and their close friendship did not warrant the liberty she had taken. But as he reasoned further, he began to frame excuses for her until he was able at least to conceal any evidence of his feeling, and to praise the group as earnestly as the rest of her friends. Yet he kept his eyes away from the face of his wife.

Later in the afternoon, however, when the first impression had somewhat worn away, he joined Agatha as she was stepping through an open window to the lawn. She was unusually pale, and he inquired if she were tired.

"Yes," she answered, "very; and I was going out for a breath of air." She took his arm as she spoke, and they strolled across the lawn beyond the other guests and entered a grape-arbor. Seating themselves upon a bench, Agatha threw her head back against the vines, and Filippo, lighting a cigarette, left her to her thoughts.

She had received a severe shock, and was bewildered. It had taken weeks to convince her that her cousin's feeling was really warmer for her husband than for herself, and only after periods of keen self-condemnation at the suspicion, had the truth been forced upon her. But she had clung loyally to the belief that Mercede's affection was very deep for her as well. Implicit confidence is not easily shaken, and Agatha had pondered and struggled through many dark hours and days, trying to reconcile Mercede's conduct with the exalted opinion she had always held of her character. The high-minded wife could not believe the logical result of facts which she was obliged to recognize. She could not, therefore, comprehend Mercede's aim. Indeed, even at this moment, as she leaned her aching head against the vines, she arrived at no definite opinion except that Mercede's regard for Filippo blinded her to common prudence. Yet it is to be remembered that Agatha was dependent for her opinion upon the complex workings of a wilful woman's mind, for so long as she did not cross Mercede's great wish, the latter manifested toward her undiminished although spasmodic warmth of feeling, thus stilling many a passing doubt that, permitted to live, would have embarrassed Mercede's purpose.

The Italians have a proverb which says that good repute is like the cypress, — once cut, it never puts forth leaf again ; and it is equally true of confidence. Mercede felt this instinctively, and was wise enough to do what she could, consistent with her own aims, to preserve the faith that she had once

prized for itself alone.   But this day's signal of
danger was one not to be mistaken.   It told Agatha
that, no matter what Mercede's opinion of her might
be, her cousin's attitude toward Filippo was one
which fully justified the whispers now floating about
Rome.   Leaving right and wrong entirely out of the
question, she could not understand Mercede's reckless disregard of public opinion ; it confounded her.
She wondered what Filippo thought of it, and waited
for him to speak.   She could not believe that he
had failed to recognize the resemblance of Tristan
to himself; while, this similarity once suggested, it
was easy, in spite of the classical type which had
been chosen for Isolde's face, to see that the pose
and lines of the figure bore a distinct suggestion of
the artist herself.

"What does it mean ? " the distressed wife asked
herself again and again ; but even now this question
failed to hold her mind.   The shock was too recent
for her to realize fully its true cause, and her mind
reverted to the less important cry, "What must the
others have thought?   What will the world say ? "

She bit her lip and clenched her fingers tightly to
restrain the indignation which possessed her.   Presently Filippo threw away his cigarette, and rising
walked restlessly to the door of the arbor.

"Shall we go back ? " Agatha asked.

"Perhaps it will be best; Mercede may be wondering where we are."

"Is it such an extraordinary thing," she could
not help saying, "for a husband and wife to go
off together for a stroll?"

" Of course not ; but some of the guests are going.
I saw them leaving a moment ago, and our absence
will be the more conspicuous."

She kept back the reply that sprang to her lips,
and rose instantly. Indeed, she preferred that as
many of her friends as possible should see her husband and herself together.

" By the bye," she said, as they left the arbor,
" we have n't spoken of the group. It 's very striking, is n't it ? "

" Very — and wonderful in its art ; but — "

" But what ? "

" I 'm sorry that the face of Tristan suggests mine,
and several people say that it does."

" Did you sit for her ? "

" Why, Agatha ! " he exclaimed sharply. Then
he added, quite calmly, " No ; and you could not
have been more surprised than I was."

She pressed his arm tightly. " Forgive me, dearest ; I really did not mean what I said."

" I should hope not," he replied.

At the threshold they met friends going away,
and passed from room to room until they found
the artist taking leave of her guests. They went
forward and joined the Duke Faviola and Gaeta (the
Duchess had sent her regrets), who were standing
near their hostess. Presently Mercede turned and
joined the group. Her color was high, for the excitement of the occasion was not without its effect
upon her.

If she had deluded herself with the hope that
Filippo's features would not be generally recognized

in the statue, she was now awakened to the truth, for the resemblance had been commonly remarked.' She therefore boldly took the bull by the horns.

"Are you not going to thank me, Filippo," she said gayly, "for having perpetuated you?"

"Thus far it's only clay," he replied; "and as you work over it the chance likeness may be lost."

She raised her eyebrows slightly. "Do you think, then, that it needs working over?"

"I supposed that sculptors always worked over their statues,—at least a little."

"Did you?" and her eye grew cold, for she believed this to be the result of his absence with Agatha. "This work is finished; I don't intend to touch it again!" She looked around the silent group and laughed quietly but defiantly. Then she realized that she was putting Filippo in opposition to herself. Therefore, with surprising intrepidity, she completely changed her tactics, and as though she had been jesting, declared that the fancied resemblance of Tristan to Filippo should have quite disappeared when next her friends had an opportunity of comparing the two faces; and as she took leave of Agatha she kissed her upon both cheeks in the Italian fashion, with no trace of the bitterness which in truth she felt.

As Loreno led his wife away, Mercede turned with a bright smile to the Duke.

"Filippo is altogether too modest," she said; "don't you think so?"

"No," said his Grace, bluntly.

"No?"

" No ; Tristan was a poacher."

" You are too literal. One cannot judge heroes of romance as a magistrate does reprobates."

" I don't; but that group, while effective, perpetuates dishonor."

" No, no ! not dishonor, but love, — that sacred force which has ruled the destinies of all ages, and which will last as long as the bronze which personifies it."

" This may be love," he answered; " but there is love of another sort which scorns selfishness and builds better than it knows. Such love is pleasing in the sight of God, and shall be more lasting than bronze."

This was positive eloquence for the taciturn Duke, and it must indeed have been a deep feeling which impelled him to forsake his accustomed reticence.

An hour later Mercede arose from the chair into which she had sunk as her last guest left her. Going to her new creation, she stood before it for a long time, drinking in its eloquence. Then she spoke as if to a living spirit.

" Are you deceiving me ? " she said.

CHAPTER XI.

" FIDELIO."

FILIPPO felt that he had wronged Mercede the day before, and he was eager to make amends to her, — at least in his own mind. She had said quite plainly that the resemblance of Tristan to himself was accidental, and he did not question her word. He was surprised and somewhat offended, therefore, that Agatha had not seemed to accept fully her cousin's statement; at least she had been noticeably quiet, not only while driving from the studio, but during the evening.

Gaeta had told them at the studio that she would go with them to the opera, and Filippo decided to suggest to Agatha that Mercede and the General should be of the party.

He had given unusual consideration as to the best method of making this suggestion, and determined to express his wish without circumlocution or inde- cision. He was quite prepared, if not for protest, at least for demur on Agatha's part, and was propor- tionately surprised when she quietly but cordially assented. He was inclined to think that he might have misinterpreted her silence of the previous night. It is not surprising, perhaps, that he reflected thus

superficially upon the incident of the day before, for
it was not to his mind, as to Agatha's, an incident of
great suggestiveness. Indeed, after Mercede's explanation, he had practically dismissed it from his
mind, for his faith in her integrity was absolute.

But Agatha was now fully aroused. At last she
felt that there was danger. Nevertheless, while a tu-
mult was raging in her heart, she realized that what
was needed, and what she must bring to the task before her, was a cool head and a patient trust. She had
the wisdom to know that in all peril, whether physical or moral, excitement is worse than inaction. She
felt as though she were rescuing a somnambulist from
a threatened fall ; should she stumble or cry out, all
might be lost. Throughout her homeward drive,
throughout the long hours of a sleepless night, she
had revolved the matter again and again, until she
compassed its gravity, and seemed to receive sufficient
light to guide her wisely, at least for the present.
Her first inclination had been, naturally, to snap off
the intimacy which had sprung up between her husband and her cousin ; but she quickly realized that
even were this possible, it would be a confession of
weakness. Nor was this idea in accordance with the
line of conduct upon which she had decided. She
would not trifle with her future happiness by playing
the part of a jealous wife. Also, she reasoned truly, by
having Mercede near her she could study her purpose
more intelligently, and to be forewarned would be an
important advantage. Nor would Mercede's presence
make any real difference in the end, for there was
nothing to be gained by delay. Sooner or later she

must stand or fall upon the strength of her husband's manhood and love.

Then the will that had once subdued that of her uncle rose in its might, fortified by the greater maturity of its mistress and the vital gravity of her cause. She decided that her faith in Filippo should be as an anchor to hold him firm ; and further, *that come what might of temptation or peril, no woman should ever become an issue between her husband and herself.*

It was in obedience to this purpose that she accepted without hesitation her husband's suggestion that Mercede should be included in the opera party, and she herself sent the invitation to her cousin.

The Apollo Theatre was thronged with an expectant audience as the Lorenos and their guests took their seats, for " Lohengrin " had not often been heard in Rome, and the German company was well liked.

Before the overture began, Agatha outlined the story to Gaeta, since the libretto did not contain the " argument " to which English and American audiences are accustomed. Mercede listened also, and as Agatha finished, remarked quietly, " Elsa was served rightly."

" Yes, I suppose so," Agatha responded, " for she should not have doubted. Yet what a punishment ! " and her voice trembled slightly.

" I mean," added Mercede, " that she seems to me, from your story, to be a miserably weak little thing, frightened lest she had made a mésalliance."

" That's one way of putting it; but to me she seems overcome by an uncontrollable desire to justify her faith in her husband."

" No man," and Mercede spoke very distinctly, " will, or at least should, permit his wife to be his inquisitor, — nor, for that matter, his monitor either."

" Whether that is the moral this story teaches or whether it is not, I quite agree with you." And Agatha's manner betrayed no comprehension of the personal suggestion of the comment, much to the disgust of Gaeta, who instantly took up the cudgels.

" *I* don't agree with you," she said boldly. " I should think it would depend upon the man, and how he behaved himself." Then, fearing she had spoken too plainly, she added, " I only hope that my knight — if ever I have one — won't try me as Elsa was tried, unless he prefers to go away from me."

" A wish. it is difficult to imagine," and Mercede's lips parted with one of her charming smiles. " Yet a man should not be too much hampered by our sensitive vanity. He must necessarily have a life somewhat apart from that of his wife. For example, do you suppose that diplomats confide all their comings and goings to their wives? And if you once recognize this principle, where will you draw the line ? "

" At what they keep to themselves, not from duty, but from lack of duty."

Madame André raised her eyebrows ominously, although she smiled again. " And pray, what conception of a man's duty has your experience taught you? I am interested."

Gaeta's little nose crept up in the air, and she looked haughtily out of the corners of her eyes, in no wise discomfited.

"He should treat me as he would compel me to treat him," she replied.

" Indeed ! You take a most serious view of married life. One might suppose you expected to marry a Turk."

"Well, whether I marry a Turk, or only a man who is tempted to behave like one, I wish to know it beforehand ; otherwise," and she gave a defiant toss of her head, "my curiosity will more than annoy him."

The General and Filippo laughed heartily, and the latter, asking Mercede for her lorgnette, hastened to comment upon some persons in the opposite box.

At this moment the conductor wielded his baton and the music began. When Elsa came upon the stage, and before she had sung a note, Mercede saw Filippo turn and look at Agatha with a significant smile. Agatha flushed with pleasure, and nodded assent.

" We heard her sing at Munich," he explained to Mercede. " She is a fine artist."

Agatha's interest in Elsa was overshadowed by the memories awakened.

They had heard this singer during their wedding trip, — an ideal episode in Agatha's life, to which she looked back with the fullest joy. Then the opera was " Fidelio," and she remembered saying to herself upon that night, so many years ago, as she was carried on by her ardent sympathy with the noble heroine, that she would do the same were her husband spirited away, and that the power of her love,

like that of Fidelio, could not fail to rescue him.
The suggestion now startled her, and her breath
came fast; but the others were intent upon the
peril of Elsa, and did not observe her excitement.

At the end of the act visitors kept the conversation in safe channels until the curtain rose again.
As the second act ended, Mr. Dow entered the box,
soon followed by Veltri.

"I think I'll go and pay some visits myself,"
Filippo remarked, rising.

"Won't you give me a turn in the corridor first?"
asked Mercede. "It's very warm here."

"Certainly."

"A good idea," said Agatha, impulsively; "let us
all go, — that is, if agreeable to every one."

So, with the exception of the General, who preferred to remain, the entire party left the box, — Mercede on Filippo's arm, while Mr. Dow captured Gaeta.
Indeed, Mr. Dow had of late become more and more
a thorn in young Veltri's side. Since the episode regarding Veltri, Mr. Dow had not only ceased to think
of Gaeta as a child, but had utterly revised his conception of her character; in fact, he stood rather in
awe of her. As his acquaintance with her had increased, he found more and more interest in her society, and was becoming more and more assiduous in
his attentions to her, although no one except Veltri
seemed conscious of the fact, — not even Mr. Dow
himself. But Veltri's brown eyes were often clouded
and his heart was made heavy by just such incidents
as that which now caused him to follow the tall
figure of his rival with bitter envy.

"I'm afraid I ought n't to have suggested leaving the box," said Mercede in a low voice as Filippo and she walked on before the others.

"Why not?"

"I don't know; but it seems strange that they should all throng after us."

"There is room enough for all," he replied rather formally.

"I only meant," Mercede hastened to add, feeling that she had blundered, "that you must n't let my coming embarrass you. Papa is still in the box, and I'll go back after a turn or two."

"I'll walk with you as long as you wish; there is n't any one I really care to see."

She bowed mockingly. "Thank you for the compliment."

"I meant," and as his eyes met hers all trace of annoyance disappeared, "that no one else offers sufficient counter-attraction."

"I refuse to accept it," she said with pretty dignity "Compliments and mirrors cannot be mended."

"Yet both are sometimes to be trusted."

"I hate anything that even suggests a mirror to me," and her voice lost its tone of banter; "my whole life seems made up of reflections. If I try to look ahead, if I even try to catch a glimpse of the hearts about me, I find only my own fears, my own hopes, thrown back at me. It's horrid!"

"What fears can you possibly have for the future?" he asked incredulously; "and as for the hearts of those about you, whose do you doubt?"

She paused, and then laughed nervously. "I don't

suppose I really fear anything or doubt any one; but have you never known anxiety about something that reason told you was scarcely possible — certainly, not probable ? "

" Often, — concerning the children, for example, and Agatha."

At that name her lips compressed.

" Precisely," she said.

They were passing the box, and opening the door she suddenly disengaged her arm and stepped inside.

" Are you tired of it ? " Filippo asked.

" Yes," she said with strange emphasis.

18

CHAPTER XII.

" MERCEDE," said the General, one evening about two weeks later, " have you changed that face of Tristan yet ? "

She looked up from her book, but did not turn her head.

"No; I have n't taken off the cage except to sprinkle the clay ; why ? "

" Nothing ; " and the old man relapsed into silence.

" There must have been some reason for such a question," she said.

" Well — " and the General hesitated.

" ' Well ' ? " she echoed impatiently.

" Have you heard any report, my daughter, that relates to you and Filippo ?   Something about — "

" There, father, that will do ! " and closing her book she flung it upon the table.   " I know all about it, and I 'm amazed that you should offer me the affront of mentioning it to me."

" Our silence will not make the world dumb."

" ' The world ' ! " she exclaimed bitterly.   " Oh, how you tremble before it !   And it 's not the first time," she added significantly.

" No, Mercede, it 's not fear of the world, but fear of being in-the wrong, that prompts me to speak.   I 'm

not concerned about Blanche and Tray and Sweetheart, but about our Agatha."

She sprang to her feet and faced him.

"It's Agatha! Agatha! Agatha! morning, noon,
and night. Does it never occur to you to think of
me a little, even at the expense of your idol?"

"Oh, Mercede!" and the old man raised his hand
reproachfully while his face grew pained. "How
can you use such language of one who is almost a
sister to you? My only happiness in the few years
remaining to me is in you both, and I never wish to
see the tie loosened that has bound you together."

"Very well; then don't take her part against
me."

"In what, my child?"

"In this report. You hear that her husband is too
friendly with me. You know how little truth there
is in it, and should scorn to annoy me with it."

"That's the trouble; I don't think it's all smoke."

"Father, I beg of you to have a care, or you will
deeply offend me!"

The old man rose and lit a cigarette; then he
resumed his seat and blew a cloud of smoke.

"Now, Mercede," he said quietly, "I've made up
my mind to speak," — he fixed his eyes upon hers, —
"and I insist upon your being dutiful and listening.
I have never approved of your riding alone with
Filippo, morning after morning; I thought it would
create remark, and I was right. I have never approved of Filippo's meeting you day after day, as you
leave your studio, and walking with you. I have
never approved of the devotion he shows you in

society. It's all very well to say he is the husband of Agatha; but you are both young, and already the strength of your influence upon him is shown by the fact that he is absolutely neglecting other affairs to enjoy these tête-à-têtes with you. This is a matter of common knowledge, and it is undeniable; and this thing, like any other wrong thing, should stop!"

The directness of his words shocked her; but a shock is an effective method of treatment under certain conditions, moral as well as physical. She was quite calm when she spoke.

"My dear Father," she began, "you hurt me more than you can know. I am not a reckless coquette, but merely a woman peculiarly dependent upon kindness and sympathy. I have, I know, both you and my dear child; but, as you say, I am still young, and I need companions of my own age. Where should I more naturally find them than in her who is almost my sister, and in her husband? I long to see them both whenever I can; but I am busy all day and so is Agatha, therefore neither can wait upon the other. Filippo happens to have a free hour in the morning and another in the afternoon, and he seems to enjoy the companionship of a disinterested and loyal friend beyond that of a set of fawning politicians or foolish philanthropists."

"He used to help Agatha in her charitable work in these hours," interposed the General.

"At the expense of his health. No one can reproach him with idleness," she went on; "but it seems that they do wish to dictate how he shall use

the little freedom he has; while as for me — well,
as Goethe says, —

> 'Laziness, you know, is not my sin,
> But somehow, when great things I would achieve,
> I find some fool from whom I must ask leave.'

As, witness my Tristan; I happen to choose a type
which to the vulgar herd suggests a familiar face.
Basta! I must change it. And now the dear souls,
finding how omnipotent they are, wish to direct all
my affairs, and not daring to come to me they sneak
in behind my back to you. Do you blame me for
resenting it? Can you wonder that I am pained at
your giving them your sympathy and using your
authority to humble me?"

"God keep me from humbling you, my child!" he
responded; "I have it only in my heart to keep you
from humbling yourself."

"But I am not a child."

"Yes, you are *my* child, and I would stand between
you and future sorrow. Friendship is a relation resting on honesty, — a relation upon which the blessing of
God may be invoked each day. Sentiment and ardor
attend it, but they should ever be its servants; otherwise it becomes indefensible license."

She was silent a long time, sitting with fixed eyes,
pondering deeply.

"What do you suggest?" she asked presently.

"That you should deny yourself some present
pleasure for the sake of the truer happiness of all."

"I cannot see the necessity," she replied. "You
look at the relation between Filippo and me in a

most distorted way. Is he not devoted to Agatha? Am I likely, even had I the right, to encourage a sentimental relation with any man? But friendship, in other words sympathy, is as essential to some characters as is sunshine to the growth of flowers. My nature can either be opened under the warmth of a friendly force, or be shrivelled up by the chill of timidity and prudery."

She rose, and began to pace up and down the room.

"Why am I so?" she continued; "and if I beat down these natural impulses and deny myself the little happiness granted me, what will the world give me in exchange? Don't for Heaven's sake reply piously, 'A calm conscience,' or suggest, 'The sweet consciousness of right doing.' I deny both! I need and I deserve some real, living, present force, which can draw my sore heart from its incessant repining. For me this force is not to be found in work nor in religion, nor does it hide even in obscure places needing only patient seeking. It has revealed itself; I have found it; I have even stretched out my hands to it. And now I am bidden to deny this, my purest instinct; to fold my arms across my breast and make a mockery of resignation." Then turning suddenly she advanced toward him with absolute defiance in her manner, her eyes blazing, her face white with passion. "I refuse to make this sacrifice," she cried, her voice deep and clear as a bell. "Do you understand me? I will not make it. I will not!"

It was in vain that her father tried to argue with her; she continued to pace the room, but would not open her lips. Presently he went to her and gently laid his hand upon her arm. She paused and looked at him inquiringly, — she had even forgotten his presence. Then going towards the door and without looking back, she left him and went to her own room.

Before sleeping, however, she decided, as a sort of sop to her conscience, to make another effort to draw nearer to Agatha. The next day this resolution was somewhat distasteful to her, but still she held to it, and in so doing felt that she merited commendation. That afternoon, as she was leaving her studio, she saw, as usual, Filippo walking toward her.

" I 'm going to make a call," she said.

His face fell. " Then are we to lose our walk ? "

" I am going to see Agatha ; but perhaps she will not be home so early ?

"Not before six. She has her violin class this afternoon. She is teaching eight or ten children."

" Very well. Then let us walk a little until I find a cab ; I want an old-time chat with her, and you would be in the way."

Filippo seemed disappointed. " I 'm sorry you chose this time. I 've had a vexatious day, and anticipated the change."

Her face brightened, but her tone was solicitous.

" What has been the matter ? " she asked.

" I 've had some important work and could n't bend my mind to it."

" I don't wonder ; it is difficult to do two things well."

" I don't understand you."

" Why, you are trying to combine statesmanship,

which taxes all the resources that any man can bring
to it, with philanthropy, which is an occupation of
itself. They interfere with each other, and the combination takes too much out of you."

"I don't agree with you; and if I did, I should n't
see my way clear to drop either."

"You amaze me!" and she regarded him with
genuine surprise. "I don't see how you can hesitate
an instant. Cut off the luxury, and devote yourself
only to work worthy of you."

"Both are worthy, — equally so," he replied earnestly. "They have the same end, — the good of
one's fellow-citizens."

Her nostrils dilated slightly. "Yes," she said, her
voice singularly clear, "perhaps they may be said to
have the same object, like man and wife laboring for
the common family. But the statesman stands before
his fellowmen and measures his strength with the
strongest, while Philanthropy remains at home looking after the house, and the children, and the flower-
pots."

He winced a little at the picture. "In fashioning
a great work," he said, "many tools are needed; don't
you think it juster to regard statesmanship and philanthropy as two of them, each fitted for its especial
purpose?"

"Possibly!"

This adverb is to a nimble disputant what the pali-
sade is to a chulo. When the animal we are worry-
ing lowers his horns, we have only to vault behind
this word and we leave him discomfited, with nothing
to hit. Mercede had too much knowledge of human

nature to pursue the subject further. She reasoned rightly that it would be better to leave the contemptuous impression which she had created, to work its way into his mind, rather than by driving it further (as was her inclination and habit in dispute) to risk putting him into an antagonistic mood. Daylight, she knew, will creep through a small hole.

Therefore she branched off suddenly to other topics, and he believed that she was trying to atone for her sarcasm. It is curious how black a man can paint the devil, and how brightly he will gild a sympathetic woman.

There was no indication of bitterness in Agatha's manner as she received her cousin.

"Did you see Filippo this afternoon?" she asked.

Mercede flushed slightly. "Yes; I met him on my way here."

"You meet every afternoon, I believe."

Mercede hesitated. "Yes, we do; that is, nearly every afternoon."

"He often speaks of your walks. He seems to enjoy them very much, and they do him good. He doesn't get enough fresh air."

"So it seemed to me, and I felt the same about myself. Indeed, it was under Dr. Maretti's advice that I decided to take more exercise."

"Yes, I remember; do you feel its good effects?"

"Oh, yes; I am much better than I was."

"I have a plan in mind that I think will put you quite right again. Has Filippo told you that we are going to the country next week?"

" No," and Mercede's lips lost their color.

" That's his frightful memory. Yes, we go next Tuesday to Varese. The people there really seem to need us."

Mercede tried to smile. " It sounds charming," she said. " I quite envy you."

" Do you? Then I hope that you will consider the plan I have to propose. Why won't you run away from work for a month and come to us ? "

The dark eyes opened with genuine surprise. " It is very kind of you," — and she paused to collect her ideas, — " but it is so unexpected ! I have n't thought of abandoning work so soon, and I don't see how I can leave just yet, but — "

" Does the idea tempt you ? "

" Yes, indeed ! It would be a most grateful rest, but I fear I can't spare the time. Yet I 'd like to think it over."

She had little realized until now, when the matter stared her in the face, what it would be to have day after day drag itself slowly by without bringing Filippo to her. This was what she kept before her mind all that evening, and the more she thought of it the less tolerable it seemed. Ugh ! what miserable, heavy, hopeless hours they would be, whole days and nights full of them. She needed all her sophistries, all her self-deceiving theories, to disguise the feeling that now stirred her so powerfully ; for ere she slept that night she knew that were she compelled to choose between abandoning her artistic career forever and losing this month with him whose presence was her chief delight, she would not hesitate ; and she marvelled as she remembered that when with Agatha only a few hours before, her hesitation had been genuine. These two fixed points startled her, bringing as they did vividly before her mind the distance she had moved in her moral orbit during these intervening hours. Yes, the realization startled her, but it did not frighten her; it did not even grieve her. On the contrary, her mind whirled with joy. In addition to the excitement of the theme was the buoyancy which so often comes with decision, — a buoyancy enhanced in this instance by Mercede's impatience under self-denial.

> " Shoot your own thread right through the earthly tissue
> Bravely : and leave the gods to find the issue."

This was the thought that possessed her. She attempted no justification, she made no apology in the present hour ; she simply nerved herself with these lines. They seemed inspired and addressed to her. They were of the wisdom of Goethe.

CHAPTER XIII.

LOOKING NORTHWARD.

MERCEDE did not sleep well. Nearly the entire night she lay with her open eyes fixed upon the flickering night-light, thinking. Slowly, but with hopeless certainty, there had crept over her joy a sullen cloud. Finally she arose from her bed and tried to throw off her wretchedness, but the cloud hung about her. Nervous from lack of rest, and worn by intense mental excitement, she suddenly flung herself upon the sofa and wept.

She was oppressed and torn by self-dissatisfaction which only a proud struggle kept from becoming self-condemnation; but at last she throttled her better nature, and then her mind was seized with a morbid jealousy that utterly mastered her. She no longer denied that she envied her cousin to the depths of her nature, and felt that she could not bring herself to enter Filippo's house to be an hourly witness of Agatha's exercise of her wifely rights — yet the thought of separation from Filippo was unbearable.

What, then, should she do? Time and again her better self struggled for recognition; but this only added to her torment, and with obstinate fury she crushed it down.

Throwing on a wrapper, she opened a window and leaning her throbbing head upon her arms tried to think. How could she accomplish these conflicting purposes? How could she have Filippo without becoming Agatha's guest? At last with the gathering light of dawn came relief to her perplexity, and rising to her full height, she stood with her hands folded behind her head, gazing at the dim stars that faded without her knowledge.

Presently a noise in the street below recalled her from her oblivion, and she watched with strange interest the trifling incidents that mark an awakening city. Her mind was clear; her purpose taken. Filippo must come to Erba, and since Agatha seemed to have conquered her desire to monopolize her husband, the peculiar sentiment she felt for Erba would probably induce her to accept an invitation to go there for her usual summer visit. In regard to the invitation to Varese, which would undoubtedly be pressed further, Mercede decided to postpone a definite reply. She felt that a happy solution of her difficulty had thus been reached; for while she should secure Filippo's society, she would be spared the humiliation of being in Agatha's home under circumstances which would scarcely be — honorable is what she meant, but the word she used was "agreeable."

Nothing remained, therefore, but to see her father and secure his co-operation. She looked at her watch, — he would not breakfast for three hours; so, lowering her curtains, she lay down upon the bed and soon fell into a deep sleep. When she awoke, it

was late, and hastily ringing for her maid she learned
that the General was still at home; whereupon she
sent him word that she wished to speak with him,
and would dress immediately. Her sleep had not
refreshed her much, and her head ached viciously;
but she swept into her father's presence with a bright
smile and bade him a cheerful good-morning.

"Papa dear," she began, "you have invited Agatha to Erba every summer since her marriage; why
have n't you invited her this year?"

"Well," and he hesitated. "Perhaps I ought to
do so."

"Why, papa! you speak as though it were a
duty."

"You see, my dear," and he avoided her eye,
"things are a little different this year."

"Different? In what way?"

"You are with me, and I don't need Agatha so
much."

"That is not your reason. Why not be frank
with me?"

The old gentleman lighted a cigarette and smoked
rapidly, as was his habit when in trouble. Then, after
a few moments' consideration, he answered her.

"If you will have the truth, Mercede," he said, "I
was n't quite sure that you would find it pleasant to
have Agatha with us. You know she is devoted
to her charities, and they pertain to Erba as well
as to Varese; and I feared you might disapprove,
and—"

"And make my disapproval offensively known?
Now I understand. But what an injustice you do

me! I trust I am a better hostess than that. Besides, I don't object to charity in its right place; and the country is just its place, for there one is away from one's other duties."

The General's eye brightened, and he protested that he needed no urging to invite Agatha to Erba. It was soon arranged, therefore, that he should see her during the day, and then go to Mercede's studio.

The General called upon Agatha in the afternoon, and later made his promised report to Mercede. Agatha had recounted the pressing demands of Varese affairs, but offered no personal opposition to the proposed delay, agreeing to leave the decision to her husband. As Mercede listened, her heart grew light; she felt that her desire was practically accomplished, and when a few hours later she joined Filippo for their usual walk, her step was light, her face bright with happiness. She lost no time in unfolding her plan, scarcely paying him the compliment of putting the matter suggestively.

To her amazement he received the idea with objections, but not, as she had expected, based upon Agatha's probable opposition to it. He had, he said received news from Varese that morning, and his presence there seemed necessary. Mercede, annoyed at the need of argument, nevertheless yielded to the inevitable; but her words seemed to make no impression upon his resolve. As she argued, her purpose grew more intense, for behind this strange opposition she believed Agatha to be intrenched. Agatha, she thought, desiring to take her husband

away, had played upon his kindness of heart for her
own purposes; and now he believed himself to be
guided by his own sense of duty, and was as obstinate
as he could be.

As the realization of parting from him came to
Mercede afresh, she shifted her ground and began
to plead, — appealing to him not to disappoint her
father; and thereupon she drew so touching a picture of the Count's happiness at gaining Agatha's
consent, that for the first time Filippo showed signs
of faltering. By a skilful use of this potent argument, — for Loreno was very fond of the Count, and
felt that Agatha owed to him the duty of a daughter,
— reinforced by the power of her own personality,
which came into full play through the emotional
direction which the discussion had taken, Mercede
succeeded in gaining two points: He consented,
first, that Agatha should visit Erba before going to
Varese; then, that he would write immediately to
Varese, and if possible would himself accept the
Count's invitation. Exultant, she pressed him harder, — all her influence over him, all her fascination
for him vivified by the full intensity of her aroused
jealousy. Little by little she won her victory, — the
most noteworthy by far she had yet won with him.
He promised unconditionally to visit Erba for at least
a few days.

Rome gossiped a little more sharply when it became known that Madame André and Filippo were
to be together at Erba; but sober second thought
gradually asserted itself, as the critics began to ask

themselves what was more natural than that the Marchesa Loreno should visit her uncle at the villa which had once been her home? Even the most eager fault-finder could not justify criticism of this fact, and was, moreover, obliged to admit that Loreno's absence would be more noticeable than his presence.

The principal actors in the affair did not, however, stay to note the ebb and flow of the gossip, but took themselves off to the sweet air and sweeter moral atmosphere of the Northern hills. Their going made at least three hearts that were left in Rome very heavy, because it suggested the approach of another parting. One heart was Gaeta's; another was that of Signor Veltri; while the third belonged to Mr. Peter Dow.

There are certain flowers containing small glands in which a drop of etheric oil is secreted. When the flower is young, these glands are but little developed, but they grow with the flower, and become fully developed only when the blossoms begin to fade. If at that time a light be held near, a flame is kindled which flashes vividly like miniature lightning. And there seem to be hearts closely analogous to such plants. They are susceptible to the touch of love only when the blossoms begin to wither; but then, if the conditions serve, they answer bravely, and suddenly illumine with exhaustless bounty the darkness which has hung over them.

Of some such species must have been the heart of Mr. Peter Dow: for not until now, when the blossoms of his youth were undeniably fading, had it

19

responded to the ever-searching flame. Yes, Mr.
Dow had at last become the victim of a new and
most incautious habit, — he thought day and night
of the fascinating little creature who of late had
treated him so kindly. He knew that the great difference between their ages was against him so far as
Gaeta herself was concerned; but Italian girls are
not so bigoted as American girls about that sort of
thing, and he assured himself that the continental
idea of marriage was much more prudent, if sometimes less sentimental, than that which prevailed in
his own country. Gaeta had developed wonderfully,
and was mature and wise beyond her years. Mr.
Dow acknowledged that she had an enthusiasm for
her young music-teacher; but this enthusiasm, apparently, was shared by her father and mother, and
surely they would not smooth the way of their only
child to a *mésalliance*. Therefore it was most unlikely that Veltri was to be regarded as a rival,
whereas Mr. Dow, in fairness to himself, felt bound
to admit that there was much to justify the hope in
his heart. Although he had no title, he had money,
and so far as birth was concerned — well, it was
something to have been born in Boston. Then his
thoughts were wont to fly away to the future, and
he smiled with grim anticipation as he pictured to
himself the hospitable way in which exclusive Boston
doors would be flung open to receive the daughter of
a Duke. Not that Bostonians value titles as New-
Yorkers do, making themselves breathless in their
eager seeking after the imported luxury; but then
no one — not even a Bostonian — would hesitate at

a Faviola. Why, Gaeta's ancestral tree would make
the best one in Boston seem like a blackberry-bush
beside a Salem elm. No; Mr. Dow had no concern
about Gaeta's reception at home; and besides, they
would only cross "the pond" now and then for a little change. America would n't be bad, taken in that
way, especially with a Duke's daughter.

But Mr. Dow was not merely ambitious, he was
genuinely in love. It seemed as though life had
been dark until the presence of Gaeta bright eyes had
fired the hidden treasures of his soul. Of late, when
he awoke, and looked upon the mellow Southern sunlight, it seemed to him to be indeed blessed, for it
brought a renewed hope of seeing the little maid
to whom his thoughts turned always. The flowers
seemed more lovely than before, as he walked around
the Piazza-di-Spagna, gazing into the baskets of the
flower-boys or into the windows of their more pre-
tentious rivals, seeking for a bunch that might fitly
be offered to her whose color rivalled that of the
rich dark roses which he so carefully selected. Then,
too, what joy to see her fresh beauty, and watch
each new indication of her increasing regard! That
she did not always greet him with fervor meant absolutely nothing, for she was a little queen in her
domain, doing precisely as she chose, and apparently having no concern regarding the impression
she might create. But usually she was most gracious and winning toward him, and he felt that her
variableness of manner was evidence of their intimacy. She always seemed glad to receive the flowers he brought to her, and now and then had put

some of them in her dress. True, he had twice known of her giving the young musician a flower from her bunch; but, after all, that was nothing. Indeed, Mr. Dow told himself, it showed a very platonic feeling toward Veltri, otherwise she would not dream of showing him such an attention. Mr. Dow dreaded the summer, since the daily glimpse of Gaeta, to which he had acquired the habit of looking forward so eagerly, must necessarily cease unless he could manage to be near her. He hoped the Duke and Duchess would invite him to make them a short visit; and that it would be a momentous visit he felt sure. Yet another and bolder plan crossed his mind; but he postponed its consideration, at least for the present. He would sit a little longer on the bank before actually taking the plunge. True, in this case it did not seem a likely way of "getting there;" but something might happen to reveal to him the depth of the water into which he proposed to venture.

CHAPTER XIV.

JUNE DAYS.

TEN days later Padre Sacconi stood on the porch of the Villa Ricci with Mercede, who was waiting to receive her guests. The General had gone to the station to meet them, and now they were here.

As Agatha caught sight of the priest she kissed her hand to him, and having greeted Mercede, came to him with the old happy look in her eyes. But she seemed rather nervous of manner, and turning back even as he answered her, looked toward Mercede. The latter was standing at the side of Filippo while he gave some directions about the hand luggage. Presently he finished and turned to her. She extended both her hands, which he took, and for an instant they stood looking into each other's eyes. They spoke a few words, and as the Marquis came forward to speak with Padre Sacconi, Mercede turned and slipped her hand familiarly through his arm, her face radiant, her manner denoting security.

The keen glance of Padre Sacconi had followed that of Agatha, and now as he looked again into her troubled eyes he read her distress. Nor was his judgment shaken by the rapidity with which her expression changed, nor by the light-hearted manner she assumed as her husband and cousin approached.

" This is like old times ! " exclaimed Filippo heartily, as he shook the priest's hand.

" Yes, and may the present leave as pleasant a
memory."

" It cannot be more pleasant ! " was the cordial
reply. There was a sudden pressure upon his arm,
and he added, " Except because of Madame André's
presence."

" You overpower me," she replied with a light
laugh ; then pausing an instant, added with peculiar
seriousness, " I sincerely trust, Padre, that your wish
may come true, and that this visit may leave memories worthy to be compared with those already associated with the old place."

" Talking of memories, Agatha," said Filippo,
" you must dress yourself in white some afternoon,
take your violin down to the iron gate, and with the
Padre give Mercede a full-dress representation of a
certain tableau that is worthy of her genius."

" Pray excuse me," interposed Mercede, whose
smile suggested bitterness, " but no more family re-
semblances for me ! An experienced monkey is
never tempted twice by a cabomba."

" Come, Mercede," called the General, stepping
outside the door, " bring in the travellers, or they
will be late for dinner, and the children must not be
kept waiting."

" But surely, papa," she protested, " the children
are not to eat at our table."

" Now, don't oppose me," he said amiably, " for
it is useless. They have been invited and have
accepted."

" But not the baby," said Agatha, who saw that Mercede was annoyed.

" And why not?" demanded Filippo.

" Why not, indeed?" said the Count. " I have invited Miss Teresa to sit at my right hand."

" There is really no reason except your fatigue, Agatha dear," said Mercede, changing front as she caught Filippo's wish ; " I 'll sit next the baby."

Agatha felt the hot blood fling itself to her cheeks, but without deigning to answer, she turned and went indoors. Filippo thought she might have thanked her cousin.

Yet dinner was a merry meal; every one seemed in good spirits, and only the fleeting expression which now and then darted into Agatha's eyes, and an occasional slight contraction of the lips as her glance fell upon Filippo, told Padre Sacconi that her heart was heavy. The young Marquis was certainly imprudent. He could have been friendly enough without devoting himself so ardently to his engaging neighbor ; but both Mercede and he seemed, with occasional intervals, to forget that they were not dining apart.

During the evening, also, they showed the same inclination to be alone. First, they strolled off together while Agatha was upstairs in the nursery ; and later, when the moon rose, Mercede, leaving the group upon the veranda, walked to the edge of the terrace overlooking the lake, where Filippo soon joined her. Presently Padre Sacconi suggested that they should all go and see the effect of the moonlight upon the distant water; but after a few general remarks both

Filippo and Mercede became quite silent, and presently Mercede, saying that she was chilly, took Filippo's arm and they walked back and forth behind the rest of the party on the broad path which skirted the terrace.

The next morning, when Agatha awoke, she was startled to find that Filippo had already risen, and glanced hastily at her watch. It was not yet eight o'clock, and the breakfast-hour was nine. She looked into her husband's dressing-room, and a sharp pain shot through her heart as she saw that he was not there. As breakfast was announced, Filippo and Mercede came across the lawn, and seeing Agatha upon the veranda, gayly waved their hands.

" We've been to the lake, and Filippo has been teaching me to row," exclaimed Mercede.

" You must be hungry ; " and Agatha strove hard to appear natural.

" Ech — cosi, cosi," and she shrugged her shoulders slightly. " I did so well, that Filippo has promised to give me another lesson before dinner."

Agatha turned to her husband. " Shall we be back so early from Villincino ? "

" I think so," he answered. " We can go immediately after luncheon, and if we give two hours, it will be enough."

" But it's our first visit this season, you know, and we have usually found a great deal to do."

" I suppose," he said doubtfully, " that it 's really necessary for me to go with you. Yes, of course it is," he added quickly, " for the houses have to be gone over for the winter prizes ; I forgot them."

"Then let us give up the row," Mercede said grimly. "It's of little consequence as compared with the pleasure of these contadini."

"Could n't we postpone our visit for a day?" Filippo suggested.

"No," and Agatha spoke firmly. "I'll go alone willingly, but I won't neglect these poor people; knowing that I arrived yesterday, they will expect me."

"Then that settles it; and if I am late to-night, I'll give Mercede a lesson to-morrow."

Further discussion was postponed by the appearance of the Count; but Filippo soon found that he was out of favor with Mercede.

"I'm going to explore some of my old haunts," said Agatha to her husband, when alone with him after breakfast; "don't you want to come with me?"

"Are you going alone?"

"Not if you will come with me, dear."

"I'd like very much to go," he began; "but —"

This was more than she could stand.

"But what?" she demanded.

"I have something — some writing to do this morning," and he smiled mysteriously.

"I will go alone," she said gravely, and turned away to hide the trembling of her lip.

As she left the house it happened that she saw her husband bending over Mercede's shoulder, reading a passage from a book, while his companion watched his face earnestly. Agatha had often seen the book in Mercede's hands, and knew it to be the

" Elective Affinities." Filippo watched his wife furtively until she disappeared ; then he left Mercede
and went to the library, where he busied himself
writing some verses.

By and by Mercede entered the room as though
unconscious that he was there. As he looked up she
apologized and made a show of withdrawing.

"Don't go," he said, " I wish to say something to
you." She returned, and he continued, "I'm very
sorry, but I think we must postpone our rowing."

" I don't mind such a trifle," she replied ; " you
could n't have done differently, since Agatha was so
firm. Perhaps we had better not go at all."

" Why not, pray ? "

" Not unless Agatha can go with us."

He paused a moment, looking at her with an
incredulous expression.

" Why ? "

Mercede shrugged her shoulders in her expressive
way. " She is a young wife, and young wives sometimes have strange notions."

" Then they are different from Agatha ; she 's
above such nonsense."

" Are you sure, Filippo ? " and she watched him
closely ; " are you quite sure ? Not that Agatha
would willingly yield to a weak or selfish notion ;
but may she not be narrow, like most other women,
in her views of friendship ? Happily, I have forced
my way out of this terrible conventionality, and am
able to stand with you on the higher plane ; but is
she also able to do this ? "

" Agatha's idea of friendship," he replied sternly,

" is shown by her loyalty to you. That plane seems
to me to be high enough for any one."

Mercede was frightened. "Doubtless my fears
make a coward of me," she said hastily; " but I have
too little of the happiness of life to spare any important factor," and she studied his face intently.

" No one begrudges you any factor of your happiness, Mercede, so put such notions out of your mind;
they are not worthy of you. Agatha is definite whenever duty comes in. That is all her decisive words of
to-day meant; and to-morrow you will see how little
she will trouble herself whether I give you a rowing-
lesson or not." ·

" I don't doubt you are right; but can't you understand that I am tenderly sensitive to anything like a
rebuff?"

He made a gesture of impatience. " For Heaven's
sake, Mercede, don't be morbid!" he said. " If there
is anything I can't stand, it's that. Don't get into the
habit of looking over your shoulder for spooks, or
you'll knock your head pretty often, besides the
wear and tear on your nerves. If you would be rid
of spectres, drive them once and forever out of your
mind; that's where they are fed and made strong."

Mercede was not clear as to whether he was un-
willing to acknowledge Agatha's jealousy, or still
partly blind to it. Of one thing, however, she was
convinced; that he would not permit any reflection
upon his wife, no matter what he thought of her
conduct. She deemed it wise to throw a sop to
Agatha's jealousy, and thereupon set herself the
task of framing some method whereby the young wife

might more often accompany her husband without embarrassing his freedom. She decided that an escort for Agatha must be provided; it mattered little who he was so long as his presence secured a fourth member to the party. Mr. Dow seemed the most practicable person for the purpose, as he had nothing to keep him in Rome and would probably come without delay.

In Rome, the weather had become enervating, and the Faviola's were on the eve of their departure for Erba.

Gaeta had just finished her last music lesson, when her mother came into the room.

"Of course you will keep the same hours for me next autumn," said Gaeta to her master.

"With pleasure, Signorina."

"That reminds me," the Duchess interposed. "I intended speaking with you, Gaeta, about your music next winter. I doubt if you will be able to take two lessons a week."

"And why not?"

"You will be much more occupied, now that you have been presented.

"But I prefer not to neglect my music."

"We had better discuss the matter another time. For the present, Signor Veltri will perhaps permit us to leave the hours open."

"I am at your service," he replied; "pray take your own time." Then he went to Gaeta and extended his hand. "Good-by, Signorina," he said.

"Are you not coming to the train?"

"Remember, dear," the Duchess said, "that Signor Veltri is a busy man."

"But not too busy to come to the station if you will permit, Signora."

"Certainly, come if you can; but don't let the child's wish influence you."

"It will be a pleasure." And he bowed and left the room.

"Now, mamma, what does it mean?" asked Gaeta, dramatically.

"That you must go more into society next season, darling. You are becoming a young lady, and must do as the others do."

"But, mamma, at the expense of my music?"

"Not necessarily; but at the sacrifice of a lesson a week."

"Oh, I am beginning to hate society!" and Gaeta clenched her fingers viciously.

"Don't be a silly girl. Most girls would be delighted at the prospect."

"But most girls don't care for music as I do. I'd rather take a lesson than — than — there isn't anything else I care a fig for."

"Then that shows the necessity of broadening your interests."

"But it isn't necessary to break my heart doing it;" and she flung herself upon the sofa, and burying her face in the cushion, sobbed bitterly.

"Why, my darling," exclaimed her mother, going to her and stroking her hair, "what does it mean? You surely can't feel so badly at the mere thought of taking fewer lessons. It's most extraordinary!" and her brows contracted. "What is it, darling? tell me."

"I don't know," sobbed Gaeta, "but I'm very unhappy."

"'Unhappy'! Come, Gaeta, look up and talk with me;" and the Duchess seated herself beside her child.

The sufferer heaved a convulsive sigh, and lifting her head laid it upon her mother's shoulder.

"Tell me, pet, why this suggestion affects you so strangely."

"I don't know, I'm sure, except that I love my music."

"But I have n't proposed that you give it up."

"Not in so many words, no! But the effect will be the same; it will kill the enthusiasm," and she sighed deeply.

"Then you don't truly love music?"

"Well, then I must be crazy, and you'd better have the doctor," was the smothered comment.

"Why crazy, dear?"

"To go on so about something I don't care for."

"I don't wish to make you unhappy," she said, playing with the black tresses; "but think the matter- over. We will speak of it again in the course of a week or two."

"No, I don't want to wait," and Gaeta sat upright. "I'd a hundred times rather settle it now. I could n't endure the uncertainty."

"What would you propose?"

"Would you not agree to two lessons a week until Befana."

"Well, perhaps so. And then possibly you will find one a fortnight sufficient."

"No, I sha'n't," was the positive reply. "But I'll try to reconcile myself to one a week."

"Very well, dear, then arrange it so." She hesitated a moment, and fixing her eyes closely upon her child's face, added, "But why not take an occasional lesson from Sgambati?"

"No, no, mamma!" and her face grew pale. "Don't suggest my changing. I'm perfectly satisfied with Signor Veltri."

"I think you must be;" and the mother's eyes grew anxious.

CHAPTER XV.

SOMETHING OF A HERO.

WHEN Mr. Peter Dow received an invitation to the Villa Ricci he regarded it as a special grace, since he had failed to win from the Duchess Faviola anything more than an expression of the general hope that they might meet somewhere during the summer. Then his maxim, like a white-winged angel, had beckoned him to a phantom seat where he should as usual "sit down to get there." And now, lo! the unfolding hours had either brought to him the opportunity for which he was waiting, or had carried him abreast of the coveted chance; he knew not which it was, nor did he care.

He was more powerfully impressed than ever with the fact that his maxim rested upon a great principle; and going to the Piazza-di-Spagna he decorated himself with a blushing rose such as had often rested upon the heart of her to whom a beneficent fate seemed to be carrying him. Then jauntily swinging up the hill leading to the Pincio, he found a shaded seat near the fountain which splashes upon the chubby little Moses in his wicker ark, and settling himself comfortably he re-read Madame André's most welcome invitation.

" My cousin and her husband are with us," she wrote, " and we are bronzing ourselves like your Indians with our outdoor life. But my father is scarcely inclined for as much exercise as the rest of us, and thus occurs an " opening," as you sometimes say, for a congenial friend who will enjoy our quiet and informal life, and share our pleasure in this respite from society. Do we mistake in turning to you to complete our party? If not, send me a line to announce your early arrival."

Agatha had been consulted about the invitation, but instantly fathoming its purpose, had assented without hinting at the surprise she would otherwise have felt; for Mercede, while civil enough to Mr. Dow, had never shown any special desire for his society. On the other hand, the Count enjoyed the companionship of the American, who had a fund of quaint anecdotes of which the former never tired; and this fact gave Mercede an excuse for her proposal. Loreno was indifferent, but readily accepted Mercede's right to invite any one whom she chose to her home. And thus a week from the day the plan was broached, Mr. Peter Dow became the guest of General Ricci and his distinguished daughter.

The new-comer, however, scarcely fulfilled the expectations of his hostess. He early developed a tendency to wander off on his own account, and when no pre-arrangement was made he vanished with vexatious regularity in the direction of the Villa Faviola. One afternoon, a few days after his arrival, he found the Duchess alone and evidently preoccupied; for although she tried to sustain a conversation with her visitor, it was evidently not easy for her to do so.

20

Seeing this, Mr. Dow was about to make an excuse for returning to the Villa Ricci, when he summoned up courage to ask if Gaeta were at home.

"Yes, I think she is at the coffee-house," the Duchess replied; "at least, she went in that direction."

"Is the Duke with her?"

"No, she is alone."

"Would you mind my strolling over your lovely place?"

"Go, by all means, if you wish to; but it's rather warm, and you'll pardon me if I remain here, won't you?"

"Certainly; I may look Gaeta up later."

"Yes, do so," was the quick response; for the Duchess was not sorry to have her daughter's meditations disturbed, while she had hesitated to be the intruder.

Mr. Dow's pretence of taking a roundabout course to the coffee-house was a hollow fraud, and within ten minutes he stood behind the pensive figure of Gaeta seated upon a bench near the spot where, as the Duchess had told him, Loreno and Agatha had come the day they first met.

As Mr. Dow went forward Gaeta sighed and turned listlessly.

"You have certainly chosen a charming spot for a retreat," he said, lifting his hat, "but isn't it a trifle warm?" and he regarded solicitously the dark head bared to the powerful sun.

"Oh, it doesn't make any difference," said Gaeta, sadly.

" No ? "

" No; I 'm indifferent."

He took a chair near her, braving the sun for the sake of his purpose, and sat looking at her silently for a minute or two.

" What makes you so reckless ? " he ventured.

" Trouble," was the laconic reply.

" 'Trouble'? Why, what has gone wrong ? "

" I 'm not understood."

" What a pity ! I wish I might help you."

" It 's too late," and her tone was lugubrious.

Mr. Dow lacked nothing of sympathy, but he was utterly non-plussed.

" It is never too late," he remarked on general principles.

" Then it 's you who are too late," she said cynically.

His heart gave a bound. Could the misunderstanding refer to him ?

" Let me understand you clearly," he exclaimed. " In what way am I too late ? "

" The storm has broken, and no one can recall its shock."

" Who is at the other end of the storm ? " he inquired, trying to grasp the facts without sacrificing the metaphor.

" You would n't believe me if I told you ; no one would — it 's too unnatural."

" You know how much your friend I am."

" Yes ; but if love be but a name, what a mockery is friendship."

He sank back into his chair bewildered. He tried

twice before he could command his voice. "Has some one been deceiving you?"

"No; even that would have been better."

"Who has hurt you so, — a man, or a woman?"

She continued to look far off upon the opposite hills without replying. Then she said stoically, "Never mind."

His heart was deeply stirred by her misery, and he failed to see the childishness of her mood. Moving nearer, he leaned forward and tried to look into her face.

"When did it occur?" he inquired sympathetically.

"After luncheon."

"Did any stranger lunch with you?"

"No."

"Then the trouble was, as it were, domestic?"

"Yes."

"In that case I ought not to press the matter." He waited, and then moved a trifle nearer. "Gaeta," he said nervously, "my dear Gaeta, I wish I had the right —" as he called her by her Christian name she turned and looked at him in a way that quite disconcerted him, — "I wish, I say, that I had the right," he steadied himself and proceeded boldly, "to share even your domestic trials."

"It's very kind of you, and in a world of disappointment a stanch friend is not to be undervalued."

"I am some years older than you are, Gaeta —"

"I know that," she interrupted with marked dignity, "or I shouldn't permit you to address me so familiarly."

" Yet you know that a companion of experience is often a wise counsellor and guide."

" Yes, I suppose so ; and I 'll tell you frankly that I 'd trust you in this especial thing before any one else in the world, not excepting Aunt Agatha."

He stared at her in amazement.

" And the reason I 'd trust you," she continued, " is because we spoke of the matter once before, and I won you over to my side, and you 've been perfectly lovely ever since."

" Have I ? " he murmured.

" I need advice to-day," she continued freely ; " I feel that I need it very much, and as you are a man, and say you 'd be glad to aid a helpless girl, I 've half a mind to confide in you."

His heart was sinking, but his consequent gravity seemed to her quite appropriate.

" You 've heard about ' The Pilgrimage of the Rose,' to be given at Varese on Aunt Agatha's festa ? "

Although his throat was dry, he managed to utter the expected assent.

" Well, it 's really about that, but indirectly about something — " she looked again steadily at the hills — " about some one else."

Hope fluttered again in his heart, and he waited eagerly.

" Mamma, like all mothers, I suppose, is always on the alert to guard her daughter from committing some faux pas, and to-day she went too far ; " and the dark eyes grew bright with indignation.

He did not trust his voice, but his face convinced her of his sympathy.

"Yes; I regret to say such a thing, but mamma forgot herself."

"Indeed!"

"You know, of course, that Madame André is getting up some tableaux to illustrate the music, and she very kindly asked me to be the Rose. Now, of course I'm going to the festa, and the rehearsals would only take me to Varese a few days earlier, and Aunt Agatha urged mamma to let me go with her when she goes, and — and mamma simply won't.'"

"She has some good reason, I suppose."

"That's what one would suppose; that's what I supposed, and that's what I must deny. Her reason is shocking!"

The listener pursed his lips, but discreetly kept silent.

"At first she was merely negative, — and mamma can be negative and positive at the same time, — but little by little I got at the truth; it's because she has your old prejudice against Signor Veltri."

"Ah! he leads the orchestra, does n't he?"

"He leads the orchestra; and naturally he will also be there a few days before the performance," — she turned away her flushed face, — "and mamma does n't think it nice for me to be so friendly with one whom she calls a mere music-teacher."

Mr. Dow smiled slightly in spite of his low spirits. "Egad! she's in the dock this time, and things have a different look to her," he thought. He failed, however, to understand how the Duchess had committed the indiscretion of stating her objections so frankly; so he questioned Gaeta on this point.

"I saw through her veiled objection in a moment," she said, "and hating nonsense, I put the truth to her, and she could n't deny it; and so I left her and came out here to have a good cry."

Peter Dow rose abruptly, and walking to the wall on the brink of the steep fall to the valley, stood leaning upon it for fully five minutes, reasoning with himself and trying to regain his self-control. Presently he turned back and went to the young girl. His eye shone kindly, and he answered her inquiring look with a slight smile.

"Gaeta, my child," he said firmly, "I understand it all now, and perhaps I can help you. Will you trust so delicate a mission in my hands?"

"Yes, if you are willing to bother about the troubles of a mere girl like me."

"Yes, I 'm quite willing," and there was a quality in his voice which she failed to understand. "'If you don't win, at least cheer the victor,' is my motto," he continued somewhat blindly; "and I 'll try to say a good word for our friend Veltri, and rescue a sweet rose from a frost that threatens to nip it in the bud."

"How will you manage?"

"I can't tell without thinking it over; but if you wish to help me, you must be good friends with your mother and avoid seeming to take her words too much to heart."

"But mamma reflected upon Signor Veltri; and I want her and every one to know that I 'm willing, if it 's necessary, to stand right up and say that I 'm his friend."

" I don't doubt it; but that is n't necessary, and under the circumstances it would n't be friendly."

The young girl remained silent, evidently considering his words.

" I agree with you," she replied presently, " and I'll act upon your advice." Then turning impulsively, she put both of her hands into his, and added fervently, —

" Thank you so much, you dear old friend ! "

CHAPTER XVI.

FRANCESCO'S FRIEND.

IT was the afternoon of the feast of the Virgin, and the guests at the Villa Ricci went with their offerings to the little church of San Pietro, where, in obedience to an ancient custom, the parishioners were gathered in force to participate in the ceremony.

Although simple in its furnishing, the church was made gay with crimson hangings and flowers, while many candles illumined the building, from which the sunlight had been shut out.

As is usual in northern Italy, there were rows of wooden benches for the congregation, and these were filled with swarthy men and boys, and bright-eyed women and girls, the heads of all females being covered with shawls or scarfs of bright colors. An excellent copy of Guido Reni's Crucifixion — a gift from the Count Ricci — hung over the first altar to the left, while on either side of the chancel were two interesting frescos, one illustrating the conversion of Saint Paul, the other Christ blessing the Apostles. The altar was of gray marble, and this had been decorated with lovely flowers sent by Agatha's orders from Varese that morning, while about the chancel-rail of red marble the Duchess and Gaeta had wound garlands of white roses.

After vespers had been sung, Padre Sacconi announced that offerings would now be received. Then the people filled the aisle and moved slowly to the altar, before which they left their gifts, while the organ pealed merrily, and the priest sprinkled holy water upon the procession. Mr. Dow, who had never before seen this ceremony, noted the gifts with great interest. There was every sort of produce, all decorated with nosegays; some givers offering only a gourd or a turnip, in which, however, a sum of money was known to be hid. The richer members of the parish bore gifts of greater value, from wax torches to pieces of plate.

When all the donors had regained their places, Padre Sacconi blessed the gifts, and then (as was his privilege) proceeded to select one for himself. The choice was watched with anxiety and hope by all, and a murmur of approval arose as the honored father selected a little linnet in a cage, which a child had brought.

Then he announced that in accordance with custom the offerings would be sold to the highest bidder, for the benefit of the church, and he exhorted those present to bid often and liberally. In the sale which followed each youth tried to gain possession of the gift of his sweetheart, the result telling many a deep secret and causing many a pretty blush. The gourds and turnips created genuine excitement, but were usually captured by their donors, unless the sum bid exceeded the sum of money hidden within them, in which event the buyer was the object of great laughter. And now a rich mouchoir-case, which Agatha had made, was put up; and Mr. Dow, whose mercantile spirit was revived, and who permitted nothing to go cheap, girded his loins anew. As Loreno bid, Mr. Dow followed him; and thus they vied with each other until the prize reached a figure at which Filippo thought it best to resign, leaving Mr. Dow in possession.

Agatha was greatly disappointed, for she had made the case for Filippo. Yet she gave no sign of her regret, and was grateful that she had not when Mr. Dow, bringing his prize to her, said, —

" Now, Marchesa, you can make your husband a veritable gift; no, don't decline it! I bought it with that idea."

There was no time for further words, for he placed it in her hands and turned eagerly toward the priest to bid on Gaeta's gift. It was a gold pencil, and Mr. Dow, who was over-anxious, occasioned wonderment as he exclaimed hastily and in English, —

" I bid twenty-five dollars! "

" I said twenty-five dollars! " he repeated, as Padre Sacconi paused, bewildered by the unfamiliar tongue.

" You mean lire, I think," suggested Gaeta, behind him.

" No, I don't," he persisted; " I mean dollars."

" Why, that 's ever so many lire," she said.

" Well, I 'm crushing opposition," he replied, with a nod. " Let — me — see," he continued, as the priest waited expectantly. " Five times five — twenty-five; five times two — ten; and two are twelve — oh, call it one hundred and fifty lire! " he announced aloud in Italian.

The peasants looked at him as though he were crazy. "The Signore offers a year's rent for a pencil-case," they said one to another.

There was naturally no opposition, and he serenely tucked away his prize in his pocket. "I'd like to keep it myself," he thought; "but when you've once put your hand to the plough, it's a bad habit to look back."

Presently a small wax figure made by Mercede was offered for sale, and again Mr. Dow and Loreno were rivals; but this time Loreno showed no sign of faltering, and fairly routed his rival.

As Mercede turned and looked into his eyes her own eyes sparkled, and her color was uncommonly high.

"I think I'll go now," said Agatha, gravely.

"I shall wait to buy the drawing Francesco made," Mercede replied.

But Agatha was too much hurt to regard appearances, and without another word moved away. Seeing Filippo about to follow her, Mercede laid her hand upon his arm. "Wait, won't you?" she said; "I have counted on you to bid on the picture for me. I am sure Mr. Dow will gladly go with Agatha."

"Certainly," Mr. Dow replied, hastening after the retreating figure.

"Why did n't you buy Agatha's gift also?" Mercede asked in a low voice; "you should have done so, in spite of that idiot."

"I thought I should contribute enough by buying this statue."

"Oh, you men! you men!" and Mercede tapped her foot impatiently.

They had not long to wait before Francesco's drawing was displayed.

"Bid ten francs for me," Mercede whispered, "and then find Francesco and we will go."

Loreno made the bid, which was instantly answered by another for double the amount.

They looked at each other incredulously.

"Bid twenty-five," she whispered.

"Fifty!" answered the strange voice from the other side of the church.

"Who is it?" asked Mercede; "the drawing is of no value."

"Shall I bid again?" Filippo inquired.

"No," she said; "if some one else wishes it, let it go."

As she rose to her feet to leave the church, she looked toward the purchaser to see who he was; she saw Francesco talking to a gentleman, as they both examined the sketch, and at that moment the stranger looked up and their eyes met.

Mercede stood as though petrified, her cheek blanched, her lips slightly parted.

"What's the matter?" Filippo asked in alarm.

When she spoke, it was with great effort.

"I was looking for Francesco," she said; "but never mind — let us go."

The following morning General Ricci received a visitor. He was a square-shouldered man of about thirty-three years; his eyes were blue, he wore a large

moustache, and his bearing was soldierly. He came
to the villa on foot, and upon receiving his card the
General gave orders that he should be shown to
the library. They were together for more than an
hour, when the General went upstairs and presently
returned with Mercede; then another hour passed
before the door was swung open, and the General
accompanied his visitor to the loggia where the others were sitting.

The stranger was not only a handsome man, but
there was also something essentially easy and amiable about him that prepossessed one in his favor. As
he bowed and walked away, Francesco came around
the corner of the house, and catching sight of his
friend of the previous night ran joyously toward him.

"That's a friend I have n't seen for years," exclaimed the General as he joined the others; "and
here he turns up straight from Africa, where he 's
been burying himself; and strangest of all, happening in at the church last night he made friends with
Francesco, and then discovered that he was talking
with a grandson of mine."

While the General was speaking, the visitor was
chatting with Francesco as they walked away hand
in hand.

After waiting a few moments, Filippo entered the
house and looked into the drawing-room. It was
empty, and he went to the library. No one was there,
and he wandered on through the other rooms with
growing dissatisfaction.

"I wonder where Mercede is," he muttered. "It
does n't seem reasonable that my thoughtlessness

about the mouchoir-case could so upset her. Yet
she certainly has not been herself since last night. I
wish she would come down!" he said half aloud.
"I believe I'll send and ask her to go for a walk."

Thereupon he rang the bell and sent his invitation; but the maid brought back word that Madame
André was resting, and begged to be excused. He
was disappointed, and inclined to be cross. Going to
the library, he threw himself into a chair near the
window and tried to read; but he found his eyes
wandering from the book, and his thoughts reverting
to Mercede "resting" in the room over his head.
"It's a strange way to rest!" he exclaimed half
aloud, for the sound of footsteps in her room, as of
some one walking back and forth, did not cease.

Mercede was pacing the room, her face drawn, her
eyes burning. Now and again she would sob con-
vulsively, as though her nerves were unstrung, and
several times she wrung her hands in helpless anguish. She had expected the visitor, and was quite
prepared to be summoned to the library; but for
the question suddenly laid before her she had not
fortified herself.

"This gentleman is now a colonel," her father
had said to her after she had bowed formally to the
visitor, ignoring the hand he extended.

"Mercede," he exclaimed, "I acted shamefully
toward you and the child. I have come to ask your
pardon, and to do what I can to repair the wrong
you have suffered. My uncle is dead, and with his
property the title of Baron has come to me. I have
not played a game of cards since you last saw me,

nor have I a debt. Will you not let me make
amends to you and the child?"

"You may not be aware, sir," was the cold response, "that I have made a name far more honored
than yours, and far more to be prized by my son
than a title; therefore we are now independent of
you. Furthermore, I am no longer a mere woman,
but an artist; and my art is sufficient unto itself."

"That cannot be, Mercede," interposed her husband; "your art has only what you bestow upon it.
Its effect is relative to its borrowed power; through
it you lift or cripple those to whom you appeal. Your
art is most sensitive to your life, and the nearer you
fashion your life to God's natural laws, not only the
more happy you will be as a woman, but the more
influence you will have as an artist!"   · ·

"You will pardon me if I deny point-blank that
marriage has any effect upon art except a mischiev-
ous effect."

"You misunderstand me," he explained. "Of
course marriage bears no direct relation to art, but
character does; and I say that your life has been
gnarled and unsymmetrical, that it must have affected
your character and been woven into your art. What I
urge is, that you should make your life as near the
ideal life of a woman as is possible, if you would catch
the living spirit of Truth and stamp it upon your
work."

"I don't understand you," she said indifferently;
"and, any way, all this seems irrelevant. Be good
enough to come back to the original subject."

"You have missed the application of what I said;

I hoped to show you that even in your art-life the resuming of your full wifely relations would serve your purpose better than the life you propose leading."

" I do not agree with you," was the firm reply.

" But, Mercede, for God's sake don't be rash!" exclaimed her father. " Think of your son!"

" He being my son, the son of Mercede André needs nothing and asks nothing," was the proud answer.

" But," asked the visitor, " will Francesco think so when he is no longer a boy?"

She drew herself up haughtily. " God only knows what he may become, with such blood as is in him!"

" I haven't come to anger you, Mercede," was the soft answer, " and I wish we might consider this grave matter without bitterness."

" So we may, sir, if you and my honored father will only grasp the question as it is. Once I was dependent upon my father; now I am not. Once I was dependent upon you; now I am not. I have made — unaided — position, money, and an honored name. You come and ask me to sacrifice the result of my labor by exchanging independence for a bond from which I have worked so hard to escape; to take again a name I have striven to bury; to accept a condition it has been my aim to annihilate. Ask this for my own sake, and I laugh at you: you are wise, therefore, in asking in the name of Francesco; for his sake, I should, perhaps, consider before refusing."

" Cannot you forgive me, Mercede?" and he

21

looked at her yearningly. "It is not duty alone, but love that brings me back. Once you came to me of your own free-will; you obeyed your heart. Will the old love avail me nothing now? Let me try to bring it back to life. It was only when temptation overcame me that its fulness and sincerity were challenged. For my conduct I offer no excuse, yet can I never atone for it? That you have suffered terribly I know, and this knowledge has scourged me through all these years. Only my determination to wait until I had something to offer you and the child has kept me from coming to you long before. I am again regarded with respect as a man and as an officer; I am wealthy; I am able to offer you a position equal to your own. As a husband, I feel that I can make some amends for the past; as a father, that I can aid you in making our son what you would have him, and thus secure your present joy in him."

Such words could not fail to impress her. As she listened, her face lost its hardness, and for the first time she kept her eyes upon the speaker.

"If," he continued, "you have not a spark of love left for me, — which God forbid! — still let the lad's love be mine. Give him a father and me a son. Be generous, Mercede. Don't visit the sin of the father upon the child! Don't for pride's sake *risk the future of your child.*"

She started. His words were the very words with which Filippo had warned her in Paris. This repetition made her superstitious.

"What do you mean by that — about the child?" she asked.

"That a son needs the guidance and advice of a father as well as that of a mother; and also, that if we live apart his position will soon become painful, if not intolerable to him. You call yourself André — his name is Finelli. Does he never ask about his father?"

"Sometimes, in a childish way. But if you care so much for his happiness, why enlighten his present ignorance?"

"Because he is my son and heir."

"Born out of wedlock."

"Legitimatized by our subsequent marriage; and I am his legal guardian."

She grew white, and stared at him as the truth rushed over her.

"Then you mean to insist upon your rights as his father?"

"I do not mean to ignore my duty as his father."

"Whether I live with you or not?"

"Your living with me is a matter which affects my personal happiness, not my duty to my son," was the firm answer.

"In other words, you intend if possible to coerce me."

"Nothing is further from my thoughts. I shall wait for you to come to me, longingly but patiently."

"Will Francesco be taken from me?"

"Not necessarily. But I shall expect to see him freely, and to have a voice in his education and training."

No one broke the silence that followed, and for fully fifteen minutes each sat buried in thought.

Then their further communication was without bitterness, and resulted in the granting to Mercede of
such time for consideration as she might desire ; and
on her part she granted Colonel Finelli's wish to
come and talk with her again the following morning,
under the condition that he would not yet betray his
identity.

As Mercede paced her room, thinking of this interview and its results, the new conditions only served
to quicken her passion for Filippo. Fight against the
truth as she would, the struggle was narrowed down
to her love for him and her love for her child. She
knew well what her duty was; and although she
lashed herself into a fury at a choice being forced upon
her, this did not cloud her perception. The issue
had become too grave for self-deception of any sort.

" Yet why not live with Ernesto ? " she asked herself. " Why should it interfere with my friendship
for Filippo ? "

With the rushing, throbbing answer all further pretence or dodging was made useless. Every fibre of
her heart told her that she loved Filippo. Even to
think of joining her life to that of any other man was
abhorrent. But Agatha? Agatha had no reason to
complain. Was it not happiness enough to be Filippo's wife and the mother of his children ? Surely
Agatha need not begrudge the crumbs that fed a
famished heart! And Ernesto? He was not to be
considered. He had made his bed, let him lie in it !
And little Francesco? " Good God, good God ! "
was all the distracted mind could answer ; " what is
to be done ? what is to be done ? "

Thus she communed hour after hour, until at last relief came in the suggestion of a compromise : she would take her husband at his word, and postpone either her refusal or consent. In the mean time, hard though it would be, she would spare Francesco occasionally that he might go to his father. This would at least be a better arrangement than the one which had been suggested six years before, when her father, after paying the lieutenant's debts, had in vain tried to reconcile her and her husband. Then the young husband had unflinchingly insisted that his wife must return to his home, while she had been equally firm in refusing. She remembered that he had quoted her letter implying that she would return to him when his debts were paid ; to which she had replied, that after this promise was made he had stolen her marriage certificate, and used her maiden name in telegraphing to her, thus insulting her beyond forgiveness. In obedience to her father's wish she had gone to Rome to consider the matter further, and then her flight to Paris had put an end to the affair. She did not know that immediately after her flight her father had received a most penitent letter from the lieutenant, to which — in the first flush of anger — the General had replied that Mercede was no longer daughter of his. Yet she did know that her moral position had become vastly stronger, while her husband's was relatively weaker. He came now as a suppliant so far as she personally was concerned, and she would take advantage of the time offered her and postpone giving an answer. The necessity for this beating about the bush was exasperating, and she longed to dismiss the wanderer and have done with him ; but he was the child's father, and she knew him to be a determined man. While he had hope concerning her he would be much less exacting about Francesco, and she must trust to future events to guide her. At present, time was everything.

The more she considered this compromise the calmer she became, until at last her perturbation left her, and she prepared to go below and join Filippo.

Francesco had conceived a great admiration for the stalwart colonel who had talked with him so amiably at the church, who had bought the picture of the rabbits for fifty lire and liked it so well that he had said he would willingly have paid more, and who after the auction had walked as far as the lodge, — so interested was he in hearing of the rabbits, and the white peacock, and the pony that Uncle Filippo had promised to send from Varese. After their greeting to-day the Colonel suggested that as he had walked to the lodge last night, it would be but fair for Francesco to accompany him to the lodge now.

" Oh, but I can show you a short cut," was the reply, — " by the iron gate."

" Which is nearer from here, — the lodge, or the gate ? "

" The lodge is a little nearer."

" Then show me the gate, if your rabbits can spare you."

" I 've just left them. I don't suppose you 'd care to see them now ?"

" Would n't I, though ! But I don't think I will go

to-day; but I hope sometime to see them — and before very long," he added with a peculiar wistfulness in his voice.

Then they chatted about birds, and this led the Colonel to speak of a parrot that he had brought from Africa; and he told his wide-eyed listener several little adventures which seemed to the boy to be simply marvellous.

" I 'd like to go to Africa! " Francesco exclaimed.

" Would you? Do you know where it is? "

" Yes; it 's where the nigger-minstrels come from."

" Perhaps it is; although the minstrels look to me as though they came from London."

" Are the people of London black like them? "

" No; but the smoke of London makes one almost as black as the minstrels."

" What a jolly place! " and the youngster's eyes glistened. Then he added with a look of admiration, " You 've seen lots of places, have n't you? "

" I 've travelled a little, and so shall you when you are older."

" My papa is away travelling," Francesco remarked.

The blue-eyed stranger glanced at him quickly, and then his eyes lingered fondly on the innocent face as the boy stood holding the gate open.

" Is he? " he replied.

" Yes; he 's been away a long time."

" Indeed! "

" I wish he 'd come back," and the wish was emphasized by a little sigh; " I 'd like to see him. He must know heaps of adventures by this time."

" Do you remember him at all ? "

" No ; that is, sometimes I think I do, but mamma says it's nonsense."

" What do you think you remember about him ? "

The lad paused, and seemed as though trying to recall a dream.

" I can just remember, sometimes, some one else besides mamma, and I think he used to take me up with him on a horse, because I remember how high it was ; and I know he had spurs, although I did n't know that he only fastened them on, for I was very little when he went away."

The father's eyes looked eagerly into those of his son, and his voice was fervent when he spoke. " Did you love him ? " he asked.

The little chap closed his eyes, and had recourse to the gentle hiss whereby the Italian gives token of that which is inexpressible.

" But how can you remember ? "

" Because I love him now."

Impulsively — joyously the father bent down and kissed the upturned face.

" God bless you, little one ! " he said, — " God bless you for your loyalty ! "

CHAPTER XVII.

IN THE GROVE.

Upon going downstairs Mercede went to the library, where Filippo was still sitting with a book in his hands. He rose instantly, and came toward her.

"Don't speak to me for a moment," she said gravely, waving him off and seating herself at the writing-table. "I have a note to write."

She took up a pen, and quickly wrote the following lines: —

My DEAR FATHER, — This grave affair is one which I alone can decide, and the knowledge of which I alone should control. Therefore I write to ask you neither to mention it to me nor to any one without my consent.

Affectionately,

MERCEDE.

Enclosing the note in an envelope, she addressed and sealed it, and going to her father's room left it upon his table.

Now her heart was comparatively light, and as she entered the library again her face wore the smile which Filippo had missed since the previous evening.

" Is all your business done ? " he demanded.

" Nearly, if not quite."

" I congratulate you ! You bore its weight badly."

" I hate business, and worry over it, I know."

" Rather a nice-looking fellow, that soldier ! " he said nonchalantly.

" Yes, not at all ill-looking."

" Is he coming again ? "

" Yes ; to-morrow morning."

" Who is he ? " he asked bluntly.

" A friend of my father."

" But you had met him before this morning ? "

" Yes."

He was silent again, playing with a book upon the table.

" He 's just from Africa, I believe ? "

" Yes. He has inherited some property and a title, — and now is going in for art."

" Oh, indeed ! " and Filippo's face brightened. " What sort of a subject does he wish ? "

" Two figures."

" There 's your Tristan and Isolde."

She hesitated, and then laughing nervously replied, " I don't think that would suit him. Hagar and Ishmael would probably be more to his taste."

" Is he lugubrious, then ? "

" Philanthropic ! But I 'm tired of business ; let 's go for a row."

Colonel Finelli called the following morning and found Mercede awaiting him. She had on her hat, and proposed that they should walk away from the house. The suggestion gave him hope, and he cheerfully acquiesced. Mercede led him out of an ivy-covered door at the back of the house, and crossing a court containing fountains and beds. of flowers, stepped upon the lawn, which, broken here and there by cypress and palm trees, swept down to the grove. This part of the wood was laid out in huge aisles stretching far away until lost in the bend of the grounds. Making their way across these, they came suddenly upon a lovely outlook. They were upon the edge of a slope thickly grown with trees; beneath them the great plain of Lombardy stretched far away to the hills in the hazy distance, the fertile vineyards and poderi blending their harmonious tints until the eye failed to distinguish between them, and turned gratefully aside to the picturesque silhouette of Alzate-con-Verzago, its ancient tower seeming to be upheld by the clouds.

Mercede seated herself upon a rustic bench, and both remained silent. " I should rejoice in this view for one reason, if for no other," Mercede remarked presently,—"that the trees shut out Visconti's showy monument and the grim unsightly pile of the Villa Inverigo."

"I agree with you," was the reply. "I cannot understand how such a barrack is considered one of Cagnola's masterpieces."

" The gods can do no wrong, and Cagnola was deified by his admirers."

He longed to introduce the subject by which his thoughts were absorbed, but patiently awaited her pleasure.

Several times she made up her mind to suggest the compromise upon which she had decided, but somehow she found it difficult to do so. As the minutes passed, however, she realized that the ice must be broken.

"After so many years of separation," she began, "the principal influence in the affair you mentioned yesterday is naturally our love for Francesco."

He watched her gravely, but made no reply.

"I have, of course, given the subject hours of most anxious thought," she continued, "and I feel that with a spirit of concession governing us both we may easily come to a satisfactory conclusion."

She had spoken very slowly and distinctly,—rather as if she were reciting a prearranged speech,—and as she paused to moisten her dry lips she was conscious of being very nervous. Her listener inclined his head as she looked at him for response.

"Don't you agree with me?" she asked, unable to bear his silence.

"I am not yet clear as to what you have in mind."

"Then I will tell you simply and directly. It is Francesco whom you love; it is Francesco whom you need, and whom you can serve. As for me, if it were not for the boy I would not consider it."

She paused, but he only inclined his head again.

"But for the child's sake I am willing to consider the question of waiving my — well, my indifference, provided by so doing I do not lose the results of the terrible struggle I have made since you — since we parted."

"For which," he said, repeating the words he had used the day before, "I scourge myself day and night."

She raised her eyebrows slightly. "Be that as it may, the fact remains that I no longer need you."

"But, Mercede —"

"Nor do you need me."

He leaned toward her, his eyes bent earnestly upon hers and his hands trembling. "As God is my judge," he exclaimed, "I do assure you — "

"Pray remain calm," she interposed; "we can discuss the matter much more satisfactorily without excitement."

"But is your love truly dead?" he asked. "Is there no living ember left?"

"The *sentiment* I had," she replied with corrective emphasis, "although it survived disgrace, was scarcely likely to survive insult."

The calm reply struck deep, and his eyes fell.

"Am I to understand," he said presently, "that you will not consent to live with me?"

"Not yet, — I cannot!"

"Oh, Mercede!" and his voice showed the depth of his disappointment.

"If you wish to withdraw your offer of time to me, pray do so," she said quietly; "or if you wish further time to consider this subject, by all means take it."

"I need no time!" he exclaimed, rising and standing before her. "It's the old question, and I have thought about it a thousand times. My duty is to do justice to Francesco, and I will do it; but my desire is to prove my sincere love for you as well as for

him. I have made your life bitter, Mercede ; may I
not make some atonement by years of devotion ? I
cannot believe that the old love is dead. We are
still young, and I dare hope may have many years of
happiness. I shall rejoice in your great talent, and
never embarrass your artistic career in the slightest
way. Although now you feel that I am nothing in
your life, my love shall rekindle yours ! Your life
shall grow fuller and richer, and even your art shall
be the gainer."

" I will think about it," was her brief response.

He looked at her silently, and then sighed. " I
suppose," he said, " that the only course open to me
is to leave everything to your pleasure."

" Thank you," she said with chilling politeness.

He lingered, searching her face for some sign of
relenting.

" I suppose I must leave you and be patient," he
said ; " but may I see Francesco before I go ? "

" Yes ; but be guarded. He is at the lodge waiting for you."

He stepped forward quickly, his face bright with
hope. " This was very thoughtful, Mercede," he
said.

" I am not without feeling ; I remember that you
are his father."

Impulsively he seized her hand. " Give me hope,
my darling ! " he exclaimed. " Give me hope that I
may also be a husband to you ! " He looked down
upon her longingly, hoping to see her resolution fal-
ter ; but without sign of relenting she withdrew her
hand.

His eyes filled with pain. "Before I return, Mercede," he said, "try to think more kindly of me, for no one on earth loves you as I do."

"Possibly," she remarked.

He lingered a moment longer; then summoning his strength of will he turned away and left her.

CHAPTER XVIII.

THE VILLA LORENO.

MR. Dow felt the weight of the responsibility he had assumed in regard to Gaeta's theatrical career, and having conned various plans for the fulfilment of his promise, determined at last to follow his golden rule, and await the development of circumstances. His maxim seemed fraught with fortune, for a few days later Agatha opened his way.

It was during a long ride, and the Marquis and Mercede having galloped on ahead, Mr. Dow and Agatha were left in the rear together.

Agatha had spoken of the fête to be given her at Varese upon her birthday, and expressed the hope that Mr. Dow would arrange to be present. He accepted with becoming gratitude, and this led them to speak of the preparations which were making. Among the other incidents of the occasion, Agatha mentioned the "Pilgrimage of the Rose," describing the tableaux which were to illustrate the music.

"Who will be the Rose?" asked Mr. Dow.

"Gaeta."

"Then this is what she referred to," he said, "when she told me that her mother objected to her giving the time necessary for rehearsal at Varese."

" Did she? " and Agatha seemed perplexed.

" Yes ; and I suspect that it was on account of your charming conductor, Signor Veltri."

" What! the Duchess objects to him ? "

" So I understood from Gaeta."

" How extraordinary ! Why ? "

" The Duchess thinks discretion is advisable, I believe."

" How absurd ! Did you gather the impression from Gaeta that there is any reason for this? "

" Her mind seemed full of the spectacle."

" Of course. I 'll see my sister-in-law and talk with her. Gaeta must keep the part, for there is no one to take her place."

" I hope you will succeed, for her heart seems set upon it."

" Poor little thing ! "

" Yes," answered the hypocrite, blandly ; " it is n't to be supposed that she comprehends her mother's real reason, but all the same it 's the worst possible course to pursue."

" You are quite right ; the Duchess will simply suggest the thing to her."

" And by making it forbidden fruit, make the temptation irresistible."

" Precisely."

Thus it was that Mr. Dow sat quietly " waiting to get there," while Agatha wound the machinery.

That same afternoon she walked over to the Villa Faviola, and while the General, who was her escort, talked with the Duke in the library, Agatha argued with her sister-in-law in the latter's boudoir. What-

22

ever form of argument she chose, proved to be the
right one; for at the end of thirty minutes the
Duchess agreed to permit Gaeta to go to Varese a
few days before the Duke and herself, provided
Agatha and Mr. Dow would watch her sufficiently
to keep her out of mischief.

"I shall be rather busy," Agatha rejoined, "but
I'll delegate Mr. Dow, who will have nothing else to
do, to be her guardian angel until you come."

This decision Mr. Dow received with preternatural
gravity, but upon communicating it that same evening to the eager Gaeta, his features relaxed.

. Since Filippo's arrival at Erba nothing apparently
had been further from his thoughts than the idea of
shortening his visit and leaving Agatha behind him.
As the time drew near for the departure of her
cousins, Mercede grew more reconciled to the idea of
going to Varese. To be a mere guest in Filippo's
house, and to see Agatha presiding over it as its mistress, would no doubt be hard to bear; but Filippo at
any price was better than no Filippo. Besides, what
excuse could she give for absenting herself from
Agatha's fête?

"I hear that Varese is greatly excited about the
fête," said Filippo to his wife one evening when they
were alone.

"I suppose so; it is so quiet there."

"We shall have our hands full, shall we not, — you
with the decorations and the rest, and I with the
open-air theatre?"

"Yes, indeed; but Signor Veltri wrote from Milan,
you know, that the orchestra is engaged, and he will

bring it with him next Monday, and my part of the preparations is already well in hand. You are not anxious about the stage, are you?"

"No—not about the stage itself," he said dubiously; "that can be arranged."

"About anything else?"

"I must confess I wish the tableaux could be taken off my hands."

Her heart sank, for she saw what was in his mind.

"Don't you think," he added, "that Mercede might be willing to go over and help us?"

She had been dreading this. She felt quite equal to the task before her, provided her mind was relieved from the strain of Mercede's presence; but simply to transfer to Varese the galling trials of the past few weeks would, she felt, blight her spirit and paralyze her energy.

She felt that the wear and tear of this constant self-repression was undermining her strength; that she should break down unless she had relief, if only temporary, from the anguish of seeing Mercede's complacency at her influence over Filippo. Yet she did not lose sight of her general purpose, and believed that to oppose her husband's wish would be most unwise. If he were conscious that she had reason for pain, he would be doubly sensitive to anything that might seem a protest from her; and his apparent indifference, or, to say the least, his blindness to her humiliating position, was a sufficient indication that any protest — even though indirect — would be most ill-timed and reactionary. Nevertheless, she could not reconcile herself to the thought of losing her anticipated respite, and could have cried with disappointment. The first temptation to oppose Filippo's wish was conquered, yet not completely: she did not lose sight of her purpose, but risked a compromise.

"I think Mercede's aid would be invaluable in the tableaux," she said, breaking the long pause, "but I'd rather not have her come until two or three days after I get home. You see, she has never been to the villa, and I should like to look it over."

"Still, Mercede is n't like company. You need n't feel sensitive about her."

"Perhaps not; but any woman will tell you that after an absence of many months she would wish time to glance over her house before receiving even a near relative as a guest."

"I really don't see good reason for such formality. If you have n't confidence in your housekeeper, get another."

"Don't be impatient with me, dear boy!" she said pleadingly. "I only suggest that we go, say on Friday, and ask Mercede and my uncle to follow on Monday, the day Veltri arrives."

"How about Mr. Dow and Gaeta?"

It had been her intention to take them with Filippo and herself, but she changed her plan on the instant.

"They won't be needed before Monday, either."

He was somewhat surprised at her answer, but he made no further opposition to her wish.

The Villa Loreno, overhanging the hamlet of Gazzada, and four miles distant from Varese, was the pride of its district, and when the family was absent, visitors to the neighborhood were brought to see it. The grounds were beautiful, and thirty gardeners were always employed in keeping the place in perfect condition. This number was not indeed needed, but the Marquis made it a training-school for young men around Varese, who being trained at the Villa Loreno, were in great demand, even as far as Como and Lugano. He was opposed to the giving of money without some return, believing it to be harmful rather than beneficial to the recipient, and in obedience to this theory gave employment to as many of the poor as he could. No young man felt that he need be idle, with the chances opened up to him by the Marquis; and Filippo's efforts compared very favorably with Agatha's work for the benefit of the Varese damsels, the aggregate of their efforts really adding much to the welfare of the surrounding district.

Filippo had driven to the station to meet the General, Mercede, Mr. Dow and Gaeta,— the first arrivals for the festa. Mercede seemed unusually grave, and this fact was made conspicuous by the high spirits of the others. When the carry-all swung past the lodge and entered the grounds, an involuntary exclamation of delight sprang to Mercede's lips. A vast English lawn, bordered by a dense grove, swept up to the distant villa, beyond which the swelling outline of the lower Alps climbed higher and higher until its soft purple green merged into dazzling white as it mounted to the tip of the Fleischhorn, on to the peaks of the great Mischabel, and then shot upwards, verily to the clouds, as it skirted the stupendous precipices of Monte Rosa the Majestic.

"There it is! Isn't it a magnificent view?" exclaimed the General, who had been discoursing upon it since leaving Erba.

"It seems much the same that we have, except that the mountains are nearer," Mercede replied.

"Perhaps,—just in front. But look, Mercede! see how the range comes up as we move. See!" and the old man rose to his feet, carried away by enthusiasm.

"Where does it end, Marquis?" Mr. Dow asked impressively, as mountain after mountain was revealed, until the whole Pennine range was in sight, while yet other ranges appeared beyond.

"Do you see that needle-point rising high beyond the others?" Filippo said, pointing behind them; "it looks like vapor, but I can see it distinctly."

"Yes. Well, what is it?"

"Monte Viso."

"Nearly two hundred kilometres from here!" exclaimed the General.

"How many miles is that?" asked the American.

"About one hundred and ten," said Filippo.

"And I see mountains even farther."

"Yes; from the tower yonder,"—and he indicated a granite tower upon a knoll, — "on a clear day, one gets a fair view of the Maritime range."

"Yet one tires of such a long view," Mercede said listlessly;—"at least I do;" and she turned her eyes

away from the mountains and glanced critically at
the house which they were approaching. "There's
Agatha!" and she waved her hand.

As Mercede entered the house she could not but
be struck with the splendor of its proportions and
effect.

Filippo joined her, and ushered the way into a large
ante-sala like that of some old feudal castle. The
ceiling was panelled, and from the centre hung a
chandelier of beaten iron. The walls were covered
with tapestries of rich design, and lined on two
sides by a carved wainscoting, against which stood
long and highly-carved benches, upon which a dozen
or more cushions were thrown. The floor was of
marble; the doors were broad and built into the
room like storm-doors, the sides of the frames and
the doors themselves being triumphs of the carver's
skill. A long hinge of brass ran the entire width of
each door, both at the top and bottom, while a flat
handle of the same metal hung upon a hinge and
required to be lifted when used. Above each door
was an elaborate over-door rising, not unlike a cathe-
dral window, to the ceiling. Great brass fire-dogs
stood under a massive chimney built out into the
room and decorated with the Marquis's coat of arms.
In front of this fireplace stood another bench with
cushioned seat. The window-hangings were of an
antique fabric of dull colors that blended with the
general tone of the room, and at this moment the
casements of colored glass were thrown open to
admit the summer air.

Agatha, who had entered behind Mercede, glanced

at her face with interest as she looked about her critically.

"It's charming," she said coldly.

"I suppose you are tired and would like to go to your own room," said her hostess.

When Mercede was alone she sank into a deep arm-chair and looked about her. The room was large, the ceiling wainscoted, — as were most of the rooms through which she had passed, — the fireplace was open and large, with a cushioned bench before it, as in the ante-sala. The walls were hung with fine old silks from the looms of Varese, the floors were of polished wood, and the furniture of quaint design. The bed was covered by a rich canopy, and protected on all sides by damask curtains. Rising, she went through a door leading to a luxurious dressing-room, beyond which was a diminutive private chapel. She glanced carelessly around it, pausing only to examine a carved crucifix above the prie-Dieu, and then closing the door she turned the key and went back to her bedroom.

"It's undeniably splendid," she thought, "but I should think she would feel lost in it. A cottage, with roses and a cat and some bird-cages, is more in her style. This dwarfs a woman like Agatha, — 'Agatha Page,' as he used to say in Paris." She lay back in her chair, her eyes fixed upon the wall. "Ah! what a fool I was!" she exclaimed, suddenly clenching her fingers. "Yet how could I know? I played into her hands; I praised her; I excited his fear of losing her. I must needs meddle, and now I have my reward. He loves me, I love him; and she stands between us, — she and Ernesto. But what of it? Which is better worth having, — the shadow, or the substance? What, I wonder, will be the outcome of it all? On one thing, however, I'm determined," — and her eye shone coldly, — "neither Agatha nor Ernesto nor any one nor every one shall come between Filippo and me! Let Agatha keep his name and his keys; his heart is mine."

It is to be hoped that Mr. Dow did his duty conscientiously during the next few days, for neither Agatha nor Filippo had much time for anything except the arrangements for the coming festival. The music was entirely in the hands of Signor Veltri, while Filippo devoted himself to the arranging of the stage upon the lawn in front of the house. Yet an orchestra cannot rehearse without intermission, nor can the most willing of subjects pose without rest. Both Veltri and Gaeta, therefore, had many a tempting opportunity for pleasant chats and walks in which Mr. Dow was supposed to participate, but as Gaeta had unearthed from her uncle's library a famous novel by Manzoni, which she advised him to read, while the " youngsters," as he called them, talked together, he became so absorbed in his book that he failed to interrupt them. Then too he developed a sudden lameness of the right leg, — an inconvenience too trifling to mention to his hostess, but which soon after starting for a walk with his young companions necessitated his resting upon some shady bank which they should repass on their homeward way.

Gaeta as the Rose was sure to be charming, while the other characters of the tableaux were gladly undertaken by young neighbors of the Marquis, whose ardor and assiduous rehearsing under Mercede's direction made amends for the shortness of the time granted them for preparation. Mercede certainly worked with enthusiasm, while Filippo was here, there, and everywhere; but both found frequent need of consulting together, while Agatha worked alone, with pain in her heart and a song upon her lips.

CHAPTER XIX.

OLD ASSOCIATIONS.

AT last the morning of the festa broke, bright and clear; and as Veltri left his room for an early stroll, he found the servants moving about noiselessly, strewing freshly-cut flowers over the mosaic floors, and twining garlands about the balusters of the stairs, while growing plants and spreading palms almost hid the walls, and outside upon the veranda thick festoons hung between the pillars.

"It must delight her eye," thought the youth; "but will anything gladden her heart, even on this day?" Then he walked on slowly, thinking as he went. "They are inseparable," he muttered; "they stroll together before breakfast; at the meal they talk together; then she hovers about him while he smokes; when at work they are constantly consulting together; dinner finds them ·absorbed in each other; the evening emphasizes the devotion of the day; while the brave wife smiles into the faces of her guests, and all try to ignore that which cannot be hidden. What a painful time it has been! I fear there is trouble near for these dearest of my friends."

He heard a footstep approaching, and looked up. It was the Marquis, who held in his hand a large bunch of forget-me-nots.

"Good-morning!" Loreno exclaimed cheerily; "are they not making the house beautiful?"

"Beautiful indeed!"

He held up the flowers. "And see these," he said. "On the Marchesa's birthday I always gather flowers for her with the dew upon them. It baptizes the new year!"

"Then God's peace go with it!" exclaimed the youth, fervently.

Loreno raised the flowers admiringly, and as Veltri looked at them his face became sad,—a fact which aroused his companion's interest.

"Don't they please you?" he asked.

"I recalled the old legend which gave the flower its name,—at least in poetry."

"I don't remember it."

"A knight in reaching for a bunch upon the bank of the Danube fell into deep water, and as he was swept away by a heartless current he flung the flowers at the feet of his lady, crying, 'Vergiss mich nicht!' Yes, they are very pretty, but it was a poor exchange."

"You are more poetical than I am."

"I confess flowers seem symbolical."

"And diabolical, I should think, from your point of view."

"In some cases even that."

Their eyes met for an instant, and then Loreno, coloring slightly, moved away, but immediately turned back, and said quietly, " I don't believe, Veltri, that I interpret your meaning rightly. But I won't stop longer, for I don't like your mood." And turning on his heel he strode toward the house.

As he ascended the steps of the veranda Madame André came out of the door.

" Are these not lovely? " he asked, holding up the flowers.

She glanced at them and her manner changed.

" Yes, very pretty indeed," she answered coldly.

" I hope," he exclaimed, " that Agatha will appreciate them more than the rest of you seem to."

She raised her eyebrows slightly. " Who else has seen them? "

" Veltri; they made him very mournful."

She evidently did not care to dwell upon the flowers, and asked where he had met Signor Veltri.

" He was going toward the garden."

" I'll go look for him," she said, walking down the steps.

" Very well; I'll take these upstairs and then join you."

" You've evidently had your walk," she said, without looking back; " I'll go alone this morning."

He stood looking after her with a puzzled expression upon his face. " Early rising doesn't seem to agree with this household," he muttered dryly, as he went into the house.

When Agatha opened her eyes, her first glance was toward her dressing-table, and as she saw the flowers her heart gave a quick bound. Hastily going to the emblems of her husband's thoughtfulness, she bent down and kissed them with a sense of joy she had not known for many a long day. She told her maid to lay out a white muslin dress; and as she stepped from her room with a bunch of the forget-me-nots on her breast and the old bright expression lighting up her face, she seemed to have caught the freshness of the morning.

Her heart beat rapidly as she saw her husband in the corridor below awaiting her coming. He came forward to meet her, and kissing her whispered, " Many happy returns — Agatha Page." Then tucking her arm within his own he led her forward to receive the congratulations and compliments of the others.

In the centre of the table was a huge basket of flowers sent by the peasants of the neighborhood, and around her plate were ranged various gifts.

She thanked each giver in turn, and at last gave her attention to a lovely copy upon porcelain of the Sistine Madonna, which did not bear any name.

" Oh, how beautiful ! " she exclaimed, "and my favorite painting. Whom have I to thank for this ? "

No one spoke.

" There seems to be something written on the back," suggested Mr. Dow.

She turned the picture and read silently some birthday verses written by her husband.

They were dated at Erba. This, then, was the mysterious " writing " that one morning while there he had remained at home to finish.

Agatha was humbled, and without comment turned and kissed him fervently. It seemed as though a new era of happiness had opened with the new year.

" Read the verses to us," suggested the General.

" I protest ! " exclaimed Filippo.

A chorus of entreaty, however, overruled his modesty, and Agatha read the verses aloud.

" What sort of metre do you call that? " inquired Mr. Dow, critically.

" Ante - Chinese Imperial," responded Loreno, gravely.

Mr. Dow smiled, although doubtfully, for he rather dreaded tilting with this scornful young Marquis.

" What do you mean? " the Count asked.

" Upon the Chinese stage," explained Filippo, " royalty is expressed by the walk of the actor personifying it. He moves in a set fashion, lifting each foot high and throwing it forward with a motion not unlike that of a pawing horse. His movement, therefore, is embarrassed by the need of keeping to his Imperial step. In the same way real poetry is recognized by its metre. But mere poetical expression is but a peasant, and may walk as naturally as it pleases ; while my homely thought shuffles humbly on in the way most easy to it, without for an instant presuming to appropriate the recognized step of royalty."

This explanation seemed to amuse every one except Agatha and Mercede, — the wife, because she thought the lines were charming ; the artist, because even this slight defiance of conventionality gratified her.

It had been arranged that the morning should be passed quietly, as the afternoon and evening would be fatiguing. At three o'clock the peasantry were to offer their congratulations, and Loreno had arranged to give them a luncheon in the grove, followed by games for prizes until sunset. At dark there were to be fireworks such as the simple peasants had never dreamed of, and at nine o'clock a hundred or more of the gentry of the surrounding country had been invited to attend the performance of "The Pilgrimage of the Rose," to be followed by a ball, for which preparations had been making for several days.

"Well, Agatha Page," said Filippo, taking both her hands in his, "where shall we go, and what shall we do this morning? This afternoon, I fear I shall be very busy."

"Let us go for a stroll," she said, "and then to the boat-house, where you shall read to me."

So while Mercede was sitting on the piazza talking with Mr. Dow and Veltri, and wondering where Filippo could be, she caught sight of him and Agatha going across the edge of the lawn.

Suddenly her face lighted with pleasure. "He's coming for me," she thought, as she saw Filippo turn and come back. "Shall I go, or shall I give him to her for this whole long morning?"

He came straight toward her and ascended the steps. She followed him with her eyes expectantly. He smiled pleasantly and nodded.

"I forgot something," he said, and passed into the house.

Mercede scarcely concealed her chagrin. Then it flashed across her mind that his words were only a cloak to his real purpose in returning, and that he was waiting for her. Making an excuse she left her friends, but Filippo was not in the corridor. She smiled as she heard some one whistling in the library, and glancing through the partly-opened door saw him looking along a row of books.

She pushed the door open and entered.

" Can I help you ? " she inquired.

" Come in," he responded cordially. " You are just the one I was wishing for."

" Yes? " and Mercede thought to tease him a bit. " Do you wish me to help you to find some book ? "

" If you would be so kind."

She admired his sang froid, but appeared to take him at his word. "What book is it ? "

"The one you asked me to read to you yesterday."

The hint seemed broad, but she kept her countenance.

" It 's in my room," she replied ; " I 'll get it."

" Thank you."

As she brought it down and placed it in his hands she waited curiously to see what he would do next.

" Au revoir," he said, moving toward the door.

" Good-by," she responded, with inward amusement. Then as he stepped into the hall she called his name, and he stopped and looked back.

" Where are you going to read, — in the grove ? "

"No ; Agatha suggested the boat-house."

Her eyebrows knit with genuine surprise. " Agatha ! Are you going to read our book to her ? "

"I thought she would enjoy it; don't you think so?"

She did not reply, but stood looking at him.

"I did n't suppose you wanted it for her," she said, breaking the silence.

He came forward. "Perhaps you were going to read it yourself."

"Never mind; I can find something else."

"No, indeed; I won't consent to take it. I did n't think of your wanting it, for you said you wished to read it with me."

She looked at him searchingly yet half smilingly.

"Are you serious?" she asked.

"Certainly; did n't you?"

"I mean about reading that book to Agatha."

"I confess I was looking for it, but something else will do just as well." His eye fell upon a small volume on the shelf behind her. "There is De Musset, I'll take that;" and he went and took down the book.

Without another word or look Mercede arose and left the room. He stood staring after her for a moment. "I suppose every genius is eccentric," he said; "but she seems particularly nervous this morning." Then he started to rejoin his wife.

As he rounded a bend of a shaded path he discovered Agatha talking with what at first sight appeared to be an animated cornucopia, for a huge basket of this shape was strapped upon the back of a young girl, its capacious mouth coming above her head, while its point reached nearly to her ankles. As she turned a little he saw that her braided hair was adorned

with gay ribbons, while around her neck a white
cloth was pinned which fell to her waist and hung
loose about her arms like a primitive dolman. A
checked apron of coarse stuff nearly covered her
dress, which reached to the neatly-turned ankles, and
attracted his attention to the dainty feet clad in
striped stockings and shod with shoes of wood, the
soles of which were raised several inches from the
ground by what may be described as double French
heels, — one at the curve of the foot and the other
at the toe. Above the latter a leather band nailed
on both sides of the shoe ran over the wearer's foot,
which enabled her by the aid of a gliding motion to
keep from casting the picturesque things. She held
a small wicker basket containing wild lilies-of-the-
valley, which she was offering to Agatha. As Filippo
drew nearer, he saw his wife accept the flowers,
whereupon the delighted girl kissed both the Marchesa's hands, and with blushing cheeks and gleam-
ing teeth dropped a little courtesy and turned to go
away.

"Wait, little one!" he called.

The girl turned in surprise.

"And who are you?" he inquired.

"Bettina, the baker's daughter, Eccellenza." And
she dropped another courtesy.

"And why did you give the Marchesa these
flowers?"

"I picked them for her festa, and brought them
now, as I cannot come this afternoon."

"You are very thoughtful, but the basket is
empty."

" Yes, Signore ; the Marchesa insisted upon my keeping it."

" Well, I will ask the Marchesa to accept it ; and in its place perhaps you will do me the favor of going to Varese and buying a work-basket I saw yesterday in a window near the post-office." He wrote a line upon a card. " Give the shopkeeper this card, and he will give you your basket."

" Oh, Signore, this is too much ! "

" I wish you to be reminded of us, since you must stay away this afternoon."

She accepted the card with dancing eyes and proper thanks, and glided down the path, turning now and again to kiss her hand.

" What a sweet little thing she is ! " he said.

" And what a dear fellow you are ! " was the proud answer. " I saw that work-basket and quite coveted it."

They strolled on together and presently turned into a small open space bordered by the thick grove. From tree to tree ivy grew in low festoons, hiding each trunk from the ground to its lowest branches. At one end of the opening rose a low green bank upon which was an aviary of rare birds, while the opposite bank contained an open pagoda filled with flowers and plants ; birilli or tennis would find here an ideal home. At the moment several brilliant peacocks lay in a slant of sunshine which fell upon the turf, while others with spread tails stalked slowly about ; doves circled overhead, and the songs of birds filled the air.

" This is the historical spot," said Filippo, " to which I brought Miss Agatha Page the night she

promised to be my wife. Do you remember the
walk down the mountain that night, and then the
ride home, and after dinner the stroll we took, and
our wonderful talk here?"

Her eyes grew moist at the vivid recollection.

"I remember every happy moment," she said, pressing his arm tightly and laying her cheek caressingly
against it.

"Even the nightingale that sang to us from that
ilex-tree?"

"Perfectly."

"And how I went for your violin, that you might
play 'Du bist die Ruh'' to me?"

"Everything — Luitello."

He raised the happy face to his and kissed it
tenderly.

"Come," she exclaimed presently. "Let us go
down to the boat-house."

They followed a broad path to the edge of the
wood, where an undulating lawn led down to a little lake that seemed like a sapphire dropped from
heaven. Skirting its shore for a short distance, they
rounded a curve outlined by trees, and came suddenly upon a low rambling building half buried in
wisteria which clung to its sides and covered its
porch, while the branches of great oaks bent tenderly over its gable roof.

Running up the half-dozen stone steps, Agatha
disappeared within the boat-house, but in a moment
threw open a lattice window, and leaning her arms
upon the sill, smiled happily upon her husband, who
stood just below rolling a cigarette.

" Here is where I used to come and dream dur-
ing that first visit," she said ; and as his eyes smiled
back into hers she added, " The maidens of the
Brianza •say that when the wisteria rustles it is
Cupid dancing with delight. Do you wonder that
I came here ? "

" No; I only wonder that such a lake had no
Luitello."

" Who knows? But my eyes could see only the
one seeking me," and as he looked up at her she
daintily threw him a kiss.

" Where shall we read," he asked, — " in the old
place ? "

" Yes."

So, going up the steps of the porch, he seated
himself upon a rustic bench, where Agatha joined
him. They sat and chatted as they looked through
the vines upon the rippling water and its wooded
banks, until an hour slipped by; the charm of the
sweet poet failing to allure them from the spell of
their happy communion.

Their tête-à-tête was disturbed by the sound of
oars, and Filippo, going to the corner of the boat-
house, saw Gaeta calmly rowing a boat, in the stern
of which sat Veltri.

" Where have you two truants been ? " he inquired, as the boat glided under the house and came
to rest.

" How do you do ? " and Gaeta nodded. . " What
have you done with Mr. Dow ? "

" Have you been rowing around the lake looking
for him ? "

"No; we were misdirected by him. I wanted to speak to Aunt Agatha, and Mr. Dow said she had gone with you for a walk, and he and Signor Veltri came with me to look for you. We came down here, and Mr. Dow said he thought you were across the lake, and that if we would kindly go and see, he would wait for us. It's been a terribly hot row." And she made a great show of fanning herself.

Filippo was amused. "Perhaps he grew a little alarmed at your protracted absence," he said cruelly, "and has gone to the other side in search of you. Had n't you better row over again and see?"

"I came to find Aunt Agatha," was the dignified response. "Is she here?"

"Are you looking for me, dear?" called a voice from above.

Gaeta hastened up the steps, leaving Veltri to meet the adversary single-handed.

"It's very kind of you to take such trouble to look for us," said Loreno, blandly.

"Oh, not at all; I was glad to be of assistance to the Signorina."

"And on such a warm morning, too."

"Yet no warmer for me than for Donna Gaeta."

"True enough; but why did n't Mr. Dow accompany you?"

"He said that he did n't care to go unless he rowed, and that it makes him ill to ride backwards. — Ah, here he comes!"

Mr. Dow reported the arrival of the Duke and Duchess Faviola. He had only caught sight of them in the distance, as he hurried away to inform Gaeta.

CHAPTER XX.

A WOMAN'S PASSION.

THE reception of the peasantry, the feast, and fireworks had passed off most successfully, and although rather tired, Agatha found herself borne up by the excitement and her happy heart. Filippo had devoted himself to her throughout the day; for even when he was engaged in furthering the pleasure of her humble visitors he managed to return frequently to her side, and she had been much interested in seeing how well he handled the large crowd, which he directed firmly without emphasizing the fact.

Then, too, she had been justly proud of the reply he made in her behalf to the toast proposed in her honor by Padre Sacconi, who had come from Erba that morning. Agatha had only heard her husband speak publicly a few times, and she listened with deep admiration; and as he took his seat amid a volley of *bravi* and a storm of hand-clapping, she felt that there was reason for her pride in the love of such a man.

The neighbors and friends invited for the evening began to arrive soon after nine o'clock. The trees were illuminated, as far as the eye could penetrate, by hundreds of colored lights, while the bright moonlight upon the open spaces aided in creating a ravishing effect. In front of the stage upon the lawn a hundred or more chairs were placed for the audience; and as the music rose gently in the uncertain light, its effect was charming. The singers were professionals from Milan, and they rendered their parts well; no hitch occurred between orchestra, singers, and those performing in the tableaux, while the series of pictures which illustrated the words was both vivid and artistic.

By eleven o'clock the last curtain fell, amid enthusiastic plaudits. Then some of the guests strolled through the grounds, and others went to the ballroom, allured by the strains of a waltz.

Gaeta was the belle of the occasion, and before she was aware of what was happening, her dancing-card was full. It was in vain that she mentally upbraided Veltri for his delinquency: for some unknown reason he did not enter the room, but she several times saw his dark face peering in at one of the open windows. At first she thought he was merely resting after the fatigue of the cantata; but as dance after dance went by and he remained outside, she became preoccupied, and it required an effort to keep her mind upon her steps. At last she caught sight of her aunt Agatha, and asked to be taken to her.

" I wonder if Signor Veltri is n't going to ask you or me to dance," she said with a show of gayety. " I would n't care if it were any one else, but he 's such a divine dancer." ·

Agatha took the hint. " I 'll see if I can find

him," she replied ; " I think your uncle and he must
have strolled away together."

" No ; he has been outside that window nearest the
door for half an hour," said Gaeta, completely ignoring her uncle.

" Then I 'll go presently and upbraid him."

" But don't let him know that I sent you."

" No ; I 'll talk to him entirely on my own
account."

She went outside, but Veltri was not to be seen.
She was about to enter the house again, when the
moonlight revealed a dim figure at the other end
of the veranda. She went toward it, and as she
approached saw that it was Veltri, sitting with his
elbows upon his knees and his hands supporting his
head, — a picture of utter dejection.

Hearing her footstep, he lifted a pale unhappy
face, and seeing who it was rose hastily.

" Why, Signor Veltri," she said, " are you not
going to dance ? "

" Ah, Signora," he responded wearily, " I 'm not
well."

She was truly alarmed, and looking into his face
said, " Shall I send the Marquis to you ? "

" No, Signora," he burst forth with evident emotion ; " it is of the heart."

" Poor boy ! " and she took his arm sympathetically. " Tell me what the trouble is."

" No, not here, Signora ; some one may overhear.
Will you walk a little ? "

" Yes, for a few moments."

" Let us go and hear the tower chimes from the

west terrace. The townspeople have brought the great Sereno from Venice to ring them in your honor."

"I know it. Was n't it kind of them! The guests are all enthusiastic about his playing. Come, let us go and hear him."

They crossed the lawn before the house, and walking its length entered the belt of wood, through which they passed to the edge of the hill overlooking the town of Varese, several miles distant; and while the sweet voices of the bells floated up to them upon the still night air, Veltri opened his heart and poured out his hopeless love for his pupil. That his love must be sacrificed to the welfare of Gaeta he declared that he knew. His decision had been taken that very day, and he would not again shrink from its necessary woe.

Agatha believed that her young confidant had a bright future, and that the time was coming when he would be a composer of acknowledged merit, the extent of which no one could yet measure. But above and beyond all else her heart was cast strictly in the softer mould, and the proposed sacrifice of Cupid upon the altar of false pride moved her to pour words pleasant to hear into the ear of the youth, who gladly modified his stern resolve.

" Go back to Gaeta," suggested Agatha; " I really don't mind being left, and I would like to sit and listen quietly to the bells for a few moments. Don't say anything about my being here, and no one will miss me; now, do as I say, or you will compel me to return, for I told Gaeta I should bring you."

So he left her, although not without protest, and as his steps died away she leaned her head against a tree and yielded to the charm of the silvery serenade. It seemed the fitting close to a happy day. As she sat listening, the outline of two promenaders appeared in the moonlight not many yards away. They did not approach nearer, but stood talking in low and earnest tones. She watched them listlessly, until suddenly the woman's voice grew louder and Agatha recognized it to be that of Mercede. As the moonlight fell full upon the man's face, indifference fled, and her heart beat rapidly.

The absorbed couple stood looking into each other's eyes, when — God help her! — Agatha saw Mercede's arms encircle her companion's neck. She thought to see him tear himself free and vindicate her faith in him ; but, bending his head, he spoke with deep feeling that was carried in trembling tones to the ears of his stricken wife.

With a muffled moan she turned away her eyes and again laid her swimming head against the tree. How long she sat there she never knew ; but when again she turned her eyes toward the spot where her husband had stood, there was no one in sight.

After the tableaux Filippo had gone to the ballroom to lead Agatha through the first dance. This finished, he devoted himself to the task of keeping the floor well filled with dancers, and soon had the satisfaction of feeling that his services were no longer needed. He went into the ante-sala, where Mercede sat, surrounded as usual by a circle of admirers.

" Are you not dancing, Mercede ? " he asked, joining the group.

" No ; it 's too warm for my waning enthusiasm," was her answer. " Even here it is very close. Would you mind taking me into the air for a few moments ? "

" I should be delighted — if our friends will pardon my stealing you from them."

When they found themselves upon the lawn they strolled up and down, until suddenly Signor Veltri passed near them.

Loreno stopped him and offered his congratulations upon the excellence of his orchestra.

" You are going in to dance, I suppose," Mercede remarked, eager to have him leave them.

" I was just on my way ; I 've been listening to the chimes ; " and bowing pleasantly he hurried toward the house, his steps quickened by the notes of a favorite waltz.

" Shall we go and hear Sereno ? " Filippo suggested.

" I should like nothing better ; " and off they went, nearly following in the footsteps of Agatha.

" How beautiful it all is ! " Mercede exclaimed as they passed through the grove glimmering with lights hidden among the fern and the trembling foliage.

" It *is* pretty ; " and Loreno stopped to glance about him at the mystic effect of the twinkling flames.

" And all in her honor ! " Mercede added. " Surely Agatha should be a very proud woman to-night."

He laughed lightly. " There is but one Marchesa Loreno," he said, " and she has but one birthday a year."

His companion made no answer, and after waiting a moment he glanced at her inquiringly. They had come to the edge of the wood, and the moonlight shone full into her face. To his amazement he saw that her breast was heaving, and bending forward to look into her eyes, found that they were filled with tears.

"Why, Mercede! what is the matter?" he exclaimed, laying his hand impulsively on hers as it rested upon his arm.

"It is all so beautiful, and I am so miserable!" and her voice was choked with tears.

"My dear friend, how can you speak so!" He paused and sympathetically took both her hands in his. "Think what you have in your art, think what you are to Agatha, and —" his voice grew more earnest — "and to me."

"What is my art to me?" she answered vehemently. "It is a stone given me when my soul craves bread. And Agatha's love, — what does it amount to? It is not and cannot be anything real to her or to me; we are both too proud."

"Too proud, Mercede! Surely you wrong her as well as yourself."

"No, Filippo; only you are a man and don't understand. It is a farce, a sham, and it doesn't deceive her or me. Can't you see that for the relation I demand to be possible, Agatha needs to be different, — more generous, or, if you please, more humble? But it's hopeless, and I'm the one who must suffer."

"Nonsense!" and he dropped her hands and

walked on a few steps before pausing. " You are nervous to-night, and things seem distorted to you."

" Call it what you please," and coming close to him she looked eagerly into his eyes ; " but the fact remains that you and she have each other and I am alone. Agatha is your wife, and I am practically nothing to you,— nothing in comparison to what I would be."

Her voice trembled with the power of her surging passion as she continued, "Do you not know that I must pant and thirst for love, like other women,— love in which I am all in all to some one ? My very soul, parched and dying for love, cries out for it!" she covered her face with her hands, as with broken voice she added, "and to the end of my wretched life I suppose it must be unsatisfied."

With the final words her self-control left her, and she sobbed bitterly.

He hesitated an instant, and then gently taking her hands from her face, he said with an intensity that thrilled her, —

" Don't cry so, Mercede ; is *my* friendship nothing to you ? "

She turned her wet eyes up to his and stood silent, struggling to stay the convulsive sobs that defied her, until presently the cry of her heart broke from her quivering lips, and her voice vibrated with fervor.

" Your friendship, Filippo ! It is the bread of my soul." Then creeping closer she clasped his hands firmly, and added in a voice eloquent with tears, "How should I live without it ? But, Filippo, *my* Filippo !

why do you not sometimes tell me of it? Not that I doubt it, but I yearn for its visible token. You sometimes seem to read my very thoughts, — you, my perfect friend, my other self. If I am indeed to you what I believe, give me sign of it! Don't you realize my need, dearest? Do you never feel what it is to live forever upon hope? Give me a token, Filippo; to-night, if never again, give me a token!"

She stretched out her trembling hands and gazed at him wistfully. Then suddenly the last vestige of self-restraint seemed overborne, and with a broken sob she flung her arms around his neck and sobbed upon his breast.

Without asking wherefore, without pausing an instant, he impulsively folded his arms about her. It may have been passion, it may have been only impulsive sympathy, but he clasped her in his arms, and with bated breath spoke words of comfort to her.

As she conquered her emotion he gently disengaged her arms.

"Come, Mercede, be yourself!" he said. "We should go back, for I must not stay any longer. I will wet my handkerchief at the spring, and you can bathe your eyes."

She looked up and smiled happily; but sober second thought had come, and his face was grave.

"That's more like your old self," he said. "Let us be going."

She drew her head up proudly and dashed the tears from her eyes.

" Very well, I am ready ! " and her tone was bitter,
— " ready to go back and dance."

With white face and glowing eyes Agatha moved
among her guests, doing her duty as a hostess.
Filippo had spoken to her but once since his return to the house.

" You must pardon me, Agatha," he had said,
" but I entirely forgot our waltz. I went out for
a breath of air, and the fact is that — " But turning her eyes full upon his, and without a word, she
walked away and left him.

" Oh, very well ! " he thought, turning on his heel,
and annoyed that she should take such a trifle to
heart. Therefore during the rest of the evening he
avoided speaking to her.

At last the guests were all gone, and Filippo and
his visitors were upon the veranda chatting about the
events of the evening, when Agatha came out of the
house and joined them.

" No, thanks," she said, as several chairs were
offered her. " I won't stay. I 've only come to bid
you all good-night."

" Why, Agatha, what 's the matter ? " exclaimed
the Duchess. " You are trembling from head to foot.
Are you ill ? "

" Not in the least," and she tried to smile. " I 'm a
little over-tired. I 'll go to my room."

" Take my arm," Filippo said, springing to her
side.

" Thank you, I don't need it ; " and she turned
and walked unsteadily toward the door.

24

" I insist ! " he said, following her.

But without reply she sank into a chair, and as her husband bent over her the failing nerve gave way and consciousness fled.

A little later Loreno brought news to the awaiting group that his wife was conscious, and resting quietly. She had asked that no one should speak to her, and had forbidden him to send for the doctor.

"She has certainly overtaxed her strength," suggested the General.

"I fear," Veltri added, "that I am greatly to blame. I took the Marchesa to the west terrace to hear the chimes, and she persuaded me to leave her there ; she had no shawl, and when she came back I saw that she was shivering ; but later she seemed quite herself again."

Two pairs of eyes turned eagerly toward the young musician.

"When was this ? " demanded Loreno.

" When I met you and Madame André."

" And where did you leave my wife ? "

" On the terrace near the spring."

It was Mercede's voice which broke the silence.

"It was very imprudent of her," were the words she uttered.

" If the Signora is ill I shall never forgive myself," Veltri answered sadly.

Loreno started to his feet and strode down the steps. After a few turns upon the lawn he returned, and bidding his friends good-night went to his wife's room.

Agatha was lying with closed eyes, and he listened

to learn if she were asleep. His sister, who was sitting by the bed, rose and took him aside.

" Have you sent for the doctor? " she asked.

" No ; she forbade it."

" Perhaps it 's as well; perfect quiet is what she needs."

" I wish I might speak a word to her."

The Duchess paused to consider, and a flood of light fell upon the affair.

" Not to-night," she said ; "it might do much harm, no matter what it is. Wait until to-morrow."

He stole back softly and stood beside the bed, looking at the pale cheeks and at the sensitive lips that did not unclose to him. Then he turned away with a sigh and went toward his dressing-room.

As he passed a table upon which a night-light was burning, his eye caught sight of the illumined face of the Sistine Madonna, and as he recalled the tender words he had inscribed upon the picture, he hastened with flushed cheeks to his own room, and dropping into a chair buried his face in his hands. The strain of contending emotions regarding Agatha and Mercede had pulled him forward and backward until sometimes the sudden and keen realization of the fact caused him to smite his brow in shame. A man does not become a drunkard in a day, nor without moments of remorse and repulsion and ineffectual struggling. And it was so with Loreno. He had had periods of bitter self-condemnation which resulted in reaction, and sometimes even in a determination to free himself from his thraldom to Mercede. At such times he would stimulate his affection for Agatha in every way possible, straining every nerve to persuade himself that he was still honest in his attitude toward her, and that his feeling for Mercede was only of a platonic nature. But the effort was spasmodic, and after a sharp struggle faded under the spell of Madame André's fascination. She had used her power so skilfully that she had ever grown more confident and more aggressive, and he now made scarcely a pretence of opposing her wishes, while her companionship and her smiles seemed to constitute his chief happiness. Yet to have actually caressed her startled him from his lethargy. He attempted no justification, and the fact that Agatha had seen him added nothing to his disgrace. But his heart ached as he thought of his wife's stricken heart, and he despised himself. Yet he laid no blame upon Mercede. He was not the sort of man to shelter himself behind a woman. On the contrary, he palliated Mercede's transgression by recalling the story of her loneliness, and the unusual excitement which had moved her. His mind was in a state of chaos, and he knew not what to do. Although feeling that he had shattered his wife's pure faith, he was forced to admit that he found a certain consolation in the knowledge of Mercede's love. Incredible as it seemed, he felt this to be true. Great God! had it indeed gone so far? He tried to believe that he was self-deceived; but ponder as he would upon the hideousness of the fact, he still felt a sense of consolation in Mercede's ardent love. All that was evil in him arose and arrayed itself against all that was good. Nor did the passing hours bring certainty or peace. He did not

indeed dream of actually disgracing his name and
that of the sweet woman who bore it with becoming
honor, nor did he forget his beloved children; but,
on the other hand, he felt that he could not sever
his relation with Mercede. He had not suspected
until now the depth of his regard for her; but it
stood revealed, and he could not deny its power.
Accepting the fact, he felt that he must have opportunity to think. What the outcome would be he
could not yet decide. Time alone could guide him.
Time was essential. Then there came to his mind
an offer from the Prime Minister, which had been
submitted to him a few days before, to intrust to him
a special mission to Berlin. He had already discussed the matter with Agatha, who had favored his
going, as it seemed both an honor and a duty; but
for some reason, which now he knew to be unwill-
ingness to separate himself from Mercede, he had
not yet consented to undertake the diplomatic task.
It would afford him an excuse for absenting himself
from home. It was, he thought, just the thing for
his purpose. He would go to Berlin.

CHAPTER XXI.

A WOMAN'S LOVE.

MERCEDE felt that further effort to hide the struggle between Agatha and herself would be useless. Agatha had undoubtedly witnessed the interview on the west terrace, and there was no choice of action left. Filippo must choose between Agatha and her; Agatha would insist upon this, if she did not. Therefore it were better for her to take the initiative, and leaving Varese in the morning, go to Rome and await Filippo's decision. She did not doubt Loreno's love for her, in spite of the manner in which he had cut short their tête-à-tête. That was a remnant of his hide-bound conventionality; it was a last attempt to resist the force of his human nature. No matter who claimed him now, his heart, she told herself, was hers; and sooner or later a man will follow his inclination, bending everything to conform to it.

She packed up her things as well as she could, and went downstairs early, in the hope of seeing Filippo; nor was she disappointed. He was evidently expecting her.

"I'm going to Milan this morning, and to Rome to-night," she announced, after they had greeted each other.

"I hope you will reconsider your resolve."

"You do?"

"Certainly. Our walk, Agatha's sudden illness, followed by your hasty departure — cannot you see how it will excite remark?"

"But I must also consider my own dignity, and I prefer not to remain."

"No doubt; but are you not willing to sacrifice something personal for the sake of all three of us?"

"I prefer to go, that's one; Agatha would prefer to have me go, that's two; and would you not be governed by our wishes?"

"No, Mercede," he said firmly, "you ought not and must not go to-day. It will be hard, very hard for all of us, but you must stay and bear your part. If Agatha is better this morning, you can perhaps make your work an excuse for leaving to-morrow or the day following; but not to-day."

She was silent for a moment, her eyes half closed. "As you ask it, I will remain," she said; "but it is to please you that I stay, and not through fear of the rest of them. I wish, Filippo, that you could emancipate yourself from such respect for the world's opinion. Why should you regard such an unequal bargain? The world gives you nothing in return for your sacrifices. It is not a friend who glorifies your merits and excuses your shortcomings; it is an enemy searching for your unguarded point, — it strives to strike your heel, not your breastplate. If you really fear the shafts of the world, pray don't go into battle, but remain in the ranks of its courtiers, craving its sneering favor and seeking safety through its royal compassion. I don't believe it will avail you anything; but it may, and I don't wish to lead you into danger."

He tossed his head impatiently. "How you rush on!" he said; "can you really see no difference between cowardice and bravado? It is beneath me to defend myself from such a charge as yours; but in my opinion it requires more courage to stay here to-day than to run away."

She saw that she had gone too far, and the all-absorbing desire of her life was to be in sympathy with him. No courtier of the world could have exceeded in sleepless vigilance the regard she paid to his favor. She was his serf, his helot. This was not the first time she had curbed her impetuosity at his bidding. It was her indefinite idea of duty, and in yielding to him thus, she felt that she both honored him and drew nearer to him. Not without the womanly instinct to acknowledge a master, she was willing in this thing to be like other women — or at least to try the experiment.

"Very well, Filippo," and her manner was most exemplary; "if you think so, I am contented to follow your guidance. But if possible, I should like to get away to-morrow."

"I also may go in a day or so," he said; "I have been considering a special mission to Berlin offered me a few days ago, and now I am greatly tempted to undertake it."

Her eyes shone with pleasure. "How delightful!" she exclaimed. "We could go together and pass a few days in Rome before you start. How long would you be in Berlin?"

"It is impossible to tell; perhaps a month."

"And then you would return to Rome to report?"

"Certainly."

She saw her opportunity for testing him. Agatha would wish him not to go.

"I hope you will accept the mission," she said.

"I shall consult with Agatha, and decide during the day."

"I hope you will accept," she repeated impressively.

Loreno dreaded to meet his wife. He pictured to himself her face, which would be white and reproachful; and her manner, which would be cold and scornful. Yet it must be gone through with unless a break in their relations were openly acknowledged; so he hovered about the house all the morning, waiting to hear that she would receive him. The Duchess was with her, and remained until luncheon, when she reported that Agatha seemed quite herself, and was dressing.

After luncheon Filippo joined his sister, and they walked away together across the lawn.

"I think of going to Berlin in a day or two," he said; "couldn't you arrange to stay with Agatha, for a time at least?"

"How long will you be away?"

"Probably a month."

"Shall you go whether I stay or not?"

"Yes."

" Then I'll stay."

There was something so abrupt in her acceptance, without regard to her other summer arrangements, and without waiting to consult her husband, that he looked at her with surprise.

"You had better consider the matter a little before deciding," he suggested.

"No; I'll remain."

"Thank you."

"Don't thank *me*," she replied; "thank Madame André."

"What has she to do with it?"

"She has made it impossible for you to remain, and therefore necessary that I should."

"I think we had better leave Madame André's name out of the matter;" and his manner was formal.

"She and you, between you, have made that difficult."

He turned rapidly. "What do you mean?" he demanded. "Has Agatha said anything to you?"

"No; words were not needed to tell this sad affair."

He tried to look defiantly at her, but could not.

" Filippo — dear boy!" and her eyes grew soft as she regarded him, "do you realize what you are doing? If not—"

"I really don't wish advice," he interrupted.

" I cannot help that. If you don't realize your position, it's my duty to point it out; if you do, then it's my duty to protest."

" I fail to see this as you do, therefore oblige me by dropping the subject."

"Drop the subject, Filippo!" she echoed. "I, my father's daughter, not protest when I see the Marquis Loreno trifling with the name he at present represents! Drop the protest of a wife and a woman in behalf of one who cannot protest!"

"'Cannot'?" and he smiled dubiously. "On the contrary, I believe she will, and that strongly."

"Then you do not know Agatha as well as I do; but as for that, I am confident that you do not. Otherwise how could you slight — even dishonor her for the sake of a woman whose whole — "

"Pardon me," he exclaimed sternly, "I forbid any discourtesy of speech concerning Madame André."

"Oh!" and the fine features denoted infinite scorn. "Then in the name of your wife, in whose behalf I spoke, let me crave Madame André's pardon and yours."

His dark face flushed deeply and his fingers played nervously against the palms of his hands. "I will not deny," he said with a sincere effort to control himself, "that I have acted wrongly, even disgracefully; so blame me as bitterly as you please, but keep the name of Madame André out of it. She is not to blame."

"That may be manly, or heroic, or anything you choose to call it, but it's not the truth! That woman is as much to blame as you are, and that's saying a great deal. But let us keep her name out of it, if it pleases you to do so. Of one thing, however, be assured: you are being terribly deceived; whether self-deceived or not does n't much matter. Let me tell you that the crisis has come, and you

must now decide whether, in plain words, you will
sacrifice the happiness of your wife and your children — not to mention the respect of your friends
and of your sister — to an indefensible and selfish passion. I grieve for you to-day, Filippo, and
long to help you ; but if you deliberately choose
selfish shame to honor, I shall learn to despise
you."

He drew a quick breath, and the intuitive closing
of his eyes showed how squarely the blow had struck
him.

" That is strong language," he said.

" Is it unjust ? "

He turned away, and stood looking at a distant
point where the blue sky met the undulating line of
the mountains. " No," he said after a long silence,
"no; I only wonder that you don't despise me
already."

The great love she bore him welled into her eyes,
and she went nearer to him.

" Filippo dear," she said with mellow voice, "it is
not for me to praise Agatha : such a noble nature
as hers it is difficult to praise. I can admire and
describe Agatha's beauty, as I admire and praise a
lovely work of art ; but her character defies descrip-
tion, for it is as marvellous to me as the depth and
color of that sky above us. When to such loveliness
you prefer the dazzle of a gaming-table, do you
wonder that I tremble for you ? Perhaps, after all,
it may be well for you to go away a little while,
to learn what a false, unhealthy condition of mind
yours is."

They were silent for a few moments. "If that is all you wish to say to me," he said, breaking the silence, "I will go back and speak with Agatha. If she objects seriously I will promise not to go away; otherwise I think an absence of a few weeks will be wise."

"Very well," she replied; then taking his hand she added earnestly, "Filippo, you've been terribly weak, but I can't believe that you are false-hearted."

He walked rapidly away and went directly to Agatha's boudoir, but to his surprise heard that she had taken her hat and gone for a walk. He longed for the dreaded interview to be over, and chafed at the delay; but since she had gone off alone he would not follow her. Throwing himself upon the sofa he gave himself up to gloomy thoughts as he awaited her return.

At last he heard her footstep, and as she turned the handle of the door he arose and went toward her. On catching sight of him she paused involuntarily, and then smiling said, —

"Oh, is it you, dear? The room seems dark after being in the bright sunlight."

This was quite different from what he had expected.

"Yes. I'm glad to hear that you are better this morning."

"I've been having a stroll with Padre Sacconi and Mr. Dow. We went down to the pond and saw the children testing the canoe Mr. Dow gave them. It glides beautifully and very swiftly."

"I must try and see it before I go." She looked

up with a startled face, and he hastened to add, "I'm quite in favor of going to Berlin, and came to talk with you about it."

Her courage wavered for a moment, and the impulse to beg him not to leave her at this terrible time was almost irresistible; but she conquered the temptation.

"You are the best judge," she said, "for you know whether the possible advantages will reward you for the fatigue and discomfort." He had resumed his seat upon the small sofa, and having taken off her hat she came and seated herself beside him. "Still," she continued, "we shall all miss you dreadfully; so I don't suppose I'm quite impartial."

"I've thought it over, and have decided that I had better go. But," he added hastily, "if you object, I am willing to give it up."

Her heart beat more quickly and her eyes brightened, but her face was in shadow, and he could not see the effect of his declaration.

"Oh, thank you," she replied warmly; "but if it's to your advantage to go, of course I don't object. You would be away about a month?"

"Yes, if I go."

"Of course, dear, a month seems a long time; but the same reason that makes me miss you would be my reason for urging you to go."

"And what may that be?" he inquired most practically.

She leaned toward him a little and laid her hand upon his. "Because I love you," she said, looking at him with unutterable feeling.

He started. The interview was actually becoming more painful than he had expected. Could he be mistaken? Was her illness, after all, only the result of fatigue?

Her eager eyes dwelt upon his lovingly, longingly. He looked into their blue depths, and the impulse seized him to kneel at her feet and crave her forgiveness; but he hesitated, then wavered — then the feeling subsided and was gone.

" Since you really don't object, I think I 'll start on Thursday," he said.

" So soon!" and her voice trembled.

" Yes ; I must go to Rome to report, and I 've delayed already longer than I should have done."

" To Rome ! "

He caught the words, and his face grew darker. She had evidently heard of Mercede's intention.

" I shall have to go there for a day or two to receive instructions."

A day or two! Ah, what might not their result be just at this time, with Mercede at hand employing the whole power of her charm to tear away the already strained bonds which bound him to his own? Agatha grew pallid and faint with the crushing pain that encircled her heart. But her guardian angel, or whatever that beneficent force may be which sometimes rescues us from sudden peril, revived her staggering will and upheld her in her great purpose. If she abandoned her faith in the inherent power of her husband's better nature ultimately to arise and control him, if she abandoned her silent appeal to his higher qualities, then her battle in behalf of herself and her children was hopelessly lost. This conviction possessed her; she felt it, she knew it, and her purpose and faith grew strong again. She found herself pacing the floor, and going behind him she put her arms around his neck and laid her cheek against his head.

"My darling," and her voice was low, "wherever you are, you are mine, and God will guard you for me."

He bowed his head, nor could he have spoken had he not been dumb with shame.

Through the hours of the past night Agatha had lain motionless, seeming only to have power to suffer. She did not think, she only felt; the actual present alone stood out before her, without past or future.

"Take me, oh God, take me!" was the constant reiteration of her soul. The union which had made her life blessed, which she had believed would even reach into eternity, was, after all, but a creation of her own mind.

Stricken, benumbed, she lay, till a sound from Sebastiano, in the next room, roused her. Raising herself in bed she looked at Teresa, who lay in a crib beside her. Then despair past control overwhelmed her, and springing from her bed she flew to the room of her little son and threw herself upon her knees beside him. She longed to lay her cheek against his, to take his hand, to feel the warmth of his human nature, the beating of the little heart that loved her and was loyal to her; and her eager eyes dwelt yearningly upon him.

"Oh, my little boy, *our* boy!" she murmured softly; and stretching her arms out into the blackness, her anguish found utterance that must have pierced to the heart of the Almighty.

"Have mercy! have mercy!" she sobbed. "Thou worker of miracles, give me back my husband!"

Sinking to the floor, she leaned her head against the bed. Thus she sat until the morning light began to creep in at the window, and gradually her mind grew calmer.

Returning to her room, she threw a warm wrapper about her and went to her boudoir. The blinds were up, and the sight that met her eyes was one of radiant beauty; she drew to the window an arm-chair, and leaning back in it watched the rising of the sun and tried to think.

The shock of last night had subjected her faith in her husband to a supreme test. "Yet," she reasoned, "the measure of faith is not in the hour of enthusiasm, but of despair." Little by little she was able to consider the question of continued faith with toleration if not with confidence, and at last, her mind having become much calmer, she went back to her room and soon fell into a deep, dreamless sleep.

When she awoke, the morning was nearly gone. She rang for her maid, and the Duchess, who also came to her, seemed amazed at her patient's announcement that she was feeling very well, and intended to dress after drinking her coffee.

Agatha felt, in spite of her brave announcement, that she would be glad of a further respite

25

before meeting Mercede; and when the others were at luncheon she went downstairs and made her way to the grove, where she threw herself upon a bank and reviewed the all-absorbing subject.

" I must force myself," she said, " to act as though I had seen nothing. Damning as it was, I will have faith, not in what I saw, but in what I feel; if I am wise, and true to my convictions, Filippo will come back to me. This very act of faith may hasten the happy hour, who knows?"

She sat motionless for some time, and then added mentally, " My part is to keep the conditions as favorable as possible; to keep the light burning, and to await patiently the time when Filippo's true nature, challenged by my faith, shall bring him back to me."

She heard the voices of Francesco and Sebastiano, who were coming across the lawn, and rising quickly hastened toward them. Padre Sacconi was with them, and Mr. Dow was coming down the veranda steps. Farther to the left, near the greenhouses, she caught sight of Mercede and Filippo standing together, and as Padre Sacconi extended his hand tenderly, he remarked upon her unusual whiteness, and urged her not again to overtax her strength.

Mercede managed to avoid meeting Agatha until late in the day, by going for a long drive with Mr. Dow, who, to her surprise, had given her the invitation at luncheon. Indeed, it seemed a day of mysterious tête-à-têtes; for just as Agatha was settled in an arm-chair on the veranda with the Duke as a companion, Veltri joined them, and after expressing his delight at seeing her so well again, asked the Duke if he might have a few words with him, whereupon the two gentlemen walked into the house. An hour later the Duke and Gaeta left the house together, and crossing the lawn, disappeared among the trees.

When Loreno arrived in Rome, he went to his own apartment to breakfast.

He was at a loss to account for Agatha's conduct under circumstances her knowledge of which he no longer doubted. Even to the last she had given no sign of resentment, but had been both natural and lovely of manner. Indeed, he did not know how she could have been more tender with him, or more solicitous concerning his comfort during his absence. She had superintended the packing of his valise, and included among his effects various little vials containing medicines for such sudden illnesses as might overtake him; she had with her own hands done some little mending that was needed; she had filled his flask and his cigar-case, — in short, done everything she could. There must be some good reason which led her to ignore the evidence of her eyes. He knew that in such a crisis any woman, and especially a woman so thoughtful as Agatha, must realize the importance of the moment, and conduct herself in accordance with some settled purpose, be that purpose dictated by passion or by wisdom. It would not do, therefore, to brush. aside patient striving after

her reason, with an indolent theory, and for the
past two days his mind had been absorbed in searching for a satisfactory explanation of her unexpected
attitude.   As a result to his ardent endeavor, he
found himself always driven back to one and the
same theory: he was simply forced to believe that
it was the result of implicit faith.   Yes, there was
no doubt that Agatha still had faith in him; nor
was it blind faith, for she had given ample though
involuntary evidence of the terrible shock of her
awakening.   Why, then, did she still believe in him?
It was extraordinary.

Although Mercede was by no means banished from
his thoughts, he recognized the fact that the anticipation of seeing her was less active, less eager,
than it had been for months.   His mind reverted
constantly to Agatha, and when he found himself
reviewing with careful minuteness the events connected with his relations toward Mercede, it was
only as bearing upon the conduct of his wife.   He
wondered that she had not noted until now how
close his intimacy with her cousin had become.   But
had she not noted it?   His mere opinion was not evidence.   Then he recalled the unveiling of the Tristan
and Isolde, the first ride she had taken with Mercede
and himself, and a dozen other indications of her
knowledge, to which only his own selfishness had
blinded him.

Indeed, had not all Rome talked of this intimacy?
Even Veltri, while a guest in his house, had plainly
protested against it; and last of all, Costanza had
upbraided him for it.   It were childish then to doubt

the equal perception of her whose happiness and honor were at stake.

Thus it was that after hours of intense retrospection, both day and night, a rift was made in the cloud that enveloped his mind, — that a bright shaft of sunlight pierced its darkness and fell upon the golden thread of his wife's faith. As it was illumined, he saw it from end to end, and cursed his incredible selfishness.

Yet Mercede came in for no part of his censure. Even now he palliated whatever he could not justify in her conduct, both on the ground of her strong humanity and because of that mysterious personality ascribed to genius, to which general opinion permits uncommon license. In spite ôf everything, as he thought of Mercede his heart beat rapidly. Her mind was so fresh, her spirit so unflagging — she stimulated him. While Agatha was a devoted wife, a wise mother, a lovely and unselfish woman, Mercede's nature was drawn in bolder lines, and should occasion demand she would rise, no doubt, to the plane of absolute heroism. Could Agatha, for example, have faced misfortune as Mercede had faced it? Did she possess the necessary force of character? Tenderness and devotion in a woman were much, but not everything.

Yet he must admit that in her present trial his wife was displaying an unostentatious strength that surprised him. Her self-restraint was wonderful. He doubted if Mercede herself could have rivalled her in this respect. His mind, now bent upon comparison, was permitted full license; he began to search

honestly for the truth. What result, he asked himself at last, had come from the stimulus which he
claimed for Mercede's companionship? It stimulated
him certainly, but did it actually strengthen him?
Had it direction? Where did it lead him? What
had it really done for him? He pondered these
questions for hours, with increasing perception of
the truth. On the other hand, was Agatha's influence equally without worthy product? Was she not,
indeed, an active force for good in his life? Would
his interests have been the same had her interests
been more conventional? More conventional! He
was struck by the word. He had hitherto regarded
Mercede as unconventional, and admired the characteristic; yet surely the same was true of his wife.
She also was unconventional, although in a different
way. Even in this affair she had been unconventional in the highest sense, and as his mind reverted
again to that faith which nothing could shake, he
asked himself, what could account for it?

Then, as he realized the full significance of his
wonder, his eyes closed with pain. Was he indeed
so unworthy of a pure trust? He could not deny
the truth, and buried his face in his hands, overwhelmed by the weight of his shame. Little by
little, amid black anguish, his thoughts centred upon
the one vital fact, — *Agatha's faith.* Unswerving in
the face of long-accruing and absolute proof, undaunted by even the evidence of the senses, that
faith brought consciousness to his benumbed spirit;
it aroused hope. He pondered upon it, not alone
with increasing wonder, but with deep gratitude.

He dwelt upon it far into the afternoon, his mind groping nearer and nearer the light, until, at last, his feeling found vent in glowing enthusiasm.

" That is the sort of thing that both stimulates and strengthens a man," he exclaimed half aloud. " It 's splendid ! It 's superb ! By God, it 's heroic ! "

CHAPTER XXII.

"MORE LASTING THAN BRONZE."

WITH the exception of the Duchess, Mr. Dow and Signor Veltri were the only guests remaining at the Villa Loreno, and they were to start in the afternoon for Stresa. They were seated in an arbor a little distance from the house, talking in low tones, when suddenly Agatha appeared before them.

Her face told them that her news was bad.

"I'm very sorry," she began, "but I must ask you to go as soon as possible."

"Has it broken out in town?" asked Mr. Dow.

"Yes, worse; two of our tenants have just been stricken down, and the doctor says it is undoubtedly cholera."

"And you and the children; where do you go?"

"The Duchess will take the children immediately, within an hour, to Erba."

"And you?"

"I must remain," she answered quietly. "I am needed here, if only to give the people courage."

"But, Marchesa," protested Veltri, "surely you will not risk your precious life so needlessly!"

"I do not consider the risk to be needless."

" But what real good can you do? "

" I can be useful in many ways which I cannot stop to explain, for I must hurry back to the children ; I expect a cordon to be put round the place at any moment ; " and she turned away.

" Then you are determined, Marchesa? " called Veltri.

" Quite," she replied without stopping.

The two men sat silent for a moment.

" I don't like the idea of leaving her here alone," suggested Mr. Dow.

" I intend to remain," was the answer.

" You do? "

" Certainly."

" I 'm willing to stay also."

" That won't be necessary, for the Marquis will of course return. I, who owe everything I am to them, am more than happy at this chance to serve them. You have neither this reason nor the one of being needed."

" Then I 'll see the Duchess safe at Erba and stay at the inn, and you must telegraph me every day how the Marchesa is and how you are ; and I 'll see that the news is taken straight to the Villa Faviola. If you fail to send word on any day, we shall know that you are ill, and in that case I 'll come and look after you."

Veltri grasped the honest hand warmly.

" Thank you," he said ; " but don't think of doing such an imprudent thing. Your coming could n't help me."

" But it might comfort Gaeta."

They stood looking into each other's eyes for a moment.

" Very well, then let it be so," said Veltri.

" And I'll answer your telegrams every day, and give you our news."

The only answer was a grateful pressure of the hand.

" And now I'm off, for I must speak a word to the Marchesa ;" and they hurried toward the house.

Mercede sat in her studio holding a chisel in her hand, but the hand had fallen to her side listlessly, and her eyes were fixed upon the floor. Try as she would, she could not work to-day. Her thoughts were engrossed with Filippo. And so it had been since morning. She could not concentrate her mind upon anything except his sudden change of manner. It chilled her ; it did more, it almost crushed her. In the first place, he had arrived in town the previous morning and had not come to her for nearly twenty-four hours. His excuse was the engrossing nature of the mission he had undertaken. Surely he could have spared her an hour, if only in the evening ; and when she chided him, although slightly, he grew silent and at first her pride was touched. But when her heart cried out and she began impulsively to tell him how she had longed to see him and how unkind he had been, he seemed unresponsive, and an ominous fear seized her and forbade her pressing him further.

In reply to her inquiry concerning Agatha's health he had answered somewhat formally, and then abruptly changed the subject. At the end of half an

hour, during which his manner was strangely constrained, he arose, and said he must be going, pleading an engagement with the Prime Minister. She
urged him as warmly as she dared to remain longer,
but without success. What did it mean? Still, she
flattered her troubled heart with the fact that he had
promised to drink tea with her at five o'clock. Yet,
when she had suggested that he should dine with her
at seven, and that afterwards they might walk out to
the Janiculum in the moonlight and hear the city
bells from the plateau of San-Pietro in Montorio, his
brow contracted, as he replied that he feared the
walk would be a little long, and that the effect would
be dearly bought. What did it mean?

Rising restlessly, she went out upon the lawn and
walked up and down a few times in front of the studio. Presently, when passing one of the open windows of a large room in which several men were
usually at work, she missed the sound of their mallets
and glanced in curiously. The men were gathered
in a group, one of them holding a newspaper from
which he was reading aloud. She was surprised
and somewhat annoyed at this dereliction of duty,
and watched them. When the reading was finished, they stood eagerly talking together, and her
curiosity was awakened.

"What is the news?" she demanded aloud.

The workmen turned and stood silent; then one of
their number advanced to the window.

"It will interest you. Signora," was his brief reply
as he offered the journal to her.

She seized it, and looking at the place which

the man's finger indicated, she read the following telegram : —

"At Gazzada, near Varese, ten cases are reported among the tenants at the Villa Loreno. There is a cordon of military around the estate, and to get news is difficult. The Marchese Loreno is said to be in Rome, but the Marchesa is reported to be nobly devoting herself to the sick, whom she attends personally. Her heroism has restored order, but the gravest anxiety for her safety is felt throughout the district, and great excitement prevails."

At that moment the studio bell rang. She glanced hastily at her watch and whispered distinctly : " It is the Marquis ; not a word of this to him. I must break the news. Quick ! go to work before he enters ! "

Hurrying back to her room she seized her chisel, and as Filippo's step was heard upon the threshold she was hard at work. Turning to greet him, she searched his face eagerly, and a glance convinced her that he had not heard the news. She felt that it should be broken gently.

" Is the water boiling ? " he asked with a careless smile. " I 'm tired, and the tea will be welcome."

" It 's nearly ready," was the reply.

" Go on with your work," he said. " I 'll sit here and watch you ; or I 'll glance over the evening paper, if you have one."

He seemed much more like the old Filippo now, and she dreaded to tell him the bad news.

" No, I 'm tired of work," she said. " If the paper has come I 'll read it to you while you watch the water."

" Very well ; " and as she went into the ante-room
he seated himself beside the small lamp, over which
the kettle stood.

She snatched the paper from her pocket, and after
smoothing it, stood with her hand upon the door-
handle, undecided what to do. That he had left
Varese indicated much, almost everything, in spite
of his apparent apathy. Confronted as he was by
the responsibility of loosening bonds and readjust-
ing relations which had existed for nearly seven years,
a heart as tender as his would naturally have a sense
of misgiving, even of regret, that might account for
his present conduct. It was nothing more nor less
than sympathy for Agatha, and a little time was
needed to allow it to subside. Mercede did not
doubt the strength of her own power over him ; yet
she regretted more than she could tell, the unfortunate news which must add to his sympathy with the
wife to whom he had just dealt so terrible a blow.
She must not delay longer, however, and would let
circumstances guide her. Re-entering the studio, she
took a chair with her back to the light, and opening
the paper carelessly, began to read aloud.

" A very interesting discovery was made yesterday at
Tivoli, while some workmen were digging a well upon the
estate of —"

" Leave that until after you read the telegrams,"
Loreno interrupted.

" As you please ; " and she turned to another page.

" The steamship 'Gottardo,' of the Florio line, arrived
in New York. The ' Independente,' of the same line.
arrived in Gibraltar, bound for Genoa."

" How stupid ! "   And she ran her eye across the
page.   " Ah, this is better : " —

" Paris.   It is reported here in official circles that ne-
gotiations have been opened with the Vatican in regard
to — "

" Never mind those silly reports," Loreno exclaimed.   " As an ex-diplomat I know how in dull
times I gave similar reports for the correspondents to
send to-day and contradict to-morrow.   What is the
news of the cholera, — anything from Milan or around
my neighborhood ? "

She seemed a long time finding these despatches.

" Milan — Milan," she said presently, glancing
down the column.   " No, not a word."

" Nor from any part of our district ? "

"Spezia, Genoa, Poretta — is Poretta near you ? "

" No, it is this side of Bologna, half-way to
Florence."

" Oh, so it is.   But why don't you pay attention
to your duty ; don't you see the steam ? " and
crunching the paper in her hand, she used it in lifting the hot kettle.   " Blow out the light for me —
that's right !   Now put that tile upon the table, for
this kettle is heavy — so ; thank you.   Now please
bring me that bowl of sugar yonder ; " and as he
turned to obey her she tossed the crumpled newspaper upon the table.   The door was opened, and a
servant entered with a telegram upon a salver.

Rising quickly Mercede intercepted the bearer, who
was approaching Filippo, and snatching up the envelope motioned with her head for the man to with-

draw. She studied the address for an instant, and then thrust the despatch unread into her pocket.

"That's delicious!" laughed Loreno. "You receive telegrams like a veteran."

"It is something I know about already."

"What a comfort! I wish I could discount my telegrams."

"You are not expecting one?" and she looked at him furtively.

"No; but when cholera is reported to be flitting about the neighborhood, one can't help being a trifle nervous."

"Did you arrange to have them send you a telegram?"

"No; but of course they would."

"And then you would return immediately?"

"I suppose so."

"Yet why should you? You couldn't do any good, and would simply risk your life to no purpose."

"Still, duty is duty."

"If you think it your duty to undertake this Berlin mission, I should think it your duty to carry it out."

"That would depend. If cholera were actually to break out at Varese, I would let the mission go to the dogs."

"I should regard that as unworthy of you. Indeed, I'd thwart you if I could."

"Thwart me!" and he laughed. "I think not; no one thwarts me."

"Vain man!" and her face bore its brightest smile.

"No, it's only a fact for my autobiography, which,

if the Berlin mission succeeds, will be worth writing;" and he sipped his tea complacently.

"Yet you would throw it over for the sake of a senseless sentiment."

He poised his cup and looked at her with an amused expression.

"How devoted you are to strong phrases!" was his irrelevant reply.

"I confess I've no patience with halting minds or measures," she answered earnestly. "Having once put my hand to the plough I never look back; but you, while you walk forward perhaps, seem to stretch your very neck looking for letters, telegrams, or messages from the villa."

He only laughed. "You are too imaginative for a diplomat," he said; "but if your imagination had n't found a vent in sculpture, you would have made a great journalist."

"Don't treat me like a child," and she drew herself up slightly. "I may have colored the picture rather strongly, but I assure you the lines are lifelike."

But her sarcasm seemed only to amuse him now; she felt this, and was alarmed. A temporary reaction was to be expected, but it was stronger than she had anticipated. With this mood upon him, dare she trust him with this knowledge of Agatha's danger and heroism?

Her hand fell upon the telegram in her pocket and her fingers clutched it desperately. Suppose he should discover her contrivances to keep him? He might upbraid her, but she would plead her desire to keep him from danger. *From danger!* Strangely enough, in her eager thought for herself she had overlooked the danger to him; but now its realization appalled her. Without a moment's hesitation she rose, and having adjusted a book or two upon the table, picked up the tell-tale journal and flung it into the waste-basket.

Her decision was taken, — at any cost, Filippo should not go to Varese.

"When do you leave for Germany?" she asked.

"To-morrow morning."

"So soon?" There was something in her eye and tone that always appealed to him, — something which stirred him even now.

To-morrow morning! The words set her mind aflame. *To-morrow morning* he would be on his way out of Italy! If the news from Varese could be kept from him until then, the chances were against his learning it until too late to give up his mission. To risk the effect of Agatha's heroism upon his mind at this critical moment was not to be thought of, and added to this was the peril to his life. He must be induced to leave Rome instantly, and must, moreover, remain away until the morning. But how could it be accomplished?

In this desperate moment her course was, as ever, dominated by her unbending will. She had now gone too far to retreat. A crisis was inevitable, nor could the battle be a drawn one: she must either win or lose. There must, therefore, be no half measures; to be weak were to deserve defeat. What did she care for the good opinion of the world as compared with Filippo's love, Filippo's life? For such a recompense no sacrifice was too great. Yes, she herself must take him from Rome and keep him until the morrow!

Rallying all the forces of her nature, she prepared for action, stamping upon conscience and drowning its last despairing cry with the shibboleth, "I love — therefore I am right!"

"I presume," she said aloud, "if you are going to-morrow, that your business here is finished?"

"Yes, I'm quite ready to start."

"Then I have a plan to propose. Let us run out to Frascati to pass this last evening; it will be a pleasant memory while you are away."

"I'm scarcely in the mood for it," he answered gravely.

"That will soon come when we are fairly started, and I should very much like to go."

"I'm sorry to deny you," he said, trying to disguise his repugnance to the plan, "but I shall have all the railway clatter that I want without beginning to-night."

"That is no reason for denying me," she persisted. "It's not much to ask when I am not to see you for a month." Her head swam with suppressed excitement, and her eyes glowed with the intensity of her purpose. "Surely, Filippo, you won't disappoint me! It would be more than selfish, — it would be positively unkind."

"Don't urge me," he replied. "You wouldn't wish me to go unwillingly."

"Unwillingly!" Then turning away she continued

in a low voice, " No ; I should rather give it up than humiliate myself."

" Pardon me, Mercede !" he said quickly, " I did not intend to wound you ; but why not remain here quietly ? "

She came nearer. " Can't you see, Filippo, that it is more than a passing whim ? And if that were all it is, think how many days must pass before you will again have a chance to humor me."

He was silent, and her heart beat wildly. On the morrow, he told himself, he was to leave Rome, and his silence while away would indicate much to Mercede. Both his inclination and judgment were adverse to her plan ; but, on the other hand, he did not propose to adopt a radical course toward her which might embarrass the freedom of Agatha's relations with the General. Since Mercede's heart was so strangely set upon making this excursion, it might be best to humor her. Yet he wished that she had not proposed it, — and to-day of all days.

Mercede was searching his face closely. " Come," she urged, " be kind to me ; it will be a long time before I shall see you again, and who knows what may happen ? "

It was a random shot, but it struck him fairly, for he was not indifferent to the pain which would be hers when she realized his changed attitude toward her.

" I 'll send a line to my maid," she exclaimed impetuously, going to her desk, " to tell her that I won't be home to dinner ; and then let us be off ! If we hurry, we can catch the five-thirty train."

Without waiting for his reply, she began to write, when a workman entered and laid a card before her.

She glanced at it, and her face assumed the pallor of death.

" I 'll come immediately," she managed to say, and seizing a fan plied it nervously as she tried to control her wavering senses.

Filippo watched her. " Are you faint ? " he asked quickly.

" No — only the heat is awful," and in spite of her giddiness she managed to smile brightly.

Rising, she walked as steadily as she could to the door, where she turned, and, nodding familiarly, assured Filippo she would be back presently.

Entering the adjoining room she was confronted by the prim figure of Mr. Peter Dow.

" Come outside," she said, leading him through a long window to the open air.

" You have come from Varese ? " she began.

" Yes; I arrived an hour ago. Not finding the Marquis at home, I came here."

" Why here ? "

" I thought he might be with you."

" He was here this morning; I would advise your seeking him at the Prime Minister's office."

Mr. Dow looked surprised.

" Is n't he here ? " he asked.

" Here ! What put such an idea into your head ? "

" Your men said he was with you, and that you were breaking the news to him."

" What news? "

" About the cholera."

" Is there any truth in the report? "

" It is all true."

" Then I 'll tell him to-night."

" But the men said he was with you."

" So he was, but I would not alarm him so greatly upon a mere rumor."

" Has he gone? "

She hesitated an instant. Loreno's life was in her hands, she thought.

" Yes," she said firmly; " by the lawn, — five minutes ago."

Her companion rose instantly. " Then I must follow him. Where has he gone? "

" He did n't say. What do you wish with him? "

" His wife is at the villa, cholera is raging, and only Veltri is with her."

" But would you have him sacrifice his life? "

" Let *him* decide. It is my duty to inform him of the facts."

" And murder him? "

" ' Murder him '! What do you mean? "

" That to tell him is to send him into the very jaws of death."

" He will never forgive me if I don't tell him, and his place is by the side of his wife."

She drove her nails into her hands and ground her teeth, but controlled herself.

" He will come to me again this evening," she said; " leave me to break the awful news to him."

" No; I must see him myself."

" Then come to the Palazzo this evening at eight
o'clock. Now I must ask you to excuse me, for I
have an engagement."

" Will you prepare him ? He should take the
night train."

" Yes."

" Very well ; I will be prompt. And in the mean
time I 'll go look for him."

" Quite right," and giving him her hand she moved
away.

He was puzzled, not knowing where to go with
any chance of success. He had not stopped to eat
anything since his arrival, and his fast, added to the
heat and his fatigue, had given him a raging headache.

" I 'll sit down for a moment," he said with a dis-
heartened sigh ; and he went to a bench under a
neighboring tree. As he seated himself, Loreno appeared at the window of Madame André's studio.

" By George ! " exclaimed the astonished witness,
" it *is* the best way of getting there ! "

While returning to the studio Mercede's mind was
concentrated upon one aim, — to get Filippo away
from Rome before Mr. Dow should see him. All
her power of self-control, all her natural gift as an
actress, was brought into play to carry out her purpose. She entered the room, blithely humming a
favorite song.

" There ! " she exclaimed, " all business is finished,
and now I have nothing to do but enjoy myself.
Are you ready ? "

" Yes."

" Come, then !" and she slipped her hand through his arm ; looking up at him brightly, she added, " Won't it be delightful?"

As she spoke the words the door opened and they were confronted by the sober face of Mr. Dow.

" Why, how do you do?" Mercede exclaimed, rushing forward and blocking his entrance. " Excuse me for a moment, Filippo," she said over her shoulder, " I 've something to say to Mr. Dow;" and before that astonished gentleman could object, he found himself pushed back into the anteroom and the door closed.

" For God's sake don't tell him now !" she pleaded ; " he 's entirely unprepared. I wanted time to prepare him, you know. Come to my apartment to-night at eight, as I proposed. I was about to take him for a walk and break the news by degrees."

The shrewd American looked at her speechlessly for a moment.

" You said he was n't here," he replied, mentally associating two different trains of thought.

" I know I did.   I had n't time to explain, and took that way of using my judgment.   Leave me to break the news, won't you ? "

" Now?   On your walk ? " he asked.

" Yes ; will you ? "

He thought a moment before finally deciding.

" Yes," he said, " and I 'll go with you."

She was equal to the emergency. " Certainly, if you wish to ; although I can tell him much better alone."

" Can you ? " and he seemed to be considering the suggestion.

" Certainly. And you wait here until we come back."

She knew her plan was more than bold, — that it was desperate. But what could she do ? If Filippo learned all now, her position would be intolerable, for everything was against her, — appearances, facts, and time.

" How soon will you be back ? " inquired Mr. Dow.

" I can't tell precisely ; how can I ? "

" I think I had better go with you."

" *Santa Maria !* " and Mercede turned upon him with blazing eyes. " What is the matter with you ? Must I go over the whole thing again ? "

" No, I 've got it all clearly in my mind ; but I think I 'll go with you, or else tell him myself, for there is no time to lose."

" I 'll tell him without delay, and bring him back here within half an hour. Ecco ! "

" Still, I don't like to get into the habit of trusting others to do my business ; I think I 'll tell — "

In her wrath Mercede suddenly seized his arm.

" For Heaven's sake, Mr. Dow ! " she interrupted, " don't say that again. Talk of a habit ! You 've said that fifty times. Now you simply must not and shall not go with us ! It is too serious a thing for mere civility, and I say you shall not tell him."

" I don't insist upon telling him, only upon going with you."

" Well, that 's impossible. I don't want you."

"I 'm very sorry; but all the same I think I must go."

She felt that the crisis had come. This man's obstinacy baffled her completely. While she stood silent, trying to form some new plan of action, her cheek suddenly blanched as a tap was heard upon the door behind her and Filippo's face appeared.

"I 'm glad to see you, Mr. Dow!" he said, nodding cordially. "When you and Madame André have finished, I want the news from Varese; so don't go without seeing me again."

"It is you I have come to see," was the quick response, "and there is n't a moment to be lost, for you must catch —"

"The five-thirty train," Mercede interrupted coolly; "so please postpone your chat, Mr. Dow, until the Marquis returns. Go get my hat and cloak, Filippo," she added brightly, "and meet me upon the lawn; I 'll give you the Varese news." Filippo turned to obey her, and she whispered appealingly to Mr. Dow, "Wait here, and leave it to me!"

"Madame André, what does all this trifling mean?" he demanded with unsuspected savageness. "I have a serious errand with the Marquis, and it must be discharged without further delay — and by me."

Loreno turned instantly, and going close to Mercede, eyed her narrowly.

She was bewildered by the sudden disaster which confronted her, and stood looking irresolutely into his eyes. Suddenly he turned away, and going to the studio door held it open for Mr. Dow to pass.

"One moment, Filippo!" Mercede exclaimed vehemently. "I too have something to tell you! Hear me first — Filippo!" but without a word he followed Mr. Dow and closed the door.

"You have come from the Marchesa," Loreno said.

"Yes; that is, from Varese."

"The Marchesa has sent me a message?"

"Yes. She begs that you will not return to Varese."

"Begs me not to return! I don't understand you."

"Have you seen the evening paper?"

"Yes."

"Did you read the cholera reports?"

"Yes; that is, I heard them read."

"You did!"

"Yes; why? Great God, Mr. Dow, it's not at Varese!"

"Even worse; at the villa itself."

"But my wife and the children are away and safe?" and grasping the other's arm he searched his face eagerly.

"The children are safe."

"And Agatha —" he asked with strained eyes and bated breath.

"Is there with her people, but was well yesterday."

"Thank God! thank God!" and his voice rang through the room as he lifted his hands gratefully toward heaven. He walked away and remained silent for a moment. Then he turned and said in a calmer voice: "So the Marchesa remained among her people. Sending every one else to a place of safety,

she remains to help the unfortunate. Of course she
does ! "

" The children are at Erba, and Veltri remained
to help the Marchesa."

" Veltri ! and here am I loitering in Rome ! "

" You can catch to-night's express — "

" I must go faster," he interrupted. " I must have
a special train. Are you going North ? "

" I go to Erba."

" Will you go with me ? "

" Gladly."

" Then come ! " and he seized his hat.

But behind him stole a quiet step, and a trembling
hand was laid upon his arm.

" Filippo ! "

He turned, and his eyes fell upon a face pitiable in
its fright and woe, but the face into which Mercede
looked was utterly impassive.

" Filippo — one moment — one moment only ! Don't
misjudge me — I have nothing to ask save this:
Don't go to Varese ! " and she held out her hands
as though begging alms. " Send for Agatha. Plead
with — command her to come away ; but for my sake
— yes, for Agatha's sake, don't go to Varese ! Promise me this, Filippo ! " He drew back, and she followed him with great tears blinding her eyes.
" Filippo ! " she pleaded, her lip quivering, her deep
voice trembling and broken, " don't sacrifice your
life for those peasants ! Though you save a hundred
of them, they can't comfort us, — Agatha and me.
In her name I plead, as well as in my own. Go near
if you will, and send for her. Beg her as she loves

you to come away — beg her in the name of her children to come away; but don't go to that fatal place! Tell him not to go, Mr. Dow; please tell him not to go!"

Her nerve and her strength gave way, and she sank to the floor sobbing piteously.

Mr. Dow turned away his face, but Loreno looked upon her without a token of pity. The scales had fallen from his eyes and her spell was broken. His mind was absorbed by one thought — Agatha. At last he comprehended the fulness of her strength. There was now no vestige of blindness left. A swift vision swept across his mind of her sweet face, her heroic faith, her self-control and patience, crowned by her consistent consecration to his suffering people.

Yet he felt no resentment toward the woman at his feet. So far as he recognized the past, it was only to glorify Agatha and to condemn himself; for Mercede he had absolutely no thought, — neither of disdain nor sympathy. He saw before him only a weeping woman, whose sorrow failed to touch him. Why this was so he did not ask himself, nor did he even wonder. It was no time for small emotions. It is the heart that feels pity, and his heart was verily benumbed with fear for an incalculably precious life at this moment in jeopardy. Perhaps he might never again see Agatha alive, never crave her forgiveness, never again hold her to his heart or look into those clear true eyes as he pledged to her the unfaltering devotion of his remaining years. What, then, were a few tears to such anguish as his!

Although his eyes were fixed upon Mercede he seemed scarcely to see her. He turned to Mr. Dow.

"Come," he said, "we are losing precious time." And without another glance upon the beseeching face upturned to his, he strode from the room.

University Press: John Wilson and Son, Cambridge.

www.ingramcontent.com/pod-product-compliance
Lightning Source LLC
Chambersburg PA
CBHW030815110726
47900CB00006B/1633